WOLFESTRIKE

A Medieval Romance

By Kathryn Le Veque

De Wolfe Pack Generations

Trade Paperback Edition

Text by Kathryn Le Veque
Cover by Kim Killion
Edited by Scott Moreland

WWW.KATHRYNLEVEQUE.COM

ARE YOU SIGNED UP FOR KATHRYN'S BLOG?

You'll get the latest news and information on exclusive giveaways, exclusive excerpts, coming releases, sales, free books, cover reveals and more.

Kathryn's blog followers get it all first. No spam, no junk.

Get the latest info from the reigning Queen of English Medieval Romance!

Sign Up Here

kathrynleveque.com

Author's Notes

The de Wolfe Pack just keeps getting bigger and bigger…

Just when I think it's getting "too" big, I notice that some authors have a 50-book series, so then I think I'm falling behind! But seriously, I love the de Wolfe Pack as much as anyone and probably more, so I'm always excited to write about another de Wolfe.

Now, it's Thomas' turn!

Or "Tor" as he is now known. You'll find out why in the novel. You'll also find out that his father is the only one who still calls him "Tommy". This is Scott de Wolfe's second son, whose mother was Athena. She tragically drowned with her sister and a few children several years before this novel (read *ShadowWolfe* and *DarkWolfe* for this background), and Tor grew up looking more like Paris' side of the family than William's. He's very big, fair, with auburn hair that started going gray early, as many redheads do. It made his hair more of a strawberry blond. He's a big, gentle giant, a personality more like his grandmother, Caladora, than his grandfather, Paris – or William or even Jordan. Tor is the strong, silent type.

Until he meets Isalyn.

Fun fact about the heroine's family – you're going to meet Isalyn de Featherstone, a very unique young woman, and the de Featherstone – or de Featherstonehaugh family – really did exist. There really was a manse in the location I describe, so this is a bit of fact mixing with fiction. Currently, there is a building still residing on the spot where the Featherstone manse was built, but it has gone through many iterations over the centuries. The entire area near Featherstone and Blackpool (a new de Wolfe castle) was known for heavy Roman occupation. Hadrian's Wall isn't far from Featherstone, in fact. The history of that part of England is rich.

Speaking of double-named characters, we've got another set here – two knights with the name Nathaniel. One is Nathaniel Hage, named after Jemma's father, and the other is Nathaniel de Wolfe, son of Scott and Avrielle, and named after Avrielle's first husband, Nathaniel du Rennic. It's a common enough name in any case but, in this book, I've got both Nathaniel characters in the same scene, same place, so I have differentiated them by calling Nathaniel Hage "Nat" – and Nathaniel de Wolfe "Nathaniel". That's how you can keep track. I also have Thomas de Wolfe and Thomas "Tor" de Wolfe in the same scenes – both named for the same man, Jordan's father, but you can tell them apart easily.

Some of this story deals with plays, or "dramas" as they were once called. Back in Medieval times, these plays were heavily controlled by the church and almost always had a biblical source or inspiration. Usually, they were performed on wagons that could travel from town to town. Dramas were not, however, the preferred mode of entertainment – music and troubadours far exceeded the demand of that kind of entertainment, as did outdoor games like archery and falconry. Medieval people found their entertainment in things other than plays but, in this tale, I address "dramas" as kind of a less popular, rare type of entertainment. Just know that it wasn't the norm.

There is also something to note – the women really run the show in this story. They are fearless! Isabella de Wolfe, daughter of Blayth, is the granddaughter of Jemma Hage. Enough said there. Isalyn, the heroine, is the granddaughter of Christian St. John and Gaithlin de Gare from *The Warrior Poet*, and she is also quite bold and fearless – she got it from her grandmother, a female warrior.

This is a complex tale with a lot of twists and turns, but you're going to love the subtle humor and sweet love story. Uncle Blayth de Wolfe plays a big part in this – and I'm always up for including the de Wolfe who lived among the dragons. And in speaking of Blayth, watch for the mention of a scene from the novel *BlackWolfe* towards the end – one of my favorite scenes of all time.

With that – I hope you enjoy Tor and Isalyn's tale!

Hugs,

Kathryn

The Parents, Children, and Grandchildren of de Wolfe

(Note: Don't be intimidated by these family trees – skip over them if you wish and then refer back to them if you need clarification on a relationship)

William (deceased 1296 A.D.) and Jordan Scott de Wolfe

Total children: 10

Total grandchildren: 75 (including 4 deceased, 7 adopted, 3 stepgrandchildren)

Scott (Troy's twin) – (Wife #1 Lady Athena de Norville, has issue. Wife #2 Lady Avrielle Huntley du Rennic, has issue)

With Athena

- William (married Lily de Lohr, has issue.)
- Thomas "Tor"
- Andrew (deceased)
- Beatrice (deceased)

With Avrielle

- Sophia (with Nathaniel du Rennic)
- Stephen (with Nathaniel du Rennic)
- Sorcha (with Nathaniel du Rennic)
- Jeremy
- Nathaniel
- Alexander
- Seraphina

- Jordan

Troy (Scott's twin) – (Wife #1 Lady Helene de Norville, has issue. Wife #2 Lady Rhoswyn Kerr, has issue)

With Helene

- Andreas
- Acacia (deceased)
- Arista (deceased)

With Rhoswyn

- Gareth
- Corey
- Reed
- Tavin
- Tristan
- Elsbeth
- Madeleine

Patrick – (Married to Lady Brighton de Favereux, has issue)

- Markus
- Cassius
- Magnus
- Titus
- Thora
- Kristiana

James – (Wife #1 Lady Rose Hage, has issue. Wife #2 Asmara ap Cader, has issue)

With Rose

- Ronan
- Isabella

With Asmara (as Blayth)

- Maddoc
- Bowen
- Caius
- Garreth (known as Garr)

Katheryn (James' twin) – (Married to Sir Alec Hage, has issue)

- Edward
- Axel
- Christoph
- Kieran
- Christian

Evelyn – (Married to Sir Hector de Norville, has issue)

- Atreus
- Hermes
- Lisbet
- Adele
- Aline
- Lesander (goes by Zander)

Baby de Wolfe – (Died same day. Christened Madeleine)

Edward – (Married to Lady Cassiopeia de Norville, has issue)

- Helene
- Phoebe
- Hestia
- Asteria
- Leonidas
- Dorian
- Dayne

- Stephan
- Pallas

Thomas – (Married to Lady Maitland "Mae" de Ryes Bowlin, has issue)

- Artus (adopted)
- Nora (adopted)
- Phin (adopted)
- Marybelle (adopted)
- Renard & Roland (adopted)
- Dyana (adopted)
- Alexander
- Cabot
- Matthew
- Wade
- Tacey
- Morgan

Penelope – (Married to Bhrodi de Shera, Earl of Coventry, hereditary King of Anglesey)

- William
- Perri
- Bowen
- Dai
- Catrin
- Morgana
- Maddock
- Anthea
- Talan

Holdings and Titles of the House of de Wolfe and Close Allies as of 1300 A.D.

Scott de Wolfe – Earl of Warenton (Heir: William "Will" de Wolfe, Lord Killham)

Troy de Wolfe – Lord Braemoor (Heir: Andreas de Wolfe)

Patrick de Wolfe – Earl of Berwick (Heir: Markus de Wolfe, Lord Ravensdowne)

Blayth (James) de Wolfe – Baron Sydenham (Heir: Ronan de Wolfe)

Edward de Wolfe – Baron Kentmere (Heir: Leonidas de Wolfe)

Thomas de Wolfe – Earl of Northumbria (Heir: Alexander de Wolfe, Lord Easington)

Wark Castle (Wolfe's Eye):

Larger outpost for the Earl of Warenton. Literally sits on the border between England and Scotland.

- Titus de Wolfe (son of Patrick de Wolfe), commander
- Ronan de Wolfe (son of Blayth/James de Wolfe)

Berwick Castle (Wolfe's Teeth):

Massive border castle, strategically important, de Wolfe holding and seat of the Earl of Berwick, Patrick de Wolfe

- Alec Hage, commander
- Edward "Eddie" Hage, commander
- Hermes de Norville, second

Castle Questing (Wolfe's Heart):

Massive fortress, seat of the Earl of Warenton, Scott de Wolfe.

- Apollo de Norville, second
- Nathaniel Hage
- Owen le Mon

Rule Water Castle (Wolfe's Lair):

The largest outpost in the de Wolfe empire, known as The Lair. Seat of William "Will" de Wolfe, Viscount Kilham, heir apparent to the Earldom of Warenton.

- Magnus de Wolfe, second
- Adonis de Norville, second
- Perri de Shera, son of the Earl of Coventry and Penelope de Wolfe de Shera (squire)

Monteviot Tower (Wolfe's Shield):

Smaller outpost in Scotland, strategic. Holding of Troy de Wolfe.

- Andreas de Wolfe, commander

Kale Water Castle (Wolfe's Den):

Larger outpost on the England side of the border, strategic.

- Troy de Wolfe, Lord Braemoor, commander
- Troy also commands Sibbald's Hold, former home of Red Keith Kerr (his wife's father). A minor property commanded by son Garreth de Wolfe.

Kyloe Castle (Wolfe's Howl):

Seat of the Earl of Northumbria, Thomas de Wolfe

- Christoph Hage, second

Roxburgh Castle (Wolfe's Claw – unofficially)*

Large royal-held castle near Kelso, formerly manned by knights from Northwood, but awarded to the House of de Wolfe by royal decree for meritorious service to the crown. Volatile location, often attacked by Scots, and is manned by both royal and de Wolfe troops.

- Blayth (James) de Wolfe, Lord Sydenham, commander
- Axel Hage, second

*Note: Because of the extreme volatile location and nature of this garrison, Blayth (James) de Wolfe was given the title Lord Sydenham and the Sydenham Barony, a small but strategic barony between Wark Castle and the town of Kelso.

Blackpool Castle (acquired by Scott de Wolfe around 1300 A.D.) known as Wolfe's Strike:

- Thomas "Tor" de Wolfe, commander
- Christian Hage, second

Northwood Castle:

Massive border castle, very important and strategic. Belonging to the Earls of Teviot. Not part of the de Wolfe empire, but strongly allied to de Wolfe by marriage and blood. The Earl of Teviot is John Adrian de Longley, Adam de Longley's eldest son. Adrian's mother is Cayetana Fernanda Teresita Silva y Fausto de Longley, Princess of Aragon.

- Hector de Norville, captain of the guard (also Lord Bowmont)
- Atreus de Norville, second
- Tobias de Bocage, second

Edenburn Tower (House of de Norville):

Smaller tower on the southern end of de Wolfe properties belonging to the House of de Norville. Owned and commanded by Alec Hage

Castle Canaan (Kendal) Wolfe's Bite:

The Earl of Warenton's southernmost holding, not directly related to the Scottish border but a source of additional troops if needed. Inherited the property when he married the widow of Castle Canaan.

- Stephan du Rennic, commander

Seven Gates Castle (Kendal):

- Seat of Edward de Wolfe's Barony – Kentmere in Kendal that adjoins brother Scott's lands at Castle Canaan
- Isleworth House, Surrey

Cheswick Castle (Northumberland) Wolfe's Roar:

- Seat of Markus de Wolfe, Lord Ravensdowne, heir to Berwick earldom
- Also included in this alliance is Trastamara Castle, home of Markus' stepson, Atlas de Abril (formerly Atlas de Sauque) and wife Caria de Wolfe de Abril.

De Wolfe Pack Generations

The grandsons of William de Wolfe are referred to as "The de Wolfe Cubs". There are more than forty of them, both biological and adopted, and each young man is sworn to his powerful and rich legacy. When each grandson comes of age and is knighted, he tattoos the de Wolfe standard onto some part of his body. It is a rite of passage and it is that mark that links these young men together more than blood.

More than brotherhood.

It is the de Wolfe birthright.

The de Wolfe Pack standard is meant to be worn with honor, with pride, and with resilience, for there is no more recognizable standard in Medieval England. To shame the Pack is to have the tattoo removed, never to be regained.

This is their world.

Welcome to the Cub Generation.

De Wolfe Motto: ***Fortis in arduis***

Strength in times of trouble

PROLOGUE

Year of Our Lord 1284
August
Lioncross Abbey Castle, The Welsh Marches

IT WAS DAWN.

From the rains the previous night, the fields were green but the road was muddy, thick and uneven, like a puddle of congealed gravy. It made for difficult travel as the two-thousand-man army from Lioncross Abbey Castle returned from a nasty battle for control of Goodrich Castle, several days' journey to the south. The English held it, a local Welsh lord wanted it, and the Lord of Goodrich had called upon most of his allies, including the mighty House of de Lohr.

It hadn't been a long campaign as far as campaigns went. They'd been on longer, but this one had been particularly brutal because of the Welsh tactics. They didn't want to give up Goodrich and the English had to beat them back repeatedly. But in the end, the banner of William de Valence, Lord of Goodrich and half-brother to the king, flew proudly alongside the de Lohr blue lion standard.

The battle, for now, had been won.

But it was a battle that had taken a toll on the knights of de

Lohr. William de Lohr, son of Chris de Lohr and the great-grandson of the great Defender of the Realm, Christopher de Lohr, had sent out most of his knights to answer the call of service. Those who rode out were some of the most elite knights on the Marches – his own sons, Curt and Lucas, were leading the army along with Jorden de Russe, a mountain of a man from the legendary de Russe family, Rhun du Bois, son of Maddoc du Bois, and perhaps the best knight out of all of them, Thomas "Tor" de Wolfe.

Though it was an impressive group, the toll on their strengths and spirits had been substantial.

The men from Lioncross Abbey been gone almost three months to Goodrich, long enough so that the Welsh grew weary of fighting and of losing good men, and three months away from home was a very long time for them. All of the knights had families, including Tor, who was expecting his first child with his wife, Jane.

God, he'd missed her.

Therefore, the three months away had been difficult for him. As the army crested the rise to the south, with the massive fortress of Lioncross Abbey on the horizon up ahead, he felt a considerable amount of relief.

Finally, he was going to see Janie again.

In spite of the muddied roads and exhaustion of the army, they seemed to pick up the pace when the great stone bastion of Lioncross was sighted. Tor, who had been riding mid-pack with the wagon carrying the wounded, spurred his mud-covered warhorse forward, charging up the line until he reached the front.

His heavy Ardennes stallion kicked mud on nearly everyone within a ten-foot radius as he brought it to a halt. Mostly, men moved aside anyway when they saw Tor's horse coming because it was the biggest, most muscular horse anyone had ever seen, with legs as big around as a man's body and a chunky, powerful build. His name was Enbarr, after a horse of the old Irish gods, but Enbarr had a secret – he may have been big and powerful, but he had two distinct personalities. In battle, he was hell, but out of battle, he behaved like a puppy. He was the sweetest, most docile animal and he'd been known to follow Tor into the keep, much to Lady de Lohr's horror.

However, Enbarr was exhausted on this day, like the rest of them, and he was edgy as Tor reined him near his liege.

Curtis de Lohr, or Curt, was nearly the exact image of his famous great-great-grandsire. He had thick blond hair and a blond beard, and a size that was purely de Lohr. He was a proud tribute to a great family and as mud came flying at him from Enbarr's hooves, he turned his head away quickly so he wouldn't get hit in the face.

"Keep that big, ugly dog away from me," he said. "The last time he came too close, he tried to nibble on my face."

Tor fought off a grin. "That is because he loves you," he said. "You should be flattered."

"Yet, I am not."

Tor's grin broke through. "Then I will remove him from you completely," he said. "Would you mind if I went on ahead? Jane should have already delivered our child by now and I would very much like to see to her."

Curt looked at him, his eyes twinkling wearily. "I was wondering when you were going to ask," he said. "You have not said a word about it nearly this entire campaign. I was coming to wonder if you even remembered that your wife was with child."

Tor shrugged. "Battle is no place to speak of a pregnant woman," he said. "I needed to keep my mind on the fight and not on my wife."

"You did not even receive a missive from home, did you?"

"Nay," Tor said, shaking his head. "It would have been too

much of a distraction, so I asked that nothing be sent. If I had received word, I would have wanted to go home right away, and that would not have been good for my focus. It was my intention to make it back to her whole and alive."

Curt laughed softly. "And so you have," he said. Then he gestured towards the castle in the distance. "Ride on. And congratulations, Papa."

With a thankful smile, Tor spurred Enbarr and the horse took off. Those powerful legs could run for days and the horse thundered over the muddy road, only slowing down twice to avoid swampy sections. The section of the road that he was on bypassed the village that was nestled to the northeast of Lioncross, so it was an unimpeded ride the entire way.

All Tor could think about was his family.

This was an important moment to him.

Tor and Jane de Merrett, a former lady-in-waiting for the Countess of Hereford and Worcester, had married a little over a year ago. He had been young to be a groom, barely twenty years of age, but Jane had been pregnant and he had quickly married her so as not to cause a scandal.

The de Merretts were a big family in Manchester and even though the House of de Wolfe was larger and more powerful, Tor hadn't wanted any issues with de Merrett. Nothing would have been more embarrassing than Lord de Merrett riding to Castle Questing and demanding satisfaction for a randy son of de Wolfe.

Tor knew his father would have killed him.

Therefore, he and Jane had married in secret and her parents could not have been more delighted, fortunately. Marrying one of the heirs of the House of de Wolfe had soothed any outrage they might have felt, and Tor had dodged what could have been a bad situation purely with his familial connection. But he and Jane paid a hefty price for their youthful, lustful behavior when she miscarried the child early on.

Only a scant two months later, she was pregnant again.

It was that child that Tor was so eager to see. His older brother, William "Will" de Wolfe, already had a child and Tor, as always, was eager to follow in his brother's footsteps. Will was far to the north now, in command of one of their father's mighty bastions along the Scots border, but Tor had remained behind at Lioncross Abbey Castle where they had both fostered. It had been his home for a few years and he loved life on the Marches even though he knew it was only temporary. At some point, he'd be expected to return to the north and take his rightful place beside his brother, as the second son of the Earl of Warenton, Scott de Wolfe.

There was the heir and then there was the spare – and that was Tor.

But until then, he enjoyed the experience of life on the Welsh Marches. They were as volatile as the Scottish Marches. Maybe more so. But he loved the scenery, the greenery, the icy rivers and the flowers in the spring. He enjoyed all of those things probably more than the next man simply because, beneath that warring exterior and quiet demeanor, Tor had a gentle nature.

Considering how big he was, and he was taller than most men, with fists the size of a man's head, his inherent gentleness seemed strangely out of place. On the field of battle, he'd been trained to rip a man's head clean from his shoulders, but those same hands could hold his wife with a good deal of tenderness. The gentle nature also belied a fierce intelligence, for in a room of a hundred men, Tor was always the smartest. He knew a great deal about almost everything and tactically speaking, he was a master. That was why Curt wouldn't make a move without him. Even at Tor's young age, he was becoming quite a legend like his famous grandfather.

It was a Welsh adversary who had given him his nickname – *Tor.*

It meant a rock formation, rising up out of the ground, big and insurmountable. Impenetrable. That was what everyone called him these days.

With youth, strength, and a powerful reputation already built, Tor had the world at his feet, now with a beautiful wife and new baby. He had everything he'd ever wanted. As he rode through the gates of Lioncross Abbey, the call went up and men were scrambling. As he neared the keep, he was met by Brom Kessler, a Lioncross legacy knight whose great-grandfather, Jeffrey, had served the Defender of the Realm, Christopher de Lohr. Brom was big and auburn-haired, and he grasped Enbarr's reins, helping Tor pull the weary animal to a halt.

"We've been riding for two solid weeks," Tor said as he slid from the saddle. "The army is less than an hour behind me, so make sure you are prepared to receive them. Four wagons bearing wounded this time. You'd better let Lady de Lohr know."

Brom handed the horse off to a stable servant and whistled for a soldier at the same time. Men came running to him, prepared to do his bidding, and he gave them quick orders and sent them on their way. When he sent the soldier for Lady de Lohr, he muttered to the man under his breath so Tor wouldn't hear him. He was sending word about Tor's arrival more than the approach of the wounded. Just as he turned around, Tor was preparing to head into the keep but Brom grabbed him.

"How many men did we lose in totality?" he asked.

Tor was distracted; that much was clear. He pulled off his helm, removing the damp linen cap that he kept pulled over his hair, revealing cropped auburn hair that was aflame with white and gold streaks, making it appear much lighter than it actually was.

"We were there almost three months," he said. "We took an army of two thousand, one hundred and forty-five men and we lost a little over three hundred. Not a bad percentage given how fierce the fighting was, but Goodrich held."

Brom lifted an eyebrow. "At least for now," he said. "I heard de Lara troops from Lansdown Castle were also there."

"They were," Tor confirmed. Then, he peeled Brom's fingers from his arm, as the man was still holding on to him. "Now, if you will excuse me, I have a wife to see. Has Jane delivered my son? Nay, do not tell me. I want to see her and let her tell me. Say a word and I shall cut your tongue out."

Brom sighed faintly, holding up both hands in supplication. "I will not say a word, Tor," he said. "But if you can just tell me more about the…"

Tor cut him off, moving away from him. "Let de Lohr tell you," he said. "As I said, they're not far behind me. He'll tell you everything. I have a wife to see."

With that, he flashed Brom a grin, turning for the keep. Brom knew he couldn't delay the man any longer than he had without him growing suspicious.

He prayed for Lady de Lohr's quick appearance.

Oblivious to Brom's consternation, Tor continued towards the keep, one he was as familiar with as any of the de Wolfe properties. Lioncross' keep was oddly shaped, a long building, as it was built on the foundations of an old abbey. The entry was on the ground level, very unusual in castles, but there was a forebuilding in front of the entry that had been built about fifty years ago for more protection on the entry door. As Tor entered the narrow, low-ceilinged forebuilding, he was met by Lady de Lohr.

Deirdra de Lohr, Countess of Hereford and Worcester, was just coming from the entry. In fact, she was rushing. A pretty woman with red hair and a sweet manner, she was much loved by her vassals. She was alone, unusual for a woman who usually traveled with an entourage, and she went straight to Tor, blocking him from entering the keep.

"Welcome home, Tor," she said. Then she pointed to the heavily fortified door of the forebuilding. "Lock that door. Do it now."

Tor didn't hesitate. He stopped, turned around, and shut the door, throwing the heavy iron bolts that made it virtually impenetrable. Once it was done, he looked at Lady de Lohr curiously.

"My lady?" he said.

He wanted to know why he'd bolted the door. Lady de Lohr had him lock it because she didn't want anyone interrupting the conversation that she was about to have with him. As the Lady of Lioncross, her responsibilities were many, including the health and happiness of her vassals.

She'd been dreading this moment for three long weeks but she knew she couldn't delay.

Reaching out, she took one of Tor's hands.

"I wanted to speak to you alone, Tor," she said softly. "It's about Jane."

He looked at her for a moment before realizing she wasn't congratulating him. No well-wishes for a new child or a joyful wife. Realizing that, his features started to tense up.

"What about my wife?" he said. "Is she well?"

Lady de Lohr continued to hold his hand. "She knew you were in battle and she did not wish to trouble you," she said gently. "Although you told her not to send word because it would distract you, I urged her to do it and she would not. She did not wish to disobey you."

Tor was starting to feel something in the pit of his belly. He wasn't a man prone to fear but, at the moment, he could feel the distinct pangs of it begin. He'd returned to Lioncross with joy and anticipation, the first time in three months he'd let himself feel those emotions. They were spilling out all over the place and he had already been planning to become wildly drunk tonight to celebrate the birth of his child.

But now…

He could just tell by looking at her that something awful had happened.

"My lady," he said, struggling to be calm. "I would appreciate it if you would simply come out and tell me what has happened."

Lady de Lohr had angst written all over her face. Tor was astute and very sharp, and perhaps she wasn't doing a very good job of delivering the news she very much wished she didn't have to tell him.

She took a deep breath.

"After you left with the army to go to Goodrich, Jane started feeling poorly," she said. "She was pale and weary, and slept constantly, so the physic put her on a diet of beef broth and meat. He wanted her to eat a good deal of meat because he said her blood was weak. That was when I wanted to send you word, but she refused. We all watched her become progressively weaker until, three weeks ago, she began to labor to bring forth your child. Tor, sometimes it is God's will that these things happen. There is often no reason or cause. It simply happens. Jane struggled for three days to bear your child but, in the end, it was too much for her. The angels called her home and the child along with her. I'm so very sorry."

Tor stared at her as if didn't understand what she was telling him. But as the words sank in, his pallor became ashen. The pale green eyes flickered.

He swallowed hard.

"She is dead?" he asked. "Janie is dead?"

"She is," Lady de Lohr said sadly, squeezing his hand. "I

wish I could say something that would bring you comfort, but you must find that in your own time, with God's help. I can tell you that she was very brave. She told me to tell you that she loved you dearly and asked that you take care of her sisters. The younger girls are all alone now, with their parents and oldest sister gone. Will you do this? Will you take care of Barbara and Lenore? It was what Jane wanted."

Tor had to sit down. There was a stone bench behind him and he sank onto it, with Lady de Lohr still holding his hand. He simply sat there, dumbfounded, hardly able to process what he'd been told.

"Jane," he murmured, dazed. Then he started to blink rapidly, as if blinking away tears. "Of course she was brave. Jane was nothing else, ever since the day I met her."

"She was very brave, dear Tor. Take comfort in that, if you will."

He simply sat there, staring off into space, thinking of the wife he'd lost.

And the child.

In an instant, his entire family was gone.

"The child?" he managed to ask hoarsely. "Was it male?"

Lady de Lohr cleared her throat softly. "I do not know," she said. "She died with the child still inside of her and we made the decision not to cut her open to retrieve the babe."

He looked at her, then. "But the child could have still been alive. Jane would have wanted you to save our son."

But Lady de Lohr shook her head. "The physic determined that the child was dead when Jane's labor began," she said gently. "The child was early, you know. The labor was God's way of expelling the dead baby, but Jane did not have the strength to push him out."

"You are certain of this?"

"As certain as I can be, Tor. Please know I would have done

everything possible if there had been the slightest chance to save her or the child."

He knew that. Lady de Lohr was a caring, compassionate woman, but he had to ask. The hollowness, the grief, that was building inside of him was demanding answers and it was difficult not to give in to the pain.

But Tor had never been the animated kind.

He was, in short, a gentle giant. He was calm and well-liked, which was part of the reason this situation was such a tragedy. Tor deserved to be happy and to have the family he very much wanted. He deserved all of the good things that life had to offer and a situation like this was a heartbreak for all involved.

Having watched him grow up, it was particularly difficult for Lady de Lohr.

Tor knew that. In theory, he knew that she would have moved heaven and earth to save Jane, but there had been no hope. It must have been dire, indeed, which began to tear at him. He'd told her not to send word to him about her pregnancy or the birth.

Now, he was coming to regret that directive, very much.

"I am sure you would have done everything possible," he finally said. "I did not mean to question you. 'Tis simply that… we are speaking of my Janie. She is too young and beautiful to die."

Lady de Lohr was near tears. "She will be forever young and beautiful to us all, Tor," she said softly. "We will remember her with great love and affection. Even if you had been here, there was nothing you could have done. You could not have saved her. Mayhap it is best if you remember her as she was the very last day you left her – happy, sweet, and loving. Hold that memory close, Tor."

His eyes were starting to well. Something in Lady de Lohr's statement conveyed the horror of Jane's final days. After a moment, he looked up at her.

"She died in agony, didn't she?" he asked.

Lady de Lohr was taken aback by the question. "She… she was weary, of course. She tried to bring forth the child for several days."

"Tell me the truth."

"Tor…"

"Tell me!" he boomed.

Lady de Lohr jumped, startled by his exceptionally loud voice. She had known Tor since he'd been a boy, having grown into a man of considerable size and strength, and his shout frightened her. It was the first time she'd ever heard the man raise his voice or show a temper, ever. Given the circumstances, it was understandable.

But she held her ground.

"I told you the truth," she said evenly. "She died exhausted but brave. Of course there was pain; having a child is not a painless experience. What would you have me tell you? That her body contorted with great contractions to bring forth a child that was far too large for her to carry? That, at times, it was so painful that she screamed? Is that what you wish to hear?"

Tor's eyes widened and Lady de Lohr realized what she had said. She'd spoken honestly before she could stop herself.

She grasped him with both hands this time.

"I did not mean to say that," she said. "Forgive me, Tor. The child was large, that is true, but it was not your fault. You must not blame yourself. I did not mean to imply otherwise."

He blinked at her, still startled by her words. "Then it is true," he said. "The child was too large. *My* child was too large."

Lady de Lohr hoped she hadn't done damage with her truthful outburst. "He was very big, but women are made for bearing big children," she said. "I have given birth to my share of them and I am quite well. But Janie… as I said, sometimes these things happen and we do not know why. Only God knows."

Tor was sinking further into despair and trying hard not to. "For a man to die in battle, I understand why God permits such a thing," he said. "A man goes into battle with the intention of taking a life. If his own life is taken, it is a fitting retribution. But a woman faces childbirth with the intention of *giving* life. It is a cruel God who allows women to die in childbirth."

"Hush," Lady de Lohr said softly. "You must not blaspheme."

Tor wouldn't look at her. "I can say what I wish now that there is no longer any reason to pray to God," he said. "He should have taken me instead of Jane. I had gone to Goodrich with the intention of killing men. But Janie… all she wanted was to hold our son in her arms. Speak not to me of God, Lady de Lohr, for that is not something I wish to hear."

Lady de Lohr wasn't going to push him. She knew that he was doing the best he could under the circumstances, lashing out as much as Tor de Wolfe was capable of lashing out. She'd never seen such a controlled man, but she had heard from her husband that once the control was broken, there was no stopping Tor in anything he wished to do – kill a man, destroy a home, burn a town. He was capable of such things.

But he kept that monster tightly under restraint.

Therefore, she simply squeezed his hand and released him. "If there is anything I can do for you, Tor, you only need ask," she said. "I am here to help you in any way. If you wish for me to send a missive to your father, I shall. I have refrained from doing anything, waiting until you returned so that you can decide what needs to be done. But you must understand that we had to bury Jane. With the weather warm, we had no choice. I hope you do understand that."

He was still looking away, still staring off into space as he pondered his unexpected future without the woman he loved.

"Where is she?" he asked.

"In Lioncross' abbey," she said.

"Down in the vault?"

"Aye," she said. "You know the area under the south wing of the keep, the old abbey. It is where all of the de Lohrs for almost one hundred years have been buried. Jane is in good company down there. The knights in their crypts will watch over her."

Tor sighed faintly, realizing that he felt very much like weeping. He hadn't wept since he'd been a child. Jane was gone, their child was gone, and he had nothing left.

Nothing but Jane's younger sisters.

Lady Barbara and Lady Lenore de Merrett had come to live with them only a few months ago after their parents died of the same mysterious infection. Barbara was ten years of age and Lenore was nine years of age, small girls that Jane had coddled and fussed over. Truth be told, Tor hadn't had any real interaction with them. He didn't even really know them.

But now, they belonged to him.

Standing up, he excused himself. He didn't want to talk to Lady de Lohr any longer. He wanted to visit Jane and their child, down in the cold, dank abbey of Lioncross. They were alone down there and he needed to be with them. He wanted to talk to her, to apologize for killing her with the child he implanted within her. He knew she wouldn't blame him, for Jane had been a gentle creature who would have taken the guilt herself before she let Tor assume any of it, but he wanted to apologize to her all the same.

He did this.

It was all his fault.

The pain was beginning to consume him.

As he made his way down to the abbey, he had to pass through the massive bailey to do it. There was an exterior door, heavily fortified, that led into the labyrinth that was known as the abbey, but as he walked, he swore he could hear a collective hush come over the bailey even though the army was beginning to arrive.

Word was spreading.

Lady de Wolfe did not survive, men were saying. They were whispering from one to another, and Tor could feel their stares crawling up his back. It felt like vermin crawling all over him, knowing men were staring at him and flooding the very air around them with their pity. He hated it; he hated being pitied. Somewhere behind him, Lady de Lohr had emerged from the forebuilding to watch him make his way to the abbey, but she caught sight of her son as he rode into the bailey and she went to him. Tor didn't see her tears when Curt took her in his arms.

He didn't care about her tears.

He only cared about his own.

The abbey smelled like mildew. It was sunk deep into the ground, not quite below ground but not quite above it, either. The abbey had been dedicated to St. David, but had fallen into ruin when the builders of Lioncross had constructed their castle over it. However, the abbey had been built over Roman ruins, so the floor of the abbey had mosaic work, unusual in a Christian building.

Whatever was down here smelled old and rotten, as if the very strands of time had been buried deep into the soil. Everything about it smelled ancient. Tor didn't come into this place much, mostly because he wasn't very pious, but as he came into the abbey itself, he could see that torches had been lit. Up near the nave stood two small figures and he knew immediately who they were.

He recognized the red hair.

Barbara and Lenore had been found.

The girls heard the footfalls and turned to see Tor as he approached in the darkness. Even though he hadn't had much interaction with them, and they didn't know him very well, they still ran at him, throwing their arms around him in gestures he found both uncomfortable and pitiful. Lenore, the younger sister, was wailing.

"You came back," she wept. "You did not die in battle!"

"We were afraid you would not return!" Barbara sobbed, grasping at him. "Janie is dead! The baby is dead!"

Tor wasn't sure what to do. The children were clinging to him as if he alone could save them from their gloom, and he wasn't ready to deal with it. He had his own emotions to deal with. He didn't want to comfort two grieving children.

It was an effort not to push them both away.

"Nay," he said. "I did not die. But do not hug me so close. I have sharp things on my belt that can hurt you and my clothing is filthy. Stand back, now. Let me go."

He practically had to pry them away, but they clung to his hands. Both of them were weeping, wiping running noses and eyes, and Tor lost his patience. He pulled his hands away from them, yanking himself free, and stepped away.

"Go," he told them. "Go back to your chamber. I will come to you there when I am finished."

"But..!" Barbara started to speak.

"*Go*," Tor boomed, the word echoing off the walls. When the girls shrieked, he lowered the volume of his voice. "Please. Obey me, both of you. Go to your chamber now."

Sniffling, Barbara dragged the wailing Lenore from the abbey. He could hear the children weeping until the sounds eventually faded. Then, he was alone in that mildew-ridden vault. Taking a deep breath, he stepped over into the nave where the crypts were kept.

It was very dark in this section of the abbey, with only the ambient torchlight to bring some illumination to the darkness. Tor moved hesitantly, his eyes becoming accustomed to the extreme darkness. There was something sacred here, but there was also something eerie, as if the slightest sound could awaken the dead. His heart began to beat faster with trepidation and his carefully held control seemed to be slipping no matter how hard he grasped at it.

He was in the realm of the dead.

Jane's realm.

The family that had originally built the castle, the House of Barringdon, had family members buried in stone crypts that were built against the walls. He could see the names of some of the past lords of Lioncross… Arthur Barringdon, who'd died on crusade with King Richard was one. Tor remembered hearing that Arthur was the man Christopher de Lohr had inherited the castle from when he married Arthur's daughter. In fact, Arthur's daughter, Dustin, was also buried here in the same crypt as her husband.

They were together for eternity.

Moving further into the nave, Tor could see the crypts of other de Lohrs. He was so busy looking for a crypt that would contain his wife and child that he failed to notice the ground to his left. The floor of the nave was flagstone, the blue slate stone that was so common to Wales, and a portion of that flagstone had been moved away and the dirt beneath it disturbed.

He finally saw it.

There was a small mound of disturbed dirt on the extreme south side of the abbey, just about the right size for a lady of Jane's small build. Slowly, Tor made his way over to it, realizing as he drew closer that there were two small bundles of drying flowers on top of the disturbed earth.

Two small bundles from two small sisters left behind.

When he realized he was looking at Jane's grave, all of Tor's strength seemed to leave him. The control that he held so carefully was gone and he sank to his knees, feeling a lump in his throat. He was a man unused to emotion but, at this moment, he was feeling things he'd never felt before. This was not what he had expected when he had returned to Lioncross this day and the blow to his soul was almost more than he could take.

"Oh… Janie," he murmured. "Lady de Lohr told me what happened. Forgive me, Janie. Forgive me for telling you not to send word to me while I was away. I wish you had. God, I wish you had, but your obedience cost you the right to have me with you as you breathed your last. It cost you the right to have my comfort and I can never express my sorrow and regret. I should not have been so harsh with you. I only thought… I did not wish to be distracted because I wanted to return whole and safe to you. I swear to you that it was my only thought."

He was met with silence. The hollow echo of the cold stone walls and the icy fingers of the earth reaching up through the ground grasping at him, caused him to feel that iciness in his heart. His grief threatened to consume him but, even above that, all he could feel was unmitigated anger at himself for being stubborn enough and foolish enough to tell his wife that he was beyond her reach during a time when he should have been at her side every moment of the day.

He was absolutely right. Her obedience of his directive had caused her to die without his comfort. Lady de Lohr had said that Jane had writhed with pain as she struggled to bring forth a child that could not, and would not, be born. What terror and agony she must have felt knowing that she couldn't deliver the child. Surely she would have known that towards the end, realizing that nothing she could do would push that babe from her body.

Jane died alone, without the love or comfort of her husband, and with only Lady de Lohr and the physic as company.

That knowledge was beginning to eat him up inside.

His head fell forward into his hands, and he sat there a moment with his eyes closed and his hands over his face as he tried not to envision Jane breathing her last and knowing her husband would not come. His face would not be the last one she ever saw. It was a horrible ending for a kind, pretty, and gentle soul, one who had captured Tor's attention even as a girl.

Tor had known Jane since his arrival at Lioncross Abbey, as she had been a ward of the House of de Lohr. In that sense, they had grown up together, and he had been given the privilege of years of knowing Jane. She wasn't like the other girls who followed Lady de Lohr around and learned from her direction. She wasn't flighty or gossipy, and that was always something he had appreciated in her. She had her moments of wisdom, her moments of stubbornness, but mostly, she had her moments of brilliance and those were moments he was very much going to miss. When he'd been at Goodrich, he'd missed her, but never as much as he did at this very moment, knowing she wasn't going to return.

And then there was their child.

Given the size of the babe and the fact that Jane had been too weak and too small to push it out, he was positive that it had been a boy. A son of the House of de Wolfe that would never know his destiny. It would not be the first child of de Wolfe that did not know his destiny, and it probably would not be the last, but this particular tragedy hit closer to home to Tor than the other instances.

He'd had his share of death when it came to young males in the family.

When Tor had been a youth, he had lost a younger sister and youngest brother in a tragic accident that also took his mother's life. As a result, his father had fled the tragedy, unable to face his grief or his guilt. Tor and his older brother, William, had been away fostering at the time, so they were somewhat removed from the heart of the disaster. Tor would never forget how his father basically abandoned the family for a few years until he was finally able to come to grips with his grief.

An event he felt responsible for.

It had been Scott de Wolfe who had given the approval for the happening that had cost the life of Tor's mother and siblings, but also the life of his aunt and two cousins. The women and their two youngest children were traveling after a series of heavy rainstorms and the carriage they had been traveling in had been dumped into a river where they had all drowned. Scott was the one who had put them into the carriage and sent them along their way, and it had taken him years to get over the guilt of sending all six of them to their deaths.

Now, Tor understood how his father felt.

He was responsible for this event.

He had been the one who had impregnated Jane. He had been the one who had kept her abed, taking delight in her supple, young body and filling her with his seed on a nightly basis. He had been reckless and lustful, never once considering that anything bad could come of it. They were married and they wanted children, and Jane had been determined to give him a son.

Her determination had resulted in her death, but it wasn't her fault.

It was his.

Tor felt sick to his stomach. The sight of Jane's grave made him feel woozy. He had killed her as surely as if he had taken a knife to her. Removing his hands from his face, he looked around the old abbey at all of the knights and ladies who had lived before him, great and wise men and women. But the same couldn't be said for him.

He could feel their critical stares.

He had failed.

Leaning forward, he put his hands against the soft, cold earth of the new grave. The moment he touched it, tears filled his eyes and the lump in his throat made it so tight that he could not speak. He wanted to take her home, back to Castle Questing where generations of de Wolfes were buried. She was a de Wolfe, after all, and the right was hers to be buried with her husband's family.

But in the same breath, he realized that she needed to stay here.

Lioncross Abbey was where she had practically grown up and it was where she had met her husband, and Tor knew how happy she had been here. She had never even been to Castle Questing, so it seemed to him that this was the best place for her – where she had been her happiest. It was where he had been happy, too, but it occurred to him that he could not stay here. He couldn't stay here and face the ghost of her memories every time he turned around. Jane was imprinted here – she was part of this place. The more he thought about it, the more angst he felt.

The control he so carefully employed left him, leaving chaos in its wake.

That very day, Tor de Wolfe fled Lioncross Abbey Castle and took two small girls with him, not by desire, but by obligation. They were his responsibility and it had been a deathbed request from his wife. He had already let her down once. He wasn't going to let her down a second time.

That day, Tor de Wolfe left the Marches behind forever.

And left a piece of himself behind.

The Hunting Party

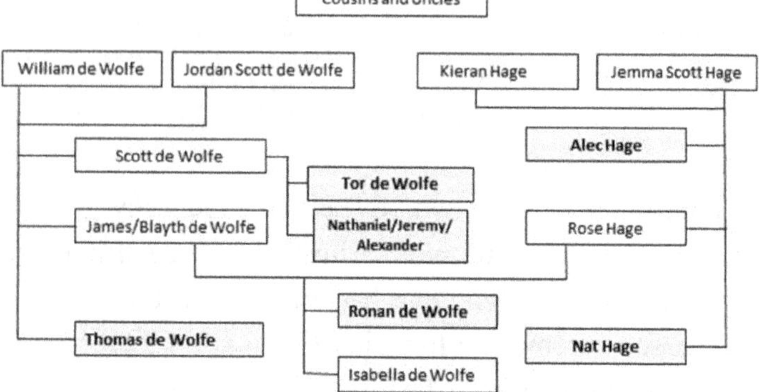

CHAPTER ONE

Year of Our Lord 1301
Northumberland

THEY WERE ON the hunt.

One of their own had been badly slandered and the de Wolfe knights were not going to stand for it.

A Hunting Party had been gathered. It had started at Castle Questing with Tor and his half-brothers Jeremy, Nathaniel, and Alexander. Tor was a product of his father's first marriage to Athena de Norville and his half-brothers were the product of his father's second marriage to Lady Avrielle du Rennic.

Tor was very close to his younger half-brothers and also to his half-sisters, of which he had several. In fact, he was close to the entire family for the first time in his life. He had been sent away at a young age to foster along with his older brother, and they had spent those formative years at Lioncross Abbey. But ever since returning home to Castle Questing, he had been given the privilege to come to know the brothers, sisters, cousins, aunts, and uncles that he hadn't grown up with.

Now, he was part of the massive de Wolfe collective.

He was one of them.

That familial bond was why they had all gathered. His Uncle Blayth's daughter, Isabella, was supposed to have been married on the last Friday of the month, but her betrothed had second thoughts and had fled south. Poor Isabella was devastated and her father, a mighty warrior who had survived a horrific wound in his youth, was bent on hell.

Blayth had called together his nephews and sons and brothers to pursue a coward who had left his daughter alone on her wedding day. Never in the history of the de Wolfe household had such a thing happened to one of their women, so the de Wolfe men were all bent on revenge. No one slandered their women and got away with it.

They were going to find the errant groom and make him pay.

Along with his three younger half-brothers, Tor was joined by Isabella's uncles, Nathaniel and Alec Hage. Since there were two Nathaniels in the family, named in honor of different men, the older Nathaniel, from the Hage branch, was called Nat. Nat and Alec were very big, very seasoned knights, and part of the reason Blayth had sent Tor and the others along was to keep Nat and Alec from tearing their niece's intended into tiny pieces.

Nat was particularly upset and he kept talking about cutting off that which was most vital to a man while his brother, Alec, who was the oldest of the siblings and the head of the House of Hage, didn't seem too inclined to tell his younger brother to calm down. Nat's rage seemed to please him.

But Nat wasn't the only one who was angry. Their posse had stopped at Kyloe Castle to collect Blayth's youngest brother, Thomas, and his oldest son, Artus. Thomas de Wolfe was the Earl of Northumbria, a title he had inherited through marriage, and he had a very large army. Artus was his adopted son, a former orphan, who had been trained as any noble son would have been. At twenty years of age, he was already a formidable knight and Thomas could not have been prouder of the young man had he been of his own blood.

The last addition to what they had deemed the Hunting Party had been the brother of the bride herself. Ronan de Wolfe was Blayth's eldest son and the fact that his sister had been shamed had the young knight's blood boiling even more than Nat's blood was. Nat was only an uncle, a brother of Isabella's mother, but Ronan was her brother. He was the angriest of all because he actually knew the groom, Steffan de Featherstone, who had been a friend. Or, at least, he thought he was a friend. It was through Ronan that Steffan had been considered a marital prospect for Isabella.

Now, Ronan was feeling like a fool.

He, more than any of them, had a score to settle.

Upon leaving Kyloe, the group of de Wolfe and Hage knights continued south to Newcastle upon Tyne. They knew that was where the groom was going because when he'd fled, he had left behind a terrified squire who had told Blayth everything because he feared for his life at the hands of too many vicious de Wolfe men. The squire had spilled his master's plans quite easily, so the pursuing knights knew where they were going.

They were going to find that bastard if it was the last thing they did.

It was late spring, and along with late spring came the storms that would turn the land into flowers in the summertime. But those same storms also turned the roads into soup and the collective party of heavily armed knights were covered in mud from their travels. The nine of them made a formidable sight as they stopped at Alnwick Castle on their way south to sup and pay their respects to Lord de Vesci. When Lord de Vesci heard the tale of a jilted de Wolfe bride, he offered them four of his most seasoned knights. Thomas, who knew de Vesci as a friend, readily accepted.

The de Wolfe Hunting Party grew.

Perhaps it wasn't necessary to have so many men, but it was prudent because Steffan de Featherstone was a seasoned knight in his own right. He served the Lords of de Royans at Netherghyll Castle and everyone knew their knights were the best. Therefore, being prepared was only wise because they were certain de Featherstone was going to put up a fight. He had fled for a reason and, for his sake, they could only hope it wasn't another lover.

As the group entered the outskirts of Newcastle on an evening with another storm on the horizon, they slowed their pace as they filtered into the village that was beginning to shut down for the night. The heady smells of the cooking fires was heavy on the air as the group plodded down one of the main avenues leading towards the center of the village, and they could hear people inside their homes, sitting down to an evening meal with the soft hum of conversation.

It all seemed rather quiet and calm, but it was the calm before the storm. As the small avenue widened and they ended up on a main street that was lined with residences as well as businesses, they were specifically looking for a tavern called The Black Bull. That was where de Featherstone's squire told them that they would possibly find their target.

Unfortunately, the squire wasn't entirely certain, and all of the threatening posturing by the irate father of the bride meant to scare him couldn't force him to change his story, so it was assumed that the squire was only guessing where they could find de Featherstone.

"He owns a big, white warhorse with brown spots on the rump," Ronan said, his blue eyes scanning the surrounding area as night fell. "We should check the liveries around here. Mayhap we can find his horse."

Tor turned to the four de Vesci knights, who had heard young Ronan. With a low whistle between his teeth and a gesture advising they do exactly what Ronan had suggested, the de Vesci knights split off and began heading in different directions, looking for the local liveries.

"I've been to Newcastle a couple times, but Uncle Tommy should know it better than I do," Tor said, turning to Thomas de Wolfe, riding next to his son. "You are the one with lands closer to Newcastle than any of us. Do you know where we can find The Black Bull tavern?"

Thomas nodded thoughtfully. "It is here, in the village center," he said. "I was last here about three years ago, so it has not changed so much that I do not recognize the place. As I recall, it was over near one of the town's wells."

The sun was almost down and the torches lit by the town's watch weren't giving off a tremendous amount of light, so the group moved forward, straining to catch a glimpse of the establishments that were still open. There was a small tavern to their left that seemed to be serving only food, and food that people were even taking home, because they had one entire side of the tavern open as they dished out food into empty pots for a few pence.

"What about sending word to the castle?" Nat Hage asked. "It's a royal garrison with hundreds of men. We could flush de Featherstone out quickly with enough help."

"Nay, lad," Thomas said. "The garrison at Newcastle is meant to defend the city, not roust it to find an errant groom. However, I will send Jeremy and Nathaniel to the castle to let the garrison commander know why we are here. I do not want word to reach them that a gang of de Wolfe knights are terrorizing the town. It would be the polite thing to tell him first."

"*Before* we terrorize the town," Tor muttered. "Informing

them will not stop us."

"Exactly."

As they grinned at each other, Jeremy and Nathaniel took exception to being sent away from the Hunting Party.

"Why us?" Jeremy said. Usually, he was a very obedient young man, but he also had battle fever. He wanted to beat up Steffan de Featherstone as much as the next man. "Why not send one of the de Vesci knights?

Thomas turned to look at him. A seasoned knight as well as a powerful earl, he was still big and muscular and imposing. Imposing enough to scare his nephews into submission.

"Because I asked you," he said pointedly. "Disobey me and I will have to tell your father. I do not think he would like it."

Scott was Thomas' eldest brother, and the two of them were close, so they knew that the threat was not an idle one. Jeremy refrained from frowning, but Nathaniel wasn't so adept at hiding his displeasure. He started to say something, but Jeremy slapped him on the back of the head.

"Come on," he said. "The sooner we inform the garrison, the sooner we can return."

As they thundered off, leaving their youngest brother with the group, who was most triumphant that he hadn't been asked to go to Newcastle, Thomas and Tor pushed forward in the search for The Black Bull.

"I am surprised that you do not know Steffan de Featherstone, Tor," Thomas said. He addressed him by his nickname, as did the rest of the family, because there were two Thomas de Wolfes, both named for the same man. "I seem to recall that they have a rather large property near Carlisle."

Tor nodded. "It is south of Brampton," he said. "And Brampton is south of my fortress. My lands butt up against Viscount Brampton's properties and I have met Gilbert de Featherstone twice at Brampton's fortress, but I am not particularly familiar with him or his son. Uncle Blayth said that Steffan serves at Netherghyll Castle. If he's part of the de Royans war machine, then he must be skilled, indeed."

Thomas looked at him. Enormously tall and muscular Tor, whose hair was now a pale red in color because it had started turning gray at an early age. He kept it neatly cut and combed back and he was, by all reasonable opinion, a very handsome man of some means.

His father, Scott, worried about him perhaps more than his other children because Tor seemed to have shut himself off from anything to do with female companionship when it came to finding a wife. They all knew why and, surprisingly, it wasn't because of the beloved wife he lost almost seventeen years ago.

It was because of a pair of vipers he kept close to him.

Tor was the only one who didn't see it.

Truth be told, Thomas worried about him, too.

"How are things at Blackpool Castle these days?" he asked casually. "Is everything peaceful?"

Tor nodded, though his gaze was searching for something that looked like a tavern. "Peaceful enough," he said. "Nothing unusual or harried, at least over the past couple of years. When Papa assumed Blackpool, it was because the former lord had been killed in a Scots raid."

"I remember."

Tor shrugged. "I must be greater than I thought because in the eight years I've been in command, I have seen an astonishing amount of peace. Not completely, but more than I should have. The Scots must be afraid of me."

He was jesting, mostly. Blackpool Castle had seen few battles over the years, but the ones it had seen had been nasty. Thomas knew this because once, he'd sent half his army over to fend off a rabid Scots attack. That particular area was full of Scots as well as de Wolfes, so there was always some conflict going on and it had earned the moniker of WolfeStrike in the short time it had been in the family's possession.

It was where the enemy met the hardest strike of all.

"Or it could be that The Lair is north of you and so is Monteviot Castle, Troy's holding," Thomas said. "It could be that those two are holding back the Scots so they do not break through to you."

Tor grinned. "Do not be fooled," he said. "I am the last line of defense between the Scots and all of northwest England. If they break the lines at The Lair and Monteviot, I can and will hold them. I've done it before. But it has been… costly."

Thomas knew that, better than most. He'd lost his share of men to combat on the Scottish Marches over the years.

"Holding the Marches is always costly," he said. "When I was in command of Wark Castle, we lost more than our share of good men. Speaking of men, do your wife's sisters still live with you? Or have you been fortunate enough to find husbands for them yet?"

Tor shook his head. "Not yet," he said. "Neither one has any real desire to leave and the few times I have brought in decent men for them to meet have not gone particularly well."

"Why not?"

He shrugged. "Barbara is very particular," he said. "She has never shown any huge interest in being married, so not any man will do. And Lenore shows even less interest. They are still young, however. They are in no rush to marry."

Thomas grunted. "They are in their mid-twenties, Tor," he said. "Already, they are spinsters. You are not doing them any favors by not forcing them to marry."

Tor cast him a long glance. "Like Uncle Blayth forced Isabella to marry and we are now chasing down her groom?" Before Thomas could answer, Tor suddenly gestured ahead of them. "Look – The Black Bull."

Distracted from the two leeches who had sunk their teeth into Tor and refused to let go, Thomas could see the two-storied establishment on ahead. Immediately, he went into battle mode.

"We must stash the horses," he said.

Quickly, he pulled his mount to a halt and slid off. To their right was a closed merchant stall and it had a hitching post in front of it, and they tethered the horses.

Then, they spread out.

The night was dark and the watch torches weren't giving out much light as they approached The Black Bull, brightly lit from within. They could hear the hum of conversation and the occasional burst of laughter.

Tor looked at the men around and behind him. Thomas was leading the way, an enormous warrior who was in his prime. He was followed by his son, Artus, well-armed and strong, whereas Nat and Alec Hage were moving faster than anyone else, ready to charge into the tavern. Ronan was sticking close to his uncles while the youngest warrior of the group, Alexander, stayed right by Tor's side. Tor glanced down at his youngest half-brother.

"You let me and your uncles do the initial fighting," he said. "Your job will be to watch our backs and make sure no one else jumps into the fray. Can you do that?"

Alexander nodded, but it was clear that he was just a little nervous. At seventeen years, he was still a squire, though his training had been very good. He knew how to handle himself in a fight.

Still…

"Wait," Thomas said, abruptly coming to a halt. He turned around, seeking out Alexander. "Alex, come here."

Alexander broke away from Tor and went to his Uncle Thomas. "Aye?"

"Do you know what Steffan de Featherstone looks like?"

Alexander nodded. "Aye."

Thomas pulled the young man's cloak up over his head, partially covering his face. "Go inside," he said. "It is crowded, so you can blend in with the patrons. I want you to see if Steffan is actually inside. Come back out to report to us."

Alexander didn't hesitate. He may have been nervous, but he knew how to follow an order. With his cloak mostly over his face at that point, he pushed into the packed tavern as the de Wolfe and Hage knights fell back into the shadows of the street to wait.

Alexander was out in less than a minute.

Concerned, Thomas pulled him into an alley next to the tavern as the others came out of their hiding spots to join them.

"What is wrong?" Thomas hissed. "Is he inside?"

Alexander unwrapped the cloak from his face. "Aye," he said. "He is sitting at a table with five other heavily armed knights. De Royans men, I believe."

Thomas sighed heavily and looked at Alec. Not only was Alec Isabella's uncle and head of the Hage family, but he was also a good deal older than Thomas and the captain of the guard at Berwick Castle. He had an enormous amount of power at his disposal, but this news wasn't good news.

Alec grunted unhappily.

"Damn," he muttered. "De Royans is an ally. I do not want to engage in a battle with several de Royans knights."

Tor spoke up. "You were prepared to engage with at least one."

He was pointing out the obvious, which annoyed Alec. "That was before we knew he brought in reinforcements," he said. "I will not go to battle with several allied knights."

"They will defend de Featherstone. If you want the man, you will not have a choice."

Alec knew that. He looked at Thomas. "Well?" he said. "This will affect you more than it will affect me if we damage our relationship with de Royans. What have you to say?"

Thomas cocked a dark eyebrow. "The de Wolfe family honor is at stake," he said. "I value that over the relationship with de Royans. Steffan broke a vow of honor to our niece. I will not let that go unanswered."

Alec sighed. "When you put it that way, I agree. Forgive me for valuing an alliance over our family honor."

Thomas held up a hand. "There is no need to apologize," he said. "You were looking at it from the correct point of view. But I am looking at it from the point of family honor."

"He compromised Isabella," Ronan said. "If you do not go in there, I will. He will not compromise my sister and get away with it, and the alliance with de Royans be damned."

They all turned to him. Ronan was a quiet one and had a somewhat gentle nature, but the young man was fearless. Positively fearless. He very much had his father in him in that respect and they could all see that their decision was made.

Thomas put his hand on Ronan's shoulder.

"Then this is not just about a broken betrothal," he said quietly.

Ronan shook his head. "Nay," he said. "My father wants Steffan to marry my sister or he wants his head on a platter. That is why he sent me. If he had come, he would kill Steffan. So I have come in his stead so there would be no killing. I am only here to capture Steffan and nothing more. But my father said that if Steffan does not return willingly to Castle Questing, then we are to return him to his father and demand compensation for Steffan's actions."

"That is the demand?"

"That is the demand."

Thomas resigned himself to that. "Then you will go into the

tavern," he said. "Confront Steffan and give him that choice. If he balks, or if the de Royans knights he is with make a move against you, then we will destroy them. We will be waiting at every window, every door, watching to see what occurs. Will you do this?"

Ronan nodded firmly. "Gladly."

With that, he pushed past the group and headed for the entry door just as Jeremy and Nathaniel rejoined the group. The de Vesci knights could also be seen down the street, heading in their direction.

It was time to move.

With Ronan heading in through the front door, Thomas issued swift orders to everyone, including Alec and Nat. Alec went to the entry door while Nat ran around to the rear with Jeremy. Young Nathaniel and Alexander went to two big windows overlooking the front of the tavern while Tor and Thomas went to the front door with Alec.

The door was propped open to air out the stuffy and smelly tavern, the scent of unwashed bodies and vomit heavy in the air. Before Thomas could stop him, Tor slipped into the tavern and immediately lost himself in the crowd near the table that held several de Royans knights.

They were identifiable by their tunics. There was no mistaking six heavily armed men sitting at a table near an open window to the south side of the hearth. The window right above the table was wide open and as he took up a seat that he had stolen from a nearby table, he could see the tops of two heads just outside that window. Knowing that Nat and Jeremy had gone to the rear of the tavern, he suspected they might have stopped by that window when they caught sight the de Royans knights.

From his position in the shadows, Tor could see Ronan approach the table. As he watched, Steffan rose to his feet as

Ronan stopped at the end of the table. Words were exchanged, but Tor couldn't hear what was being said. Whatever it was, they were being quiet and civil about it. With his sister's honor at stake, Ronan was being calm about the situation, far calmer than his uncles had been.

That calm demeanor impressed Tor. He, too, had a calm manner and was often the one sent to negotiate in difficult situations because he wouldn't become angry or aggressive no matter how stupid or insulting the circumstances would be. That was also part of the reason he had been sent to Blackpool Castle. With an easy, likable manner about him, he was perfect for dealing with the hotheaded Scots.

As Ronan was speaking to Steffan, Tor was watching the men at the table, preparing to move if they drew their weapons. They were all heavily armed, but none of them had moved for their weapons. Ronan was young, but he was seasoned, and it wasn't the fact that he could not defend himself in a fight. He could. This may have been his fight because it was his sister who had been slandered, but Thomas has been absolutely right – it was the entire family whose honor was at stake.

They were all ready to clobber de Featherstone.

Surprisingly, it wasn't Steffan who drew his weapon first. It was Ronan. Apparently, Steffan was refusing to move and Ronan intended to force him. When Ronan drew his sword, two of the de Royans knights stood up and unsheathed their weapons. Whether or not they were actually going to make a move against the young knight would be something for debate in the days to come but, at the moment, it looked very much like Ronan was in trouble.

That was when the room exploded.

Nat and Jeremy came flying in through the window over the table, their broadswords arcing in the weak light of the common room. That was all it took for Tor to jump into the fray as the entry door and the rear door blew open to reveal more armed de Wolfe and Hage knights.

In an instant, people begin screaming and scattering as the battle turned very bloody, very quickly. The crowded tavern cleared out rapidly because no one wanted to be caught in the midst of a knight fight. Not just any knights; de Wolfe knights. The tavern keep, a tall and slender man, didn't even try to enter the fight or stop it. He began screaming at his servants to clear the floor, and the frightened wenches ran for the doors. The safest thing was to clear out the place and let the knights do what they did best.

Destroy.

It was unfortunate and a little confusing for the de Royans knights, who recognized Thomas early on. They knew he was the Earl of Northumbria, so raising a sword to the earl was not only forbidden, but confusing. They didn't know what to do. Thomas noticed their confusion because when he came near, they lowered their weapons. So he used that to his advantage.

Explaining to them that this was a fight that did not involve the House of de Royans, but only de Featherstone, he ordered them away in the hopes that they would comply. Three of them did, but two of them did not, and it was those two who engaged in a nasty battle with Alec and Nat as Ronan went after Steffan.

Tor and Jeremy and Nathaniel manhandled the de Royans knights out of the tavern as Alec and Nat subdued their opponents. They didn't want to kill them, but they did move to disarm them and as their weapons fell away, they grabbed the knights and pulled them away from the table where Ronan was still battling with Steffan.

Now, it was the brother of the bride against the runaway groom.

Tor and Thomas monitored the situation, watching Ronan battle against a man who had excellent skills. Ronan may have been young, but he was a de Wolfe, and that meant his talent was limitless. He was quite skilled with a blade. Just when it seemed that Ronan might gain the upper hand, something unexpected happened.

Tor saw it first but there was nothing he could do to prevent it. He could see his youngest half-brother, Alexander, back in the shadows because he had come in through the rear entry. He hadn't engaged in the battle so far, but mostly lingered on the fringe to make sure no one else was going to try to jump in and injure any of his relatives.

But Alexander unexpectedly moved.

Before Tor could stop him, Alexander came up behind Steffan. The de Royans knight caught the movement out of the corners of his eyes and turned into panic with his sword leveled. Alexander had his sword lifted and it was enough to prevent him from being killed, but not enough to prevent part of Steffan's blade from cutting into his chest.

That brought Tor on the run.

Steffan de Featherstone never had a chance with Tor bearing down on him. Tor's sword came up and over, completely overwhelming Steffan as a man tried to defend himself from the attack. Thomas started shouting, begging Tor to back away, but it all happened so fast. Tor wasn't listening to him and the price of Steffan cutting into Alexander was Steffan's very life.

Big brother Tor wasn't going to let the man injure his younger half-sibling without consequence. He struck hard and struck fast, as he was the de Wolfe with the hardest strike of all. Before anyone had realized what had happened, Steffan lay on the hard-packed earth of the common room, bleeding out all over the dirt.

Tor had nearly sliced his head off.

"Christ," Thomas hissed as he rushed forward, crouching over Steffan to see the damage. Already, he could see that it was hopeless. "Damnation!"

But Tor wasn't listening, nor did he care. He was bent over Alexander, peeling back layers of tunic and mail to see how badly the young man was hurt. It was a nasty slice that had cut Alexander from his neck, across his collarbone, down his chest and across his right forearm.

It was a bad wound.

No one other than Alec and Thomas seemed to be paying any attention to the dead knight on the floor. Everyone was crowding around Alexander, wanting to help, wanting to see how badly he was injured. Tor sent a panicked Jeremy for hot water, wine, and boiled linen, and the young man ran off into the kitchens screaming for the items. Nathaniel, the usually hot-headed middle brother, was surprisingly calm as he helped Tor.

"You were very brave, Alex," Nathaniel assured him, hand on his brother's head. "It is not a bad wound. Simply bloody."

Alexander was pale and shaking as blood from his wound stained his de Wolfe tunic and began to splatter on the floor.

"It is not bad?" he asked, wanting to be reassured.

"Nay," Ronan said steadily, bending over him, seeing for himself that it was a fairly serious wound. But he lied about it. "It is not bad. You will heal quickly."

Alexander's trembling was growing worse. "He was trying to kill you, Ronan," he said to the man he'd virtually grown up with. "I could not let him do that."

It was a sweet and honorable intention, but the older knights knew that it had been a dangerous one that had cost him. In truth, it had been the decision of an inexperienced warrior. But now wasn't the time to scold him.

"You are very noble," Tor said steadily, grabbing a wad of boiled linen from Jeremy, who had swiftly returned. He began packing it against open chest wound. "I will stitch you up myself. You will heal quickly."

Alexander was in pain but trying to be brave about it. "This is my first real injury," he said. "It happened so… quickly."

Tor was trying not to think about the events that Alexander's youthful mistake had put in motion that had resulted in not only a dead groom, but a dead de Royans knight. Now that he realized that Alexander was going to live, he pulled Ronan forward and told him to put pressure on the wound to stop the bleeding. Leaving Ronan and Nathaniel and Jeremy to tend Alexander, he stood up and faced the results of his actions.

Steffan was dead a few feet away. Thomas, Alec, Nat and Artus were standing there, looking down at him, muttering softly. Taking a deep breath, Tor went over to them.

"Whatever you may think of my actions, know that I do not regret my choice," he said. "De Featherstone was going to kill Alexander. I was not going to let that happen."

Thomas sighed heavily. "You know that Alexander acted stupidly."

"Of course I do. Was I supposed to simply stand there and let de Featherstone gore him?"

Thomas shook his head. "Nay," he said. "You did what you had to do. But now we have a big problem."

That was an understatement. Not only had Isabella's groom been killed, but there was possibly great damage to the alliance with the House of de Royans because of it. But Tor didn't regret anything.

"I am not going to pretend that de Featherstone was innocent in all of this," he said, his usually cool demeanor hardening. "The man compromised Isabella and then ran out on her. When confronted, he made the choice to fight. What did he think was going to happen? What did any of you think was going to happen? He chose the sword and he died by it, so I have no remorse for what has happened. He got what he deserved as far as I am concerned. But the only concession I will make is that Alexander behaved stupidly. That still does not mean I would allow him to be killed because of it. I am willing to go to de Royans and explain my part in all of this if that is what you are afraid of."

Thomas shook his head, putting his hand on Tor's shoulder. "Nay," he said. "I will go. It will be better coming from me because I can try to mend whatever damage this has caused. But you… you take your foolish half-brothers back to Castle Questing and tell my brother that his son has created a hell of a mess."

"De Featherstone created the mess, Uncle Thomas. That was where this all started."

Thomas cast him an annoyed look. "I am not going to debate this with you," he said. "I know where this started but the situation is delicate. Get your half-brothers home and tell Scott what has happened."

"I'll do it," Alec said grimly. "Isabella is my niece, after all. I must speak to Scott about the situation, anyway. I will take Ronan and the de Wolfe brothers home to Castle Questing. Tor, you and Nat can return the body to de Featherstone's father. You can tell the father what happened to his dishonorable son."

Since the House of de Featherstone wasn't far from Tor's fortress of Blackpool, it made sense that Tor should deliver the bad news. Without an argument to that, Tor simply nodded.

As Thomas went to find the de Vesci knights and use them as his muscle when he sent the de Royans knights away without telling them what had become of Steffan, Tor went in search of something to wrap up de Featherstone's body with, but the care he took with it wasn't cautious or kind.

The man didn't deserve it as far as he was concerned.

The best thing Tor could find was a big, dirty horse blanket from the livery behind the tavern and between him and Nat, they managed to wrap up de Featherstone tightly and haul him back out to the livery, storing him in one of the stalls as Tor returned to Alexander to stitch up his considerable wound.

With the excitement of the night over with, it was time to deal with the aftermath.

Confiscating one of the small sleeping chambers for Alexander, the tavern keep could find nothing better than heavy woolen thread to stitch up the young squire's wound. Tor made the man boil it first, knowing that would help keep the poison away.

Alexander was very brave as Tor took that rough, heavy thread and put neat stiches from his neck to his ribcage, but it wasn't painless in the least. For every grunt of pain that escaped Alexander's lips, Tor was glad that Steffan de Featherstone was dead because if the man wasn't, he would have been before the night was over.

Thomas had been right. They had created a hell of a mess, thanks to a runaway groom. Tor couldn't help but wonder where, exactly, it was all going to end now.

A small spark often ignited a wildfire.

CHAPTER TWO

One week later
The village of Haltwhistle

"HE'S STARTING TO smell."

The words came from Tor, plodding along on Enbarr with the body of Steffan slung over the horse's rump, still wrapped up in that old horse blanket. Only now, it was held together with a good deal of hemp rope.

No one wanted the putrefying corpse escaping.

Nat, a broad man who looked a good deal like his late father, Kieran Hage, made a point of staying ahead of Tor.

"I know," he said. "Why do you think I am riding in front of you?"

Tor sighed heavily. "I hate to go through the village, but there is no other way to reach the de Featherstone manse," he said. "Hopefully, we can get through without attracting too much attention."

"Or flies."

That was something they both agreed on.

They continued along, entering the edge of town and passing by people who were going about their business. The sky overhead was relatively clear but puffy, dark clouds loomed, suggesting that more rain was in store for them.

Unfortunately, there had been a good deal of rain over the past week and part of the smell emanating from the body was because it had been repeatedly soaked from the rains and hadn't entirely dried out. Mildew was sprouting and God only knew what else, and Tor knew that they had to get that corpse into the ground as soon as possible.

"I must admit that I am hesitant to present this corpse in its current state to Steffan's father," Tor said. "I haven't looked at it in a couple of days but, based on the smell, I'm fairly certain it's not in the best of condition."

Nat glanced back at the bundle. "It's starting to seep through the horse blanket," he said. "Those fluids are beginning to leech out."

"That's a charming thought."

"Do you know Steffan's father?"

Tor shook his head. "I've met the man on a couple of occasions, but nothing more," he said. "It's my understanding that Featherstone is the de Featherstone country house. Either they are named for it or it is named for them, I do not know. But I heard once that they have another manse in Carlisle."

Nat glanced at him. "The family is wealthy?"

"From what I've heard, wildly so," Tor said. "Money made in the merchant trade. De Featherstone's main support to Brampton is financial – he pays a good deal of support for the man's army and receives protection from it for his homes and his fleets."

Nat pondered the wealthy businessman, which here in the north was a fairly rare beast. Most people this far north were either warlords or farmers, or both.

"But his son became a knight," he said. "Not only does he *not* serve Brampton, he serves de Royans."

"It is a more prestigious house."

"To be sure, but you would think the son would follow the father."

Tor shrugged his big shoulders. "Steffan de Featherstone seemed to be a man who did as he pleased," he said. "Mayhap he did not wish to become a merchant like his father, just as he decided not to honor a marital contract with Isabella. Who made that contract, anyway? Was it the father?"

Nat shook his head. "From what I heard, it was Steffan himself," he said. "Isabella is a pretty thing, you know. He saw her somewhere, I do not know where, and fancied her. He was the one who made the contract."

"And decided in the end not to honor it."

"That was my understanding, aye."

Tor looked on up ahead into the busy village at this time of day. "Then we shall make sure his father understands that," he said. "You had better let me tell him while you remain out of the manse. In case I am taken prisoner against Steffan's death, you will need to go for help."

That thought had occurred to Nat. "Or mayhap you simply dump the body at the door and run."

"I have considered that."

When Nat looked at him, he grinned, and the two of them snorted at the suggestion. Honorable knights didn't run, no matter what the circumstances, and no matter how much they wanted to.

They were going to have to face Steffan's father.

The deeper they progressed into the town, the busier it became. This was one of the larger villages in between Newcastle and Carlisle, so there were many peasants from the countryside bringing in their produce to sell. This far north, there was a great deal of agriculture and sheep, and as they entered the town center they could see big corrals stuffed with wooly, white sheep.

There were more sheep in small herds outside of the corrals, being kept closely guarded by dogs and shepherds. There were wool merchants haggling with the farmers over the quality of their wool and even as the bargains were struck, sheep were cut out from the herd and clipped by men whose entire profession it was to clip the wool from the sheep. Those men were very precise with their big, steel shears and they were in much demand by the wool merchants because they were very precise. A bad job of shearing could cost them money.

Because there was so much going on in the town, no one seemed to be noticing two knights lumbering through the village on expensive warhorses. They were both wearing de Wolfe tunics, identifying them as being from one of the most powerful families in the north. Tor was hoping that they could get through the village without being noticed at all but, unfortunately, that was not to be.

A situation arose.

It all started out of their sight, in a corral on the other side of a livery that was at the edge of the town center. A man was selling beautiful and expensive Spanish horses, brought all the way from Madrid. He'd had twenty of them with the intention of selling them to the nobility of England, but because times were rather poor at the moment, he'd only been able to sell fifteen of the twenty on his journey through England.

Now, he was down to his last five and they were the most expensive. They were fine Spanish Jennets, horses bred from Arabians and long-legged warmbloods. The resulting horse was a masterpiece of equine breeding, both fast and sturdy. At the moment, the man was trying to sell a gorgeous white mare to a woman who seemed to have a discerning eye for horseflesh. She inspected the horse, looking over every inch of it, before deciding she wanted to sit on it. The horse was only green broke and against the man's better judgment, he let her sit on the horse.

That was when all hell broke loose.

Tor was first aware of it when he heard a scream go up. He was on the road heading towards a turn off that would take them south, but he saw the horse charging towards them. It was clear the woman on the horse had no control of it, struggling not to fall off.

Tor realized that it was a runaway animal, a very dangerous situation in the midst of a busy village, and his knightly instincts kicked in. He was sworn to protect the weak and save the innocent. At the moment, it appeared to him that the woman on the horse very much needed saving.

As the horse charged in his direction, he swung both legs over his saddle. He was still sitting on Enbarr, waiting for just the right moment. As the white horse went sprinting past, he launched himself at the woman and they both went over the side of the white horse, crashing onto the street below.

It had all happened very quickly but Tor had been conscious of the position of his big body as they'd fallen. He thought he could land on his feet, but momentum had taken him sideways. Therefore, he purposely turned so he would hit the ground and she would fall on top of him.

She did, heavily.

But there was a fly in the ointment. Unfortunately, or fortunately, depending on how one looked at the situation, he had ended up planting his face right in her breasts when he'd grabbed her. Literally, his mouth was on her tit.

But that wasn't the worst – or best – of it. She had been wearing a cloak or a cape that had come up over them, entangling them both in the garment. He ended up laying on it, pinning it down and making it virtually impossible to move because of the way they were both laying.

Once they hit the ground, Tor lay there for a moment because the wind was knocked out of him. He shook off the stars, realizing there was the swell of a lovely white breast against his face.

"My lady?" he said. "Are you…?"

When the woman felt his hot breath and mouth against her bosom, she shrieked and began frantically pushing him away even as she tried to move. "You may release me," she said, cutting him off. "I am not injured. Do you hear? Release me!"

He wanted to, but the cape had them tangled. He unwound his arms and in her panic to separate herself from him, she put her hand on his face and used it as leverage to push herself up.

Tor grunted in pain as she smashed his nose, but the cape began to come unraveled as she stood up. He could see that she'd managed to put both feet on the ground and she gave a good yank on the cape, pulling it off of his head but catching his left ear.

With a hand on his stinging ear and the other one on his smashed nose, Tor looked up at the woman he'd just saved from certain death. Instead of gratitude, all he saw was indignation.

"Although I am sure you thought you were doing me a great favor, I did not require your assistance with the horse," she said, straightening up the cape that was part of her fine, and very expensive, dress. "Your heroism was unnecessary, my lord. In fact, it was presumptuous."

Tor was sitting in the gutter, his enormous arms draped over his bent-up knees as he found himself looking at what was inarguably the most beautiful woman he'd ever set eyes upon.

She was petite in size, but curvy and big-busted. This was no fragile, slender female. Her hair was blonde, long and soft and wavy, and she had several small braids decorating her hair, all of them woven with strings of pearls or ribbons that matched her red damask dress. But her face… that's what had his attention. She had delicately arched brows over dark blue eyes, a pert little nose, and full lips. But those eyes were blazing at him and he brushed himself off, rising to his feet.

"My apologies," he said.

And that was *all* he said. He wasn't going to stand there and argue with her, ungrateful wench. He didn't care how beautiful she was because she had the manners of a boar. It wasn't as if he'd expected her to fall at his feet with thanks, but a little gratitude might have been nice.

Maybe there was just a little wounded pride there.

Without another glance, he crossed the street where Nat was mounted, holding on to Enbarr.

"Did you hurt yourself?" Nat asked. "That was a hard fall."

Tor grunted. "I am not injured," he said, swinging himself onto Enbarr's back. "Let us get on with this."

He gathered his reins and prepared to move forward but a shout stopped him. Pausing, he turned to see the blonde in the magnificent red dress crossing the road towards him. She had something in her hand, lifting it up to him.

"Here," she said, though it was forced. "I am sure you thought you were helping me, so please take this for your trouble."

He could see that she had coins in her hand and, for some reason, that enraged him. Well, as much as anything could. He'd never been truly furious in his life, but the fact that she thought she was doing him a favor by rewarding him tweaked his already damaged pride. He leaned over, fixing her in the eyes.

"Keep your money," he said. "And keep off horses you cannot control. What I did was not to save you. It was to save all of those people you were preparing to trample with that wild animal. The next time a man risks his life to save yours and so many others, it would be the well-mannered thing to thank him rather than lie to him and tell you that you did not need any help at all."

She was red in the face by the time he finished with her. Lowering her hand with the coins in it, it was obvious that her prideful manner had taken a hit.

"I did not ask you to risk yourself," she said.

He lifted his eyebrows. "That is true, you did not," he said. "Nor did the townsfolk who were under threat from your unruly mount. But I am a trained knight and when there is trouble, I cannot stand by and not do anything about it. Had I known how rude and ungrateful you were, however, I might have changed my mind."

With that, he directed Enbarr out onto the road and began to move away. Nat was already several paces ahead of him, uninterested in the lecture Tor was giving the lovely young woman. Tor could see Nat up ahead and he directed Enbarr through the villagers and farmers who had resumed their business now that the wild horse had been corralled. He wasn't moving very quickly, but he did have the road south in his sights. He was looking up ahead when he heard a voice beside him.

"I am sorry that I was rude." The woman in the red dress was suddenly walking beside him. She'd caught up to him and he never even noticed. "It's just that my father will probably never let me ride a horse again if he has any sense that I nearly got myself killed. There were people standing around who might know him, as he is well-known in town, and word might get back to him. I had to pretend I had some semblance of control."

He looked down at her, willing to accept her apology with shocking speed. Usually, he was a man to hold a grudge and he'd been known to hold them for quite a long time. But looking down at that sweet face, he was willing to forget the whole thing.

"Your father is popular in town, is he?"

"Well-known, anyway."

"It must make it difficult for you to be anything less than perfect."

"Exactly."

"My name is Tor."

She looked up at him, the dark blue eyes studying him. "I am Isalyn."

He dipped his head. "My lady," he said. "'Tis an honor to meet you."

"And you. For what you did… you probably *did* save my life. Thank you."

"You are welcome."

She forced a smile, just a little one, but it was the prettiest smile he'd ever seen. "If you will not take my coins, will you at least let me purchase a meal for the man who saved me from breaking my neck? It would be very bad manners of me not to thank you in some way."

Tor had his day mapped out. Go to Featherstone, return de Featherstone's body to his father, and depart for home. If he moved swiftly enough, he might even be able to sleep in his own bed tonight. Blackpool was about twenty miles to the north, so if he moved swiftly, he could make it home that night.

All of those things were going through his mind.

But he realized as he looked at her that he might not make it home tonight at all.

Tor wasn't one to be influenced by a pretty face. For close to seventeen years, ever since the death of his wife, he'd made a habit of shutting out the weaker sex. Jane had been the only woman in the world for him and he never expected to replace her. In fact, even thinking about another wife made him feel unfaithful to Jane. She had been gone all of these years, but she still wasn't gone from his heart.

The memory lingered.

At least, that was the impression he lived with every day. But in looking at the young woman's lovely face, he could feel a tug on his heart, that cold and dormant thing that lived inside of him. He realized that he wanted to go with her and he wanted the company of a lovely young woman, and that made him feel guilty. It had been nearly seventeen years since he last held company with a beautiful young woman and he thought it wasn't something he missed at all until this very moment.

Something inside him was stirring.

Glancing over his right shoulder, he could see that Nat had already made the turn onto the road south. They were both here on business, and nothing more, and he felt a little strange deviating from that plan. But when he looked at Isalyn's face again, he didn't care that he was about to deviate.

He was rather intrigued by it.

"Very well," he said after a moment. "Let me catch up to my companion and tell him. Where would you have me meet you?"

Isalyn pointed back towards the town center. "There is a small place on the other side of the square called the Crown and Sword," she said. "It is not much to look at, but the food is excellent. My father will come to town just to eat there."

"That is as good a recommendation as any," he said. "I will join you there shortly."

With that, he directed Enbarr forward again, thinking about what he was going to tell Nat. Nat wasn't invited, of course, and he wasn't sure how he was going to break that to him. He could explain away the woman well enough – that she simply wanted to thank him for saving her – but he wondered if Nat would be able to read his thoughts.

Thoughts that suggested he was more than willing to join her.

When he finally caught up to Nat, the man fortunately didn't read his mind because he was too busy being annoyed at the delay. Now he was going to have to patiently wait for Tor as a grateful lady paid for a meal. Tor promised Nat that he would bring him food, which seemed to be the only thing to placate the knight, who now had to mind two horses and a corpse while Tor was off cavorting with a grateful maiden.

It hardly seemed fair.

But Tor really didn't care.

CHAPTER THREE

"I SWEAR TO you that I have never fallen from a horse," Isalyn said. "I've never even needed help. This was a first."

Tor wasn't so sure he believed her but, at the moment, it didn't matter. He was too busy being fascinated.

By her.

The Crown and Sword was a small establishment. It was nestled between two bakers' stalls and had the invariable distinction of always smelling like fresh bread. It was also quite warm because of the heat from the bakers' ovens that used common walls. Coupled with the heat from a hearth that was as tall as a man, it was a very warm place.

Tor wasn't quite sure if he was sweating because of all of the heat or if it was because of the company he kept. He was dressed as he normally did, in a padded tunic, mail coat, and a heavy de Wolfe tunic. All of the heavy and protective clothing that went with what a knight usually wore. He was normally comfortable in the garb because the temperatures in the north could be quite cold but, at the moment, he was sweating buckets as he sat across the table from lovely Isalyn.

He resisted the urge to strip off anything.

This wasn't the place, nor the time, for it. He remained fully clothed, wiping at his sweaty face once in a while. The small establishment they were in was really no larger than a home and there were just a few tables, all full of people enjoying what was perhaps one of the finest meals Tor had ever eaten. Unlike most establishments, which were mostly meant for drink, this one seemed to be meant mostly for food. It was quiet and there was no entertainment or boisterous behavior.

It was an interesting place, indeed.

The food came in courses and it had been coming in a steady flow ever since they sat down about an hour ago. The first course had been poached eggs on bread covered in a sweet and savory sauce. That had been quickly devoured and the second course had been hard boiled eggs stuffed with meat and breadcrumbs. Six had been brought to the table and Tor had eaten four of those because they were so tasty. The third course had been a fish pie, literally a pie crust in the shape of a fish. It has been filled with white, salty fish swimming in a sweet wine sauce.

Now, they were on the fourth course, which was a very good beef roast with sweet carrots. It seemed as if the wenches brought another course about every fifteen minutes and the talk between them had been light. Isalyn spoke of her recent visit to the tavern and the dish her father seemed to favor, which was stuffed capon. She spoke very little of herself or of her family except to say that she had a father and a brother but, other than that, Tor didn't know anything about her. He suspected that she had designed the conversation that way.

But the truth was that he had not spoken much of himself, either, although he was wearing the de Wolfe tunic. That should have told her where he came from but she never commented on it. It was one of the most recognizable standards in England, if not the most recognizable in the north, but she never said a word. He began to understand why when he asked her what her favorite dish was.

That's when Lady Isalyn began to come alive.

"There is a place in London called The Taberna," she said. "Everything they serve is modeled after the food the ancient Romans ate. They serve a dish called *Ova*, which is eggs with pepper and honey. It is delicious."

Tor was still working on the fish pie because his portion had been so large. "And that is your favorite?"

She nodded, sipping at her mulled wine. "One of them," she said. "They also serve a dish that is made from chicken legs with a sauce of vinegar and honey and mint. I could eat that morning and night."

She had such a deliciously round little figure that he could believe it. He liked a woman who loved to eat.

"Do you travel to London frequently, then?" he asked. "You seem to know a lot about the Roman tavern."

She nodded. "I live there most of the time," she said. "My mother's family has a home in London along the Thames and I live with my aunt. She has no children, so she enjoys the company."

Tor sopped up the fish sauce with his bread. "Do you like it there?"

Isalyn nodded fervently. "I do," she said. "There is no place I would rather be. I long for the bustle of the city, the way of life. I like the shops, the food, the culture."

"What culture?"

"Why, entertainment, of course," she said as if he were ignorant of such things. "There is an entire district where actors portray great works of literature. Dramas, they are called. Have you never seen one?"

He shook his head. "I have heard of them, but I have never seen one."

She was warming up to a subject she knew a good deal

about. "Mostly, there are popular ones that portray stories from the Bible," she said. "The church has a good deal of control over the content, but there is a district across the river that does Greek tragedies and scandalous romances. The church is angry about it, but they cannot do much except denounce it. No one listens, however. The dramas are performed to big crowds every night from the bed of the wagons."

He was chewing the last of the bread and fish gravy. "Ah," he said. "I have seen such wagons. They move from place to place. Sometimes they come this far north. You will see them in the larger cities. In fact, there is an ancient Roman theater near Melrose and I have heard they do great productions there from time to time, but I have never seen them."

She smiled. "In London, they do the same thing with an ancient Roman theater near the Guildhall," she said, her expression becoming somewhat wistful. "I miss the dramas. When I am in London, I sneak out of my aunt's home and take the ferry across the river to see the dramas."

He lifted an eyebrow. "In London?" he said. "Alone?"

"Of course."

"You are taking great chances with your safety, my lady."

She grinned, a delightfully impish gesture. "You sound like my father."

"He is right."

Seeing that she did not have his support, she shrugged. "I do not need an escort clinging to me everywhere I go like a shadow," she said. "I much prefer to go alone and move about unnoticed."

"You disapprove of escorts?"

"They are a nuisance."

He swallowed the bite in his mouth, eyeing her. "I was wondering why you had no escort," he said. "You are having a meal with a man you do not know and there are no soldiers around to protect you."

She stiffened, just the slightest. "I can take care of myself," she assured him, perhaps even suggesting with her tone that she was prepared to fight him should he entertain any unsavory ideas. "A woman does not need a man to protect her. Women must learn to protect themselves. They must learn to do for themselves. I do not subscribe to the notion that women always need men to save them and mayhap that is why I was so harsh with you earlier. I should not have been and I have apologized but, truly, do women always need a man to save them? I do not think so."

Tor was rather amused by her attitude. "That is a brave notion," he said. "But it could also be a foolish one with the wrong man."

"Why?"

He lifted his big shoulders. "What if you marry a man who demands complete obedience? What if he does not want you wandering around without an escort?"

She frowned. "I would never marry such a man."

"Wouldn't you?"

"Nay."

"Did you ever stop to think that such a man is concerned for your safety? He does not insist on an escort to control you, but because he doesn't want anything bad to happen to you."

She had to think on that. "I suppose that can be true," she said. "But men are conditioned to dominate a woman. That is our world. Do you, as a man, always wish to dominate a woman?"

In bed, mayhap, Tor thought quickly, but he didn't speak the words aloud. He had a feeling she wouldn't take kindly to them. Instead, he tried to keep a straight face as he answered her question.

"Men are the stronger sex, my lady," he said. "That is the

natural order of things."

"They may be stronger, but that does not mean they are more intelligent in all things."

"That is true."

Her mouth twisted wryly. "Are you married?"

He shook his head. "Nay."

"But if you were married, would you dominate your wife and suppress her natural curiosity and strength?"

"That depends."

"On what?"

"On whether or not she was foolish and reckless."

"But how do you determine if she is? Women are just as smart as men, you know. Men can be foolish and reckless, too."

He couldn't help the smile on his lips. The woman was a spitfire. He didn't sense that she was argumentative, but she definitely had an opinion she wanted heard. If she hadn't been so adorable, he would have grown annoyed long ago.

"That is true," he said. "I do not mind a woman who is curious and strong, I suppose, but I draw the line at reckless and stupid. Whether or not you want to agree with me, the fact of the matter is that this world can be a dangerous place and women need protection from time to time. It is not an insult, simply a matter of fact. And some women do not mind having a man for protection."

Isalyn couldn't disagree. As the fifth course arrived, this one an apple and cheese tart, she picked up her spoon and delved into the dish.

"Nay, some do not," she said. "And there is nothing wrong with it. I know that mayhap it hasn't been the best decision for me to travel on my own, but I find something emboldening about it. I am bright and educated, so why should I not be in command of my own life and my own destiny?"

Tor was already halfway through the delicious tart. "What

does your father have to say about that?"

She seemed to deflate a little. "He does not like it," he said. "He tells me that I will never find a husband if I continue to behave like a rebel, but I do not care. I do not much care about marriage. But if I do marry someday, he will be a man who will treat me as an equal, not as a possession."

"Then he will be a unique man, indeed."

"Mayhap I shall find him, someday," she said. "I only hope I am still young enough to enjoy it."

He looked at her, thinking that she was perhaps being suggestive in that comment, but she just started giggling. She was absolutely charming, opinions and all, and he grinned at her.

"As beautiful as you are, I am sure you will have no trouble at all," he said. "If I come across such a man, I will send him your way. Where shall I send him?"

"London," she said flatly. "I do not intend to remain in the north any longer than necessary."

"Did you come here for a purpose?"

She nodded, spooning more tart into her mouth. "My father was unwell," she said. "He sent word and asked that I come to visit him, so I did. But he is much better these days and I wish to return to London."

"You do not like it with the barbarians of the north, I take it?"

She shrugged. "As I said, I like it much better in London," she said. "Life in the north is too provincial for me. I need the excitement of the city."

"And the filth," he said pointedly. "*And* the thieves *and* the beggars *and* the crime. Why in the world should that excite you so?"

A smile creased her lips as she picked at her tart. "It just does," she said. "There is more opportunity for a woman of ingenuity there."

"What do you mean?"

She stopped picking and eyed him. "May I tell you a secret?"

"If you wish."

"You must promise never to tell anyone."

"I swear it."

She leaned towards him, lowering her voice. "Those dramas I spoke of?" she said. "It is against the law for women to act in them, and no decent woman would write one, but I have written several. The dramas I go to see are my own."

He looked at her, surprised. "I see," he said. "And no one knows this?"

She shook her head. "I write dramas under a man's name," she said. "It is so very foolish that I must conceal my name, but to openly participate in drama would bring condemnation against me and my family. It is unfortunate that I cannot be free and honest about who I am, but the truth is that I cannot. It is only acceptable for men to write and act in dramas. So, I write the dramas and give them to my friend, who is an actor. He and his friends perform them."

"What name do you write under?"

"Wellesley Fairhurst."

Tor sat back in his chair, his gaze glimmering with mirth. "Now I understand why you love London so much," he said. "You can be an anonymous playwright."

"Exactly."

"Do you make any money from this secret life?"

She nodded. "A little," she said. "It is money I stash away so that I can marry any man I choose because I can offer my own dowry."

He snorted. "I thought you said you did not care about marriage?"

She lowered her gaze, embarrassed. "I suppose that's not

really true."

His smile broadened. "Do you already have someone in mind?"

She shook her head firmly. "Nay," she said. "But I know he will be worldly and educated and like to travel."

"No provincial knights for you, then."

"There is nothing wrong with provincial knights," she insisted. "But my father is a merchant, as was his father before him. When I was young, I traveled with my father and I suppose that is why I like the bigger cities. Even as a child, there were so many interesting things to see there. I could never be happy in the wilds of England or France because provincial lords are content with their boring lives. I could never be content with such a thing."

Something she said gave Tor pause. "Your father is a merchant?"

"Aye."

"What is his name?"

"Gilbert de Featherstone."

Tor's heart sank. He had no idea Steffan de Featherstone even had a sister, a woman he just spent a wonderful hour with. She was bright and curious and vivacious, and he had enjoyed his time with her immensely.

A woman whose brother he had killed.

In truth, he was a little confused. He had enjoyed his time with her, that is true, but there was never a thought of anything beyond that enjoyment. His thoughts had not wandered to seeing her again or a more permanent arrangement, like courting her, because of his feelings for Jane. He had spent almost seventeen years ignoring any thoughts of remarrying again and it was something he was untroubled by until about an hour ago.

Now, he was troubled.

If Isalyn de Featherstone was nothing else, she was honest and forthright. The entire conversation in that overheated tavern had been an introduction to a woman who didn't think like most women of the day. She believed women should be strong and should not be dependent upon a man. Such thoughts coming from a well-bred and well-educated young lady were not normal. Well-bred young women were conditioned to be polite and ladylike and appreciate chivalry, but not Isalyn.

She had her own ideas about such things.

Truth be told, he didn't really mind.

He found her fascinating.

But no longer. Realizing she was Steffan de Featherstone's sister essentially destroyed any hope of a further relationship with her and he realized that he was grossly disappointed. He was quite certain that there wasn't much chance of a woman like that wanting to maintain a friendship with the man who had killed her brother.

"It is a coincidence that you are Gilbert de Featherstone's daughter," he said after a moment. "I was just going to visit your father at Featherstone."

"Oh?" she said with surprise. "You know my father?"

He shook his head. "Not really," he said. "I know *of* him. In case you have not recognized my standard, my father is the Earl of Warenton. My name is Tor de Wolfe."

Her eyebrows lifted. "You are a de Wolfe?"

"I am. One of those provincial knights who lead boring lives."

She heard her words come out of his mouth and her cheeks flushed a dull red. "I am sorry," she said. "I should not have said such a thing. I have never had trouble speaking my mind and it has caused some embarrassment at times, mostly mine. I am sorry."

Because she was so ashamed, he forgave her in an instant. "No harm done," he said, smiling. "But I will say that my life, and the lives of my family, are anything but boring. It can be quite exciting along the Scottish Marches when we are the only thing that stands between a Scottish invasion into those big cities you are so fond of. Did you ever think of who was protecting your freedom to write plays and cavort without an escort?"

She shook her head, properly contrite. "I suppose I have not," she said. "It seems that I have offended you twice today, my lord. Once when you saved me from that horse and now with my opinion of provincial knights."

"The day is still young. There may yet be the opportunity for more insults."

He was jesting, but Isalyn looked at him with a measure of horror. "I think two times are quite enough," she said. "I evidently owe you another meal to make up for the second insult."

He started laughing. "That is not necessary," he said. "But you could provide me with an escort to your father's home. My companion and I might need your protection."

She looked him over, noting the enormous broadsword at his side that probably weighed as much as she did. "Somehow I doubt that, but you are kind to say so," she said. "I will escort you under one condition."

"What is that?"

"That you do not tell my father I was rude to you. Twice."

He fought off a grin. "You have my vow, my lady."

"And you do not tell him what I told you about the dramas that I write."

"You said only one condition. Now you must pick which one. Either he knows about your bad behavior or he knows about your clandestine activities. I cannot withhold both."

He was clearly teasing her, fighting off a smile, and she sighed sharply. "If you tell him both, I will write you into my next drama and ensure you are killed off in the most painful way possible. I will set the de Wolfe hounds on you."

He burst out laughing, flashing big, white teeth at her clever play on words. "God, not *that,*" he said. "Very well, then. At the risk of being a corpse in your next drama, I will not tell him either of those things. You have my promise."

The ends of her mouth curled up. "Good," she said. "We understand one another."

"I think we are starting to."

Her triumphant grin told him everything he needed to know, and it was a great pity. A pity he couldn't continue this conversation and a pity he couldn't come to know a woman who very quickly had his attention. Nearly seventeen years of loneliness he never knew he suffered from had suddenly been recognized with the event of the busty blonde lass. God, how he'd missed laughing with a pretty, witty woman.

He wondered if he was going to deeply regret killing Steffan de Featherstone in the days to come.

CHAPTER FOUR

FOR A PROVINCIAL knight, he was handsome.

Quite handsome, really. If she was honest about it, he was the most handsome man she'd ever seen.

Pity he was a provincial knight.

On their ride south from Haltwhistle, she tried to pretend that she wasn't looking at him even though she was. He was very big – perhaps even the biggest man she'd ever seen, tall as well as muscular. He had a square jaw and green eyes, and in the dim light of the tavern, she thought he had blond hair. But in the light of day, before he'd put his helm back on, she could see that his hair was red with a dusting of silver and gold. Blended together, it made him look like a blond.

No matter what his hair color was, it was beautiful.

So was he.

Truth be told, she had no idea that there were men of such magnificence this far north. Although she had been born at her family's home in Carlisle, she had not spent an over amount of time in the north. Her mother, a worldly woman of some means, preferred the cities and her own family's home in London, and that was where Isalyn had spent a large part of her life.

To her, the north of England was full of barbarians. On her infrequent trips home, she had mostly spent them at the family manse in Carlisle, as that was an acceptable abode for the most part. Carlisle was a fairly cosmopolitan city, but it was nothing like her beloved London.

She loved the city life.

Isalyn's father and brother loved the country manse at Featherstone that had been in her family for over a century. It was a pretty place and when Isalyn had been young, she had spent a few happy summers playing in the elaborate garden or splashing in the brook that ran next to the property. She had been terribly young then, those carefree days of youth, and it had been before her parents decided to live separately and her mother had taken her to London.

But Isalyn did remember those younger years, like bits of a dream. She remembered her mother laughing, and her father laughing, and her brother pulling her hair. She remembered the days as seemingly bucolic and happy when they were a family.

But those days were long gone and now, she could hardly stand to return to Featherstone. She told herself it was because it was too rural. She was a lass who needed the excitement of a city, as she had told Tor. But perhaps the truth was that the memories there were just too painful because they had been so short lived. It was difficult to return to a home where there was no longer any love or laughter, and perhaps that's why she wanted to stay away most of all.

It reminded her of things that had ended.

It reminded her of a mother who had died three years ago, right about the time Isalyn was becoming a young woman. Her mother had a cancer that ate away at her until she died a painful and lingering death. Isalyn had been devastated by the death of the woman who had been her very best friend and she had spent years mourning her mother as if her death had only happened the day before. Her aunt, who was her mother's older sister, filled in as best she could, but she was devastated, too. There wasn't a lot of room for Isalyn's grief to a woman who was more concerned with her own sorrow.

And then, there was her brother.

Steffan was most definitely his father's son. Arrogant, irresponsible, and largely immune to the sufferings of the world around him, Steffan had hardly seen his mother in the time his parents had been separated and he didn't much seem to care. With their parents separated, Isalyn had gone with her mother and Steffan had remained with his father, and Steffan had lived as if he didn't have a sister or a mother. She'd hardly seen the man growing up and the last time had been a few years ago.

There had been rumors, of course. Rumors of Steffan's behavior that had trickled down to Isalyn's mother. Even in London, they had heard of Steffan's recklessness and of his inability to behave as a knight should. He was evidently a gambler and had stretched thin his finances because of it.

There were times when Isalyn forgot she even had a brother and, quite frankly, that was fine with her. Steffan had never made any great attempt to have a relationship with her and she had made no great attempt to have a relationship with him, so the siblings were ambivalent towards one another.

Even with this visit to Featherstone to see her father, Isalyn hadn't even seen her brother because, according to her father, he now served the House of de Royans. That had apparently been going on for the past two years and Gilbert seemed both proud and lonely for the fact that his son served another house. Steffan had no intention of going into the family business and that, too, seemed to weigh heavily on Gilbert.

Steffan wanted to be a knight, not a worthless merchant, as he put it.

Thoughts of Isalyn's mother and a brother faded as they

drew closer to Featherstone. They could see the big manse in the distance, a jewel nestled among the pastoral greenery. Isalyn's focus returned to Tor, riding slightly ahead of her astride one of the biggest horses she had ever seen.

She was curious about the man beyond their conversation at the tavern.

"Sir Tor?" she called.

He turned as much as he was able given the restrictions of his armor. "My lady?"

"Tor. *Tor*," she said, drawing his name out. "It is an interesting name. May I beg you to tell me who you are named for?"

He smiled weakly. "My Christian name is Thomas," he said. "I am named for my grandmother's father, but I also have an uncle who is named Thomas. When I was serving on the Welsh Marches, the Welsh gave me the name of Tor. It means a strong and impenetrable rock formation, and my family took up calling me that as well so I would be called differently from my uncle. But my father still calls me Tommy. He is the only one who does."

"You have a big family?"

He nodded. "I have nine siblings," he said. "Some from my father's first marriage, some from my stepmother's first marriage, and then some by their marriage together. I am the second eldest, my father's son by blood."

Isalyn thought on having ten brothers and sisters. "That is a lot of children."

Tor snorted. "My Uncle Tommy has eleven children although, in fairness, several of them are adopted," he said. "The de Wolfe family is quite large."

"There are de Wolfes in Wolverhampton, too."

"Those are cousins. My grandfather's eldest brother was the Earl of Wolverhampton and those are his descendants."

It seemed like a large family, indeed. Isalyn's gaze trailed over to the second knight in their escort, riding silently as she and Tor chattered away.

"And you, Sir Nat?" she said politely. "You are part of this enormous family?"

Caught off-guard by the question, Nat was certain the pair had forgotten about him. He'd barely said two words to the woman that Tor seemed to be quite interested in, so her question surprised him.

He was certain that he was a ghost as far as they were concerned.

"I am," he said. "My mother is a cousin of Tor's grandmother."

Isalyn's brow furrowed. "But you cannot be much older than he is."

Nat grinned. "I am the youngest of six children," he said. "Tor is the second eldest of the de Wolfe siblings. We were born ten years apart."

Isalyn looked between them. "I would not have guessed that," she said. "Are you married, Sir Nat?"

He nodded. "I am."

"Do you have children?"

"Seven."

Isalyn blinked. "God's Bones," she said. "Everyone has big families but me. It is only my brother and me. I think my parents must have been lazy."

Nat chuckled. Even Tor smiled. "Or brilliant," he said. "Mayhap they knew that the more children they have, the more trouble there will be."

"You think so, do you?"

"Ask my father. He'll tell you. I've got three younger half-brothers who can bring about a world of trouble."

The way he said it made her laugh. He had a humorous way about him at times, she noticed. Isalyn was thinking on how handsome he looked when he smiled, but the wind suddenly shifted and she caught a whiff of something rotten.

Her nose wrinkled.

"What's that smell?" she asked.

Tor struggled not to react to the question. He knew exactly what it was because the wind was now blowing northwest, which took that putrid smell from the back of his horse straight at her. Over on Tor's left, Nat coughed loudly, endeavoring to cover up a guffaw.

"I thought I smelled that, too," Tor said innocently. "It smells as if it is coming off the fields. Rancid water from the rains, I suppose."

Isalyn pinched her nose shut, looking off towards the west, into the great fields. "God's Bones," she muttered. "It smells positively rotten."

"It does."

Suddenly, Isalyn was spurring her little palfrey forward, trotting past Tor and moving quickly down the road and away from the terrible smell that was blowing off the fields. She still had her nose pinched shut as she kicked her little horse into a canter.

As she ran by, Tor glanced at Nat, who shrugged his big shoulders, and spurred his horse forward as well. With both Nat and Isalyn trotting on ahead, Tor was left behind. He was the one carting the rotting corpse on the saddle behind him and he didn't want to jolt it around in case something decided to fall off. It wouldn't do for a putrid arm or hand or head to come rolling out of the horse blanket and fall to the road. Therefore, he picked up the pace as much as he could without jerking the body around and followed Nat and the lady towards the distant manse.

As they drew close, the wind shifted again and dark, puffy clouds began to blow in from the west. In this section of

England, that was usually the direction that the weather came from, blowing off of the Solway Firth. The smell of rain was in the air and the very land around them begin to smell damp, signaling oncoming rain. Tor arrived at the manse just as Isalyn and Nat were crossing the bridge that led to the gatehouse.

Tor took a moment to look over the great house of Featherstone. It was much bigger than he had imagined for so remote a country house. It was built from the gray granite stone that was so prevalent to the area, the kind that turned mossy and green with age. While the front of the manse was built from stone, he noticed that the second floor was built from wattle and daub. He could see great crossbeams built into the walls, an architecture that was very common in England.

The gatehouse itself was three stories, but the rest of the house only seemed to be two. Surrounding this enormous house was a moat and as Tor directed Enbarr over the stone bridge, he looked down into a moat that was murky and full of green growth. For a country manse, it was an extraordinarily wide moat, meaning that no one could easily cross it. In fact, it was more of a lake than a moat with the odd feature being the permanent stone bridge that crossed it and led to the gatehouse.

A permanent stone bridge was not a wise safety feature, but it led to the gatehouse that had as many safety features on it as any military castle. The three-story gatehouse was protected by not only two enormous iron gates, but as he passed through it, he could see that it also had two portcullises as well. Anyone who could get across that stone bridge would face a monumental task of breaching the iron gates and iron grates.

A monumental task, indeed.

Now that he had seen it, Tor was quite impressed by the size and the architecture. Once through the gatehouse, they emerged into a large yard that contained a couple of trade shacks, a small stable, and a small stable yard. It had all of the function of a castle but on a smaller scale, and Tor was so busy looking around that he failed to see Gilbert de Featherstone emerge from one of the many doorways.

"Isalyn!" the man called, looking concerned with his daughter in the presence of two unfamiliar knights. "Is everything well? You foolish lass, I've sent Fraser out looking for you. Where did you go?"

Isalyn looked at her father, who didn't look at all like the sickly man she'd seen when she had first come to Featherstone two weeks ago. In fact, he looked better than he ever had and she was coming to think that his illness had been faked purely to lure her back to Featherstone. He stood tall enough, his cheeks with color, his red hair blowing in the wind. The more she looked at him, the less patience she felt.

"Greetings, Father," she said evenly. "I went into Haltwhistle. Where did you think I had gone?"

By Gilbert's expression, it was clear that he wasn't sure how to react to her. He was torn between being glad to see her and being angry that she had left in the first place. His gaze moved nervously to the knights, confused by their appearance. Isalyn's defiant attitude wasn't helping.

"You have my thanks for escorting my daughter home," he said to Tor, who happened to be closer. "I am Gilbert de Featherstone. You are welcome in my home."

Tor eyed the man before removing his helm. "I am Tor de Wolfe," he said, gesturing to Nat. "This is my cousin, Nat Hage. Finding your daughter in town was a coincidence, I assure you. We were passing through because we were on our way to Featherstone. We have business with you, my lord. Is there somewhere we can speak in private?"

Gilbert looked rather confused by, and perhaps wary of, the request, but he nodded quickly. "Of course," he said. "Come inside. I fear it is to rain soon, so permit me to show you my hospitality. Let us take comfort in my hall."

Enbarr was tethered next to a trough, shoving his face into the water and alternately drinking water and blowing bubbles, but when a stable servant came to take the horse, Tor quietly snapped at the man and told him to leave the horse alone. He didn't like anybody touching his horse but, more than that, he had a body strapped to the saddle and he didn't want the servants getting wise to it.

The servant backed away.

Tor and Nat followed Gilbert through a door that led to a wide, curving stone staircase. The steps were long and flat, and they followed the man up the flight until they reached what was a small foyer. The foyer opened up into a large hall that spanned the entire front of the manse, from one end to the other, including the gatehouse. There were two wells in the middle of the chamber where the portcullises would sit when they were raised, as they were now. It was like having two big grates in the middle of the chamber, which made it quite strange, but the hall was big enough that it really didn't matter.

In fact, Tor was surprised at how grand the hall was. There was an enormous hearth made from cut stone, with angels and demons carved into it in an elaborate artistic fashion. Tor was quite fascinated with it but he was distracted when Gilbert led them to a large table at the end of the hall, indicating the chairs for them to sit upon.

Tor and Nat made their way over to the dais where Gilbert was already taking a seat. It was clear that he seemed to think this was a social call, unprepared for what was to come. Already, Tor and Nat were looking for the exits in case they had to flee. Tor had originally told Nat to wait outside of the manse in case they took Tor hostage in their grief, but with Lady Isalyn as their escort to Featherstone, Nat couldn't have very well refused to go inside because it would have looked strange.

The lady might have suspected that something was wrong.

Therefore, Nat took a seat near Tor in one of the heavy, oak chairs that lined the table. They were of the finest quality, as was the table, and Tor was coming to see just how much wealth the House of de Featherstone had. Not only was the furniture some of the finest he'd ever seen, but instead of rushes on the floor, there were expensive hides. The walls contained exquisite tapestries, clearly of the finest quality, and the long lancet windows were covered with expensive oilcloth.

There were other things, too, that lent credence to the theory of de Featherstone wealth. The wall over the hearth contained shields that Tor did not recognize. He thought they might have been Germanic or Spanish because they were unrecognizable to him and he recognized almost every standard in England. If he had seen it, he would have remembered it. He had a memory that never failed, so the heraldry on the wall was curious. In fact, he pointed to them simply to be polite.

"Interesting standards, my lord," he said. "I do not recognize them."

Gilbert sent servants running for food and drink. "Nor would you unless you had fought battles outside of England," he said. "In my travels, I have purchased many pieces for my collection. Call it a hobby, I suppose, but all of those shields are from every province I have ever visited. Do you see the one on the very top?"

"The white and red?"

"Aye," Gilbert said. "That belongs to the Duke of Vilnius. I was his guest for a night."

Tor was impressed. "That is at the ends of the earth, some would say," he said. "You are a well-traveled man."

Gilbert shrugged. "More than most," he said. "My father was also well-traveled and knew many people in many places. But you did not come here to speak of travel, I am sure. You said you had business with me. How may I be of service, de Wolfe?"

The moment was upon them. Tor wanted to be concise and to the point, but that was before Isalyn appeared. He was preparing to speak when she joined them at the table, bringing expensive pewter cups with her and setting them down in front of her father and in front of the guests. But instead of leaving, she lingered to listen to what was about to be said and Tor hesitated.

Although it should not have mattered to him, he didn't want her to hear what he had to say. Perhaps he was trying to protect her, or perhaps he just didn't want her thinking poorly of him. He wasn't certain. As he fumbled for the right words, suitable for a lady's ear, Gilbert turned to his daughter and frowned.

"This does not concern you," he said. "Go to the kitchens or to your chamber. I will summon you when I want you."

Given all that Tor had heard from Isalyn at the Crown and Sword and also on their journey south, he knew that kind of demand would not sit well with her and he was right. Her face turned red and her jaw flexed but, to her credit, she didn't snap back. Tor watched her as she quit the hall, embarrassed by the way her father had treated her. He had to admit that he felt rather badly for her.

Once she was gone, Gilbert returned his attention to Tor.

"You were saying?" he said.

Tor sat forward, his arms resting on the table and his hands folded, feeling infinitely more comfortable now that Isalyn was out of the chamber. Something about her presence was distracting, but not entirely in a bad way. Quite the opposite.

"I have come about your son, my lord," he said.

Gilbert sighed heavily. "What has he done now?"

"Did you know that he entered into a betrothal with Isabella de Wolfe, daughter of my uncle, Blayth?"

Gilbert's features rippled with confusion. "A *betrothal*?" he repeated with surprise. "I knew nothing of this. When did this happen?"

Tor looked at Nat. Given that he was the jilted bride's uncle, he might know more, so he silently encouraged the man to answer.

Nat complied.

"Six months ago," he said. "The wedding was to be held last week, but your son ran out on Isabella after compromising her."

Gilbert visibly blanched. He tried to keep the expression of horror off his face, but he wasn't doing a very good job. "Oh… God," he muttered, wiping a hand over his face. "I… I do not know what to say. Has he gone back to de Royans? I shall send for him immediately. This will not go unpunished, I assure you."

"He did not go back to de Royans," Tor said. "We tracked him to Newcastle and found him in a tavern with several other de Royans knights. My lord, I will be to the point – when we confronted your son, he fought. He refused to return to Isabella and he tried to kill my half-brother, a son of the Earl of Warenton. He did not survive this attempt, my lord. Your son was killed while resisting men who were there to force him to keep his word."

Gilbert's mouth popped open and his eyes widened, the news of his son's death sinking in. When it seemed to hit him, all at once, he moaned a little and slumped back in his chair, gripping the arms until his fingers turned white.

"He… he's dead?" he finally said in an oddly strangled voice. "Steffan is dead?"

Tor nodded. "It was his choice, my lord," he said. "He could have gone quietly and fulfilled his vow. Instead, he chose to fight."

Gilbert stared at him a moment before lowering his gaze. The white-knuckled hand moved to his heart as if to hold in the pain that was threatening to explode.

"Oh, God," he muttered. "Oh, God, oh… God. Tell me my son did not dishonor himself this way."

Tor couldn't help but feel some pity for the man, who was obviously shaken. "I wish I could, my lord," he said. "I have many witnesses who can attest otherwise."

Gilbert put a hand over his face, sobbing softly once or twice before drawing in a deep breath, trying to compose himself.

"That is not necessary," he said hoarsely. "I do not doubt your word. The reputation of the House of de Wolfe is beyond contestation. But I do not understand any of this. I have not seen my son in over a year. It has been a very long time. If you please… can you tell me the story again? I must hear it again. He was betrothed to a de Wolfe lady?"

Tor looked at Nat again to do the explaining. Tor's seat of Blackpool was on the fringes of the de Wolfe empire property, so he wasn't always privy to the things that were happening at its heart. Given that Nat served at Northwood Castle, he knew more.

And he'd seen more.

Nat didn't hesitate to tell him.

"Your son seemed to spend a good deal of time away from Netherghyll Castle," he said. "My lord, I will tell you what I have heard and what I have seen, and then mayhap you can understand why we were so displeased with your son. Rumor had it that there was a woman in Berwick that had Steffan's attention, so he was a frequent visitor to the city. That is where he saw my niece, Isabella, and he made the decision to pursue her. He began showing up at Castle Questing, seat of the de Wolfe empire, asking to speak to Isabella. Her father, who is my uncle also, was unimpressed with your son and his reputation, but Isabella was quite fond of him. The more he denied your son, the more Isabella wanted to see him. You can imagine how these things go, my lord. I have three daughters myself. When they want something, it is difficult for a father not to comply."

Gilbert nodded, wiping at his eyes. "I understand," he said quietly. "Please continue."

"Isabella was enamored with him," Nat said. "Servants saw them in the garden in a compromised position and that made its way back to her father. The fact that they were betrothed was the only thing that kept her father from killing your son. You *do* realize that Blayth de Wolfe is one of the most fearsome warriors in the north, do you not?"

Gilbert nodded weakly. He was quite pale, the shock of his son's death sinking deep now. "I know of him," he said. "He did not kill my son, yet my son is dead."

"That is because he ran away on the day of the wedding," Nat said. "He was a coward, my lord. As Tor told you, we tracked him to Newcastle. When he was confronted, instead of admitting his wrongs, he fought with us. He was killed when he tried to kill a young squire."

Gilbert looked at him in disbelief. "A *squire*?"

"Aye, my lord."

"Not even a knight?"

"Nay, my lord."

Gilbert grunted, closing his eyes to the shame if it all. At this point, wine and food was being brought forth and Gilbert grabbed at the nearest pitcher, pouring himself an overflowing cup and drinking nearly the entire contents. Tor took only the drink while Nat took food as well, as he hadn't been treated to a fine meal earlier in the day. Tor had been so taken with Isalyn during their meal together, he had totally forgotten his promise of food for Nat. As they watched de Featherstone reconcile himself to his son's cowardly death, a heavily armed knight entered the hall.

Both Tor and Nat stopped what they were doing, watching the incoming knight with suspicion. That was normal when heavily armed men faced one another, and were strangers to each other, but Gilbert lifted a hand.

"Be at ease," he told Tor and Nat. "This is Fraser le Kerque, a knight who serves me. He is my only knight, but he commands the small army of men who protect me and my goods. Fraser, this is Sir Tor de Wolfe and Sir Nat Hage."

Fraser was just nearing the table as Gilbert made the introductions. He was a big man, handsome, with a square jaw, black hair, and pale blue eyes. He looked at Tor and Nat with a good deal of concern, clearly curious as to why they were here.

"De Wolfe?" he repeated. "Castle Questing?"

Tor shook his head. "Blackpool," he said. "It is north of here."

Fraser nodded. "I know," he said. "We heard that de Wolfe now occupies it."

"For eight years now."

Fraser dipped his head politely. "Then it is an honor to finally make your acquaintance," he said, but his attention returned to Gilbert. "My lord, I have just been told that Lady Isalyn has returned. How long has she been here?"

Gilbert held up a weary hand. He didn't want to deal with his headstrong daughter's behavior at the moment but was forced to by necessity.

"Not long," he said. "She was in Haltwhistle. These good knights escorted her home."

Fraser looked between Tor and Nat again, and it was apparent that he was fighting off a wicked surge of annoyance. But to his credit, he remained calm even though he had been out for hours, searching for the errant daughter of his liege. With a heavy sigh, he set his helm onto the table near Nat and began to remove his heavy gloves.

"I see," he said, taking a deep breath. "I have been all over the countryside looking for her and she was in Haltwhistle all along?"

Gilbert nodded. "At least she did not go far this time."

"It seems that all I have done since she arrived is chase her all over this valley, my lord."

Gilbert had no energy to show any concern for that situation. "She will return to London soon and we shall no longer be concerned for her," he said. "But, Fraser… these knights have come bearing news of Steffan."

"What of him?"

"He is dead."

Fraser's eyes widened for a brief moment, but he controlled himself. His attention moved to Tor, sitting across from Gilbert.

"What happened?" he asked steadily.

Tor simply repeated what he'd told Gilbert. "He entered into a betrothal with a de Wolfe daughter," he said. "He chose to flee the day of the wedding and when we caught up to him, he chose to fight rather than be forced into honoring his word. He lost the fight."

Fraser didn't seem surprised by that statement in the least, but he was shocked by the news. He ended up sitting in the nearest chair, trying not to appear as stunned as he felt. After a few moments, he finally shook his head.

"Far be it for me to speak ill of the dead, but this is not shocking news," he said. "Steffan did as Steffan pleased."

Gilbert looked over him. "Not now, Fraser."

But Fraser ignored his plea. "My lord, Steffan made no secret of that fact," he said. "He has shamed the de Featherstone name time and time again, now with the House of de Wolfe. God's Bones, do you realize how powerful they are? They could destroy us with very little effort. And your son has affronted the house? Have you asked them what they wish for compensation?"

He wasn't being belligerent, simply forthright. Tor took his question seriously.

"We have asked for no compensation," he said. "We have not come to demand it. We have come to inform Lord de Featherstone that his son has been killed and that we have brought him home."

Both Gilbert and Fraser looked at him sharply. "Home?" Gilbert said sharply. "Where is he?"

"On my horse."

Gilbert's mouth popped open again. "God's Bones," he muttered. "I came out into the bailey… I came because my daughter had been brought home… are you telling me that Steffan is on the back of your horse?"

"Aye, my lord."

"I was that close to him?"

"Aye, my lord."

He bolted up from his chair. "Then I must retrieve him at once. *At once*!"

Fraser was on his feet, as were Tor and Nat. Gilbert was muttering to himself, something about collecting his son, and began to scurry from the hall. Fraser was on his heels and because they were nearly running, Tor and Nat were nearly running as well. Everyone was nearly running at that point.

By the time they reached the entry door, they began to hear the screams.

CHAPTER FIVE

DAMN THE MAN for chasing her out of his hall.

True to form, Isalyn did not go to the kitchens or to her chamber as her father had instructed. She had spent many years away from her father and his commands, so she wasn't going to start listening to him now. Instead, she had gone back the way she had come, out into the bailey with a blustery storm gathering overhead.

Even as she stood there, she could feel raindrops falling inconsistently and thunder rolled in the distance. She glanced up into the sky, watching the pewter-colored clouds as they collected, and the wind was beginning to pick up.

It was going to be a good storm.

But it was nothing like the storm in her heart. The moment in the hall with her father was so typical of so many moments with him. It seemed to her that when her mother was alive, he had been far more congenial and sweet. She remembered the affection between her parents, something that had changed so drastically in what seemed to be such a short amount of time. She had such memories of her parents' affection and then, suddenly, it was gone.

Even though her father had summoned her from London

under the pretense of an illness, something that would indicate he wanted her with him, he still had no ability to behave towards her as a father should. Affectionately, kindly. It was as if he didn't know how to behave with her at all and considering how much time she had spent with her mother in London, she was virtually a stranger to him.

And he was a stranger to her.

Isalyn had always wished that she had asked her mother what had happened between her and her father, but the woman had been so sick in the last few years of her life that Isalyn didn't want to bring up the past. Her mother never spoke of Gilbert, as if he were dead to her somehow, but perhaps if she had asked about the situation, she might understand him a little better. As it was, she knew nothing.

He never even tried to get to know her, not even when she appeared a month ago at his summons. It was as if her coming had been enough for him, because there had been no grateful reunion or meaningful conversations.

But there had been some consternation on his part.

Isalyn wasn't a calm, obedient girl. She had a mind of her own. Consequently, her behavior confused and upset him, but he never once tried to talk to her about it. The more she did as she pleased, the more he seemed to distance himself. Isalyn's mother had given her so much freedom and so much encouragement to do what she wanted to do, and that was the way Isalyn lived her life. Her mother had known about the plays she had written and she had even read a couple of them until her illness consumed her. She had been proud of her daughter's creativity and had never tried to discourage her, something that was rare for a parent to do with a female child.

The rain began to come down a little more steadily as Isalyn reflected on her relationship with her father. It had been embarrassing when he'd spoken so condescendingly to her in front of Tor, but rather than snapping back, she had kept her mouth shut. When every cell in her body was demanding she resist, there was a part of her that didn't want Tor to see that. She had already impressed upon the man just how independent and strong she was, and she was certain that he was intimidated by that. Any man would have been. Being independent was one thing, but being sassy and disobedient was quite another.

She just didn't want Tor to think badly of her.

Why on earth that should matter to her, she didn't know. But it did.

In fact, even thinking about him made her smile. Perhaps it was the patience he had shown her since the very beginning of their association. She'd never seen a man with more patience. He had saved her life and how had she thanked him? She had been rude. *And* nasty. But she had apologized for it, bought him a meal, and he had forgiven her. Their conversation at the Crown and Sword had been one of the better ones she'd ever had.

Or perhaps it wasn't the conversation as much as it was the company.

More rain began to come down and Isalyn could see Tor's big, hairy warhorse standing over by the trough, burying his nose in the water and blowing bubbles. He was such a big horse, but with oddly short and thick legs. It seemed to her that he was just as big and strong as his master, so they seemed to fit well together.

Curious, she made her way across the courtyard, pelted by occasional fat raindrops and thinking that perhaps she should find some shelter because she didn't want to ruin the red damask she was wearing. Across the courtyard, where the horses were tethered, was a doorway that led inside and she headed in that direction.

But that path took her by Tor's fat horse and something

made her pause next to the animal. Maybe she simply wanted to get a good look at the horse, an animal he would have undoubtedly taken into battle. In London, she wasn't exposed much to the warlords or knights, so battle to her was more of a concept than something she had any experience with. Bloodthirsty knights who fought with barbaric Scotsman or uncivilized Welsh were about all she knew of the fighting class. Her world had always been a somewhat sheltered and civilized existence, where things like that didn't much exist.

She had never shown much interest in that world but, suddenly, she was.

That world had Tor in it.

At that point, Isalyn was standing at the horse's head and the animal noticed her, lifting its muzzle out of the water. It was a very pretty horse, even if he was big and hairy and strange-looking. There was something in his eyes that looked almost gentle and, on impulse, she reached out to pet him.

It was the wrong move.

The horse, startled by the hand in its face, jumped back and reared up. It was enough of a jolt to knock that enormous bundle on its hindquarters onto the ground and as Isalyn watched, the bundle became undone and part of an arm was exposed. Curiosity turned to horror as she realized that the wet blanket concealed a corpse, but that wasn't the worst of it. A big gust of wind lifted up part of the horse blanket that the corpse was wrapped in, revealing its head.

She recognized the hair and the somewhat distorted features. Even though she hadn't seen him in a few years, still, she never forgot a face.

Isalyn found herself looking at her very dead brother.

Her screams filled the air.

BY THE TIME Tor hit the bailey along with Gilbert, Nat, and Fraser, everyone seemed to be in an uproar and it all seemed to be centered around Enbarr. There was more screaming going on and, quickly, Tor pushed through a crowd of soldiers to see what they were looking at.

Then, he could instantly see what happened.

Somehow, some way, Steffan's body had been dislodged from the back of his horse. It now lay up on the ground, in the mud, and the horse blanket that had been tightly wrapped around it had partially come off. But that wasn't the worst part – Enbarr, startled by the surge of the crowd and the screams that seemed to be echoing off the walls of the manse, was dancing around in a jittery fashion. In the process, he had stepped on Steffan's body repeatedly.

What they had was a mess.

"God," Tor groaned, shoving some soldiers aside as he hastened to calm his panicking steed. He grasped the horse's head, struggling to calm the beast. "Easy, Enbarr. Be easy, lad."

Quickly, he untied the reins that had the animal tethered to a post, pulling the animal away from the body on the ground. There were horrified stable servants standing around, watching the spectacle, and he grabbed the nearest man by the collar and yanked him over to the horse.

"You will tend my horse," he growled. "Your life depends on how well you tend him. See that he is calmed and fed and watered. Is this in any way unclear?"

The petrified servant nodded, quickly taking Enbarr and leading him off towards the stables. Tor would have liked to have tended his horse personally, but he had a bigger matter on his hands. He made his way back to the trampled body on the ground, now as Gilbert bent over it, trying not to weep.

"My son," the man said tightly, looking at the rotting remains. "My poor boy."

He didn't seem to know what to do other than stand there and grieve, so Tor swung into action. He snapped his fingers at Nat and motioned to the body. Taking the hint, Nat bent over and flipped the blanket back over the body to cover it, as least as much as he was able. The blanket was matted and filthy from having been stepped on. Both Tor and Nat lifted the edges of the horse blanket and used it like a litter.

"Where do you want him, my lord?" Tor asked.

Gilbert was clearly shaken, now being forced to process Tor's question. "To… to the vault, I suppose," he said hoarsely. "I have nowhere else to put him. We must take him to the vault."

With that, he put his hand over his mouth, perhaps to hold back the horror of what he had witnessed, and turned for the door that led down into the storage vaults. Tor and Nat started to follow, but Fraser put his hand on Tor's arm.

"I will take him," he said quietly. "He has already been enough of a burden to you, my lord."

It was a soft, polite statement. Tor didn't sense anything hostile from the man, simply an offer to help. Fraser seemed to be quite on edge about a potential conflict with the House of de Wolfe, so he was on his best behavior. Therefore, Tor turned over his ends of the blanket to Gilbert's knight, who assumed the load. Along with Nat, they followed Gilbert's trail to the vault. Tor began to follow as well until he caught sight of Isalyn, standing over near a small animal pen.

His attention shifted.

Isalyn had her back turned and even from where he stood, Tor could see her shoulders heaving. It took him a moment to realize that she was weeping and it occurred to him just where those horrified screams had come from.

Her.

With regret, he made his way over to her. As he drew closer, he could hear her sniffling.

"My lady?" he said gently.

Startled by his voice, Isalyn whirled to see who it was and just as quickly turned away. "I… I do not need assistance," she said, wiping her face. "I am well enough."

Tor wasn't a man immune to emotion but, truth be told, he was good at keeping it bottled up. He wasn't one to take on someone else's grief or even show much sympathy but, at the moment, he felt a good deal of pity for Isalyn. She had witnessed something that would have turned the stomach of the strongest man, so he felt sorry for her. She may have been brave and bold, but she wasn't hardened.

Perhaps he felt a little more concern than he should have.

"I am sorry that you had to see that," he said. "Had your father permitted you to remain in the hall, you would have known of your brother's passing and you certainly would not have seen… that."

Isalyn wiped furiously at her face, struggling to compose herself and pretend as if she were completely unscathed. "It is of no consequence," she said. "Steffan is dead."

"He is."

"Then the business you had with my father was to bring his body home."

"It was."

She turned to look at him, watery-eyed. "It has occurred to me that my brother was that horrible smell you said was coming off the meadows."

Tor couldn't very well lie to her. "It was," he said. "I apologize for lying to you, but I was trying to spare your delicate senses."

Isalyn understood that but her manner suggested she was perturbed by his attempt to shield her. "I know," she said. "But I am not a weakling. You could have told me the truth."

Tor tried not to look contrite, as if he'd done something wrong. "You are definitely not a weakling," he said. "But what I did, I did to protect you, my lady. It will not happen again."

She looked at him. "Of course it will not happen again," she said. "I only have one brother. You have many, but I only have one and he was not a very good brother at that. Mayhap I should not have said that, but it is true. I hardly knew him. Steffan and I lived apart for so many years that I never really knew the man."

She was trying so very hard to pretend that none of this mattered, but her chin was still trembling, as if she were going to break down in tears at any moment. Tor wasn't sure what to say to her, so he fell back on the obvious.

"I am sorry for your loss, my lady," he said. "I hope you will forgive me my… mistake of trying to protect you from the truth."

Her gaze lingered on him a moment before drifting out over the bailey, catching a glimpse of her father and Fraser and Nat as they ducked into the stairwell that led down to the vaults, carting that putrid mess between them. The rain was falling a little harder now, thunder rippling overhead.

"How did my father take the news?" she asked. "He did not seem particularly hysterical when he saw my brother's body lying there."

"He took it bravely," Tor said. "But I am sure that he is quite troubled by it. It is his son, after all."

Isalyn's attention was on the manse, but her thoughts were elsewhere. Her dark blue eyes reflected both turmoil and truth.

"Steffan was a disgrace," she said quietly. "He always did as he pleased and my father never stopped him. Even before my parents decided to live separately, Steffan would do naughty things to me and he was never punished."

Tor found himself watching her lush mouth as she spoke. "What did he do to you?"

She sighed faintly, thinking back to that time of youth, those days she didn't like to think about. "Pull my hair," she said. "He was always pulling my hair. Once, he tied my braids in a knot and my mother had to cut my hair to get the knot out. He would catch flies and pull the wings off of them just to see them suffer. He had a dog that he would kick constantly. I finally took the dog and hid it. It became my dog, but I had to keep it in my room always so Steffan would not find it. It became a very spoiled dog who slept in my bed and ate from my plate, but someone told Steffan I had the dog and, one day, the dog just disappeared. I never saw it again. When I asked Steffan where the dog was, he told me the animal got what it deserved and would not tell me more. I loved that dog."

The memory of the dog brought tears again and they spilled from her eyes faster than she could wipe them away. Even so, Tor was coming to get a broader picture of Steffan de Featherstone. Not only was he a man who broke his word, but he was a tormenter as well. There were probably darker secrets, even more than that. Men like that usually had a few. Before he could respond, however, she looked at him and spoke.

"Do you have sisters, Sir Tor?" she asked.

He nodded. "Five, but I lost one many years ago."

"But you are kind to all of them? Even the one you lost?"

He nodded faintly. "I do not pull their hair if that is what you are asking," he said, his eyes glimmering with mirth. "I love each one, my lady. I would kill or die for them."

She gazed at him a moment with big, bottomless eyes, perhaps pondering a world where a brother could be kind to a sister. Or a family that loved one another. After a moment, she smiled weakly.

"They are most fortunate to have you for a brother," she said. "I envy them. Will you go home to them now?"

He shook his head. "They do not live with me," he said. "I live at Blackpool Castle."

"Where is that?"

"About twenty miles north of here."

"And you live there alone?"

He nodded. "Without my sisters and brothers and parents," he said. "My cousin lives with me, however. Christian is my second in command. Blackpool is an important outpost, a military outpost, so it is heavily manned."

"But you are happy there?"

He wasn't sure why she was asking so many questions, but he sensed something behind her curiosity. It seemed she wanted to hear that someone was happy, somewhere, because she wasn't particularly happy with her circumstances. A dead mother, now a dead brother, and a father who seemed distant at best. Perhaps she simply couldn't believe there really were happy families in the world.

It was a foreign concept.

She was looking for happiness, somewhere, even through a knight she'd just met.

"I am happy there," he said. "When my uncle purchased the castle, it came with herds of sheep with black faces. Funny little creatures. There are orchards and gangs of geese that like to congregate in my bailey and bite my soldiers. But it is a happy place, at least for me."

Her face was still pale and her eyes a bit watery, but she smiled at the thought of such a place. "There are some people in London that keep geese for protection," she said. "Sometimes they are better than dogs."

"If I had thousands, I'd send them after the Scots."

She giggled, displaying a sweet smile. He was simply glad that the mood was finally lightening. It had been touch and go there for moment.

"Good," he said. "You're smiling again. Now, shall we go into the hall and get out of this rain?"

She looked up at the dark sky. The rain still wasn't falling heavily, but it was enough that she agreed with him. When he offered her his arm, she didn't hesitate to take it and Tor realized, as he led her towards the entry to the hall, that he felt rather proud to have her on his arm. Little did he know that she was feeling the same way, too.

The unexpected day for them both was turning out even more unexpectedly.

CHAPTER SIX

Netherghyll Castle

"HE ATTACKED ONE of my nephews and was killed in the process," Thomas said grimly. "You cannot know how badly I feel for this unfortunate incident, Kelton, but Steffan chose his own path. It was not forced upon him. He could have come peacefully with us and fulfilled his vow, but he chose not to. I am sorry to inform you of this."

Kelton de Royans, Lord Cononley, was staring at Thomas rather dumbfounded. A middle-aged man, his blond hair mostly gone gray, he was genuinely shocked by what he was hearing. The unexpected appearance of the Earl of Northumbria should have told him something was amiss but, even so, he wasn't expecting this.

Or perhaps he was.

Given that the subject was Steffan de Featherstone, perhaps he shouldn't have been surprised at all.

"A betrothal to Isabella *de Wolfe*?" he said, incredulous. "I had not heard of this, my lord, and Steffan has served me for two years. When did this betrothal occur?"

Thomas could see that the man was being genuine in his disbelief. "Within the year is my understanding," he said. "He pursued Isabella quite seriously, enough to compromise her so that her father gave in to the demands for marriage. Then, on the day of the marriage, Steffan was nowhere to be found. Forgive me for pointing this out, but he is your knight. Did you not wonder why he was not here with you at Netherghyll?"

Kelton sighed heavily. "He said that his father was ill," he said. "He was traveling frequently to Featherstone to see to his father, but now I am guessing that was not true."

Thomas shook his head. "It seems that it was not," he said. "Steffan was pursing Isabella and then abandoning her. When we caught up to him, he chose to fight, as I said, rather than honor his promise. The decision cost him his life."

Kelton's expression of shock began to turn to one of rage. He turned to the five de Royans knights that had returned to Netherghyll with the earl.

"You lot were in Newcastle," he said through clenched teeth. "You met Steffan there, did you not?"

The knight in the lead nodded to the question. He was young and intimidated by an angry lord but, then again, all five of them were young men newly knighted. Netherghyll was known as a training port for new knights, bachelor knights, and the like. In exchange for service, they received more advanced training from an arsenal of senior de Royans knights, much as Castle Questing and other castles provided. It was a way of strengthening ranks while giving new knights more experience, but the caveat was that sometimes those younger knights had a lot to learn in both battle and ethics.

This was clearly one of those times.

"We were in Newcastle, my lord," the young knight said. "We were at Alnwick at your request, if you recall, but we were preparing to depart when we received de Featherstone's missive to meet him in Newcastle."

"Did he say *why* he wanted you to meet him?"

"Nay, my lord. I swear it."

Kelton wasn't convinced. "You were friends with de Featherstone, Powell," he said. "Do you mean to tell me that you knew nothing of his activities?"

"He told me that he was visiting his sick father as well, my lord."

The young man was pale with fear, but neither Kelton nor Thomas sensed he was lying. Just nervous. In fact, Thomas sought to take Kelton's anger off the knight.

"I believe him," he said quietly. "We had the opportunity to speak after the encounter at the tavern and I am convinced your men believed they were being attacked by de Wolfe knights for some unknown reason. They appear to know nothing about Steffan's activities so I would say you have men who trusted the wrong companion. That is their only crime."

Kelton still wasn't convinced but he let it go. He knew that Powell and Steffan and another knight named Joah de Brayton had been good friends, so he honestly couldn't believe that Powell knew nothing. After a moment, he waved them off.

"Go," he said. "Out of my sight. But do not leave this castle. I may have more questions. Do you understand me?"

The five of them nodded fearfully. "Aye, my lord," Powell said.

Dismissed, the five knights nearly ran from the room. An enraged de Royans was never a good thing. Four of the knights headed out into the bailey to tend to their horses but Powell paused a moment in the entry, sighing heavily as he ran his fingers through his dark hair. He felt as if he'd barely survived his bout with an angry lord. In fact, the entire situation had him reeling. Just as he went to follow his colleagues outside, he heard someone hissing.

Turning towards the sound, he could see an older knight standing in a doorway that led to a servant's passage. The man was hissing at him and Powell looked startled to see him. His eyes darted around to make sure no one was watching before he swiftly headed in the older knight's direction. When he drew close, the man reached out and grabbed him, pulling him into the darkened passage.

"What *happened*?" he hissed. "Where is Steffan?"

Powell sighed sharply. "Dead," he said. "The de Wolfe pack caught up with him and when he refused to return to marry the de Wolfe girl, he was killed."

The older knight's breath caught in his throat. That wasn't the answer he had expected. His eyes widened and he slumped back against the passageway as the color drained from his face.

"Nay," he breathed. "Tell me it is not true."

"It *is* true," Powell whispered. "I just lied to de Royans, Joah. I told him I knew nothing of Steffan's activities and thank the sweet Lord that he believed me. Or mayhap he did not. I suppose time will tell, but I will deny any knowledge to my grave."

Joah de Brayton put his hand over his mouth, closing his eyes as tears popped forth. He lost his composure while Powell stood there, completely unmoved by the tears. In fact, he yanked Joah's hand from his face, his eyes blazing.

"Don't you dare act as if you are crushed by this," Powell hissed. "This was all a plot between you and Steffan to get your hands on a de Wolfe dowry and Steffan lost his nerve. I wish you had never spoken of it because now I am part of this… this dishonorable mess."

Joah was a master knight at Netherghyll, a man with twenty years of training and battle experience. His credentials were good. But he was also a man who had grown disillusioned with his post. For the past few years, he wanted something better, the opportunity for riches and leisure. He found a partner in that dream, and in his bed, in Steffan de Featherstone.

But clearly, that dream had somehow shattered.

"You were agreeable enough to be part of it with the promise of the reward," Joah reminded him. "You are not innocent, Powell. You overheard Steffan and me speaking of the de Wolfe lass and the dowry she would bring. You were eager enough to be part of it when we offered you a prestigious post with the de Wolfe army once Steffan married her. Nay… not only are you not innocent, you are complicit. Remember that."

Powell knew that. God help him, he did. But he felt as if he were getting sucked deeper and deeper into a quagmire that he would have no hope of ever escaping. Joah and Steffan had been conniving, unscrupulous men and being young and ambitious, Powell had fallen into a dangerous trap.

Now, he was part of that filth.

"I have not forgotten," he said after a moment. "But Steffan must have had a change of heart and ran out on the marriage at the last minute. We did not have time to speak in private before he was killed. We'll never know why he decided not to marry the de Wolfe lass."

Joah's eyes started to well again as he thought on his lover. "How… how did it happen?" he asked. "His death, I mean. How was he killed?"

Powell couldn't help the disgust in his eyes. "I do not know," he said. "It looked as if his throat had been slit, but that was the only obvious wound. I do not know who did it, but we were set upon by the House of de Wolfe. They were all de Wolfe men."

Joah wiped at his eyes, quickly. "Do you know who?"

Powell thought a moment. "The Earl of Northumbria was one," he said. "I recognized several from a meeting with the king last year, when he gathered his northern warlords at Alnwick. They were all from Castle Questing or Berwick. I saw two Hage knights and the son of the Earl of Warenton was there; one of the older ones. I think he has his own command now near Carlisle, from what I heard. I think they call him Tor."

Joah recognized the names. He'd served de Royans long enough to recognize most of the de Wolfe men and their allies – Hage, de Norville, and de Longley. They were all family, all thick as thieves.

"Isabella de Wolfe is the daughter of Blayth de Wolfe," he said. "He's the one who made a name for himself in Wales years ago, the de Wolfe brother believed to be dead. He is a powerful warlord. He was not part of this assassination contingent?"

Powell shook his head. "Nay," he said. "But I believe his eldest was, Ronan. The lad looks just like him."

"Ronan," Joah repeated slowly. "How young?"

"Mayhap seventeen or eighteen years."

Joah grunted. "Young and impressionable," he muttered. "They are teaching him to be a good little killer, just like the rest of the de Wolfes."

Powell wasn't sure what to say to that, but something told him that Joah was sinking into the well of blame. It would consume him, surround him, and cover him. He would hold Steffan completely blameless for his own death.

"Northumbria is in the solar with de Royans," Powell said. "If I were you, I would distance myself from Steffan. De Royans is not pleased and he knows that you are close to Steffan. He will ask you what you know."

Joah was calming somewhat, but it was only the first wave of peace before the grief hit him again, later, and he would be swamped with it. But at the moment, he was looking to place the blame for his beloved's death. In his mind, Steffan wasn't to blame. He surely had a perfectly good reason for fleeing Isabella de Wolfe before the marriage could take place. What that reason was didn't matter.

In fact, there was part of him that was glad Steffan fought marriage to a woman. Joah didn't particularly want to share his lover, but the lure of de Wolfe wealth and prestige had been great. It would have taken him away from de Royans, where his talents and life were stagnating.

Perhaps Steffan had come up with a better idea or had a better offer.

Better than a de Wolfe.

And they had killed him for it.

"Do not worry about me," he said after a moment. "Go, now. Tend to your horse and your men. I can handle de Royans and Northumbria if they come calling. You needn't worry."

Powell studied the man for a moment, wondering where the suddenly burst of steeliness had come from, but he didn't have the inclination to ask. The further he remained away from de Brayton, the better.

The man was trouble.

Without another word, Powell headed out into the bailey, leaving Joah still in the servant's passage because he could hear anything coming in and out of the solar.

He wanted to hear what Northumbria and de Royans had to say.

This may have been the end of Steffan, but it was not the end of the situation. Steffan was, in all things, above reproach in Joah's mind. The more he thought about it, the more he knew that the de Wolfe pack must have unfairly cornered him. He was positive that Steffan had a good reason for running.

He only wished he knew what it was.

But that was of little consequence now. His lover was gone, his plans were laid to waste, and the common denominator to both of those things was the House of de Wolfe. Certainly, Joah could not attack any number of their fortresses to exact his revenge. He had no army, no men sworn to him. He was only one piece of a much larger war engine, a war engine that the House of de Royans controlled. Personally, he had nothing.

It was that sense of emptiness that had started this entire scheme.

He'd lost whatever connection he was going to have to the House of de Wolfe. He had lost a man he had loved very much for the past two years. Now, he had nothing more to lose, but that did not stop his sense of vengeance. As he saw it, Steffan was a victim in all of this. A victim of de Wolfe greed and ambition. They had everything – money, power, properties, and titles. They had everything and Steffan would have asked for so little. Marriage to a de Wolfe daughter would not have mattered in the grand scheme of the House of the Wolfe.

It would have been hardly nothing.

But now that nothing was gone.

Joah was, if nothing else, sly. He knew how to manipulate men and he knew how to concoct a scheme. This entire de Wolfe betrothal had been his idea, after all.

He was going to have to think of something else to get back what he had lost.

The House of de Wolfe had outposts and castles all along the Scottish Marches, including two that were closer to Carlisle. Everyone knew of Rule Water Castle, known as Wolfe's Lair. That was perhaps their biggest outpost. There was another one they had acquired a couple of years ago near The Lair and Joah remembered this because at the same gathering at Alnwick when King Edward gathered his warlords, he had heard talk of Blackpool Castle and that the de Wolfe family had purchased it.

The House of de Wolfe just got richer and richer.

Joah wasn't sure who the garrison commander was, but surely it was another de Wolfe. Perhaps if he made his way to Blackpool, which was about one hundred miles directly north, he could pose as an injured allied knight and seek shelter. The land up there was fairly remote, so perhaps there would be an opportunity for him to seek a little retribution against those who had ruined his plans and killed his lover. If not, then he'd move on to the next de Wolfe property and seek opportunities there. After twenty years as a de Royans knight, he was ready to move on.

He was finished with Netherghyll.

More than that, it was time for Joah de Brayton to evolve.

With as big as the de Wolfe family was, perhaps he could find a bride amongst them. Where Steffan had failed, he would not.

He was going to make them pay.

CHAPTER SEVEN

Featherstone

"IS THIS USUAL?"

The question came from Tor. On a misty morning, with a heavy layer of dew covering the countryside, Tor and Fraser stood in the muddy courtyard of Featherstone, waiting for their horses to be brought out.

"Aye," Fraser said, resignation in his voice. "Ever since Lady Isalyn arrived, she has thrown all of Featherstone into turmoil. She is used to doing as she pleases and sees no need for an escort in anything she does. She doesn't even see any reason to tell anyone where she is going."

Tor wasn't surprised to hear that and Fraser sounded genuinely worried. "She is a woman of independence," he said. "I recall hearing stories of my grandmother also being a woman of independence, escaping my grandfather and doing as she pleased."

"And your mother?"

Tor shook his head. "My mother also," he said. "The grandparents I speak of are my father's parents. My mother, however, was a strong and forceful woman. She did as she pleased no matter what my father said. Unfortunately, it cost her in the end."

Fraser looked at him curiously. "What do you mean?"

Tor could see the stable servants bringing out Enbarr and Fraser's long-legged stallion through the mist. "She wanted to go on a visit after heavy rains and my father tried to discourage her," he said. "She decided to go regardless of his advice and her carriage was lost in a river. She drowned alongside my younger brother and younger sister, an aunt, and two cousins. It took my father years to come to terms with what had happened. He once said he wished he had forbidden her to go on that day. Not that it would have mattered; she probably would have gone, anyway."

Fraser's expression of curiosity turned to one of sympathy. "That is a terrible story," he said. "I am sorry for you."

Tor nodded politely. "Thank you, but it was a long time ago," he said. "I think my point was that strong women often run into trouble because they do not know what is good for them, so I will help you look for Lady Isalyn on my way home. I have to go through Haltwhistle, anyway."

"What about your cousin, Nat?"

Tor grunted. "He drank too much last night," he said. "He is sleeping it off, still. He will head back to Castle Questing when he feels better, so we do not travel in the same direction."

"Questing is quite far north."

"About eighty miles. It will take him a few days at the very least."

The horses were brought around and the knights mounted up, heading out into the cold, misty dawn. Yesterday's rainstorm had turned the road into a swamp, so they mostly traveled on the shoulder because there were some massive puddles to avoid.

The ride was silent for the first several minutes. Tor was thinking ahead to the Crown and Sword, wondering if that was where Isalyn had gone, when Fraser broke into his thoughts.

"My lord, I must say something, if you will indulge me," he said.

Tor looked at him curiously. "Speak."

"I must apologize for Steffan's actions," Fraser said hesitantly, as if he weren't sure he should speak on such a matter. "If Lord Gilbert has not, I will. Steffan was a complicated and difficult man. He has caused his father much grief, so do not judge the entire family by Steffan. He is not representative of Gilbert."

Tor glanced at him. "Lord de Featherstone is not being judged, at least not by my family," he said. "You needn't worry."

"Thank you, my lord. May I tell Gilbert that?"

Tor nodded, but his gaze lingered on the black-haired, blue-eyed knight who seemed proper and professional. He had since the beginning of their association and Tor was growing curious about him. It seemed to him like such a knight should be serving in a big house with a big army, not serving a wealthy merchant. There was a definite division of class there.

"What is your story, le Kerque?" he asked. "Not to be nosy, but you seem far more loyal to Gilbert than his own son. Steffan was a knight and did not even serve his father."

Fraser nodded. "I know," he said, somewhat quietly. "Steffan did not wish to follow in his father's footsteps and become a merchant, so Gilbert paid Lord de Shera of The Paladin near Chester to train Steffan as a knight. He went to foster there at twelve years of age, very old for that kind of training, but he learned quickly."

Tor's eyebrows lifted. "The Paladin?" he repeated. "That is a prestigious castle and the House of de Shera is very powerful. So that's where Steffan trained?"

"He did."

"How did you come to serve Gilbert?"

Fraser smiled wryly. "My family is an old one," he said. "Once, we were wealthy, but now all we have is our good name. The fortune was gone long ago. My father used it to obtain a position for me in the House of de Winter. I trained at Norfolk Castle and my reputation is without compare, but I have a fortune to build. When my father dies, I will inherit Welton Castle, but only the property and the title of Lord Faldingworth. There is nothing else – no money, no wealth to speak of. Therefore, I serve the lord who pays me the most."

"De Featherstone?"

Fraser nodded. "He is quite wealthy. The money he pays is better than most."

Tor couldn't fault the man for doing what he had to do. "Do you see much action?"

Fraser gave him a long look before snorting. "With de Featherstone?" He shook his head. "I've been with him for a few years and have yet to see a serious battle. I drill the small contingent he has constantly so our skills stay sharp, but I will be truthful. I wish I was back with de Winter or served some other great house, like de Wolfe. I miss the camaraderie of other knights and I miss the smell of battle. I miss doing what I was born to do. With de Featherstone… there is little action. I am a guard dog and little more."

"You are going to grow weary of that after a while."

"I already have. But I need the money."

Tor could understand that and he felt rather sorry for the man. But in the same breath, he respected him for doing as he must. Each knight had a story and that was Fraser's.

From that point on, the rest of the ride into town was silent. As they drew near Haltwhistle, the road grew more crowded as they began to blend with the farmers coming in off the fields, bringing in their produce to sell. The mist had lifted a little more by this time and patches of bright sunlight were streaming through the soupy mess, revealing a busy village. As they entered the outskirts of town, Tor paused.

"I am going to inspect a couple of places," he said, pointing. "You check the stables. Yesterday, I happened to know she had some interest in a man selling horses there, so she may have gone back there."

He refrained from mentioning the wild Arabian and Fraser nodded. "Where are you going?" he asked.

Tor looked towards the east end of the village. "There is a tavern over there I am going to check."

"The Crown and Sword?"

"Aye," Tor said. "I swear I have never eaten so much in my life."

Fraser snorted. "That place will make a glutton out of you."

Tor grinned. "If she is not there, I will make my way down the avenue and see if I spy her. I would suggest you do the same if you do not find her in the stables. Sweep until the end of the avenue heading west and I will meet you right here when I am finished."

It seemed like a good enough plan. Fraser nodded as he headed off towards the livery and Tor turned in the opposite direction, heading for the Crown and Sword.

The tavern seemed like as good a place to start as any. He really didn't know where else Isalyn could go this early in the morning, but the entire town seemed to be open for business at this early hour.

If she was here, she could be anywhere.

The Crown and Sword was empty at this hour, at least of diners, but there were a few people sleeping on tables and in the corners. Isalyn was not among them, so Tor headed down the street, planning to check in every stall he could find.

As Tor had noted yesterday, Haltwhistle was a surprisingly busy village, but not so surprising considering it was the largest village on the road between Newcastle upon Tyne and Carlisle. Leading Enbarr behind him, Tor came to a row of stalls whose sole business was precious metals. There were heavily armed guards all around, and they eyed him suspiciously. Unwilling to be seen as a threat, he stayed clear of them as he moved down the avenue.

Across the street were more stalls that seemed to have a good deal of wool. Raw wool, woven wool, and woolen thread, and they were advertising the fact that they could dye the wool whatever color one might wish. Two men stood out in front of one of the stalls, calling to women passing by, promising that they could dye thread the color of the sky or the color of their eyes. They seemed to be very enthusiastic, pulling in customers for their colored wool.

But still, no Isalyn.

Further down the street came an area that had more to do with the heavy wool trade in the region – beaters, sorters, and washers of wool were spread out in an organized fashion, overseen by managers, and there was a good deal of business going on. At this time of year, sheep were being brought to market, as he'd observed yesterday. He had his own sheep at Blackpool to take to market, but last year he took them into Carlisle. He thought that this time, he might bring them here because they clearly had a heavy wool trade industry. Thoughts of bringing his sheep down here were interrupted, however, by what he thought might have been a cry.

A scream.

Tor paused, ears cocked. There were crowds around him, so he thought he might be hearing things until he heard it again.

He'd heard that scream before.

Yesterday.

He was on the move.

THE DAY HAD started out as a good one.

Isalyn had awoken before dawn, rising in a chamber that was already warm because the servants had stoked the hearth in the wee hours while she'd been sleeping. Her father always made sure that she was well-tended when she visited, which meant the room was warm, fragrant, and richly appointed in all aspects.

As the daughter of a merchant, luxury was a given, and that was readily apparent at Featherstone. Covering the wooden floor were fluffy hides and expensive woolen carpets that had been imported from points east. Because her father had many suppliers all over the known world, and supply trains that traveled all over the continent, they often had exotic items from the Holy Land and even further east.

Things from the lands of the pagan gods.

One of those items was beneath her feet at that very moment, a rug from Baghdad. It was elaborate and beautiful, magnificent in every aspect. Featherstone had at least four of those rugs that she knew of, including two in her father's bedchamber and one of them hanging on the wall in the great hall. When she walked the floors of Featherstone, her feet never touched the floor because of all the rugs and hides.

Her father always insisted on that.

She was thankful for the floor coverings this morning because it had dawned cold and misty. She made her way over to the hearth to see that a thoughtful servant had put a pot of water over the flame to heat and it was already steaming. Hissing with the cold, Isalyn removed her sleeping shift and washed with the hot water and a soft, white bar of soap that smelled like flowers. She was quick and vigorous in her grooming because today was going to be a busy day.

She had things to attend to.

It seemed to be a rather strange deviation from her usual routine because her thoughts this morning were not of returning to London. As long as she had been at Featherstone, she had awoken every morning thinking that this was going to be the last day at her father's manse. She very much wanted to return home and she had made no secret of that, so nearly every day since her arrival, she had thought that this particular day would be her last.

It hadn't worked out that way.

This morning, her thoughts lingered on Tor and not her return trip home. After the distasteful shock of her brother's death yesterday, she and Tor had retreated to the great hall for the remainder of the day and into the night. It was clear that he was trying to be kind to her because of what had happened and, truth be told, she was going to let him. Tor de Wolfe was beginning to grow on her, just a little, and she was starting to appreciate his company.

Provincial knight or not.

In fact, she had come to see that he was no backwards knight. He watched her with a gaze so intense that surely it could have driven nails through stone. He missed nothing, remembered things she said from yesterday to the last detail, and generally seemed to be one of the smarter men she'd ever met.

Their conversation in the hall had been a continuation of their other conversation from the tavern in Haltwhistle. That conversation at the Crown and Sword had been a little stiff and perhaps even a little uncertain given the circumstances, but the continuing conversation in the great hall had been anything but stiff and uncertain. Tor was becoming more comfortable with her, so the conversation had been more animated.

And that's when Isalyn figured out just how smart he really was.

Even so, she realized that she had done most of the talking while he had done most of the listening, but it seemed to her that he'd had a smile on his face the entire time. That enormous, handsome, rural knight had her attention and she had no idea why. She wasn't even really sure if she liked him. Well… that was a lie.

She *did* like him.

That was why she traveled to Haltwhistle on this misty morning. She had departed Featherstone just as the sun rose and headed north to the village. Suspecting that she would never see Tor de Wolfe again after this day, there was something inside of her that wanted the man to remember her. Perhaps it was feminine vanity and nothing more. It wasn't often that she met a man she could converse so easily with and who was so attentive when listening to her speak of her silly hobbies or independent opinions, but Tor had done both of those things. He had listened to her spout off and he had never said a word to the contrary.

That took a special man.

Therefore, she was determined to get something for that special man that she had seen in town the day before. There was a metalworker near the eastern end of town who specialized in unique things. He was more than a blacksmith because not only did he fashion beautiful weapons, but he also fashioned other objects made out of steel, including women's hair pins, combs, and she even saw a pair of beautiful metal bracelets on display. But the one thing that had had her attention was a lovely steel dagger with a dog's head on it. Set within the dog's head, as it was a profile of a dog, was one big sapphire blue eye. She thought the weapon had been rather strong and unique, much like Tor de Wolfe.

When Isalyn reached the town, it had just been coming alive with farmers from the fields and other people who were there to do business. The metalworker's stall was towards the eastern end and she made her way down the avenue through the cold, dark morning, plodding along a street and being lured by the smells of the bakers who were churning out their bread for the day.

Isalyn was so used to traveling by herself and never having any trouble that she wasn't particularly watching her surroundings. She was usually so good at staying unobtrusive and out of sight that she became accustomed to focusing on her destination and not the world around her. It seemed strange that she had never had any trouble in all the time she had traveled alone, it was the truth. Therefore, she functioned under a false sense of security, as her father had told her.

She thought he worried like old women.

Even when she had traveled north from London to Featherstone, it had been with Fraser and a few of her father's men because Gilbert had sent Fraser to London to summon his daughter. Had her father not sent an escort, she would not have hired one. She saw nothing wrong with traveling alone at a time when even men did not frequently travel alone, so she was a unique soul, indeed.

And a bothersome one, according to her father.

But Isalyn didn't care what he thought.

In a few days, she'd be heading back to London, probably to never see him again. Therefore, as she neared the metalworker's stall, she didn't notice three soldiers who were also approaching the stall. She was hunting for the dog's head dagger and didn't see the three men as they looked her over, elbowing one another. She was looking at daggers and they were looking at her.

Her lack of observation was going to be her grave mistake.

"What's a sweet young miss doing all alone this morning?"

A burly soldier with a big scar on his cheek had sidled up beside Isalyn without her even noticing. Startled, she looked at the man, who was too close for comfort, and started to move away. But in doing so, she bumped into one of his companions, who was on the other side of her and looking at her rather lasciviously.

Startled anew, she backed up but the third soldier was right behind her. Frightened and enraged, she threw her elbows out and began kicking and shoving.

"Back away," she barked. "How dare you stand so close to me. I do not recall inviting you to do so. Get back!"

She said it so viciously that they instinctively did as they were told, but their obedience was brief. The man with the scar on his cheek frowned.

"You have no cause to behave like that, girl," he said. "We were only saying good morning."

Isalyn's heart was thumping against her ribs. She knew, just by looking at them, that they were up to no good. She struggled not to let her fear get the better of her.

"I do not know you and I do not wish to speak with you, so go spew your morning salutations on someone else," she said. "Go away."

They didn't move, but they didn't advance, either. "You're an uppity little chit, aren't you?" the man with the scar asked. "You need to be more mannerly. When someone wants to be nice to you, it is polite to be nice in return."

Isalyn had a choice at that moment – continue to bark at them or simply turn away and hope they got the message. She was afraid that if she continued being combative, they might grow angry with her, so she turned her back on them and moved to another side of the stall. Her decision was to ignore them.

They followed.

"You're all alone," Scar-Face said. "Don't you need protection? We're willing to give it for a price. Always for a price."

The men snickered lewdly, but Isalyn continued to ignore them, moving away even as the trio followed. They followed her all the way around the stall until she came back to where she had started.

By this time, the metalworker and his apprentice were watching and when the trio passed close to where they happened to be standing, the metalworker held out an iron rod, putting it between the soldiers and Isalyn. When they looked at the man in outrage, he cocked a bushy, dark eyebrow.

"The lady said tae leave her alone," he said in a Scots accent. "Go about yer business, lads."

The soldiers eyed the big, burly metalworker and his apprentice, who was clearly a son because he was simply a younger version of the man.

"'Tis none of your affair," Scar-Face said. "Mind your own business."

The metalworker didn't move the iron bar. "Ye're harassing one of my customers," he said. "Move along."

Scar-Face shoved the iron bar out of the way. "I don't take kindly to a Scots dog telling me what to do," he said. "And how do you know I wasn't going to be a paying customer? And what makes you think she is?"

The metalworker lifted the iron rod, wielding it like a club. "I willna tell ye again tae move along," he said. "I've got more weapons at my disposal than ye do, so consider yer answer carefully."

Scar-Face's answer was to unsheathe his sword. His companions followed. Seeing this, the metalworker and his son unsheathed two gorgeous broadswords that they had displayed in the center of the stall. People began to scatter as metal began to flash.

A fight was in the air.

That is, everyone scattered but Isalyn. She was outraged and frightened, but the metalworker had defended her so she couldn't very well leave him. She was standing by a display of beautiful daggers, including the dog's head, and she grabbed it. Her other hand took up a long and very sharp dirk. She wielded both of the weapons threateningly.

"You have been told to leave several times," she said. "You are not welcome. If you do not leave immediately, I will summon the watch and they shall run you out of town."

The soldiers looked at her with a mixture of impatience and annoyance. "I'll deal with you after I've taken care of these bastards," Scar-Face said. "Put those daggers away before you hurt yourself."

Truth be told, Isalyn had never used a dagger in her life. She didn't even own one but, even so, she wasn't afraid to use it. Hopefully, it wouldn't be turned against her, but she was willing to take the chance. She couldn't let the metalworker's noble defense go unaided.

"If you do not leave now, I am going to summon the watch," she said steadily. "You have your last warning."

"Better listen tae her, lads," the metalworker said. "I can use a sword as well as ye can, so dunna think I'll make an easy target."

He'd meant it as a deterrent, but it only seemed to act as a threat. One of Scar-Face's companions brought his sword to bear on the table in front of him, one that held metal bracelets and combs. The table broke and the items went flying, and people began to run in earnest.

The metalworker flew into action.

Swords began flying and a table dumped over onto Isalyn as

men engaged in combat. Frightened, and surprised by the tipping table, she let out an instinctive scream. It was enough to cause one of Scar-Face's companions to swing his sword in her direction, right at her head. Isalyn hit the ground when she saw it flying at her and she screamed again, simply because it was very frightening. She wasn't used to combat of any kind. Her thoughts turned towards summoning the watch to break up the fight, but that was the last thing she remembered thinking before the entire stall exploded.

Suddenly, there was a fully armed knight in their midst.

A massive broadsword was arcing in the direction of the soldiers in a skilled and offensive fashion. Caught off-guard by an enormous and enraged knight, they struggled to defend themselves from the onslaught. But their actions were for naught. They were no match against the knight bearing the colors of the House of de Wolfe. Scar-Face was the first one to go down, sliced across the neck, down his chest, and into his belly.

He hit the ground right in front of Isalyn.

She yelped again, hit in the face by Scar-Face's hand as he fell. She rolled away, now scrambling to get out of the way as a vicious battle took place over her head. She was crawling through the mud, trying to get clear and get to her feet so she could run away. At some point, she made it far enough away to stagger to her feet, but she made the mistake of turning around to see what was happening.

All she could see was Tor killing everything that moved.

It was hypnotic.

A second soldier went down as she watched, leaving the last soldier fighting against Tor with all his might. The metalworker and his son wisely cleared the stall, running over to stand with Isalyn as she stood there and watched Tor with awe.

She'd never seen a fight in her life.

Now, she was getting an eyeful.

The remaining soldier was a big man and he wasn't going down as easily as the other two had. The metalworker's stall was completely destroyed at this point, with product and broken tables littering the ground. The soldier was fending off Tor more than he was actually waging an offensive against him because, at this point, he was just trying to stay alive. However, the ground littered around him was impeding his ability to keep solid footing. He kept tripping over daggers and combs and other things that had fallen from the broken tables.

But Tor wasn't showing the man any mercy. He was swinging that sword with great skill and tremendous power, and it was only a matter of time before he gained the upper hand. The soldier took a misstep and Tor was on top of him, using that big sword to slice into the soldier's right arm, severing tendons and muscle. The soldier had the presence of mind to grab his sword with his good arm, taking a swipe at Tor, but he was too slow. Tor kicked him in the belly, sending him onto his backside. Before the soldier could pick himself up, Tor gored him right in the chest.

The battle was over.

It had been a skill level and a fight not usually seen in these parts. Tor de Wolfe was a man with the kind of talent that was used to fight for kings, so as much as the fight had been terrifying in many ways, it had also been a feast for the eyes. It had truly been something to watch.

Even for Isalyn.

She stood there a moment, mouth hanging open in shock, watching Tor kick his opponent to make sure he was dead, before wiping his sword off on the dead man's tunic. Then, he went to the other two men he'd cut down to make sure they were dead, too. Only when he was sure they were not going to rise up against him did he look over to Isalyn.

Their eyes met and, for a moment, they simply stared at one another. Then he made his way over to her, that deadly broadsword still in-hand. As he came near, he reached out and touched the corner of her mouth with his thumb.

"They hurt you," he said simply.

Isalyn had no idea what he was talking about. Her hand flew to her lips, coming away with smears of blood. Then she remembered being hit in the face by Scar-Face when he fell.

"Not intentionally," she said. "It was an accident. Tor… *what* are you doing here?"

He sighed heavily and sheathed his sword before speaking. "To find you," he said. "You ran off before dawn, so your father sent Fraser and me out to find you. I was heading home, so the stop in Haltwhistle was along my way. What in the hell happened? Why were you fighting these soldiers?"

He was being calm and collected, not at all like the beast she'd just seen slay three men. She had expected shouting at the very least, but there was none. That left her feeling somewhat disoriented and she endeavored to answer his question.

"I do not know, really," she said. "I was looking at the metalworker's wares and those three would not leave me alone. They were quite… aggressive."

"Did they touch you?"

Before she could answer, the metalworker spoke up. He and his son were still standing there, still with those beautiful broadswords in-hand.

"They boxed her in and tried tae assault her," he said. "When I tried tae stop them, they thought tae fight me. That is when ye came in, Sir Knight. Ye were a welcome sight."

Tor looked at the man, and his son, and then turned to look at the shambles of their stall. "From the look of your place of business, somehow I doubt that," he said. "But you understand I could not let them threaten the lady. She was in distress."

"Ye saved her," the metalworker said. "The rest, I can fix. I'll have it rebuilt in a couple of hours. But tae see ye fight like that… 'twas impressive, Sassenach."

He said it with a smile so that Tor knew he wasn't trying to offend him with the Scots term for English, which they usually meant as an insult. Tor simply nodded his head and the pair walked past him, back to their destroyed stall.

But Isalyn was still standing there and he turned his attention to her. He looked at her for a moment before finally shaking his head.

"Had I not come along when I did, this situation would have had a considerably different outcome," he said in a low voice. "I found you in town yesterday and I saved you from a wild horse. Today, it was from soldiers who more than likely would have happily molested you. What is going to happen to you when I go home and am no longer around to save you?"

Isalyn was trying not to look ashamed. "I have survived this long without you," she said. "But I do appreciate your assistance."

That wasn't the answer he wanted. "Why did you come to town this morning, anyway? What is here worth risking your life over?"

Isalyn realized she was still holding one of the daggers. Looking to her left hand, she could see that it was, indeed, the dog's head dagger. She had no idea what happened to the other one. She had dropped it somewhere in her panic. She lifted the dagger up so that he could see it.

"I came to buy this for you," she said, thinking it sounded stupid even as she said it. "I wanted to thank you for yesterday and for… well, for everything. You have been kind and attentive and I wanted to thank you for it. I wanted to give you a token of my gratitude."

Tor was looking at the dagger with the sapphire eye. When

he realized that she'd come to town to purchase a gift for him, it doused any irritation he felt.

But not completely.

He was still wound up from the fight.

"You did not have to do that," he said, somewhat gentler. "A kind word would have sufficed."

Realizing the gift did not have the same meaning to him as it did to her, Isalyn suddenly felt embarrassed. She wanted the man to remember her, but not as a foolish lass who needed constant saving. She had thought… she had *hoped*… that he rather felt some attraction to her as she was feeling for him. But realizing that was not the case, she immediately lowered the dagger and her gaze.

"I am sorry, then," she said. "I did not mean to cause you such trouble. You have been kind and I have very much enjoyed conversing with you, so forgive my boldness in thinking to purchase you a gift. It was wrong of me."

She pushed around him, quickly, heading back to the metalworker's stall just as the metalworker and his son were starting to pick up things that had been scattered. She handed the metalworker the dagger, apologized profusely for the mess, and gave the man about half the contents of her purse to pay for the damage. The man was grateful, but he tried to give her the money back and she wouldn't take it. She insisted. Leaving the metalworker looking concerned, and a little confused, she tucked her head down and headed down the street.

But Tor caught up to her.

"Hold, my lady," he said, grasping her by the arm. "Where are you going?"

Isalyn was deeply ashamed and, truth be told, still upset about the fight. Something about it had damaged her sense of safety, the one that permitted her to travel alone whenever she pleased. Tor had been right – had he not come along when he had, her personal well-being at this moment would have been decidedly different. In fact, the entire morning had been upsetting and she simply wanted to go back to Featherstone.

"Home," she said, unable to look at him. "I am going back to Featherstone, pack my belongings, and return to London where I belong. I do not like it up here in the wilds of Northumberland. I want to return to the city that I know."

Tor could see that she was fighting off tears. She still had blood streaked on her cheek, which fired him up again. But knowing she was safe and the threat was vanquished brought him back down. He'd fought for her, defended her, and he felt as if he'd never done anything more worthwhile in his life. Even though her actions had been foolish… well, he wasn't one to point out the obvious. She knew she had been foolish.

… didn't she?

It occurred to him that this probably wouldn't be the last time she charged out on her own. If he left her now, he was going to worry about her. Probably for the rest of his life. Somehow, this beautiful, bold woman had managed to get under his skin and he'd only known her for a day.

But… oh, what a day it had been.

"Come with me," he said softly, reaching out to grasp her arm.

Isalyn found herself being swept along. "Where are we going?" Before he could answer, she dug her heels in and pulled her arm from his grip. "Tor, I am going back to Featherstone. I've already created enough of a…"

He cut her off, latching on to her again. This time, it was her hand. "Shut up," he said quietly, but there was a glimmer of mirth in his eyes. "You talk too much. Just keep your lips shut and come with me."

Isalyn would have yanked away from him again had she not thoroughly enjoyed the feel of her hand in his. His hand was gloved but, even so, the power and warmth against her flesh was something she'd never experienced before. And the way he looked at her…

Maybe she had been wrong.

Maybe he *did* feel attracted to her as she did to him.

But it was worse even than that. She felt safe and wanted. Her hand in his seemed so natural that she never wanted him to let her go. She could have kept her hand there forever and a day, just to feel the man's strength against her.

How could she even want such a thing from a man from the wilds of Northumberland?

As he pulled her down the street, they came to his horse, tethered next to an animal's trough. True to form, the horse had his face buried in the water, blowing bubbles. Tor untied the beast and they continued along, nearing the Crown and Sword. That was where Tor caught sight of Fraser and he paused, waving a big arm over his head until Fraser saw him. The de Featherstone knight made haste in their direction.

"Lady Isalyn," Fraser greeted, disapproval in his tone, before he looked to Tor. "Where did you find her?"

"Down the avenue," Tor said without elaborating. "We are going to find something to eat. Will you join us?"

Fraser's gaze returned to Isalyn. Suddenly, his eyes narrowed and he dismounted swiftly, coming to look her right in the face. His jaw began to tick.

"*Why* is her lip split?" he said, turning to Tor. "Why is there blood on her face, de Wolfe?"

Even Isalyn could see that Fraser thought Tor had struck her. It was written all over his face. To avoid a catastrophe, she threw up her hands.

"Because I caused a fight and Tor saved me," she said. "Do you really think the man would strike me, le Kerque? You must be mad!"

Fraser looked at her, frowning. "What fight?" he said. "*Who* struck you?"

She sighed sharply. "I am not in the habit of explaining myself to my father's hired men, but just so you do not think Tor hit me, I will tell you what happened," she said. "I came to town to make a purchase. Three unsavory soldiers tried to accost me at the metalworker's stall. Tor came around just in time and saved me from them, but not before they destroyed the stall and scattered everything within it. If you do not believe me, then go ask the metalworker. He is piecing his stall together as we speak."

The situation was laid out in that simple but shocking explanation, but Fraser believed every word. Tor de Wolfe didn't seem to him like a man who would strike a woman, but he'd only known him a very short time. Sometimes, men kept things hidden. He looked at Tor.

"My apologies," he said sincerely. "But you must know how this looks."

Tor nodded. He wasn't offended. "I know," he said. "I have never lifted a hand to a woman in my life and no matter how foolish and stubborn she is, I never will."

That was enough for Fraser. "I am sorry I assumed otherwise," he said. "As for your invitation to join you for a meal, I must decline. I must return to Featherstone and tell Lord Gilbert that his daughter has been found. Again."

Tor shook his head. "I do not intend to return to Featherstone and the lady should not travel home alone," he said. "Therefore, we will forego the meal and you can take her with you now."

Isalyn turned to him, her eyes big. "You… you are going home?"

Tor nodded. "I must," he said, thinking that she looked as if she didn't want him to go. Something in her eyes made his heart race, just a little. "We are very close to my home, about twenty miles to the north."

"Then… then you want to go home?"

He shrugged. "It is time," he said. "I have been away the better part of three weeks chasing your brother around, so it is time."

"Of course," she said, deflating a little with disappointment. But after a moment, she forced a smile. "Of course you want to return home. I suppose I was hoping you would sup with us again this evening."

He smiled faintly. "I would love to, but there are things at home that require my attention," he said. "But now that we know one another and are friends, I should like to invite you and your father to sup with me at Blackpool. Le Kerque, too, if he can behave himself."

While Fraser rolled his eyes and tried not to grin, Isalyn took the invitation very seriously. "Truly?" she said. "After all of the trouble we have caused you, you would still invite us to sup?"

"Absolutely."

"But… but I was planning on returning to London shortly."

"Then we must make it soon," Tor said. "You will come before you go, will you not?"

Isalyn found herself wishing that Fraser would go away. But he was standing there, listening to everything that was said, and Isalyn wanted this conversation to be just between her and Tor. She didn't want to sound like a fool in front of Fraser, or even in front of Tor, but she was quite intrigued by the invitation to visit. She wanted to go very badly. It was a struggle not to sound like she was too eager.

"If you wish," she said. "As I said, I was planning on returning very soon. Mayhap even next week."

"Then you must come in the next few days. Tell your father

that I insist."

Something about the way he said it left no room for debate. Isalyn realized that her heart was pounding against her ribs again but, this time, it wasn't because she was afraid.

It was because of the way Tor was looking at her.

Would she come in the next few days?

She was going to come as fast as she could.

"I will," she said. "Thank you for your kindness. My father and I would be honored to sup with you."

"Fraser, too?"

She passed a glance at the knight. "Fraser, too."

The corners of Tor's eyes crinkled, a smile playing on his lips. "Good," he said. "I shall expect you shortly."

Isalyn simply nodded, trying not to look as if this invitation of all invitations she had ever had pleased her beyond reason. She pretended it was nothing to get excited over even though her palms were sweating and she felt very much like smiling. She'd never felt so giddy. Instead, she tried to play it off as if it were nothing of importance.

"Twenty miles to the north, you said?" she said.

He nodded, pointing to a road that broke off from the main avenue and headed north. "Follow that road," he said. "It will twist and turn a little, but stay on it and follow it to the end. You will see Blackpool Castle."

Isalyn dipped her head graciously. "I am looking forward to it," she said. "And thank you again for… for everything, my lord. You have gone above and beyond with regards to my safety and I am grateful."

Tor dipped his head in response, his eyes glimmering at her for a moment longer before mounting his horse. That hairy, stocky, muscular beast that he loved like a brother. With a nod at Fraser, Tor directed Enbarr towards the road north. Isalyn watched him until he disappeared from sight.

"My lady?" Fraser said. "Lady *Isalyn*?"

He was trying to get her attention and Isalyn realized that he'd caught her staring at Tor. Slightly embarrassed, she turned to him to see that he was already mounted on his horse. He held out a hand to her to help her mount behind him, but she shook her head.

"My palfrey is at the livery," she said. "I will fetch her."

She did, quickly, with Fraser trailing behind her, but all the while, she was thinking of the next time she saw Tor.

She picked up the pace.

It was going to be sooner than he realized.

CHAPTER EIGHT

HE COULD SEE it in the distance.

The approach to Blackpool Castle, as he had told Isalyn, was literally at the end of a road. It could be seen for miles because the topography in this area wasn't as hilly as it was in some parts of Northumberland. It was flat moors with an occasional rise now and then. Therefore, there was a wide field of vision and the great bastion of Blackpool Castle was easily seen.

That did not mean that it was vulnerable however. Quite the contrary. Castles along the Scottish Marches all tended to be built the same way – heavily fortified, with massively thick stone walls, stubby and compact, as if they were burrowing down into the earth to gain a foothold against the Scots.

Carlisle Castle was a perfect example of a fortress looking as if it were hunkering down, preparing to take an onslaught. But then there were castles like Northwood and Questing and Berwick, that were massive places, soaring above the land with four and five-storied keeps, or in the case of Questing, sitting atop a big hill. Breaching it was impossible because an attacking army had to mountain climb in order to get to it, and once they reached it, the walls were twenty feet high.

It was a great deterrent against attack.

Blackpool was much in the same vein as the rest of these Marcher castles. It wasn't sitting atop a big hill and it didn't have a soaring keep, but it was built from the beige sandstone that was so common to the area, reinforced by gray granite. It had an enormous curtain wall that was eighteen feet high, being twenty feet thick in some places. Having been built by William Rufus, it also used an ancient man-made structure to its advantage: the wall across the northern part of England built by the ancient Romans.

At this section of the old wall, it was still several feet tall and had what they called a gatehouse, or a mile house, built into it. It was essentially a fortified gatehouse. When William Rufus had built Blackpool, he'd used this ancient wall to protect his fortress by adding on to it and making it encircle his new garrison. Therefore, an army had to pass through the ancient Roman gatehouse before it could even arrive at the fortress itself. All of that protection was exactly why Scott de Wolfe had purchased the property.

It was a sight to behold.

And it belonged to Tor for the most part even though, technically, it belonged to the Earl of Warenton. Scott had given it over to his second son to command and Tor had taken to it immediately. He had reinforced the fortress by having his army dig a moat around the eighteen-foot walls, something that had to be carefully engineered so the walls wouldn't collapse, but Tor was brilliant that way. His army had dug out the moat in a little under six months and the massive walls were as steady as they ever were. The moat was fed by a small river called the Black River, hence the name of the fortress.

Blackpool Castle had become one of the more formidable castles in Northumberland.

Tor derived great satisfaction from the sight as he and

Enbarr trotted down the road, drawing closer to the outer ancient wall. Already, he could see movement in the outer gatehouse and as he rode up to the thick, squat gatehouse, his men were more than happy to open the heavy iron gates. He passed through, greeting his men, as he continued on to the second, and main, gatehouse.

This gatehouse was thick and impenetrable, two stories tall, with a platform on top of it so the gate guards had easy access to unruly visitors. It was a simple thing to position archers atop the gatehouse for just that purpose but, in this case, the double portcullises were lifted, admitting Tor into the courtyard beyond.

There was only one courtyard at Blackpool, but it was a big one. Surrounded by those tall walls, it was well-protected. In addition to a three-storied keep, there were separate living apartments built by the former owner, a separate great hall, kitchens, and a stable yard tucked into one corner. In the vast space between the fortress and the ancient Roman walls, there was a larger stable and a vast garden to supply the fortress with fresh produce.

"Welcome home!"

Tor turned to see his second in command approaching. Christian Hage was his cousin, the youngest son of his aunt, Katheryn, and her husband, Alec. Christian was named for two dead uncles, a brother to his grandfather and then also brother to his father. Both men had lost their lives in battle. Katheryn and Alec thought long and hard before naming their last child after two dead men because that particular name seemed to be cursed within the Hage family. But they finally decided that curses could be broken and the dead uncles needed to be honored.

So far, this Christian Hage hadn't seen any trouble.

Though young at twenty years and five, he was mature and

seasoned beyond his years, as all Hage knights were. He had his grandfather's size, with enormous shoulders and a muscular body, but he had his mother's honey-colored hair and emerald eyes. There was no shortage of female admirers for Christian Hage.

"Greetings," Tor said as he reined Enbarr to a halt. "How is my fortress?"

"Well," Christian said. "And its commander?"

"Well."

The smile on Christian's face faded. "I heard about de Featherstone," he said. "You should know that Uncle Blayth and Isabella are here."

Tor looked at him in shock. "Here?" he repeated. "What on earth are they doing here?"

Christian sighed heavily. "All I could get out of Uncle Blayth is that he wanted to talk to you," he said. Then, he lowered his voice. "Ronan told him that you killed Steffan."

Tor wasn't intimidated. "Because he tried to kill Alexander," he said. "I was defending my half-brother."

Christian held up a hand to ease him. "I know," he said. "I heard everything. Ronan is here, too. I think he came so his father wouldn't be too angry."

Tor's eyebrows lifted in disbelief. "Angry for what?" he said, incredulous. "He blames *me* for this fiasco? He should thank me. The things I have heard about Steffan de Featherstone since that time are unsavory at best. Even his father apologized for the man's behavior. Where is Uncle Blayth?"

"In the apartments," Christian said. "But he has probably heard the sentries. Mayhap you should go to him before he hunts you down."

Tor rolled his eyes, but the point was taken. He removed his saddlebags before Enbarr was led away and handed them off to Christian.

"Put those in my chamber, if you will," he said. "I will find our loving uncle and discover what kind words of praise he has for me."

It was a sarcastic remark, one that had Christian grinning as he headed off to do Tor's bidding. Only Tor wasn't grinning.

He was bracing himself for what was to come.

The apartments of Blackpool were built into the northwest corner of the bailey, a two-storied building that had four rooms on each floor. The keep was large and powerfully built, but it only had one giant chamber on each floor and the previous lord of Blackpool had twelve children. He needed somewhere to put them all.

The chambers were comfortable and well-built, and whenever there were visitors at Blackpool they were always housed in the nice, cozy chambers of the apartments. Tor had the apartment block in his sights as Ronan spilled from the entry.

Tor wasn't so sure he wanted to speak with Ronan if the man had blamed him for Steffan's death. His cousin was going to have to do some fast talking.

"Tor!" Ronan called out, heading in his direction. "How did it go with Gilbert de Featherstone? You told him about his son?"

Tor came to a halt. "I have a better question," he said. "What did *you* tell your father, Ronan? Why is he here?"

Ronan tried not to look too guilty or apologetic. "He asked," he said. "I wasn't the only one who told him the truth. Alec told him, too, and…"

"Tor!"

They both turned to the apartment entry in time to see a lovely young woman emerge holding the hand of a big, battle-scarred man. The young woman was waving at Tor happily, finally letting go of the man and rushing to Tor for a hug.

"Bella," Tor said, kissing her on the cheek. "It is a nice surprise to see you, lass."

Isabella Anne de Wolfe was genuinely a sweet girl who looked exactly like her grandmother, Jordan, had in her youth. With big green eyes and a sweet smile, she was a beauty. She also looked a lot happier than Tor had expected given she'd just lost her fiancé.

"Father wanted to talk to you about Steffan," Isabella said, holding Tor's hand. "We heard what happened, that he fought to escape the de Wolfe pack. Ronan said he tried to kill Alexander."

"That's enough, Bella." Blayth de Wolfe was close enough to hear the conversation. "I will speak with Tor alone. You and Ronan go somewhere else and make yourselves useful."

Isabella frowned at her father. "Doing what?"

"I don't care what. Play in the mud for all I care. Throw rocks at each other. Just go away."

Isabella's frown deepened. "Father, this discussion concerns me. I wish to stay."

Blayth didn't say a word. He simply pointed to the keep, silently directing her to leave, and Ronan took her by the arm and dragged her away. But it wasn't without resistance and Isabella struggled and complained the entire time, at least until they were out of earshot. She just didn't think she needed to leave and was quite angry about it.

Blayth shook his head.

"She's worse than her mother ever was," he muttered. "She acts just like her grandmother, Jemma, at times. God help us."

Tor smiled faintly as he looked at his uncle. Born James de Wolfe, twin of Katheryn, he was blond, bright, powerful, and handsome. He had been a fine tribute to the House of de Wolfe until he died. At least, that had been the belief for five long years. James and the rest of the de Wolfe knights had gone into Wales and been in an ambush where James had been struck down.

Because of the dangerous conditions, he'd been left behind, felled by a morning star that had caved in the left side of his helm. William de Wolfe had been forced to leave his boy behind with the strict belief that he had left a body, but the truth was that James had been alive.

Saved by a Welsh warlord, James had been strong enough to overcome a horrific head injury, but the cost was the loss of his memory. He had been healed by the Welsh with no memory of who he was and the Welsh called him the Welsh word for "wolf" because it seemed to be the only word James could remember. *Blaidd*, or phonetically pronounced Blithe or Blayth, became his name. James de Wolfe had transformed into a scarred, rugged Welsh warrior who had returned to his family purely by chance.

But that had been twenty years ago. He'd come home a different man in many ways, but the heart of him was still a de Wolfe. His memory had gradually come back but it had taken many years. There were still things he didn't remember, and he'd married in Wales because he didn't remember that he already had a wife, but it had all worked out in the end. His first wife and Isabella's mother, Rose Hage, had remarried to good man named Owen le Mon who served at Castle Questing while Blayth commanded Roxburgh Castle.

The dynamics had been a little strange, that was true. It wasn't often a man came back from the dead and found himself with two wives. But Blayth's Welsh wife, Asmara, and Rose had gotten on splendidly from the beginning and there had been nothing strained. Ronan and Isabella, children of James and Rose, had been raised lovingly by two sets of parents for the most part. They called Owen "Papa" and Blayth "Father", and in the case of Isabella's reluctant fiancé, Owen had deferred to Blayth completely.

And that was where they were at this moment. Tor could see that Blayth was in full angry-father mode simply by looking at him.

"So," Tor said quietly. "You want to know why I killed Steffan."

Blayth looked at him, folding his big arms over his chest. "I know why you killed him," he said in his deliberate speech, the result of his head injury. "I cannot say that I blame you, lad, but surely there had to be another way. Did you have to kill him?"

Tor shook his head. "Nay, there was not another way," he said firmly. "You know how it is in battle, Uncle Blayth. You know that you only have a split-second to make a decision, and that was all the time I had. It was either Steffan or Alexander, and I was not going to watch Steffan kill my half-brother. I am sorry if you are angry with me for it, but that is the truth. I would kill any man who tried to harm my younger half-brothers."

Blayth sighed faintly. "I understand, I suppose," he said. "But Steffan… damn the man…"

Tor could hear the distress in his tone. "Honestly, Uncle Blayth," he said with some passion. "Do you really want a man like Steffan married to your daughter? He ran from her, for Christ's sake. And you were going to force him to return and marry her? Do you really wish that for your daughter?"

Blayth eyed him unhappily. "He made her a promise."

"And he broke it," Tor said flatly. "I would not want that kind of man for my daughter. That was a complete and utter show of Steffan's true colors – a coward and a liar. In fact, when I took his body home, his father apologized for his son. Gilbert de Featherstone was greatly distressed at Steffan's behavior. It seems that his son has been a ne'er-do-well all his life, arrogant and ambitious. Not even the man's own father showed any great regard for him. And you *still* want him for your daughter?"

Blayth cast Tor a long look before rolling his eyes and averting his gaze. "I do not," he said. "But I wanted the privilege of punishing him myself."

Tor's eyes twinkled with mirth when he realized exactly *why* Blayth was angry. "Is that what this is all about?"

Blayth grunted dejectedly and Tor burst into soft laughter. Then, Tor put a big arm around his uncle's neck and kissed the side of his scarred head.

"I love you very much, Uncle Blayth," he said. "You have the same thoughts as all the rest of us."

"Inflicting pain on those who offend our women?"

Tor continued to snort. "Exactly."

"He deserved everything I could do to him."

"He did. But I must say… Isabella does not seem too upset about all of this."

Blayth shook his head. "She is not," he said. "She and Matha had a long, detailed conversation on the day that Steffan fled. Matha convinced her that she doesn't want such a man because he would only bring her heartache. Isabella agreed. Truthfully, she seems most relieved about it now."

Matha was what the de Wolfe grandchildren called Jordan de Wolfe, wife of William. She was still alive, though extremely elderly, and was the matriarch of a great and powerful family. Her word was law, no matter how powerful her sons were, and she was deeply loved by all. In truth, Tor wasn't surprised to hear that his grandmother had been involved in Isabella's change of heart.

In fact, he was glad for it.

"There seems to be a history of men being punished for wronging the women of our family," he said. "I recall a story about Poppy and Uncle Alec. He was sweet on Aunt Katheryn before they started courting and although she was sweet on him, she evidently would not give him any indication. Do you recall this story?"

Blayth was smiling reluctantly. "I do not believe so," he said. "One of the many things I do not remember from long ago. What happened?"

Tor pulled his uncle along as he began heading towards the great hall. Now that the crisis was averted, they were going to drink.

"From what my father told me, Alec decided to make Aunt Katheryn jealous, so he called upon one of the de Reyne women," he said. "You know the ones – from Throston Castle? Beautiful women with dark hair and pale eyes. Anyway, Alec went to mass at their church and made sure he was seen with the eldest daughter. Just for show, mind you, but word got back to Poppy and from what I hear, he made Alec pay dearly with help from my father and you, Troy, Atty, and Tommy. You do not remember this?"

Blayth was trying very hard to, but he eventually shook his head. "I wish I did," he said. "I would have liked to remember beating on Alec, the big dolt. Poppy would have spared nothing to make sure Alec was properly punished."

Tor shook his head, grinning. "Poor Uncle Alec," he said. "All he wanted to do was make Aunt Katheryn jealous and all he ended up doing was angering Poppy and the de Wolfe brothers. I heard that Uncle Kieran had to step in to save him. The way Matha tells it, Kieran tried to hide Alec until Poppy's anger cooled, but it did not work. Poppy found him and took his pound of flesh."

"How did he do it?"

Tor was laughing again. "He told my uncles that they couldn't use their fists or weapons, and whatever they did couldn't draw blood or leave marks that couldn't be covered by clothing, so they tied him up in a stall and took turns spanking him. Somewhere in the midst of that, Poppy produced a big paddle and they yanked his breeches off and took turns paddling him. I am hesitant to say this, but I was told that you lathered Alec's head and shaved it clean down the middle, leaving a big bald strip right down the center of his head."

Blayth looked at him in surprise. "I did that?"

"That is what I was told."

"That does not sound like me. I would not do anything like that."

Tor snorted at that lie because everyone knew that Blayth had a wicked sense of humor. "Not much, you wouldn't," he muttered. "Alec's punishment went on and on until Kieran finally came to beg for his son's dignity. God, I'm surprised he married Katheryn after that. In any case, mayhap that was why Alec was so eager to return the favor with Steffan."

"Alec can be quite formidable when roused. I have seen it."

"That's what you were hoping for."

"I was."

They shared a laugh at Alec's expense as they walked across the compound, but Tor found himself sobering at the memories of his grandfather, the great knight William de Wolfe. It was difficult not to think of the man when reflecting on the remembrances of the past, good or bad or hilarious, as the case may be.

"It's things like this that I wish I could tell Poppy," he said, glancing up into the crystal-blue sky. "About Steffan, I mean. I wish I could tell him all about it and hear him tell me that what we did was justified. Sometimes I still cannot believe he is gone. I thought he would live forever, Uncle Blayth. I truly did."

Blayth's smile faded as he thought of his father, the greatest knight the north had ever seen. His memory of his father was so deep that not even the terrible head injury could take it away completely and although the vast majority if his memories of his father were gone, some remained. There had been a special bond between them, one not even death could break.

"He lived a very long time," he said after a moment. "He was so very old, but still, you are not alone in your wish. We wanted him to keep on living. I think, in the end, that he just wore out. It was his time. I miss him, but I am grateful for the time we had with him."

Tor's smile was gone completely by that time, remembering the day he'd been told of his grandfather's passing. "There are three events I remember very plainly in my life," he said, feeling the pangs of sorrow claw at him. "The first event is the day I was told that Jane had passed away giving birth to my son. That sticks in my mind as if it only happened yesterday. The second event is the day we received word that Bonny had passed away, four months to the day after Poppy died. The third is, of course, the morning I was told of Poppy's death. I was at Castle Questing at the time, you know."

"I know."

"It was dawn and I was heading out to my post," he continued, seeing that morning vividly in his mind. "I was not quite to the door yet when I heard my father call to me. He was on the steps leading to the upper floors and as I went to him, I could see that he was weeping. I thought something had happened to Avrielle. It never even occurred to me that he was weeping for Poppy."

Blayth patted the big arm that was still around his shoulders. "Poppy went the way he wanted to go," he said. "Not in battle. Not in great pain. He simply went to sleep and never woke up. Mother was with him. He was in her arms. That was exactly the way he wanted it – with her, on his own terms."

They were nearing the hall but talk of William always upset Tor, one of the very few things that did. Although he had loved his grandfather, Paris, very much, the bond he had shared with William had been special. That day five years ago was engrained in his mind as if it had only happened a few moments ago.

"I suppose I should be grateful for that," Tor said after a moment, feeling tears sting his eyes. "I remember running up to his chamber and Matha was sitting there, still in her bed clothes, her arms around him. And she wasn't weeping… she was just sitting there, looking at his face, and when I came into the chamber, I will never forget her expression. As if she was… joyful. I cannot explain it any better than that. I must have made a noise because she shushed me softly and told me that it was okay because he was with Uncle Kieran now. She told me that they were young and strong again, and more than likely off on one of their adventures again. And she was *happy*, Uncle Blayth. I never understood how she could have been so happy for his passing. I was not happy when I lost Jane, so I never understood that. I still do not understand that."

By the time he was finished, the tears were starting to come. That strong, silent knight had a well of emotion buried deep, but it came forth when the subject was one that meant something to him. Blayth came to a halt and turned to face him, cupping his face between his two big hands.

"Your loss of Jane was different, Tor," he said softly. "Mother's loss of Poppy was joyful because the moment he breathed his last with her, he put his hand into Uncle Kieran's and they embraced, as brothers who had missed one another deeply. She took comfort in that. But with Jane, she was young and her death was unexpected and tragic. She hadn't lived a full life. You did not have the joy of having her by your side for years and years. But when she died, did you ever stop to think that she took her last breath and in the next moment, she was in her parents' embrace? Wouldn't they be there waiting for her?"

Tor blinked away the tears that threatened. "They would," he said. "I guess I never really thought of it that way. To be truthful, I try not to think of it at all."

"Does the thought give you comfort?"

"I suppose it does."

Blayth dropped his hands. "Then now you understand why Mother was joyful," he said. "Poppy had lived such a rich, full life, but he had missed Uncle Kieran terribly. Then Uncle Paris joined them four months later, followed by Aunt Jemma. Now they are all together again, waiting for Mother to join them. She's the last one left of that generation."

Tor's eyebrows flickered with distress. "How can you speak of her death without feeling grief to your very bones?"

Blayth smiled. "Simple," he said. "Poppy will be waiting for her. 'Tis the circle of life, Tor. When you die, Jane will be waiting for you and the two of you will begin a new adventure. Death is nothing to be grieved over, at least in the years to come. Of course, it hurts us when it happens, but that is because we are selfish. We only weep for ourselves. But for those who have died – what a life of great joy they must experience in God's heavenly kingdom."

"Do you truly believe that?"

"I do."

Tor thought on that a moment before taking a deep breath. "I suppose you look at it in a way I have not yet become accustomed to," he said. "I hope that will come with time."

Blayth patted him on the cheek. "With time, many things will come," he said. "You are still young yet. You see, I have already been dead, so there is no great mystery to me."

Tor broke down into soft laughter. "You have a point," he said. "But let us put aside this morbid subject. I have some fine Spanish wine I have been saving. Will you share it with me?"

Blayth took him by the arm and began moving towards the hall entry. "Quickly before Ronan catches wind of it. The lad likes his fine drink."

Arm in arm, the two of them headed into the hall.

The world was right once again.

CHAPTER NINE

"YOUR HALL IS always so beautiful and warm," Isabella said. "Tor is very fortunate to have you both."

She was speaking to two young women who were fussing over the table on the dais. And fussing and fussing.

They wanted everything to be perfect.

Lenore was the closest and she smiled at Isabella's praise.

"Thank you," she said. "Your visits are always welcome, Isabella. I wish you would come more often."

Isabella smiled in return, watching as Lenore went back to feverishly arranging the food that was on the table as her older sister, Barbara, poured wine from earthenware jars into cut crystal pitchers. Everything had to be right for the pair, who fussed and flitted over every single inch of Blackpool's keep, apartments, kitchens, and great hall on a regular basis.

It was the domain of The Vipers.

Isabella knew well what the pair were called. Everyone in the family did. She'd visited more frequently than most because the vast majority of the de Wolfe family didn't want to see the pair, or deal with them, but Isabella and her mother, Rose, would come along with Tor's parents on occasion. Everyone loved Tor but they didn't love what The Vipers did to him.

Or, more correctly, what he allowed them to do.

Isabella knew.

Oh, but she knew.

Tor had raised the pair after their sister, Tor's wife, had died. He'd brought them all the way from the Welsh Marches because they had nowhere else to go. But the trouble had started when Lady de Lohr had said something to Tor that he had taken literally – *Jane asked that you take care of her sisters.* Tor had, bringing them to Castle Questing almost seventeen years ago, where they had been raised as wards of William de Wolfe. They had been educated and taught the finest skills that all young maidens were expected to know.

But something strange had happened in the meantime.

When they had been young, they had been inordinately attached to Tor. It was understandable given the fact that he was their dead sister's husband, but as they grew into young women, it wasn't just attachment they felt for him.

It was possessiveness.

Tor belonged to them. It wasn't that they lusted for him in a sexual sense. It was simply that he was *their* possession and they had a duty to protect their sister's husband from other women. Jane had died so, in their mind, she had passed Tor down to them. Isabella had grown up alongside Barbara and Lenore, living in the same castle for several years, and they had always been friendly with each other. Barbara and Lenore could be very gracious and kind to women they didn't view as competition for Tor. Since Isabella was a cousin, they did not view her as a threat.

But Isabella had seen what they could do to women who were.

That was when The Vipers' fangs came out.

There had been a lass from the House of d'Umfraville of Prudhoe Castle. She and her family had simply come to visit on their way to Berwick. Lady Heather d'Umfraville, named for the vibrant heather that covered the northern moors, had been a very pretty girl who had struck up polite acquaintance with Tor. Her family was only at Castle Questing for the night, so it wasn't as if they'd had a huge amount of time to get acquainted.

But that was enough for Barbara and Lenore.

Pretty, lively Heather d'Umfraville awoke the next morning, put her feet on the floor, and promptly fell into the corner of a table, mouth-first. Somehow during the night, an oil lamp had been tipped over and she had slipped on the oil. The fall had knocked out three of her teeth, an absolute mess and the end of a lovely smile. Everyone agreed that it had been a terrible accident at the time, but Isabella had seen Barbara and Lenore giggling about it. Coincidentally, they had been in the vicinity of Lady Heather's chamber that evening.

That had been the start.

After that, any woman who looked twice at Tor ended up somehow disfigured or injured. There had been Lord Lanchester's daughter who had come at the invitation of Sorcha du Rennic, Scott's adopted daughter. Sorcha knew Lady Violet le Marr from the days when she had fostered at Alnwick Castle and she had been very excited to have her friend visit for a few weeks. Violet was tiny, dark, and quite lovely, something that hadn't gone unnoticed by some of the single males at Castle Questing.

Tor hadn't paid any attention to the woman, but that hadn't mattered to Barbara and Lenore. Perhaps he would and they had to prevent that at all costs. Violet had been pushed down a flight of stairs and she'd broken a leg, hitting her head so hard that she lost some hearing in her right ear. She couldn't say who had pushed her because it had been at night, and the stairwell dark, but someone had. She'd known that for certain because she'd felt the shove.

Scott had turned Castle Questing inside-out looking for the culprit, but no one had been named and no one confessed. Barbara and Lenore had found Violet at the bottom of the stairs after her fall and they pointed fingers to a mute male servant who couldn't defend himself. With no other choice, or suspects, Scott had banished the man from Castle Questing, but Isabella knew the truth. She had seen the way Barbara and Lenore had stalked Violet during her visit and although she didn't see them push her, in her heart, she knew it had been them.

And that's when she had told her father.

Given that Isabella hadn't actually seen Barbara and Lenore do any of the heinous deeds, Blayth had to be delicate about approaching Scott with the situation. He wasn't even sure it was the truth because Barbara and Lenore looked like innocent angels. Therefore, he held off saying anything until a particular incident at mass at Kelso Abbey when the de Wolfe family had attended for Martinmas.

A pretty Scots lass from Clan Scott, the clan of Jordan de Wolfe, had been speaking with Tor after the mass. She had been speaking with Ronan and a couple of others, too, but she seemed to bat her eyelashes mostly at Tor.

It had been her undoing.

When Emma Scott left her de Wolfe cousins and went back into the church to see what was delaying her mother, Barbara and Lenore were nowhere to be found. But they did show themselves, eventually, and the House of de Wolfe returned to Questing only to hear, on Christmas Day, that Emma Scott had met with an unfortunate accident the last time she'd been in Kelso's abbey. In the hunt for her mother, an entire bank of candles from the nave fell on her and she had been badly burned when part of her clothing had caught fire.

That was when Blayth finally told Scott.

You have vipers in your bosom, Brother.

Given the evidence and circumstances, Scott had been forced to agree that all fingers pointed to the pair. It was made easier by the fact that they had all seen the way they acted towards Tor. Scott didn't feel it was his place to punish them, but he told his son of their suspicions with the expectation that he would punish them.

That was when the real trouble started.

Tor couldn't bring himself to punish Barbara and Lenore for one very good reason – no one had seen them commit the crimes and he couldn't bring himself to punish Jane's younger sisters based purely on rumor and speculation. It had to be a mistake, he said. Scott never told him where he got his information, so no one knew it had come through Blayth from Isabella.

Which was a good thing. As Isabella watched Barbara and Lenore make sure the dais was perfect in Tor's great hall, she was glad they didn't know it was her or she'd find herself shoved down a flight of stairs, too.

The Vipers wouldn't hesitate.

"I come as often as I can," she said belatedly, lost to her reflections about the pair. "You must come and visit me at Castle Questing sometime. You have not returned since Tor took command of Blackpool."

Barbara, who was making her way down the table with the crystal pitchers in-hand, answered. "We are quite busy, Isabella," she said. "As you can see, there are a thousand things to do. You do not have the responsibilities that we do so you are freer to travel."

Isabella nodded. "That is true," she said. "Can I help you with the wine, Barbara?"

Barbara smiled at her, shaking her head. "No, dear Bella," she said. "This is my task and you are a guest. In fact, I have not had the chance to tell you how sorry I am about your broken betrothal. How heartbroken you must be."

The focus shifted to Isabella's recent troubles and Isabella knew she had to be on her guard with Barbara especially. Lenore was a little less devious, but Barbara had a dark streak in her. She was pretty and red-haired, just like her younger sister, and she looked quite innocent and angelic.

But that was where people made a grave mistake with her.

Isabella, however, wasn't so naïve.

She knew better.

"I suppose I was at the time," she said, trying not to sound emotional. The truth was that she had been more embarrassed than anything. "But I realize now that Steffan is not a man I wish to be married to. He was not a good man, though it took me some time to realize that."

Lenore had stopped fussing with the food and was looking at her sadly.

"But… but I heard he compromised you, Bella," she said, distressed. "What a terrible man to do such a thing and then not marry you!"

Isabella frowned. "He did *not* compromise me," she said flatly. "Some servants saw us kiss in the garden of Castle Questing and, suddenly, everyone has me with child and the fact that I *must* marry. But it is not true, I say. I have sworn this to my father and mother and brother. I am not certain Ronan believes me, though. Men always think the worst."

Barbara stopped working, too. Both she and Lenore sat down near Isabella, enthralled with a shocking tale of a jilted bride.

"But your uncles and cousins and brother went after him," Lenore said, excitement in her tone. "I heard rumor that they killed him!"

Isabella looked at her, careful in her reply. "They went to force him to either marry me or demand compensation," she said evenly. "Ronan was there. He told me that Steffan put up a terrific fight rather than capitulate. When he tried to kill Alexander, Tor killed him. But he was only defending Alexander and had Steffan not fought them, it would not have been necessary."

While Lenore looked scandalized at the tale, Barbara wasn't so shocked. "You do not seem very upset about it," she said. "Why are you not more upset?"

Isabella turned her attention to Barbara. The woman was watching her very closely. Even suspiciously. She shrugged.

"I was at first," she said. "I was upset that he had fled on our wedding day, but I spent the day speaking to my grandmother and she helped me to see that Steffan was no great loss. In fact, now I am quite happy he fled. He would have made a terrible husband. While I am not happy for the man's death, he should not have tried to kill Alexander. It is his own fault."

Barbara was looking at her as if she expected something more – more emotion, more drama – but Isabella gave her nothing more. Lenore, however, sighed sadly.

"Were you not in *love* with him, Bella?" she asked.

Isabella thought on that. "I thought I was," she said. "But when he ran away, I realized that he was not worthy of my love. He told me that he loved me and if that was true, he would have never left. I cannot waste any tears over a man so unworthy, Lenore. It was a harsh lesson to learn, I suppose, but I am better for it."

She sounded firm, resolute. Lenore nodded as if in complete support while Barbara stood up to resume her tasks.

"You are so right," she said. "He did not deserve you, Bella. You are being very brave about this."

Isabella watched Lenore rise to resume her tasks, also. "There will be more suitors," she said. "I will simply be smarter the next time."

Barbara glanced at her. "Do you have any in mind?"

Isabella grinned. "I do not," she said. "But the north is full of eligible men. And speaking of eligible men, we must find you two suitors as well. You do not want to stay at Blackpool for the rest of your life as Tor orders you around, do you?"

She said it lightly, but given what she knew about the pair, it was anything but a light subject. She watched Barbara's face as the woman smiled thinly.

"It is a good life here," she said. "I do not think I shall ever marry."

"But why not? Don't you want children and a home of your own?"

Barbara shook her head. "I am content," she said simply. Then, she looked over at Lenore as the woman arranged the last of the bread that had been brought out. "Take care and put a cloth over that bread, Lenore. It will get cold before Tor eats it."

She was making it clear that she had no desire to discuss marriage and Isabella let the subject drop. There wasn't much more she could say on it, anyway, and she didn't want to be pummeled with more questions about Steffan. She was more damaged about it than she let on, but she didn't want Barbara and Lenore to know that.

She didn't want The Vipers to know her weakness.

Just as Lenore was covering up the bread with a cloth, Ronan entered the hall. He had deposited his sister in the great hall before making a quick run to the stables to check on his horse, which had come up lame on the ride from Newcastle. But he was back now, making haste towards the crystal wine decanters. Like a good hunter, he had them in his sights.

Her brother was a wine connoisseur.

Barbara didn't seem too thrilled that Ronan commandeered an entire decanter for himself, but she didn't protest. She simply stood there and frowned at him as he drank it and smacked his lips. Perhaps she was thinking about berating him, but he was saved from a lashing when Tor and Blayth appeared.

Then, Barbara forgot all about Ronan and Lenore forgot all about the covered bread.

After that, no one else, and nothing else, in the hall existed to them but Tor.

"Welcome home, Tor," Barbara said, indicating the fine wine on the tables. "Please sit. Surely you must rest and relax after your harrowing adventure. We heard all about it."

Tor barely glanced at her, but that was usual. The women were fixtures in his home but that was all. He didn't even really consider them family members. Simply Jane's sisters, his obligations. Never let it be said that Tor de Wolfe hadn't fulfilled his wife's dying wish.

He sat at the table and Blayth with him.

"It was simply a task," he said with disinterest. "What food do you have for us?"

Barbara was pouring the wine into fine pewter cups. "We butchered the old sow," she said. "I have pork with beans cooking, boiled carrots, peas, stewed apples, and bread. I will have the servants bring it out."

She waved at Lenore, who promptly called to the servants. Guests had arrived and the food was to be presented, so the sisters went into full chatelaine mode. As Blayth commented on the delicious wine, Barbara interrupted the conversation.

"We heard what happened to Steffan de Featherstone," she said as if there were no one else in the room. "What you did was a brave and noble thing, Tor. We are very proud of you."

Tor looked at her. "You will not speak of that here," he said. "In fact, you will not speak of it at all. It is none of your affair, Barbara. Please keep silent on it."

Barbara lowered her head, properly rebuked, but coming from Tor, it didn't even sound like he was scolding her because he said it in such a way that it sounded more like a request. The man didn't get worked up over anything, not even a statement that rudely interrupted his conversation with his uncle.

"Of course," she said. "My apologies."

"Please make sure the food is brought to us and then you may leave."

Barbara wasn't offended; that was usual with Tor. They rarely all ate together. "As you wish," she said. "Do you require anything else?"

Tor shook his head, about to wave her off, but he suddenly stopped. "Possibly," he said. "Are all of the chambers in the apartments prepared?"

Barbara paused thoughtfully. "Not all of them," she said. "We usually keep them void of bedding when not in use so that the rats do not nest. Why do you ask?"

Tor picked up his cup. "Because we shall have visitors in the next few days," he said, but he turned to Blayth as he continued. "I have invited Gilbert de Featherstone and his daughter to visit."

Blayth's eyebrows lifted. "They would visit the man who had a hand in Steffan's death?"

Tor shrugged. "I did not tell them that part," he said. "I only told them that Steffan was killed when he tried to kill Alexander. I did not say who delivered the death blow."

"Ah," Blayth said. "Then he does not know."

"He does not."

"But why invite him here?"

Tor took a drink of his wine before answering. "Because the man seemed genuinely horrified at his son's behavior," he said. "His knight was positive that the House of de Wolfe would seek some kind of retribution for it. They both seemed very worried about it and apologized profusely for Steffan's behavior. I received the impression that both Gilbert and his knight were decent men. Steffan seems to have mistreated his father terribly. I thought mayhap an invitation to sup here would ease their fears that we are going to take our armies and burn them to the ground. Moreover, they are close to Blackpool and I am always willing to make an ally."

Blayth didn't think that sounded strange. "That is not a bad idea," he said. "But you should probably be honest with the man and tell him you are the one who actually killed his son. Better to hear it from you than from someone else. You were not the only man in the tavern that night, and word can get around."

Tor conceded the point. "True enough," he said. "I will tell him myself."

"That is wise," Blayth said. "You mentioned a knight. Who is it?"

"Someone by the name of Fraser le Kerque," Tor said, sipping more wine. "I've never met the man, nor have I heard of his family, but he told me that his noble family lost their wealth and that is why he serves de Featherstone. He must make his fortune."

Blayth looked thoughtful. "Le Kerque? From where?"

"Welton Castle," he said. "The man trained with the de Winter war machine and they are very selective of who they train. That means he must have talent."

Blayth nodded. "True enough," he said. "Welton Castle… I believe that is in Lincolnshire. I seem to remember hearing about it, once."

"You cannot remember shaving Uncle Alec's head, but you can remember a castle from Lincolnshire?"

Tor was grinning as he said it and Blayth burst into soft laughter. "Such is the nature of my memory sometimes," he said. "What about the daughter? What do you know of her?"

Tor thought on that question. He probably knew a lot more

than anyone else who knew her did, as she had confided in him about many things. He realized that he was eager to see her again, hoping she and her father would come sooner rather than later. Or perhaps they wouldn't come at all and she would forget about him altogether.

He didn't like the thought of that.

He was more eager to see her than her father, but he didn't want to let on.

"All I know is that she has lived most of her life in London with her mother," he said casually. "She's a beauty, though. An intelligent young woman."

"Married?"

"Nay."

"Mayhap a prospect for you, Tor?"

Tor lowered his gaze, chagrinned to realize that he was fighting off a blush. "Certainly not," he said. "She is young and beautiful, and I am far too old. Besides, she called me provincial. Not exactly romantic talk."

Blayth snorted. "You *are* provincial, but you are also the smartest man I have ever known and one of the best warriors I have ever seen," he said. "That will count for something for the right young woman someday."

"Do not worry about me, Uncle. I was married once. I will not marry again."

Wisely, Blayth changed the subject. Speaking of Jane or marriage or even of Lioncross Abbey were taboo subjects with Tor, so the family avoided them for the most part. The brief topic of Isalyn de Featherstone was forgotten.

At least, by Tor and Blayth.

But there were others who had been listening.

Isabella had been one of them. She was seated opposite her father and Tor, listening to them talk as she ate a big slab of bread and butter. She wasn't much interested in the conversation until they mentioned Gilbert de Featherstone's daughter. The moment Tor said she was a beauty, Isabella found herself looking at Barbara, who hadn't yet left the hall. She wasn't close by, but she was close enough to hear what was being said.

Isabella remembered seeing that expression on her face somewhere before.

Around the same time Violet le Marr had fallen down those stairs.

If Isalyn de Featherstone came to visit as Tor said she would, Isabella just knew there was going to be trouble.

CHAPTER TEN

Featherstone Manse

"WHERE IS MY daughter now?"

Gilbert sounded exhausted even as he asked the question.

They were in his solar at Featherstone, a beautiful chamber that faced out over the front of the manse so he could watch all of the activity. One of those activities had been Fraser and Isalyn returning from Haltwhistle, with no indication as to the mayhem that had happened there that morning. The truth was that Fraser wasn't sure how to bring it up in a way that wouldn't send Gilbert spiraling out of control. The man had just lost his son. Fraser thought that perhaps the idea of his daughter in a knight fight might be too much for the man to take.

He cleared his throat softly.

"The last I saw, she was heading to her chamber," he said evenly. "Tor de Wolfe found her, in fact. She told him that she had gone into town to… purchase something."

Gilbert didn't even ask what it was. As the daughter of a merchant, there was no reason for her to be purchasing anything he couldn't give her for free. She had everything she could possibly want. He shook his head, exasperated, and returned to the missive he had been scribing.

"She is becoming more trouble than she is worth," he grumbled, scratching out something on the vellum. "She has said repeatedly that she wishes to go home. I wish she would. It was a mistake to bring her here. I should have known better."

Fraser watched him as he wrote out something in his deliberate script. "I never did ask you why you wanted her to come to Featherstone, my lord," he said. "It is none of my business, of course, but it seemed to me that you were eager to have her here. Was I incorrect in that assumption?"

Gilbert dipped his quill in his ink pot. "She is my daughter," he said simply. "My son wanted nothing to do with me and I had hoped that she… it was a foolish hope. When Millicent took her to London, years went by before I ever saw her again and with her mother gone these three years… I thought that I could get to know my daughter again and that she would want to come and live with me. Aye, I was eager to have her here. I am her father, after all. And she is my only living child now."

The day after learning of his son's death, Gilbert seemed steely for the most part, but that last sentence was muttered and, in it, Fraser could see that the pain was still there no matter how much Gilbert tried to cover it.

"My lord, we do not have to discuss this now," he said. "Yesterday was a… difficult day. Your daughter is safe now and we can discuss this at a later time, if you wish."

But Gilbert shook his head. "We will discuss it now," he said, glancing at Fraser. "You need not worry about me, Fraser. I have accepted Steffan's death, although to be perfectly truthful, it seems to me that he left me a long time ago. I will overcome this grief. You needn't worry."

Fraser didn't press him. Gilbert had been known to be rather cold where his children were concerned, a dysfunctional life that had left him distant from both of them. Therefore, he simply nodded.

"As you wish, my lord," he said. "What more do you wish to discuss about your daughter?"

Gilbert continued scratching on the vellum. "I don't know," he muttered. "Mayhap there is nothing more to discuss at all except my frustration with her."

"I know, my lord," Fraser said. "It seems that she is a woman grown with many bad habits she has formed from her years in the city."

"Like traveling without an escort."

"And doing whatever she pleases, whenever she pleases."

Gilbert sighed sharply as he stopped writing. "And what skills does she have?" he asked, looking at Fraser. "She never fostered as far as I know. If she did, her mother never told me, but what skills does she have as a wife and chatelaine? A husband is going to want a woman who will not be a burden to him and I fear all my daughter can do is wander around like the village idiot. No man will want her for a wife."

Fraser lifted his shoulders. "She is astonishingly beautiful, my lord," he said. "Based on her beauty alone, she should command a high price."

Gilbert cocked an eyebrow. "Why do you say that?" he questioned curiously. "Do *you* want her? Nay, forget I asked that. I would not burden you with her because she would drive you mad and I think too highly of you, Fraser. But I have been thinking…"

Fraser wasn't quite over the question he'd just been asked. *Do you want her?* Gilbert hadn't given him the opportunity to answer. *Did* he want her? She was magnificent, but she was as headstrong as a bull. Fraser had always hoped for a woman who was a little more cultured and knew her place in a man's world. Isalyn did not. He also wanted a marriage with some political connections, perhaps connecting him to a fine warring family where he could find his place in the world.

If he married Isalyn, he would have a few manses, a merchant business, and unlimited wealth. But that wasn't the life he wanted. Like Steffan, he didn't want to be a merchant. He was trained for warfare. He pushed aside the confusion he felt at Gilbert's question in order to focus on the rest of his statement.

But I have been thinking…

"What have you been thinking, my lord?" he asked.

Gilbert paused a moment before setting his quill down. Then he stood up, stretching his legs as he made his way to the lancet windows that overlooked the courtyard. There was a yew tree outside of this set of windows, one that created flickering shadows when the sun was in a certain position in the sky. Often times, he liked to sit in front of this window, watching the sunlight through the leaves.

At the moment, however, he wasn't thinking of leaves or sunlight.

He was thinking on something far more serious.

"I was thinking that if I could marry my daughter into a great house, like the House of de Wolfe, it might be the very best thing for her," he said. "Great houses like that would not tolerate a foolish young woman. They would mold her, shape her, and make something respectable out of her. I would not be ashamed of her."

Fraser's brow furrowed. "*Are* you ashamed of her?"

Gilbert shrugged. "She is unruly and unconventional," he said. "How else am I supposed to feel? Everyone who meets her probably thinks my daughter is a wild animal."

Fraser could see his point somewhat. "Sir Tor did not seem to think she was a wild animal," he said. "At least, that is not the impression I got from the man. In fact, I heard him invite you and Lady Isalyn to feast with him before she returned to London. He made her promise to come soon."

Gilbert looked at him, astonishment on his face. "He did?"

"I heard him myself."

Something in Gilbert's eyes seemed to light up at the very thought. "Perfect," he said. "We can go to Blackpool and sup with him. De Wolfe is the greatest house in the north. Mayhap he has a nephew or a brother who would be a viable marital prospect for Isalyn."

"Mayhap he himself would be."

"Is he married?"

"I did not ask him, so I do not know. But if he is not married, he seemed to be attracted to Isalyn."

That was what Gilbert wanted to hear. "Then that is what we shall do," he said decisively. "We shall take him up on his invitation immediately and I will discover if he has a brother or nephew or cousin who would be a viable prospect… or if he is one himself."

"He is a de Wolfe," Fraser reminded him. "They are in great demand, my lord. I doubt there isn't one male or female in that family already taken."

Fraser pointed a finger at him. "But they owe me," he said. "Steffan may have jilted a de Wolfe bride, but the de Wolfe pack killed him. They did not have to do it, but they did. Therefore, they *owe* me. They took away one de Wolfe marriage. They shall provide me with another – to Isalyn."

Fraser could see that Gilbert was going to work the guilt angle. Already, he wasn't entirely sure that was a good idea. When he had mentioned Tor de Wolfe's invitation to sup, he hadn't expected this turn in Gilbert's perspective of the situation.

"I would be careful in how you negotiate that, my lord," he said. "After all, Steffan was running from a de Wolfe bride. Mayhap you should simply try to negotiate a betrothal without trying to guilt them into agreeing. You may want to leave

Steffan out of it entirely."

Perhaps deep down, Gilbert knew that Fraser was right, but he wasn't going to admit it. Not yet. He was still willing to use Steffan's death as leverage.

"No promises," he said, waving Fraser off. "Go and tell my daughter that we are departing for Blackpool tomorrow at dawn. Make sure that she, and the escort, are prepared."

"Aye, my lord."

"And bring a wagon packed with gifts," Gilbert said thoughtfully. "Capes, furs, anything a prospective de Wolfe husband might want. Isalyn comes with an enormous dowry. Let us give him a taste of it."

"Aye, my lord."

"And, Fraser?"

"My lord?"

"You will not speak of this plan to Isalyn. Not a word."

"Nay, my lord."

Gilbert flicked a wrist at him, sending him off. As Fraser went to carry out his orders, Gilbert stood by the window, watching the activity in the bailey, wondering if he'd just found the solution to rid himself of the burden of his disobedient, willful daughter.

He was about to set a de Wolfe trap.

CHAPTER ELEVEN

Blackpool Castle

ISALYN WONDERED IF her father realized just how eager she was to come to Blackpool.

Strangely enough, he seemed quite eager as well. When Fraser came to tell her that they would be accepting Tor's invitation to visit immediately, she had been thrilled to hear it. She had retreated to her chamber when they had returned from Haltwhistle, fully anticipating her father to verbally lash her for running off yet again, so Fraser's good news from her father had been unexpected.

But most welcome.

In truth, given the fight she had caused in Haltwhistle, Isalyn wondered if Tor had reconsidered his invitation in the time they'd been apart. Once he reached home and realized she was a handful of trouble. Regardless, they were accepting the invitation so the sooner they went to Blackpool, the better. Perhaps there was some way she could prove to him that she wasn't all mayhem, all the time.

But that was essentially what he'd seen from her.

She was eager to change that perception.

Still, that fight had opened her eyes in many ways. She had

never seen a fight before, at least not a fight with a real battle-experienced knight in the middle of it. Having spent most of her time in London, the atmosphere there was different than it was up north. The people there were different, and although she saw knights frequently in the street, guarding lords or moving in packs as they headed to Westminster, it wasn't like she saw them on a regular basis and she most certainly never saw them fight on a regular basis.

But here in the north, the land was wild and the people were wild, and the knights seemed to be stronger and tougher. Fighting, and life and death, seemed to be far more of a reality here than in London. Certainly, there was a comparable share of life and death in London, but it seemed to her that it was a different *type* of life and death. Life in London was hard-fought and death came easily with thieves and robbers and disease. But here in the north, death seemed to have a more brutal and unexpected flavor.

There was something abrupt about it.

It was strange, really. When she realized those soldiers meant to harm her, she hadn't been given the time to be afraid. All she could think of was getting through the situation alive. She hadn't known what she was getting into and, fortunately, she never had to experience what could have been a deadly end result because Tor had saved her life before it could get out of hand.

When she had seen him flying into the center of the fight like an avenging angel, it had been something to witness. He had been enormous and strong and skilled, and he had used his sword as if it weighed no more than a feather. She knew for a fact that sword was very heavy, and it was almost as tall as she was, so it was a heavy weapon meant for a skilled warrior.

And what a warrior he was.

Even when Tor had been battling three men, Isalyn had

never felt true fear. There was something about him that just seemed immortal and invincible, and there had never been a doubt in her mind that he was going to emerge the victor. It had been fascinating to witness it and, in a sense, a privilege as well.

For someone who wrote plays and often watched them from the shadows, Isalyn knew when she saw talent. Of course, actors upon the stage for a different kind of talent, but Tor had shown her a talent that she never knew to exist and it was far more impressive than anything she had ever witnessed before. Like a well-choreographed dance, he'd slain the soldiers with grace and movements where there had been no wasted effort. Every action had a reaction. That kind of skill took years of training and hard work, and she admired that greatly.

Somehow, during that violent mix, Tor had become much more than a provincial knight.

He had become a hero.

Perhaps he didn't live in London and didn't give grand parties, nor did he have learned friends or immerse himself in culture and philosophy, but he had something else that was more impressive. Qualities in a man that she once thought were so important, like dramatic talent or a highly educated scholar, didn't seem to be that important any longer.

Tor de Wolfe opened her eyes to a great many things.

Therefore, she was more than willing to accept his invitation – immediately – but she was surprised her father had been so eager, too. Gilbert had even brought a wagon that not only carried their trunks of clothing and personal possessions, but there were other trunks that he told her were gifts for Tor.

His reasoning was because the man had been helpful in finding Isalyn in Haltwhistle, but Isalyn thought it seemed like an excessive amount of gifts for simply hunting her down. Perhaps it was really just to ingratiate the family to Tor, and considering what Steffan had done, Isalyn couldn't argue with the logic.

The de Featherstone siblings had been a trial to Tor from the start.

Loaded with gifts and good intentions, the journey from Featherstone to Blackpool had mercifully taken less than four hours. They had departed at dawn when the land had been covered with a mist, as it usually was this time of year. It was cold and dank and damp, but the party from Featherstone had traveled swiftly northward on a road that was still surprisingly good, arriving at Blackpool by midmorning.

Emerging from the fog and rising above the misty fields like a mythical fortress, Blackpool came into focus just as the mist was burning off. In truth, Isalyn was shocked by the size and breadth of Blackpool Castle. Somehow in her mind, she had imagined it to be just another simple garrison when, in fact, it was one of the bigger border castles she had ever seen. She had been to Berwick many years ago and she had also seen Carlisle Castle, many times, and both of those castles were quite large. Blackpool Castle was on that grand scale, a vast and highly protected place.

In fact, it was quite a sight to see it dominating the landscape once the mist had cleared. The sun's warming rays dried out the muddy roads fairly quickly, and it was spring, meaning the weather could be unpredictable at best, but the last half-hour of their journey to Blackpool had been in mild and pleasant weather.

As they drew closer, Isalyn found herself studying the fortress closely. Blackpool had two sets of walls from what she could see, enormous walls that stretched skyward. Whereas most concentric castles usually had the walls closer together, Blackpool's walls seemed to be spread out in quite a distance, creating a giant outer bailey between them. Their party reached an ancient gatehouse on the outer wall first. Once they announced themselves and why they had come, they were admitted into the vast outer bailey.

They continued on towards the second set of walls and the second gatehouse, which were surrounded by a moat, passing the gaggles of geese that Tor had once talked about. The second gatehouse was larger, and Fraser announced them again. But this time, they had to wait quite some time before they were admitted through this gatehouse. As they waited, the geese began to move in their direction and Isalyn wondered if they were about to be attacked. But the noise from the big, iron double portcullises lifting chased the geese back towards the moat and the party passed through the gatehouse, emerging into the large inner bailey.

They were met in the yard by a knight who was young and handsome. He was also quite big and quite muscular, and Isalyn was starting to wonder if that just wasn't how the men up north were bred. As big as Tor was, this knight was also quite large, so she was starting to think that perhaps that great size was simply a prerequisite to being a de Wolfe knight.

The knight was very polite, however, and well spoken. He called forth servants to help with the animals and the wagon before moving to Fraser and introducing himself.

"I am Christian Hage," he said. "Tor told me to expect guests from Featherstone, although I did not think it would be so soon. Welcome to Blackpool."

Fraser dismounted his expensive warmblood. "I am Fraser le Kerque," he said, turning to Gilbert as the man dismounted and came around his horse. "This is Gilbert de Featherstone, Lord de Featherstone."

Christian dipped his head politely. "My lord," he said. "Welcome to Blackpool. We are honored by your visit."

Gilbert was dressed in his finest – fine silks, a heavy robe with a fur lining, and gilded chains around his neck and waist.

A heavy silk purse hung from his belt. He was looking around Blackpool as if inspecting it, as impressed by the sight as his daughter was. Behind him, a soldier helped Isalyn from her palfrey and she came to stand silently next to Fraser. When he caught a glimpse of her from the corners of his eyes, he indicated her.

"This is Lord de Featherstone's daughter, Lady Isalyn."

Isalyn smiled politely for the handsome, young knight. "My lord."

Christian bobbed his head in greeting. "My lady," he said. "Tor has been told of your arrival. In fact, I…"

He was cut off when Gilbert and Isalyn caught sight of something behind him. He turned in time to see Tor as the man emerged from the keep, heading in their direction. But he evidently didn't seem to think he was moving fast enough because he picked up the pace and jogged the rest of the way.

"My lord," he said as he came near, addressing Gilbert. "I see that your daughter told you of my invitation to feast. How good of you to come."

Gilbert greeted him pleasantly. "It was Fraser who told me, in fact," he said. "I was told you wished for us to come visit very soon, so here we are. I hope it is not *too* soon."

Tor shook his head, his gaze moving to Isalyn. "Nay," he said, smiling at her. "The timing is perfect. You are welcome whenever you choose to visit. I do not have many visitors, in fact, so your company is a pleasure."

Isalyn had to bite her lip to keep from smiling too broadly. He didn't sound like a man who had entertained second thoughts about extending the invitation to visit.

"Thank you, my lord," she said since he was looking at her. "We are honored to dine with such an esteemed ally."

Tor hadn't taken his eyes off of her. "I do hope you'll stay long enough to enjoy other diversions and not simply my food," he said. "I have some very fine horses and a falconry. My birds are some of the best in the north. Only my Uncle Blayth has birds as fine as mine; well, *almost* as fine as mine. Truthfully, mine are much better. In fact, my Uncle Blayth is also here at Blackpool with his daughter and son."

"Ah," Gilbert said, retaking the conversation from his daughter. "Another de Wolfe. I look forward to meeting him."

Tor looked at the man, his smile fading. "It is his daughter who was betrothed to Steffan," he said. "I have not yet told them of your arrival, but I thought you should be aware of who he is."

Gilbert lost some of his pleasant expression. "I see," he said. "Then mayhap this is not an opportune time. We can return home and come another day."

Tor shook his head, reaching out to boldly take Isalyn's hand and tuck it into the crook of his elbow. "Not at all," he said. "Come into the hall with me. I am looking forward to coming to know a new ally under more pleasant circumstances than the one we experienced two days ago. And let my uncle come to know the father of the knight who deserted his daughter. You want him to think favorably of your family, do you not? Then show him you are an honorable man. Please stay."

Gilbert had little choice because Tor was leading Isalyn away, but Fraser remained behind because of the extreme value of the contents of the wagon as he and Christian began to work on the logistics of where those treasures would reside when removed from the wagon.

With Fraser off with Christian and Gilbert trailing behind, Tor took a moment to study Isalyn. To say her appearance had been a surprise was an understatement. Tor had told her to visit soon, but he hadn't expected her to come the very next day. Even so, he was happier to see her than he realized he would be.

She sparked something within him, something he thought was long gone. A fire that had once burned in his heart, something passionate and deep and longing for a woman's touch.

Something he thought had died with Jane.

But it hadn't died. It was only waiting to be reborn. Isalyn was clad in a dark green damask gown with long strands of pearls around her neck and a cap made from tiny pearls and gold thread upon her head. Her hair was long, down her back to her buttocks, and she had tiny braids woven into it, catching the sunlight with the golden threads woven into them. It brought him pleasure simply to look at her.

He was becoming smitten even if he didn't have the courage to admit it.

Yet.

"I told you to come soon," he said after a moment. "You took me at my word, I see."

Isalyn looked up at him, her dark blue eyes glittering like sapphires. "It was my father's decision," she said. "He was the one who wanted to come today."

"And you are opposed to this?"

She smiled, looking away modestly. "Nay," she said. "I agreed with him."

Tor could see the faint mottle of a blush in her cheeks and he was enchanted. "Good," he said. "You have just made my day a little brighter."

She looked at him again. "Have I?"

"My hall has never been graced with a more beautiful woman."

She blinked, surprised. "That is a kind thing to say.

"It is the truth."

He smiled at her, a warm glimmer in his eyes, as they reached the entry to the hall. Since their arrival had only been announced within the hour, servants were scrambling to light the hearth and bring food and drink to the table. Lenore was there, but not Barbara, as Tor took Isalyn and her father to the dais, making sure they had the most comfortable chairs.

"Please, sit," he told them. "You must have left Featherstone early. Surely you did not have the opportunity to break your fast yet."

Isalyn shook her head. "Nay," she said. "We left before dawn."

Tor emitted a piercing whistle between his teeth and Lenore, at the end of the dais, came running.

"Aye, Tor?"

The warmth in Tor's eyes faded as he looked at the woman, but he was polite when he introduced her.

"This is Lenore," he said to Isalyn and Gilbert. "She is a de Wolfe ward. If you need anything, she will be honored to be of service. Lenore, this is Lord de Featherstone and his daughter, Lady Isalyn. Make sure they have chambers prepared immediately in the apartments. They will want to rest after their morning's journey."

Isalyn nodded politely at the flame-haired young woman. But the moment their eyes met, she sensed something more than curiosity.

She sensed scrutiny.

But Lenore lowered her gaze before Isalyn could figure out what, exactly, the woman was thinking. She dipped her head in greeting, as it was the polite and expected thing to do.

"Welcome to Blackpool, my lord and my lady," Lenore said. "My sister is already seeing to your accommodations. I apologize they are not yet ready for you. We did not know you were coming."

Her last sentence sounded like… an excuse? A rebuke? Tor interrupted her before anything more could be said.

"See to their food," he said, decidedly colder. "And hurry

about it."

Lenore scurried off, heading towards the servant's entrance to the hall. Gilbert was in the process of settling down when he suddenly stood up again.

"The garderobe, if you please," he said. "I'd better before I sit down. It has been a long ride."

Tor whistled for another servant, who escorted Gilbert from the hall to show him to the garderobe built into the wall turret to the east of the hall. As Gilbert vacated the hall, Tor turned to Isalyn, sitting at the big, scrubbed table.

Finally, they were alone.

"Well," he said, smiling. "It seems as if I have you all to myself, at least until your father returns. How was your journey?"

Isalyn couldn't adequately describe how she felt when she looked at Tor. As she knew, something had changed yesterday when he'd charged in to save her from the soldiers, something that made her feel giddy and warm in his presence.

"It was quite pleasant, thank you," she said. Then, she lowered her voice. "Before my father returns, you should know that he does not know about the fight in Haltwhistle. Fraser has not told him and I certainly have not, so…"

His grin broadened. "So you do not want me to mention it."

"I would appreciate it."

"Your secret is safe."

Isalyn smiled in return, flushing simply from the way he was looking at her. "If I did not thank you adequately for your assistance, allow me to do so," she said. "That is twice you have come to my aid. I really do wish you would have let me gift you with the dog's head dagger. I very much wanted to."

He shook his head, sitting opposite her just so he could look at her unimpeded. "I told you that it was not necessary," he said. "It was my honor to help you."

"You are gracious," she said. "I feel as if I have been nothing but trouble since we have met."

He snorted softly. "You have certainly kept me alert," he said. "But please do me a favor."

"What is it?"

"Do not leave Blackpool unescorted," he said. "Please. As a personal favor to me. I want to be able to sleep tonight and I will not be able to unless you promise me."

Isalyn shrugged. "Where would I go? Back to Haltwhistle?"

"That was *not* a promise."

"Then I promise," she said, watching his smile return. "But if your food is lacking, I shall run all the way back to the Crown and Sword. I am very hungry."

He laughed. "It may not be as fine as you are used to, but it will be tasty and plentiful," he said. "But if it is not to your liking, I will take you to the Crown and Sword myself. I will not subject you to food you are not happy with."

It was a sweet thing to say, a chivalrous declaration that seemed so natural coming from him. "I promise I will eat whatever is put in front of me," she said. "I was only jesting."

"I was not."

She giggled. "You needn't worry over me so. I know it seems as if I take quite a bit of attention, but I assure you that I do not."

He was watching her, his gaze drifting over her face. "Tell me something."

"What?"

"When you are in London, what do you do every day?" he asked. "Do you go to your dramas every day? How do you spend your time?"

It was a change in subject, but one she was more than willing to speak of. "I live with my mother's sister," she said. "It is a house owned by my mother's family."

"Where is it?"

"On Watling Street near Bow Street," she said. "My mother's family was from the north, much like my father's family, only my mother's father was a St. John, a warlord. The St. John home in London has been there for one hundred years. I had a great-great-grandfather who built it with permission of King Richard."

He cocked his head curiously. "The St. Johns of Winding Cross Castle?"

"Aye," she said. "Do you know them?"

He nodded. "They are allied with my father," he said. "Eden Castle is also part of their property. In fact, it is not too terribly far from here."

"That is my mother's family," she confirmed. "My grandfather was head of the family, but he only had two daughters – my mother and my aunt. My grandfather's cousin is now head of the family."

It was interesting information, yet another facet to this woman he found so fascinating. If her mother was a St. John, then war was in Isalyn's blood. The House of St. John was notorious for their passionate knights and warring ways. It was starting to make some sense to him as to why Isalyn was so fearless in everything she did.

She came from warrior stock.

His respect for her grew.

Before he could speak, however, Lenore appeared with a pitcher of wine and cups. She was followed by servants with trays, each tray bearing something different. There was bread, cheese, stewed apples and cherries, hard boiled eggs that had been rolled in salt and herbs, and another tray that carried what looked like little pies. All of this was set down between Tor and Isalyn, and Lenore seemed to make sure she was still between them even when the other servants dropped their load and moved away.

In fact, it began to get odd. She was fussing with a plate of bread on the table between them, seemingly making the presentation perfect but all she was doing was brushing away crumbs. Tor finally moved the platter out of her reach.

"That will do, Lenore," he said. "I would like my guests to have more hot food, so please see to it."

Lenore looked at him, almost wounded, but she swiftly moved away. When Tor looked back to Isalyn, he could see that her attention was on the young woman. Curiously. When their eyes met once more, she smiled weakly.

"A relative?" she asked. "You introduced her as a ward. She seems very… attentive."

Tor picked up the pitcher of wine and collected two cups. "She and her sister are my wife's younger sisters," he said as he poured. "My wife died almost seventeen years ago and her sisters became my responsibility. They are my chatelaines here at Blackpool."

Realizing he had been married, once, brought Isalyn pause. He was a widower. She was inherently curious about it but sensed, simply by his manner, that it wasn't an open subject, so she refrained from asking about it. The fact that he had been married, however, didn't surprise her. He was quite a bit older than her twenty years. With the silver in his hair, he could have been twice her age for all she knew, but he didn't seem old. In fact, he seemed to be a man in his prime to her, but if he had been married seventeen years ago, that was near the time Isalyn had been born, well, within three years. He must have married at a very young age.

Curious, indeed.

"I am sorry to hear about your wife," she said after a moment. "How lovely of you to accept responsibility for her sisters. That speaks so very well of your honor."

He handed her a cup, full to the rim with wine. "What else was I to do?" he said. "They had nowhere to go, so they came to live with me. But let us not speak of them. We were speaking of you. I want to know what you do in London when you are not writing plays and attending dramas."

Gilbert picked that moment to return to the hall and Isalyn eyed him. "My father does not know that," she whispered, flicking her eyes towards the entry to let Tor know that Gilbert was returning. "I would be grateful if you did not speak of such things so openly."

Properly rebuked, Tor nodded quickly. "Of course," he said. "My apologies."

She smiled at him, sipping at the sweet red wine. "No harm," she said. "But in answer to your question, I have a good many friends in London. We do many things."

"Such as?"

She shrugged. "We play games sometimes," she said. "My aunt has a lovely home and my friends often gather there."

"What types of games?"

"Cards, Fox and Hounds. Do you play games?"

Tor thought on that. "Not since I was very young," he said. "Unfortunately, in my vocation, there is not a good deal of time for trivial pursuits."

By that time, Gilbert had joined the table and he sat heavily, accepting a cup of wine from Tor and drinking down half the cup before he stopped to take a breath. He smacked his lips.

"Excellent drink," he said. "Where do you get it?"

"From a merchant in Carlisle," Tor said. "It comes from the Bordeaux region of France. It is my grandmother's favorite wine."

Gilbert eyed the red liquid with approval. "Now it is mine."

As her father and Tor begin to toss around a variety of subjects, Isalyn sat back and watched. With Tor occupied by her father, she had the privilege of watching him unobstructed. She had very much wished her father had not interrupted their conversation because it was just starting to get interesting and from the way he was acting, she suspected that her father was going to monopolize all of Tor's time from this point forward, which was disappointing.

She was very much hoping that *she* could monopolize his time.

But that was not to be.

So, she ate the eggs, some bread and cheese, and had more wine as her father and Tor rattled on about different subjects. In truth, it was her father doing the rattling and Tor doing most of the listening. Then she realized that in her past conversations with Tor, she had also done most of the speaking and he had done most of the listening. He was most definitely the strong, silent type, only speaking when he had something he considered important to say. He was not a man of inconsequential conversation.

That was something more to appreciate about him.

And the morning marched on. They had been in the hall perhaps an hour or less when they were joined by more people. Isalyn tore her gaze from Tor long enough to notice an enormous man entering the hall along with another young man and a lovely young woman.

As they drew closer, she could see that the man in the lead was older, with blond hair, a gray beard, and the entire left side of his head badly scarred. He was missing almost all of his left ear. His face was handsome enough, but he looked as if he'd been through a horrible battle and barely made it out alive.

But the gaze in his razor-sharp eyes was fixed plainly on Gilbert.

Tor, whose back had been to the entry, realized the man was nearly upon them when Gilbert stood up. Tor quickly rose to his feet, facing the battle-scarred warrior.

"Ah," he said. "Uncle Blayth, I am glad you have joined us. This is Gilbert de Featherstone and his daughter, Lady Isalyn. At my invitation, Lord de Featherstone has come to put to rest your poor opinion of his family. Lord de Featherstone, this is my uncle, Blayth de Wolfe, Lord Sydenham. He is the fourth son of William de Wolfe, Earl of Warenton. A greater warrior you will never meet."

Blayth hadn't taken his eyes off of Gilbert and the tension in the air was obvious.

"I was not aware you would be here today," Blayth finally said. "I was just told of your arrival."

Gilbert was the least bit intimidated by the enormous warrior. He almost couldn't blame Steffan for running from him. *Almost.* But since he knew his son had been in the wrong, and Blayth had every right to be angry, he did the only thing he could do under the circumstances.

He groveled.

"I am honored to make your acquaintance, my lord," he said. "I am also glad that you are fortuitously here today. It gives me the opportunity to apologize to you in person for my son's actions. Please believe me when I say I was completely unaware of the betrothal. What Steffan did was inexcusable and it is my greatest hope that you will accept my apology."

His polite pleading took some of the wind out of Blayth's sails. He had just been informed by Christian that Steffan de Featherstone's father had unexpectedly arrived and given that his anger on the matter was still fresh, he was fully prepared to berate Gilbert de Featherstone for raising such a dishonorable son.

But Gilbert didn't give him that opportunity. Although the man was clearly appalled by his son's actions, Blayth's anger still wasn't appeased.

"It is well within my rights to demand compensation," Blayth said. "Your son abandoned my daughter. I have every right to demand a pound of flesh."

Gilbert nodded. "I realize that, my lord," he said. "And I heartily endorse your right of compensation. I have brought all manner of gifts with me. I would consider it a personal favor if you would accept them as a token of my deepest apologies. If that is not enough, I would willingly give more."

The gifts meant for Tor would now have a new and perhaps more important purpose. Gilbert had met Blayth's anger with more groveling and now there was nothing more Blayth could say, to be truthful. It was clear that Gilbert's apologizing knew no limits.

The man was all but pleading.

Blayth looked at Tor, who shrugged faintly. Blayth sensed that he was somehow siding with Gilbert. After a moment, he sighed heavily.

"Sit down, de Featherstone," he said gruffly. As both Gilbert and Tor reclaimed their seats, Blayth pointed to his daughter. "This is Isabella, whom your son shunned. Look at that face. She is as sweet as she is beautiful. Your son has hurt her deeply."

Gilbert looked at Isabella, who was a bit wide-eyed at her father's dramatics. "My lady," he said, putting his hand over his heart. "My son was a fool. He had no right to treat you so poorly. He has paid for this foolishness with his life. I pray you can forgive, with time. Steffan was a good lad when he was younger, but as he got older… I do not know why he did what he did. I wish I could give you a reason, but I have not seen my son in some time. Men change. Clearly, he changed and I am sorry you bore the brunt of that."

Isabella looked to her father with some uncertainty before returning her focus to Gilbert. "Your apology is appreciated, my lord," she said. "I… I am sorry that Steffan is dead. I did not wish that upon him."

"I did," Blayth muttered, sitting at the table. "He deserved what he got, de Featherstone. He tried to kill Tor's half-brother and Tor had every right to run him through. I'm sure he has told you that by now."

Tor grunted softly, looking to his blabber-mouth uncle. "I have not yet had the opportunity," he said deliberately. "Thank you for being the bearer of that particular bit if news."

Across the table, Gilbert stiffened. "You?" he said to Tor. "*You* killed him? Why did you not tell me that?"

Tor shook his head. "As I said, I have not yet had the opportunity," he said, but there was no remorse in his manner. "Your son tried to kill my half-brother. I was perfectly within my rights to protect Alexander. The cost, unfortunately, was Steffan's life. But that is the price he paid for attacking my half-brother."

He said it firmly. Gilbert looked at him with some exasperation before finally shaking his head and returning to his cup. He drained the contents and moved to pour himself more.

"I am not disputing you," he muttered. "I understand. Then it was your half-brother who was the squire?"

"Alexander is only seventeen years of age."

Gilbert rolled his eyes. "My son not only ran away from a beautiful bride, but he tried to kill a child." He waved his hand at them. "Oh, I know that your half-brother is a man. But seventeen years… so young. I simply do not understand what was in Steffan's mind. I do not understand how and where he got the idea that attacking a squire was the honorable thing to do. I always thought the House of de Royans stood for honor and courage, but where else could he have learned it? What are they teaching their men at Netherghyll Castle?"

No one had an answer for him. As the men began to drink

and mull over the situation at Netherghyll, thankfully resolving what could have been a terrible situation between Blayth and Gilbert, Isabella took a seat across the table from Isalyn. She smiled timidly at the woman, who returned her smile without hesitation.

"I know most of the young women from the families in this area," Isabella said. "I cannot believe I have never been acquainted with you in all this time. But I suppose you do not travel easterly towards Castle Questing much, do you?"

Isalyn shook her head. "Nay, my lady," she said. "And… and may I say that I, too, am sorry for my brother's behavior? It was a terrible thing he did to you and I am very sorry."

Isabella smiled, but it was without warmth. It was a rather sorrowful smile. "Thank you," she said. "May I say that I am sorry he is dead? This whole situation has been… unpleasant and sad."

Isalyn was relieved to see that Isabella wasn't crushed by what her brother had done. Depressed, of course, but she didn't seem too terribly grieved.

"I am sure it has been," she said. Unsure what more to say on the matter, she sought to change the subject. "You mentioned that you knew most of the young women in this area, but I do not live in this area. I live in London. I am only here visiting my father."

Isabella's eyes lit up as thoughts of Steffan were forgotten. "London," she breathed as if it were the most beautiful word in the entire world. "How fortunate you are. My brother, Edward, has a manse outside of London, near Windsor Castle. I have visited him on occasion. I find the excitement of the city quite agreeable."

In spite of the odd situation that had brought them together, Isalyn could feel herself warming to Isabella, who seemed kind and friendly. She was also quite lovely, with dark hair and flashing green eyes. Isalyn could hardly believe her brother had taken advantage of such a sweet-seeming soul.

"As do I," she said. "I miss it. I was planning on returning shortly, but Tor invited us to visit Blackpool and we were happy to come. It is a very nice fortress."

Isabella looked around the elaborate and well-built hall and shrugged. "I suppose," she said. "I have been in halls like this my entire life, so they hold no fascination for me. But London – that is of great interest to me. So many interesting people. The last time I visited Uncle Edward, he took me into the city to show me the sights and we saw people from other countries. There was a man dressed in silks and he had servants following him with a matching silk canopy to shield him from the sun. Uncle Edward told me that the man was from Constantinople."

Isalyn grinned. She liked the enthusiasm in Isabella's expression. "I met a man once who told me he was from a place called Kashmir," she said. "It is so far away that it took him months and months to come to London. Not even the men of Richard's crusade made it as far as Kashmir."

Isabella was entranced. "Kashmir," she said, rolling the name over her tongue. "It sounds wonderful and exotic. And he spoke our language?"

Isalyn nodded. "He did," she said. "He played an instrument that looked like a citole and sang songs in his language, of far off lands and beautiful women."

Isabella was listening with great interest. But then, she sighed heavily. "There is no chance of meeting a man from Kashmir in Northumberland," she said with disappointment. "Are you returning to London soon?"

Isalyn's gaze flicked to Tor, who was listening to his Uncle Blayth speak with great animation. *Was* she returning to London soon? Much depended on what happened with Tor in the next few days. Perhaps she would be able to convince him to visit her in London. Perhaps he might even like it and stay a while, and she could show him the world she was part of. But that was all speculation – *hopeful* speculation.

Quickly, she returned her attention to Isabella.

"At some point soon," she said after a moment. "It is my home, after all."

Isabella leaned forward. "Would it be too much of an imposition to visit you sometime?" she asked. "When I go to see my Uncle Edward, I mean. Would it be too much trouble to visit you so I could mayhap meet your man from Kashmir?"

Isalyn grinned. "I would love to have you visit me," she said. "In fact, you do not have to wait for a visit to your Uncle Edward's. You are invited to come and stay with me at my aunt's home any time you wish. It is on Watling Street, near Bow Street. Do you know where that is?"

Isabella shook her head. "I am sorry to say that I do not." Her face lit up with a smile. "But I will find it!"

She seemed so enthusiastic that Isalyn giggled. It was comforting to find someone who was as excited about the large city as she was. Isabella giggled in response and soon they were giggling together. Under the most peculiar, and uncomfortable, of circumstances, they had found something to bond over. There only seemed to be genuine interest between them, the lure of a new acquaintance and a new conversation. But that quickly came to an end when Isabella caught sight of a pair of women entering from the servant's alcove.

Isalyn turned to see what had Isabella's attention and she recognized Lenore returning to the hall. She was with another woman who looked just like her, perhaps a little older, and both of them were heading for the dais. She turned to say something to Isabella but refrained when she saw the look on the woman's face. That warmth and friendliness was gone, replaced by something that could only be construed as wariness.

The woman was on her guard.

Isalyn was shortly to find out why.

CHAPTER TWELVE

"I AM TELLING you that she has that same look upon her face that the Violet woman did," Lenore hissed at her sister. "The only difference is that Tor is looking at her with equal interest."

"Who?"

"Lady Isalyn!"

Barbara was standing next to a bed in the upper floor of the apartment block at Blackpool. She had come to prepare two chambers when she had been informed that Tor had visitors. Lenore had gone to the hall to prepare refreshments and Barbara had gone with the servants to clean out two dusty chambers, that were now mostly swept and made up in preparation for their guests.

But Lenore's words had Barbara pausing in her duties.

"*She* is interested in him?" she repeated, concerned. "It will do her no good. He clearly said that he was too old for her."

Lenore was shaking her head. "Mayhap that is what he said, but he lied," she said. "He is looking at her with great interest, Sister. I saw it myself."

Barbara was the more devious of the pair, the one who made the plans and led by example. Lenore was simply a follower. However, it took Barbara some time to act, like a slow burn. She had to be absolutely clear before she was motivated. As her sister's words sank in, she set down the pillow in her hands.

"That does not sound like Tor," she said. "I cannot ever recall him looking at a woman with great interest. At least, not *that* kind of interest. Mayhap he is only being kind because he killed her brother."

Lenore shook her head firmly. "Listen to me," she said. "He is looking at her as if he wants to kiss her. I have seen men look at women in such a way. The soldiers who take after the serving wenches, for example. They have the look of a predator."

"And Tor is looking at the woman as if he is a predator?"

"He is looking at her in a most interested fashion. You must see it for yourself."

Barbara thought on that a moment. Lenore wasn't one to act in haste, so if she said something was true, it usually was. Then Barbara looked around the chamber. This room was on the corner of the apartment block, with windows that faced both west and north. To the west was a yew tree that had sprouted up between the building and the wall, and to the north were the livestock and kitchen yards.

In fact, the pen that kept the goats and pigs butted up against the north side of the building. The ground floor didn't have windows on that side, so it didn't matter, but the first floor did. Barbara made her way over to the windows, examining them for a moment. Each window had exterior iron shutters with a lock that could be closed in the event of a siege or bad weather. The key for the lock was on a large key ring in Barbara's possession. But in the case of the shutters over the animal yard, the lock had rusted away and no one had ever fixed it.

Barbara inspected the shutters, pulling them closed. Unable

to lock the one over the yard, she locked the one by the yew tree. The shutters were designed in a pattern that was pretty to look at, making it an interesting view even when they were shut. When she turned back around, Lenore was looking at her curiously.

"Why did you lock those?" she asked. "What are you doing?"

Barbara didn't answer her right away. She went to the chamber door and inspected the latch on it. It was a warded lock, meaning there was a complex series of tumblers and several ways to lock it. Being that this was a border castle, and sieges and invasions were common, there were times that one might want to lock oneself in a chamber for protection, or lock someone *into* it for safekeeping. Therefore, the elaborate lock worked from both sides.

Each door in the apartment block had the same complex lock.

"What is the woman's name again?" Barbara finally asked.

"Isalyn," Lenore said, watching her sister with interest. "Isalyn de Featherstone."

"How long is she to be here?"

"I do not know. That has not been discussed."

Barbara took out her enormous key ring and began fumbling through it. "Do you remember how we discovered these doors could be locked from the outside?" she asked.

Lenore nodded. "It can be locked from the inside or the outside," she said. "All you need is a special key to…"

"To disable the latch on the inside," Barbara said, cutting her off. She finally found what she was looking for, an oddly shaped key, and put it in the lock from the inside. "I will disable the latch so she cannot leave the chamber, at least for tonight. When she does not come to the feast, it will be assumed that she was too weary to attend. She can spend the night alone in this chamber, without food or fire. One night spent like that should prompt her to want to leave quickly, don't you think?"

Lenore nodded, a smile on her lips. "I should not have doubted you," she said. "You always find a solution."

Barbara turned the key, disabling the latch from the inside. "Always," she said, looking at her sister. "The bed is made and there is an extra coverlet, so she will not freeze to death, but being trapped by a broken lock will surely convince her to return home quickly."

Lenore's smile broadened. "Shall we go greet our guest, then?"

Barbara nodded graciously. "By all means," she said. "Let us show her Blackpool hospitality."

Leaving the door open, the sisters headed towards the great hall, confident that yet another eligible female for Tor's attention would soon be gone by morning.

Unfortunately for them, their victim would not make an easy target.

CHAPTER THIRTEEN

"THIS IS BARBARA," Isabella said, rising from the table. "Barbara, this is Lady Isalyn de Featherstone. Barbara is Lenore's sister, my lady. They are both Tor's wards."

In the great hall of Blackpool, introductions were being made between Barbara and Isalyn. It wasn't an unpleasant moment, but it was a strangely tense one. Isalyn forced a smile at the redheaded woman who was smiling thinly at her in return. There was something in the air between them, though it was difficult to discern what, exactly, it was. All Isalyn knew was that there was a hint of disquiet.

She was intuitive that way.

"Sir Tor has explained Barbara and Lenore's situation to me," Isalyn said evenly. "He told me that they are his chatelaines. Ladies, you are to be commended for the state of the hall. It is as clean and pleasant as any I have seen."

Barbara dipped her head graciously. "You honor me, my lady," she said. "I am pleased that it meets with your approval."

"You have done an excellent job," Isalyn reiterated. "I am sure that holds true with every corner of the fortress and not simply the hall."

Barbara swept her hand in the direction of the apartments.

"That is why I have come, in fact," she said. "Your chamber is now prepared, as is your father's. If you would like to rest, I will happily show you to your chamber."

It sounded innocent enough. Isalyn turned to her father, still sitting with Tor and Blayth. "Father?" she said. "Your chamber is prepared. Would you like to rest?"

Gilbert waved her off, still talking to Tor. Isalyn shrugged and returned her attention to Barbara.

"It seems that he wishes to remain, but I will go with you," she said. "My father's knight should have my satchel."

"I will send someone for it."

Isalyn stood up and moved to follow Barbara and Lenore, but Isabella was suddenly by her side.

"I will go with you," she said, looping her arm through Isalyn's companionably. "I would like to hear more about London. Will you tell me?"

Isalyn nodded, feeling some comfort that Isabella was going with her. She was feeling uneasy with Tor's two wards for reasons she couldn't explain.

Perhaps it was only nerves.

The four women headed out of the hall, out into the bright day. Now that the fog had burned off, the view was limitless and Isalyn found herself looking at the inner bailey with interest. There was a massive, square keep nearly dead center in the middle of it and several large outbuildings.

"This is such a large place," she said, shielding her eyes from the sun as she looked up at the keep. "I had no idea that it would be so big."

Isabella looked to see what had her attention, squinting in the sunlight. "It is a very big keep, but each floor only has one large chamber," she said. "That is why guests stay in the apartments."

She was gesturing towards a two-story stone building built

close to the wall. There were a few outbuildings near it, but Isalyn noticed that the apartment block butted up next to the kitchen yard.

"Do you come here often, my lady?" she asked Isabella.

Isabella shook her head. "Not too often," she said. "My father divides his time between Castle Questing and Roxburgh Castle."

"And you travel with him?"

"Sometimes," Isabella said. "I like Roxburgh a great deal, but it is a dangerous place. The Scots are always trying to gain control of it, so my father prefers that I stay at Castle Questing with my mother."

"And the Scots are not always trying to gain control of that one?"

Isabella grinned. "Not that one," she said. "Castle Questing is impossible for them to get close to. It is the safest castle in the north, you know. It has never known a serious siege, mostly because the Scots would have to climb a mountain to get to it and, by that time, they would be too exhausted to fight."

Isalyn's eyes twinkled. "Given that I was born in Northumberland, one would think I would know a little something about these big border castles and military tactics, but alas, I know nothing."

"Do not worry," Isabella reassured her. "While you are here, I will teach you. The first rule is to never go outside of these walls without an escort. This far north, the Scots linger everywhere. They would be thrilled to pluck a ripe English lass and take her home."

Isalyn remembered what Tor had said to her; *do not leave Blackpool unescorted.* Now she was coming to see what he meant. A lass like Isabella, who spent all of her time in the north, knew not to wander away alone. Isalyn had done it from Featherstone, but Featherstone wasn't quite as far north as

Blackpool was. Here, they were very close to the border.

Isalyn would have to remember not to wander alone and resist her natural instinct.

She didn't want to be plucked like a ripe berry.

"You are kind to take the time to teach me," she said. "You can teach me about the north and I can teach you about London."

Isabella liked that idea a great deal. "An excellent suggestion," she said. "Teach me everything so that when I visit London the next time, I will look as if I belong there."

They grinned at each other, quickly becoming fast friends, when a shout came from behind. They paused, turning to see a big knight with black hair on the approach.

Isabella's eyes widened.

"Who is *that*?" she asked.

Isalyn lifted her hand again to shield her eyes from the sunlight. It was a very bright day. "That is my father's knight, Fraser," she said. The same hand at her eyes waved at him. "Here, Fraser!"

Fraser was carrying a satchel with him. Clad in a mail coat, tunic, and with his elaborate broadsword affixed at his side, he was moving swiftly. When Isalyn saw that he was carrying her bag, she went to him to collect it.

"Thank you," she said. "My father is still in the hall, but he will be staying in this building as well. Those two women ahead of us are the chatelaines. They can tell you which chamber is his."

Fraser nodded, catching sight of the dark-haired lass a few feet behind Isalyn. When their eyes met, he nodded his head in her direction.

"My lady," he greeted politely.

Isalyn made the introductions. "This is Lady Isabella de Wolfe," she said. Then, she lowered her voice as she turned away from Isabella. "This is the woman who was betrothed to Steffan."

Fraser's dark eyebrows lifted. "It is?" he muttered. "God's Bones… he ran out on *that*?"

There was something in his tone that made Isalyn take a second look at him. He was focused on Isabella as if he'd never seen a woman in his life and Isalyn fought off a smile, realizing there was some manner of instant attraction there. She'd never seen anything spontaneous from Fraser for as long as she had known the man, so this was an event.

She wouldn't waste it.

"Come with us, Fraser," she said, grabbing his arm and pulling him along. "Lady Isabella, you do not mind, do you? Fraser can see where my father is to sleep so that he can have his baggage brought there."

Isabella was looking at Fraser much the same way he was looking at her. "I do not mind at all," she said, her cheeks tinged pink. "It is a pleasure to make your acquaintance, my lord."

Fraser dipped his head at her again. "For me, also," he said. "Do you live here, my lady?"

Isabella, on the other side of Isalyn, shook her head. "Nay," she said. "I was telling Lady Isalyn only a few minutes ago that I spend my time between Castle Questing and Roxburgh Castle. My father is Blayth de Wolfe, brother to the Earls of Warenton, Berwick, and Northumbria. He is the fourth son of William de Wolfe, the great Wolfe of the Border. Have you heard of him?"

Fraser nodded. "Everyone north of Leeds has heard of William de Wolfe," he said. "Young lads are raised on tales of his valor. You are his granddaughter?"

Isabella nodded. "I am," she said. "Did you ever met him?"

"Alas, no," Fraser said. "I wish I had been given the opportunity. I am sorry to hear that he passed away only a few short years ago, but he has left a great legacy."

Isabella was smiling at Fraser's gracious compliment of her grandfather. He had a deep, silky voice, one that was quite pleasant to listen to, in her opinion.

"Thank you," she said. "I quite agree with you."

Fraser smiled at her, one that was bit more flirtatious and a little less polite, but there was nothing more to say at that point so he looked away, only to catch Isalyn grinning openly at him.

Realizing she was aware that he thought Isabella was quite pretty, his smile vanished unnaturally fast and he cleared his throat, looking on ahead to the apartment block. Anything but Isalyn's smirking smile. As they arrived at the apartments, the two red-haired chatelaines were waiting at the door.

"This is my father's knight, Sir Fraser le Kerque," Isalyn said as they arrived at the entry. "He is to be shown where my father will sleep. Fraser, this is Lady Barbara and Lady Lenore, wards of Tor de Wolfe. They are his chatelaines."

Fraser greeted them politely, but not with anywhere close to the zeal that he had greeted Isabella. As Lenore took him into the apartments to show him where Gilbert was to sleep, Barbara led Isalyn and Isabella up the stairs to the first floor.

Although Barbara seemed to be behaving herself, Isabella walked up the stairs behind Isalyn, remembering what had happened to Lady Violet. She was nervous that Barbara had put Isalyn on the upper floor, but it wasn't as if she could say anything. She could only hope that Barbara wouldn't maneuver Isalyn anywhere near the stairs for the duration of her stay. She simply didn't trust her not to. In fact, Isabella was going to make sure her father knew of her concerns. Perhaps he could relay them to Tor.

Or perhaps not.

It wasn't like Tor was apt to do anything about it.

As Isabella lost herself in memories of the women Barbara and Lenore had targeted in the past, Barbara led Isalyn into a large chamber on the northeast corner of the apartment block. It was quite roomy, with a big, fluffy bed and an enormous wardrobe against the wall.

"This is where you will sleep, my lady," Barbara said, standing by the open door. "I will have servants bring fuel for the fire and a few lamps for light. You will notice that I closed the shutters that face the wall; soldiers are sometimes on the wall walk and they can look through the window if they try, so I thought it best to discourage them from peeking at you."

By this time, Isalyn had moved to the bed, setting her satchel upon it. "That was thoughtful of you," she said. "Thank you."

Barbara gestured to the one open window. "That window faces north, so you will have excellent views all day," she said. "It also faces the kitchen yard, so if it becomes too noisy, do not hesitate to inform me."

Isalyn went to the window, which was a big one. To the north, she could see mostly the walls and treetops and the brilliant blue sky. It was a nice view. But that was only if one was looking straight ahead or up. Looking down gave the view of most of the kitchen yard and the pens where the goats and pigs were kept.

And then there was the smell.

Not wanting to complain, however, Isalyn didn't say a word about it. She wondered if the placement was on purpose considering she felt there was something off about these women from the start. Still, she was gracious.

"It is quite fine," she said. "Thank you again for your kind attention to my comfort."

Barbara was still standing by the open door as Isabella went to look from the north window. Realizing the kitchen yard was right there, she frowned.

"Barbara, surely you did not have to give her the room that overlooks the pigsty," she said. "There are seven other chambers in this block. Can she not have one of those?"

It was clear that Barbara didn't like being questioned. She stiffened. "You and your father and your brother occupy three of them," she said. "Lord de Featherstone was given the big, comfortable chamber on the ground floor. One of the smaller chambers on the first floor has been used for storage and the other two share a leaking roof, so this is the best and only place I can put Lady Isalyn unless you would like her to share your chamber."

Isabella almost agreed but thought better of it. She had just met Isalyn and to insist she share her chamber might be a little too much, too soon. She had a good feeling about Isalyn but she didn't want to force the woman to be her very best friend in the first day of knowing her, so she simply smiled and turned to Isalyn.

"You may take my chamber if you wish," she said. "It does not overlook the pigsty."

But Isalyn shook her head. "Do not worry so much," she said. "Truly, this chamber is fine. I am most appreciative."

"Are you certain?"

"I am. But you are very kind to worry so much."

Isabella smiled at her, thinking that perhaps the woman might like to be left alone since she had spent all morning traveling. "I am sure you wish to rest now," she said. "I will take my leave, but I look forward to seeing you tonight at the feast. You promised to tell me all about London."

Isalyn smiled. "And I will," she said. "I am looking forward to it as well, my lady. And, again… I cannot apologize enough for what my brother did. You are so very gracious not to bear a grudge."

Isabella paused, lifting her slender shoulders. "My grandmother says that life is too short to live with regrets or grudges," she said. "I suppose everything in life happens for a reason.

Even having a prospective husband run away. I will see you this evening, my lady."

"Please call me Isalyn."

"And you will call me Isabella."

With that, Isabella turned for the door, pausing to let Barbara pass through first before following her. Quietly, she shut the door behind her, leaving Isalyn alone in the vast, well-swept chamber.

Truthfully, Isalyn was glad to finally be alone. Not that she hadn't liked becoming acquainted with Isabella, because she had. Very much. She was a sweet girl and Isalyn was feeling increasingly bad for what her brother had done to her, but Isabella seemed to be taking it very well. She had a mature outlook for one so young.

Isalyn liked that.

Feeling happy that she had come to Blackpool, Isalyn untied her satchel and began to unpack.

As she unrolled the garments that she had packed and went to hang them up on pegs inside the wardrobe, her thoughts begin to drift from Isabella to Tor. Isalyn had been as close to giddy as she had ever been in her life when they had first arrived at Blackpool and he had come out to greet them. The way he looked at her made her heart sing in a way she never realized it could. She had spent her entire life in London, around male friends of her aunt's, and she had also spent time with her own friends, many of whom were actors. Never once had she had the same reaction to them as she had to Tor.

All Isalyn knew was that a look from him made her heart race. A word from him was like music to her ears. And when he smiled… that was when the moon and the stars and the heavens seemed to open up and all she was faced with was utter brilliance. What made it even better was that he seemed to be quite attentive to her also.

Was it possible that he was feeling the same giddy ardor that she was?

Isalyn was eager for the feast to begin that evening, but she also knew that feasts simply weren't a meal. They were events. They would start in the evening and sometimes go all night, and if that was the case tonight, she wanted to enjoy every single minute of it. She wanted to stay up all night, talking to Tor and coming to know a remarkable man. Therefore, she knew that it would be wise for her to try and sleep this afternoon, just a little, so that she would have the ability to stay up all night and speak to the provincial knight who had quite ably captured her attention.

Therefore, she put away all of her belongings and stripped off the dark green traveling dress that she was wearing. Underneath it, she wore a very fine lamb's wool shift that was both lightweight and warm. It was one of the finer garments that her father imported and she had a few of them. When he sold them in his stall in Carlisle, he could barely keep them in stock.

Stripped down to just the shift, Isalyn climbed into the big, fluffy bed only to realize that the mattress was not stuffed with feathers as she had hoped, but stuffed with straw. Stuffing a mattress with straw or dried grass or even rags was not unusual, but it was usually done in the poorer households. In a fortress like this, she had expected a little better, but she resigned herself to it and lay down, listening to the straw crackle and feeling it poke.

In fact, realizing that the mattress was stuffed with straw made her realize that the two chatelaines, Barbara and Lenore, might have done it deliberately to make her feel unwelcome. Perhaps they did that to all of the female visitors, or perhaps they only did it to women they had taken an instant dislike to. Whatever the case, the room with a view of the pigsty and the scratchy straw mattress belonged to her and it would be a great tale to tell her friends in London. She would regale them with the story of the two harpies of Blackpool Castle.

It sounded like a great play in the works.

Giggling to herself, Isalyn drifted off to sleep in the early afternoon. Contrary to what Barbara had suggested, the noise from the kitchen yard didn't bother her in the least and she slept for a few hours before awakening in the late afternoon.

Yawning, Isalyn awoke to the sounds of goats bleating. Nonetheless, she felt rested and content, but it occurred to her that the room was a little chilly because of the stone walls and the lack of any direct sunlight into the chamber. With the covers up around her neck, it further occurred to her that no fuel for a fire had been brought as Barbara had promised.

Realizing this, she rose from the bed and quickly put her traveling dress back on. She wasn't entirely sure that servants hadn't come while she was sleeping, knocking on the door and not receiving an answer. She assumed that must have been what had happened, so she went to the door to summon a servant to let them know that she was awake and that they could stoke her hearth. Putting her hand on the door latch, she tried to lift it only to realize that it was fixed in place.

The latch wouldn't budge.

Curious, Isalyn tried to force the latch to lift several times before realizing that it was a futile effort. Peering at the lock itself, she could see that the bolts were firmly in place, meaning the tumblers had been turned in order to move the bolts into their locked position. She could not imagine why the door would be locked, so she assumed that it was merely a mistake. Someone had accidentally locked her in. She began to knock on the door, calling to anyone who was within earshot and asking for help with the door.

That went on for several minutes before she realized there

was nobody within earshot to help her. She wasn't frightened, nor was she angry, but she was annoyed. The sun would soon be down and her chamber would be plunged into chill darkness, so it was important for her to catch the attention of a servant to help her. She didn't want to be stuck in a freezing tomb all night.

Giving up on the idea of banging on the door and yelling for help, Isalyn went to the shuttered window that faced the wall walk, thinking that she could open up the shutter and speak to one of the soldiers and ask them for help. That seemed to make the most sense, so she made her way over to the shuttered window only to discover that the shutters were locked.

Just like the door.

And the only window that was open was facing over the pigsty.

Now, it was starting to occur to Isalyn that this was no accident. She had received a strange sense of scrutiny from the chatelaines since she had arrived, and now she was in a chamber that was cold, without a fire or food, and with a locked door and one locked shutter. She would have not been suspicious had it only been the door, but now she was starting to put the pieces of the puzzle together and realize there was a pattern.

Her hostesses were making sure that she was not only uncomfortable, but trapped.

It was starting to make sense as to why Isabella had accompanied her to her chamber. The woman had known something that she had not. When Barbara and Lenore had come to the hall to take Isalyn to her chamber, Isabella had looked at the women with an expression that suggested a coldness.

Guardedness.

Considering how friendly Isabella had been towards her,

that change in manner had been sudden and strange.

Maybe there was a reason for Isabella's coldness towards them.

Isalyn was thinking that perhaps she should have given Isabella's change in manner more credit. This was her first visit to Blackpool and she didn't know the people, nor did she have any reason to be suspicious of anyone. But in hindsight, there had been signs all around her that she had ignored. She didn't want to be immediately suspicious of a new place and new people.

Now, she was paying the price.

Going to the window that overlooked the pigsty, Isalyn peered over the ledge to see just how far of a drop it was down into the pigsty. Had her hostesses put her on the ground floor, she could have simply jumped out the window with little effort, but being that she was on the first floor, there were more logistics involved with it. She had no doubt that the pair had known that.

But she wasn't going to let that stop her.

The yew tree was at the window that had the locked shutters. Isalyn could see it through the pattern of the shutters. Locking those shutters had been to keep her from climbing out onto that tree and making her way to the ground. When she remembered that she had thanked Barbara for shutting them, she felt like a fool.

She had thanked the woman for locking her in.

Sheer rage was beginning to take over at this point. Thinking quickly, she ripped the linens off of the bed in preparation for her escape. The coverlet and the two linen sheets beneath were firmly and carefully tied end to end, creating a rope that she tied off on one of the legs of the bed.

Throwing the rope from the window, she climbed onto the ledge and noticed servants out of the kitchen yard going about their business. She called to them and waved her arms, but when she shouted, the goats and pigs below would make noise because they were startled by the sharp sound of her voice. She shouted four times but, each time, she was drowned out by a frightened animal. Frustrated and impatient, she grabbed the rope and began to lower herself out.

Truthfully, she'd never done anything like this before and quickly discovered that it was not as easy as she had thought it would be. It took upper body strength and a good grip. About halfway down, the bed must have slipped because the rope suddenly gave way and snapped her right off. Isalyn fell the last few feet to the ground, landing on her backside in the mud as the pigs squealed and scattered.

For a moment, she simply sat there, a wee bit stunned at hitting the ground so hard. But her shock was momentary. She was out of the chamber and that was all she cared about. Struggling to her feet, she was also so angry that she was quite certain the devil himself would have run from her at that moment.

Now, she was on the hunt.

Storming out of the kitchen yard, she found herself in the inner bailey, heading for the great hall. Her entire backside was soaked with mud, and it covered most of the back of her head and her hair. It was on her arms and hands, and the only thing it didn't seem to be on was her chest and face. By the time she entered the great hall, there were flames of fury shooting out of her ears.

She had come to do battle.

Unfortunately, the hall was empty except for the knight who had greeted them when they had first arrived at Blackpool. He was sitting at the table eating the remnants of a meal, but he caught movement out of the corners of his eyes and looked up just as Isalyn approached the table.

His eyes widened at the sight.

"My lady?" he gasped, rising quickly. "What on earth happened to you?"

Isalyn was ready to explode. "What is your name, my lord? I have forgotten."

"Christian, my lady. Christian Hage."

"Christian," she said through clenched teeth. "I will explain the situation to you – the door to my chamber was locked. The shutters were locked except for the ones overlooking the kitchen yard. I had to climb from the window to escape the chamber because no amount of screaming or banging would bring anyone to my aid. I had no fire, no food, and no way to communicate with anyone. Where are those two chatelaines?"

His wide eyes grew wider. "You… you were locked in?"

Isalyn nodded. "The latch would move, but the bolts were in place," she said. "I can only assume that someone, whoever had the key, had locked the door from the outside. But things like that do not happen by accident. Did they think I was going to simply sit there all night and weep because they had locked me in?"

Christian sighed heavily, closing his eyes as if to ward off what he was being told. He didn't say what he was thinking; *The Vipers strike again.* Only this time, they had struck on a woman who wouldn't take it lying down. Christian could see that simply by looking at her.

Lady Isalyn was fit to be tied.

Before he could answer, however, Barbara and Lenore chose that moment to enter the great hall. They entered through a servant's entrance that was behind Christian so he didn't see them.

But Isalyn did.

Suddenly, she was rushing around him, mud and all, running towards Barbara and Lenore as they came into the light.

Christian ran after her.

"You!" Isalyn boomed, pointing to Barbara. "I want you to listen to me very carefully and answer only when spoken to. Do you understand me?"

Barbara and Lenore, caught off-guard by a very muddy and angry lady, were taken aback by the sight of her.

"My lady!" Barbara gasped. "What…?"

"Silence!" Isalyn shouted. "You do not ask any questions. *I* will ask the questions. You are chatelaine of Blackpool, are you not?"

Barbara was looking at her with wide eyes. "Aye, my lady."

"Does anyone else have control over your duties?"

Barbara cast a nervous glance at Lenore. "My… my sister is also chatelaine."

"Who prepared my room today?"

"I did, my lady."

"Are there locks on all the doors in the building you call the apartment block?"

"There are, my lady."

"Who carries the keys?"

Barbara blinked. "I-I do."

Isalyn stood aside. "Get into that apartment block. Do it now."

Barbara had never been spoken to that way before by another woman. Not ever. She was used to being in charge and in control but, at the moment, she had lost both. Isalyn had the power and Barbara was moving to do her bidding out of sheer shock.

"My lady," she said calmly. "If you would tell me what this is about, mayhap I can…"

"Shut your lips!" Isalyn snapped. "You are not speaking. You are doing as you are told. Where are your keys?"

Barbara licked her lips nervously. "With me, my lady."

"Were they ever out of your possession?"

"Nay, my lady."

"Then get into that apartment building before I drag you over there by the hair."

Barbara's mouth opened in outrage and she looked at Christian, standing behind Isalyn. But Christian had a stony expression, certainly not one of support, and Barbara was starting to feel cornered. Without another word, she tucked her head down and began to move, very quickly, from the hall. Lenore scurried after her, with Isalyn following closely.

Christian brought up the rear.

It made for a very odd parade across the inner bailey as the sun set. They were nearing the stone building just as Tor emerged from the keep, seeing the four of them at a distance and wondering what was going on.

Curious, he began to follow.

But Isalyn didn't see him. She was focused on Barbara and Lenore, up ahead, as they entered the apartment block. She came in right after them, directing them up the stairs to her chamber. Slowly, the pair made it up the stairs with Isalyn and Christian behind them. Once they reached the door, however, Barbara came to a halt.

"My lady, if you would only stop shouting and tell me what this is about, mayhap there is a logical explanation," she said. "Surely this is all a great misunderstanding."

Isalyn wasn't having any of it. She folded her muddy arms over her chest. "You told me that you have the only key to this chamber, correct?"

"Correct, my lady."

"And no one else has had the key."

"Nay, my lady."

"Then it stands to reason if this door is locked, you did it."

"I have no reason to do such a thing, my lady."

"Pull out your keys and unlock this door."

Barbara sighed heavily. Reaching out, she simply lifted the latch and the door opened wide.

"You see?" she said. "The door is not locked, my lady."

Isalyn was not appeased in any way. "Then give me your keys."

Barbara looked at her curiously. "Why?"

Isalyn held out her hand. "Give me your keys," she said. "I want you to give me your keys, go inside the chamber, and shut the door. If the door is not locked from the inside, then I will apologize profusely."

Barbara drew in a long, deep breath. She was about to refuse but she caught sight of someone on the stairs behind Christian. Everyone turned to see Tor standing on the top step behind Christian, silently observing the situation.

But he was looking straight at Barbara.

"Do as you are told," he said in a low, rumbling voice. "Give her the keys and go inside and shut the door."

Lenore gasped, looking at her sister fearfully. Barbara hesitated a moment before fumbling on her belt and pulling forth a chain that contained a ring of many keys. She unclipped the chain and handed it over to Isalyn before stepping inside the chamber and shutting the door.

"Open it," Tor said loudly.

Barbara could only rattle the latch because the door was, indeed, locked from the inside. Tor pushed between Christian and Isalyn, lifting the latch and shoving the door open.

"This is warded lock," he said. "It can be locked from either side, either to keep someone in the chamber or to keep someone out of it. But in order to be locked from the inside, it must be deliberately set."

"It must have been an accident," Barbara pleaded as her composure began to fracture. "The servants and I cleaned the room thoroughly, so somehow, the lock must have been set."

Tor sighed heavily as he looked at her, but he didn't reply. He looked to Isalyn, standing there muddy and cold.

"Would you be so kind as to tell me what happened, my lady?" he asked softly.

Isalyn's point had already been proven as far as she was concerned, so she didn't need to gloat. But she wanted Tor to know how rotten his chatelaines had been to her.

"Barbara brought me to this chamber and left me with a bed but nothing else," she said. "No food, no fire. She told me those things would come later, but they never did. When I tried to leave the chamber, I discovered that it had been locked. I also discovered one of the shutters had been locked, the one overlooking the yew tree so I could not climb down it and escape. I was forced to make a rope from bed linens to escape, but I ended up falling into the pigsty. That is why I am covered with mud. Had I not tried to escape, I would still be shut up like a prisoner in this chamber and no one would ever know. I suspect that when it would come time to feast tonight, Barbara would tell you that I had decided not to attend."

Tor looked straight at Barbara. "Did you do this?" he asked, incredulous. "Did you truly shame me so badly in front of Lady Isalyn?"

Barbara was beginning to tremble. "It was an accident, Tor, I swear to you!"

"Nay, it was not."

The voice came from the stairs. Isabella was coming up the steps, having heard Tor's voice and Isalyn's subsequent explanation of what had happened. She had been downstairs in her chamber when she had heard the commotion and followed the voices. She looked right at Barbara as she spoke.

"It was *not* an accident," she said. "Barbara, I know that you and your sister are capable of such things because I have seen it.

I know that you are responsible for Heather d'Umfraville losing teeth when she slipped on oil *you* put on the ground, and I know you tried to kill Lord Lanchester's daughter by pushing her down the stairs. There have been others, for I saw them myself when we were fostering at Castle Questing. Anyone who looked at Tor in a manner you did not like fell victim to your treachery. Therefore, I knew you were going to try to do something to Lady Isalyn and that is why I escorted her up here to her chamber. What I did not count on is you locking her in. Admit it was no accident, Barbara, please. You and Lenore have been doing this kind of thing for years and we all know it."

Lenore burst into tears and Barbara just stood there and trembled. "Isabella," she gasped. "I thought you were my friend. How can you say such things?"

"Because it is true," Isabella insisted. "You and your sister are terrifying and wicked, and I have no idea why Tor allows you to do such things. You have hurt so many people and, still, he does nothing. Come with me, Isalyn. You are staying in my chamber tonight. At least I am willing to protect you."

It was a firm rebuke, an insult directly at Tor. Reaching out, she grasped Isalyn by the muddy hand, pulling her back down the stairs. But Isalyn was looking at Tor, who was watching her go with great sorrow.

Great, great sorrow.

CHAPTER FOURTEEN

"SHE COULD HAVE been killed falling out of that window," Gilbert said. "Although I do not fault you for Steffan's death, my daughter's would be quite another matter. The House of de Wolfe seems to want us all dead."

An hour after Isalyn's plunge from the apartment window, Gilbert was in the great hall, furious at what had happened. He was speaking to Tor, but there were others there – Fraser, Christian, Ronan, and Blayth, all of them listening to Gilbert rage about what had happened.

Not that anyone blamed him.

Tor least of all.

Because Gilbert was standing, he was standing. He faced the man's anger head-on because he deserved it. Whatever happened at his castle was his responsibility, and Barbara and Lenore's wickedness reflected on him directly. But that was something he'd always known about.

It had been hard for him to admit.

But today, he had to face it.

Oh, he knew the family called the pair The Vipers. He'd known that for years, ever since the bloom of womanhood had come upon them. But something else had come upon them, something jealous and possessive and dark. Tor knew it but he'd tried to be sympathetic. He'd tried to be understanding. No one had actually seen them commit the crimes they'd been accused of and that was why he wouldn't punish them, but the truth was even deeper than that. Jane's memory was preventing him from lifting a hand to them. He didn't want to hurt Jane and he knew that if he punished her sisters, it would have hurt her greatly.

But today, they'd made a great misstep.

They'd gone after Isalyn.

Tor realized he wasn't afraid to punish them any longer. They'd crossed a line and he'd been forced to act, especially when Isabella had testified against them. He believed his cousin implicitly, for she wasn't the type to lie.

Therefore, Barbara and Lenore were currently in the same chamber they'd locked Isalyn in, only Tor had sealed up the shutters overlooking the pigsty so they could not escape. He wasn't sure what he was going to do with them, but he wasn't going to allow them to run free any longer. Seeing Isabella protect Isalyn when she felt he wouldn't had been like a dagger to his gut.

It was at that moment that he began to see things clearly.

He'd been a fool.

That being the case, facing an enraged Gilbert de Featherstone was something he welcomed. He deserved every last lash of the man's tongue.

"My lord, let me assure you that we do not want the entire House of de Featherstone dead," he said. "The offenders are being punished. It will not happen again, I assure you."

But Gilbert was not assuaged. "What are you doing about this?" he asked. "I discover that your chatelaines have tried to harm my daughter, so I want to know what you intend to do about it. And I hear they have a history of this? Why have you allowed this to go on?"

Tor could feel Blayth and Christian's eyes upon him. They knew the history. They had probably been wondering the same thing for years. Tor wasn't oblivious to that. It was time to finally acknowledge that which he had long refused to.

Quietly, he cleared his throat.

"About seventeen years ago, my wife died in childbirth while I was away in battle," he said, his voice low. "I returned to a dead wife, a dead child, and my wife's two younger sisters, who were only children at the time. They became my responsibility and not a welcome one. I suppose… I suppose much of this is my fault. I looked at them and I saw Jane, which meant I did not want to look at them at all. They had no parents, no sister, only a brother-in-law who paid them little attention. What I am trying to say is that they ran amok and I refused to believe it. I denied it, ignored it, and made excuses for it. But no more. Believe me when I say that I will take their offenses very seriously, my lord. I will not let their actions against your daughter go unpunished. You have my word."

By the time he was finished, Gilbert didn't look so angry. Tor wasn't a man for a lot of words, nor was he a great orator. In the short time Gilbert had known him, he had seen that. Therefore, that rather impassioned speech meant something.

He believed him.

"I am sorry for you," he said. "I did not know you were married."

"It was a long time ago, my lord."

Gilbert could feel himself giving in to Tor's tragic tale, prepared to forgive him completely, but something stopped him. He'd had a plan when he had come to Blackpool and it was the entire reason he had come – to find a husband for his unruly daughter, and now he saw the perfect opportunity to press that agenda.

Tor was a widower. He was eligible and wealthy, and Gilbert wasn't a fool. He'd seen how his daughter had looked at the man.

Now was the time to strike.

"Be that as it may, my family has suffered devastation at the hands of the House of de Wolfe," he said. "I understand that my son wronged Lady Isabella and I make no excuses for him, but his death was by your hand. Would you agree?"

Tor nodded. "In order to defend my younger half-brother, it was."

Gilbert lifted his shoulders. "It is quite possible that, given the proper persuasion, he could have returned to the lady to fulfill his promise. Would you not agree?"

Tor looked at Blayth, who simply shook his head in annoyance. Gilbert was grasping at straws given how Steffan had behaved and they all knew it.

"I suppose it is possible, in theory," Blayth said, answering for his nephew. "Given that he ran and then fought the men who had come to force him to honor his promise, I would say the possibility of him admitting wrongdoing is very small, but I will concede the fact that it might have been possible."

Gilbert's attention turned to Blayth. "That being the case, my lord, you will understand that this betrothal was taken from my family," he said. "If anyone should feel wronged, it should be me. My son could have married into the House of de Wolfe, but that chance was taken from me. Your men killed my son before he was given a chance to mend his ways."

Blayth grunted and looked away, wanting to tell the man how ridiculous he was and struggling to refrain.

"I suppose it could be viewed that way," Blayth said, irritated. "But the reality is that your son ran. He did not have to run in the first place, so do not make this out like he was a noble lad set upon by the de Wolfe pack. He ran and was punished for it."

Gilbert was fixed on him, unblinking. "But he was never given the chance to mend his ways."

"He never gave us the chance to speak with him!"

Gilbert's gaze moved between Blayth and Tor. "A beneficial betrothal was taken from me," he said. "My *son* was taken from me. I only have my daughter left and considering everything that has happened at the hands of the House of de Wolfe, I demand satisfaction. You took one betrothal away from me and I demand another."

Tor frowned, perplexed. "You want another betrothal?"

Gilbert was focused intently on him. "You are the common element in all of this, Tor de Wolfe," he said. "My son's death, and now my daughter being set upon by your wards. *You* owe me."

Tor's eyebrows lifted. "Me? *I* do?"

"I demand a betrothal between you and my daughter. You have much to make up to my family."

Tor's mouth popped open, his initial reaction one of outrage. But just as quickly, he shut his mouth. He wasn't a man given to whims or fits of aggression, so he took a moment to digest what Gilbert had said as Blayth began to condemn Gilbert's suggestion for being outrageous and idiotic.

But not Tor.

A marriage to Isalyn.

God help him… as he thought on it, he realized that it wasn't an unattractive proposal.

"Tor," Blayth said, interrupting his thoughts. "You had better speak up, lad. Your future is at stake here."

Tor looked at his uncle a moment before finally looking at Gilbert, who was standing stiffly with his arms folded across his chest. Tor could tell just by looking at him how serious he was. He had stated his position and he was going to dig in against any opposition.

But perhaps there wouldn't be any.

In fact, Tor was at a sort of crossroads – he had never expected to remarry after Jane's death, nor had he wanted to. He'd never even considered it and it had never entered his mind where it pertained to Isalyn.

Certainly, he'd responded to her more than any other woman since Jane. In fact, he couldn't even remember responding this quickly *to* Jane. His relationship with dear Jane had been something of a slow burn, from the time they met as children until the time they were of marriageable age. He'd had years to warm up to the idea of marrying Jane.

But with Isalyn, it had barely been a few days. He'd just met her and, already, the idea of marriage between them had been brought up, by her father no less. Tor wasn't one to act impulsively, and he didn't consider this an impulse, but he had the ability to think about his life in a year, in five years, and even ten years and wonder what it would be without a good woman by his side.

Without Isalyn by his side.

He didn't like the look of a future without her.

Perhaps he'd only known her a matter of days, but he trusted his gut where she was concerned. He liked the way she'd handled Barbara and Lenore. He liked the way she'd handled herself in the fight in Haltwhistle. He'd seen some life-changing situations with her over the past few days and throughout it all, Isalyn had been composed, thoughtful, and brave.

Very brave.

That was the kind of woman he wanted to be married to.

"My lord," he finally said, scratching his head thoughtfully. "Your argument about Steffan being given the opportunity to mend his ways is hollow. We all know he never, at any time, would have considered returning to Isabella, so I reject your notion that he could have possibly changed his mind. Had you seen him at The Black Bull in Newcastle, you would have seen what we all saw – a man running from a commitment. Therefore, what you suggest is not so and I will not be coerced into marriage. However… I do find a betrothal between your daughter and me… intriguing."

Gilbert, who had been gearing up for a battle, was suddenly slapped in the face with Tor's interest to his betrothal demand. He had thought for certain that Tor was going to tell him to go jump off a bridge to permanently shut his foolish mouth, but that's not what Tor said.

The man was actually interested.

… interested?

"She comes with a very large dowry," Gilbert said eagerly. "She will make you a very rich man. After my death, my merchant business will go to you. It is quite profitable."

Tor shook his head. "I have wealth," he said. "Making more of it is of no particular interest to me. But a marriage to her would ensure an alliance with you."

Gilbert looked somewhat baffled. "But I have no great army."

Tor nodded. "I know," he said. "But you have a great manse at Featherstone and I have heard of an even bigger one in Carlisle. If I wanted to keep men at either place…"

"You could. I would pay for their keep."

"And if I needed more funds to increase my troops…"

Gilbert cut him off. "I would happily provide you with funds for your army."

Tor passed a glance at Blayth to see how he was reacting to all of this. The de Wolfe uncle seemed to be as intrigued as Tor was with the idea of a wealthy ally, and family member, with funds to funnel into armies and more men. That would be most beneficial to the de Wolfe war machine.

Gilbert de Featherstone was one of the richer merchants in

the north, so even if the marriage wasn't one that provided military support, it would provide excellent financial support. Blayth began to see what his nephew was driving at and it was quite cunning.

He nodded faintly.

That was what Tor wanted to see – approval from someone he trusted. He wanted the man to think he was only in this for the gains and not for the fact that Tor found Isalyn attractive. Nay, more than attractive.

She had sparked a fire within him that he thought was long dead.

"Then speak with your daughter," Tor said. "If she is agreeable, then I am as well. I will give you twenty minutes with her before I join you to speak to her myself."

Gilbert nearly tripped in his haste to leave the hall with Fraser on his heels, leaving Tor behind with Blayth, Christian, and Ronan. When the men had cleared the hall, Blayth turned to his nephew.

"An excellent bargain, Tor," he said. "De Featherstone has nearly unlimited wealth. With it, he could help you expand your empire. Exceptional thinking on your part."

Tor sighed heavily and perched his bottom on the edge of the feasting table. "Henry is always looking for money for his wars," he said. "I would prefer that he didn't know I was married to a gold mine, but I suppose he would find out soon enough."

"Did you do it because of Steffan?" Ronan wanted to know. "Because of what he did to Bella? Did you do it to appease him?"

Tor could see that Ronan was concerned that perhaps Tor was paying the price for a broken betrothal. But Tor smiled faintly at his cousin.

"I do not do anything I don't want to do," he said. "You

needn't worry, Ronan. I am not sacrificing myself for the common good."

"It is not a bad bargain," Christian spoke up. He'd been watching the entire situation unfold but, more than that, he'd seen the way Tor looked at Isalyn. There was interest in the man's heart. "It's not simply the wealth, but Lady Isalyn is a beautiful woman. She is quite a prize. But are you sure about this?"

Tor remained neutral as talk of Isalyn's beauty was introduced. "I am," he said. "But if she is not, then I will not pursue it. The woman lives in London and I have no intention of living there, so she may very well be opposed to a union that will keep her in Northumberland. This may be all for naught."

Even as he said it, he genuinely hoped not. Surely he couldn't have imagined the warm smiles and glimmer in Isalyn's eyes that told him she had interest in him, too. But he was a good deal older than she was – she had seen twenty years and he had seen thirty-eight, so there was quite a spread. Even so, she didn't seem young and juvenile in manner, but rather a woman of poise and maturity.

Every moment he'd spent with her had been a moment of joy that Tor hadn't experienced in nearly seventeen years. It didn't take a man of great intellect to realize the years of his life since Jane's death had been dull and colorless. He had been existing, not living.

He wanted to live again.

He only hoped Isalyn felt the same way.

"*MARRIAGE*?"

"That is the fourth time you have asked me, Isalyn. Are you hard of hearing?"

No, she wasn't hard of hearing, but she was having difficulty believing what her father was telling her. Sitting in the chamber she now shared with Isabella, who had been chased from the room when Gilbert arrived, she was looking at her father as if the man were speaking in tongues.

She could hardly believe it.

"But…" she stammered. "But you cannot mean it."

"Of course I can."

"He is a de Wolfe, Father. The males of the family are more in demand than royal princes."

"And this one has agreed to a betrothal with you," Gilbert said. "Tor is the second son of the Earl of Warenton, do not forget. Behind his older brother, he is in line to inherit a vast empire and the prestige you would know as his wife is something the finest and most well-placed women in England would kill for. Don't you realize what this means?"

Isalyn did, in fact. Living in London made her very aware of excellent marriages, politics, lords, and ladies. Aye, she knew it well.

London…

"Father," she said, trying to find the right words. "I do not like living in the north. I would feel lost and out of place here. My home is in London."

Gilbert could see that she wasn't as excited as he had hoped. "You live with your spinster aunt," he said shortly. "If you are not careful, you will be a spinster, too. Is that what you want? To live alone for the rest of your life and die alone? Isalyn, I have found you the greatest husband you could possibly hope for and he does not even seem to mind that you are rather old for a bride. Do you not understand this, lass?"

Now he was starting to lob insults at her. "I understand,"

she said. "I understand very well. But… I must think on this."

"What is there to think about?"

She eyed him, growing annoyed. "When I came to Featherstone to visit you, it was because I was told that you had been ill and you were asking to see me," she said. "I did not come north for any other reason than that, and certainly not to marry a provincial knight and spend the rest of my life in the wilds of Northumberland."

Gilbert frowned. "Is that all you see? A provincial knight? We are speaking about a de Wolfe."

"I know who he is."

"Then do not be stupid about this!"

She stood up. "Being stupid would be to agree immediately," she said. "I… I am simply not prepared for this. It has all happened so fast. I must think on it."

"Do you not like the man? He is big and handsome and wealthy. God's bones, what is wrong with you?"

"If you like him so much, then *you* marry him!"

Gilbert threw up his hands. "Does living in London mean more to you than having a fine husband and a powerful position?" he asked. "Would you really turn down this offer and return to London to live in that smelly house with your smelly aunt? Isalyn, there is nothing to think about. I am accepting this betrothal on your behalf."

"Don't you dare!"

A knock on the door interrupted their building argument. With a growl, Gilbert went to the door, throwing it open to reveal Tor standing on the other side.

"I am sorry," Tor said, smiling timidly. "I could not stay away. May I have a word with your daughter?"

Gilbert nodded his head with frustration. "Go," he said, indicating Isalyn standing on the other side of the chamber. "Talk to her. Tell her what an excellent husband you would be and how foolish she would be to turn down the offer. Tell her she will die alone and unloved if she does, and that I will never speak to her again!"

With that, he stormed out of the room, leaving Tor standing by the open door. His eyebrows lifted as he looked to Isalyn.

"Is this true?" he said. "You will die alone and unloved, and ignored by your father?"

His eyes were twinkling at her as he said it and Isalyn broke down into a weak smile. "Apparently," she said. "I am not happy about being alone and unloved, but it might be worth it if he really did ignore me for the rest of my life."

Tor grinned and shut the door to give them some privacy, but he remained by the panel. He made no move to enter the chamber any more than he already had. He gazed at her a moment, his smile fading.

"May I make a confession?" he asked.

She nodded. "Of course."

"I was listening outside of the door. I heard everything."

Her smile vanished. "I see," she said, averting her gaze as she went to sit down on the only chair in the chamber. "You must understand that I did not mean to insult you. Never did I mean to insult you. But this has all happened so quickly. It is simply not the way I had ever envisioned my life to be."

He leaned back against the door. "You want to return to London."

She looked at him, then. "That was my intention," she said. "But I have made no secret of that. My life is there. My dramas are there, as are my friends. Everything is there."

He nodded in understanding. "I cannot say that if I was taken away from my family and friends that I would be so agreeable," he said. "Then… it is nothing I have said or done to make you question this betrothal?"

She shook her head firmly. "Nay," she said. "I swear it, my

lord. Nothing you have said or done. In fact…"

"In fact… *what*?"

"Would you consider moving to London?"

His grin was back because her question gave him hope. "Not all the time," he said. "But if my wife loved London so much, I might be convinced to build a home there, one we could stay in while we visited her friends."

Her eyes widened. "Would you really?"

He nodded. "Of course I would," he said. "My lady, I was married once and one of the things I remember from that relationship was that it was necessary to compromise if I wanted my wife to be happy. I know that most men view marriage as a monarchy – the man is king and everyone does as he commands. But I found that marriage was better when it was more of an alliance and a partnership. Sometimes I had my way, and sometimes Jane had her way. But the main thing was that we were willing to compromise. I believe that keeps everyone happy."

Isalyn was listening intently. "And you found that it worked well enough?"

"Indeed, it did."

She thought very hard on that. "And you would be willing to compromise with me?"

His eyes glimmered at her from across the chamber. "For you and you alone," he said quietly. "Isalyn, I realize we have not known each other for very long but, in that short time, I have come to see that you have some very good qualities. You are brave and you are honest, and I respect that a great deal. You are also cultured and literate. I know of no other woman who writes dramas. Do you know why I invited you and your father for a visit?"

Isalyn had been hanging on his every word. "Nay… I do not think so."

He stepped away from the door, moving slowly in her directly. "I invited you because I did not like the thought of never seeing you again," he said. "You were planning on returning to London and I wanted to see you before you went. But the truth is that I did not want you to go at all."

Her eyes widened. "You didn't?"

"Nay."

Isalyn wasn't sure what to say. Her cheeks flamed an obvious shade of pink and she grinned, putting a hand to her warm face. She was so flattered that she was actually speechless for a moment. Never in her life had a man said to her what Tor just had. But if he was being so honest, perhaps she should be as well.

His candor gave her the confidence to speak her mind.

"Why do you think we came so soon?" she said, lowering her gaze bashfully. "I did not want you to forget about me."

He smiled broadly. "You?" he said. "Never. Never would I forget the woman who introduced me to the Crown and Sword."

She laughed softly. "At least my culinary knowledge impressed you."

"Everything about you impressed me."

She looked at him, feeling a good deal of disbelief. She could hardly believe the man was as interested in her as she was in him.

"Truly?"

"Truly."

She looked him over, picturing him as her husband and the very idea made her heart swell with pride. The provincial knight who had changed her mind about provincial men. He was anything but the rural bumpkin she had imagined knights in the north to be. After a moment, she sighed.

"Did you mean what you said about having a home in London?" she asked softly.

He nodded. "There is one thing you should know about me immediately," he said. "I never say anything I do not mean. And I will never say anything I will not follow through on. My word is my bond. If it would make you happy, then I will buy or build a home in London where we may stay when we visit. But know that I will not live there all year. My home is here, at Blackpool, and this is where I will spend the bulk of my time. But a few months a year spent in London, if it will make you happy, is something I would be willing to do. As long as you would be willing to come back to Blackpool with me."

He was being truthfully and incredibly sweet. Already, he was speaking to her as if she meant something to him and it was endearing like nothing else.

"I would be willing, of course," she said. "But you do not have to come to London with me if you do not want to. I would not force you to. I know you have obligations here and that it is your home as much as London is mine."

He took a few more steps and ended up sitting on the bed, closer to her. "Would you really want to spend so much time away from your husband?"

She shook her head. "Nay," she said. "But I would not force you to go with me if you did not want to."

"You are that determined to spend time in London?"

She shrugged. "As you said, it is my home."

"Would you be happy with just a few months a year?"

She thought on that a moment. "I would," she said. "Summers are miserable in London, but the spring and autumn are lovely months. But would you be happy there, happy away from Blackpool?"

"I think I could be happy wherever you were."

More sweet words. She could hardly dare to hope that they were true. "If you are certain, then we have a bargain."

His smile was back. "If *you* are certain, then we do."

"I am."

"No lamenting a marriage to a provincial knight?"

She winced. "You are not going to let me forget that, are you?"

He laughed softly. "Not for a while, anyway," he said. Then, he sobered. "And about what happened with Barbara and Lenore... if I seemed inactive in any way against punishing them, you have my deepest apologies. I have spent so long simply trying to ignore them that I fear it has become habit. Nay, that is not entirely true. Because they are Jane's sisters, I felt guilty even thinking of punishing them and they know it. But no longer – you are to be my wife and their reign of terror is at an end."

Isalyn averted her gaze. "I will be truthful with you," she said. "To have them continuing living here with you... with us... is concerning. I do not mean to speak against them or disparage them, for my experiences with them are my own and they are limited, but I will not go the rest of my life looking over my shoulder and wondering what they are going to do to me next. I realize they are your dead wife's sisters, but do you think she would have approved of their behavior?"

Tor immediately shook his head. "Nay," he said. "I know she would not have. And I will not have you fearful in your own home, so we will have to come to a pleasing solution to the problem of Barbara and Lenore."

"Have you thought of finding them husbands?"

He grunted. "They do not wish to marry."

"That is because they have you. Why should they?"

He looked at her, sharply. "I am not their husband, nor am I bound romantically to either one of them."

She shook her head. "Forgive me," she said. "I did not mean that the way it sounded. I simply meant that they tend your home, they fulfill the roles that a wife would normally fill, so mayhap they view you as a husband-figure in a sense."

As much as he didn't want to admit it, that made sense. But after a moment, he simply shook his head. "That is my fault," he said. "I should have had them married off long ago. But they are my last link to Jane and I suppose I was in no hurry to do it."

"And now?"

"Now, I can see that I failed them in that respect. And I cannot have them around any longer if you and I are to enjoy a happy marriage."

"I am not trying to force you to rid yourself of your last links to Jane if that means something to you. I would never ask that of you."

He nodded, reaching over to boldly take her hand. His hand was easily twice the size of hers, maybe more, but that giant appendage held her with a good deal of tenderness.

"You are not," he said quietly. "But I know that what I have done… it was not healthy. It is time for Barbara and Lenore and I to go our separate ways, because they cannot come where I am going. And I am going with you."

Isalyn's heart was racing at his touch. "As you wish," she said. "But I will defend myself against them should the need arise."

He smirked. "After what I witnessed today, you are more than capable of doing so," he said. "You have my permission."

"Thank you."

The conversation lagged, but it wasn't uncomfortable. They simply sat there, together, lingering on what the future might bring. Tor was studying her face closely, acquainting himself with the woman he was to marry.

He was still in awe of it.

"What are you thinking?" he asked softly.

She cocked her head, amused. "I was thinking that it did not occur to me when I came home to visit my father that I would find something much more interesting here in Northumberland."

He laughed softly. "And it did not occur to me when I visited Featherstone with your brother slung over my horse that I would come away with the greatest prize Featherstone had to offer. But I think I will be a better man for it."

Isalyn squeezed his hand at the hopeful and chivalrous declaration. "Will you tell my father, or shall I?"

Tor's gaze took on a mischievous twinkle. "Let him worry about it," he said. "I am in no hurry to leave you. Let us speak more on what activities you enjoy while you are in London because, coincidentally, I will be doing the same activities. I should like to get to know what it is I am going to be doing."

Isalyn thought that sounded like a marvelous idea. There were so many things to tell him, so much she wanted him to know. It was a moment she never thought she would face and the joy of it was difficult to describe. All she knew was that she never wanted the moment to end. It was surreal to realize that if she married him, it never would.

But that tender moment was interrupted when a knock on the door summoned Tor.

A situation was afoot.

CHAPTER FIFTEEN

SHE WAS HIDING.

Well, not exactly hiding, but Isabella was trying to stay to an inconspicuous spot so she wouldn't be noticed. Once Gilbert had chased her from her own chamber because he wanted to speak to his daughter, Isabella came out to the bailey but she didn't go any further.

Something was in the air.

Gilbert had been angry, or agitated, or… something. It was difficult to tell with him because ever since he had arrived at Blackpool, the man seemed to be in a perpetual state of distress. Isabella was certain that it had something to do with what had happened with Barbara and Lenore, and he was probably concerned for his daughter's safety. At least, that's what Isabella thought.

But she didn't really know.

That's why she was trying to stay out of sight.

When she had come out to the bailey, it looked as if nothing was amiss. Men were still going about their duties as they always did and nothing seemed out of place. Isabella probably should have gone to the great hall to wait out the situation, but she couldn't seem to get away from the apartment block because something was happening inside.

She was curious to know what it was.

She hadn't been out in the bailey for more than a few minutes when Tor came running from the great hall, heading towards the apartment block. Isabella had been standing out in plain sight, but he hadn't even looked at her. He'd simply continued into the apartment block, looking like a man with a good deal on his mind.

That made her more curious than ever.

Casually, she made her way around the side of the building, heading in the direction of the windows of the chamber she shared with Isalyn. The chamber was on the western side of the apartment block and there was just one set of windows that faced out to the inner wall. The last she had seen, the windows had been open, so she thought that perhaps she could crouch down below them and listen to what was being said.

It was naughty and she knew it, but there was so much excitement going on here that never went on at Castle Questing or even at Roxburgh. Those places tended to be very regimented, and very boring, so the opportunity to partake of a little bit of drama was alluring.

For a moment, she lingered at the southwest corner of the apartment block, peering around the corner and straining her ears to see if she could catch anything that was being said. She could see a couple of soldiers on the wall, but they were far enough away that they probably would not see her, or even if they did, they probably wouldn't care. Isabella stood there a moment, listening for any strains of conversation coming from chamber. Feeling bolder, she took a step around the corner when a voice stopped her.

"Greetings, my lady."

Startled, she very nearly tripped over her own feet as she whirled around to see Fraser standing right behind her. She'd never even heard him come up. Hand over her thumping heart, she grinned.

"Greetings," she said breathlessly. "You startled me. I thought that I was quite alone."

He smiled at her, flashing big, slightly crooked teeth that made his smile look absolutely charming.

"You were until I saw you over here," he said. "What are you doing?"

What *was* she doing? Isabella wasn't going to confess her naughty intentions to a knight she thought was quite handsome. He would think her a fool.

Even if she *was* behaving that way, just a little.

"I… I was waiting," she said, throwing a nervous thumb in the direction of the apartment block. "Lord Gilbert asked me to leave so that he could speak with Isalyn privately."

Fraser nodded in understanding. "Ah," he said, but his gaze seemed to linger on her. "I hope this will not embarrass you, but I heard what you did, my lady. Standing up for Lady Isalyn, I mean, against de Wolfe's chatelaines. That was very brave."

Isabella felt both flattered and humbled by his praise. "It was the right thing to do," she said. "I am just glad the situation was not worse."

"What do you mean?"

Isabella shrugged. "That she was not injured," she said. "That those two didn't do more damage. They are capable of much worse. In fact, I have known them to… oh, forgive me. I should not speak so. I do not want you to think I am a gossip."

"I do not," he said. "But it is clear that you know something about that pair."

"I do."

"Yet you did not warn Isalyn."

Isabella sighed faintly. "If you really want to know, it is an old story with Tor and those vipers," she said. "I suppose I would rather gossip a little than have you think I withheld information from Lady Isalyn about the danger she might face. You see, I have known Barbara and Lenore since they came to live at Castle Questing, almost seventeen years ago. I was only a baby at the time, but I grew up with them. If they believe a woman is looking at Tor in an amorous way, they will do all they can to discourage her. Everyone knows that. They treat Tor as if he were their property, but Tor is the only one who refused to believe it."

Given that Fraser had heard Tor's confession in the great hall about that very subject, he nodded. "I have heard," he said. "Tor has explained his position. It is understandable, I suppose, given they are his wife's sisters."

"Then you do not disagree with the way he has handled things?"

"I did not say that. I only said that I understood his reasons." He sighed. "I suppose if I had a dead wife, I might treat her remaining siblings different as well. Tor is in a difficult position."

"I suppose."

"I did not know that his wife died."

Isabella nodded. "In childbirth," she said. "He was very much in love with her from what I've heard my father say. Poor Tor has had a difficult life. He lost his mother and two siblings in an accident when he was a young lad, and then he lost his wife. He has suffered through more than someone should at his age. But he is truly a kind and generous man in spite of everything. Everyone loves him very much."

"He seems pleasant enough."

"He is." Isabella paused, her gaze moving over Fraser, studying the man at close range for a moment. "As for not warning Lady Isalyn, I could not risk angering Tor, as he is very sensitive when it comes to Barbara and Lenore. But I did escort her to her chamber to make sure Barbara did not pull any tricks, although I did not take into account that she would lock Lady Isalyn inside the chamber. I suppose I should have. Several years ago, Barbara and Lenore took offense to a young ward of Castle Questing and locked her in the buttery during a cold winter's night. When she was found the next morning, she was nearly frozen to death. Barbara swore it was an accident and she was believed, but those of us who knew her knew better. Lady Isalyn was fortunate that locking her in her chamber was all they did."

Fraser shook his head at the thought of two vicious women. "And you have managed to stay in their good graces?"

Isabella smiled wryly. "No longer," she said. "If given a chance, I am sure they will turn their tricks on me now that I have taken a stand against them."

Fraser smiled faintly. "Not to worry," he said. "I will make sure they do not get close to you."

Isabella's heart began to beat, just a little faster, at his chivalrous declaration. "You will?" she asked, sounding breathless. "But why?"

"Because you saved Lady Isalyn. That is reason enough."

Her face fell. "Of course," she said, feeling foolish for thinking he might have meant something personally. "I like Lady Isalyn a great deal. I would not want to see her come to harm."

Fraser looked at her for a moment before speaking. "And this coming from a woman who was badly wronged by Lady Isalyn's brother," he said quietly. "Are you always so forgiving, my lady?"

Isabella averted her gaze, pondering his question. "I wasn't, not at first," she admitted. "But my grandmother convinced me that men like Steffan de Featherstone are not worth grieving. It was my own fault, really. I met Steffan when I was visiting my uncle and cousins at Berwick Castle. We all traveled into town one day because my Aunt Bridey wanted to go to the fish market, so the whole gaggle of us went along. You must understand that in my family, males dominate. I have far more male cousins than female, and those who are female are mostly younger than I am. So many of my male cousins are getting married to beautiful young women and when I met Steffan, I suppose I was feeling a little left out. He was very attentive, mayhap *too* attentive, but it was nice to feel wanted. I suppose, in hindsight, I was not in love with him. When he left me on the day of our wedding, I was humiliated more than anything. Truthfully, I am very glad my brother and cousins and uncles did not bring him back."

Fraser had a smile on his face as he leaned casually against the apartment wall. "Truthfully, so am I," he said. "Although I should not speak ill of my liege's son, you have been honest with me so I will be honest with you. Steffan was a callous, selfish man. Had he married you, I am quite sure you would have regretted it. You deserve a much better husband."

She grinned bashfully. "There are only de Wolfes and de Norvilles and Hages where I live and I cannot marry a cousin," she said. "Lady Isalyn promised that I could visit her in London. Mayhap I will find a husband there."

Fraser scowled. "Have you ever been to London?"

"Aye, several times. My Uncle Edward has a home there."

Fraser shook his head. "The only men you'll find in London are arrogant prigs, dandies, pickpockets, or crusty old lords," he said. "You'd do better finding a man to marry in Northumberland. There are fine families this far north other than de Wolfe, de Norville, and Hage. You should have your pick."

She cast him a dubious look but ended up breaking into soft laughter. "I doubt my father will let me select my own husband again," she said. "I failed miserably with Steffan. He will not trust me again."

Fraser was grinning because she was. He was rather enchanted by her silly little giggle. "Then mayhap some fine man will select you instead."

She looked at him with interest. "Do you think so?"

"Possibly."

"Do you know of one?"

"That is very possible."

Her eyes lit up. "Do you really?"

"As I said, it is very possible."

"I am intrigued," she said. "Tell me more."

Fraser was becoming upswept in the gentle game of flirtation when sentries from the inner gatehouse began to send up a cry. They could see the gatehouse from where they were standing and they could see a bit of commotion.

The portcullises were open and a soldier was coming through the opening, heading for the hall. As he came closer, he caught sight of Isabella and veered in her direction. Curious, Isabella came away from the wall and went to meet the soldier halfway.

"My lady," the man was breathless because he had run. "We have a seriously ill man at the outer gatehouse. Would you come and see to him, my lady?"

Castles were beacons of food, shelter, and help, so it was unthinkable to turn away a sick traveler. It simply wasn't done. But Isabella balked.

"I do not know anything about healing," she said. "I would not do any good."

"But he needs help, my lady," the soldier said. "We can put him in the troop house, but someone should see to him."

Fraser was standing behind Isabella, listening. "Who is the man?"

The soldier shook his head. "He gave his name as Joe or Joseph," he said. "It was difficult to tell, as he could not tell us more. The man seems delirious."

"Feverish?"

"He seems to be, my lord."

Fraser looked at Isabella. "You do not want a fever spreading among the men," he said. "I would recommend not putting him in the troop house. Is there anywhere else you can put him?"

Isabella knew Blackpool fairly well, but not as intimately as if she lived here. "I do not know," she said. "Barbara and Lenore would know better than I would and they would tend him as well. I know they have done that sort of thing. Mayhap he should be brought to Lady Isalyn's former chamber where Barbara and Lenore are?"

"That is reasonable," Fraser said. "He can be isolated there. Who has the keys?"

"Tor does, I think."

Fraser gestured to the apartment block. "I saw him go inside," he said. "Find him and have him unlock the chamber where the chatelaines are being held. I will bring the sick man to the chamber so those two can tend to him."

Isabella nodded quickly and fled, running into the apartment block as Fraser headed for the gatehouse.

A dramatic day was about to get a little more interesting.

"WHY SHOULD WE tend him?" Barbara said stiffly. "Clearly, we have been removed from our duties. You do not expect anything more from us."

"I expect you to be useful," Tor said flatly, keys in hand from so recently unlocking the chamber door. "I am still putting a roof over your heads and food in your bellies, so you will do as I say. What do you need to tend to this man?"

Two soldiers were carrying a limp knight between them as Fraser followed, helping them put the man upon the uncomfortable straw-stuffed mattress that had been so thoughtfully prepared for Isalyn. Fraser instructed the soldiers to remove the knight's protective gear, gloves, belt and helm, as Tor faced off against Barbara and Lenore.

A battle was brewing.

"We do not know what is wrong with him yet," Barbara said, eyeing the man on the bed. "I do not know what I need."

Tor was losing his patience. "Then look at him and figure it out," he said. "Do it now."

Barbara hesitated for a moment but the look on Tor's face told her any semblance of rebellion would not be well met. Still, she wasn't going without a fight, so he would know how displeased she was at being sequestered with her sister.

Slowly, she moved.

The knight on the bed was unconscious as his clothing was stripped away. As the soldiers pulled off his boots, Barbara and Lenore leaned over the man, visually inspecting him before Barbara gingerly reached out to touch his forehead. It was clammy to the touch. She then used her fingers to prop open his eyelids, peering into his eyes.

"Well?" Tor said.

Barbara's gaze was still on the man. "I am not certain," she said. "He does seem feverish."

"What do you require to heal him?"

She turned to look at him, then. "If you want me to heal him, then I must be permitted to move about freely," she said. "There are herbs and medicines to gather, and I must have access to the kitchen so I can brew a potion. If I tell you what to bring me, there is no guarantee it will be done correctly."

She had a point, but Tor wasn't thrilled with giving her the ability to roam freely about Blackpool, not after what she had done. Therefore, he crooked his finger at her, beckoning her to him. When she and Lenore timidly came near, Tor pulled them aside and lowered his voice.

"I want you two to listen to me very carefully," he said. "I know what you are capable of. I have known for years and, God help me, it has taken me this long to acknowledge the truth, so I want you to understand me clearly. I will release you so that you may go about your business. You may return to your chatelaine duties. But if you so much as look, speak, or act in a way that displeases me towards Lady Isalyn or even Isabella, or any other woman for that matter, I will put you in the vault and you will stay there the rest of your lives. You will never know freedom again. Your days of vindictive and appalling behavior is over. Is this in any way unclear?"

Barbara's expression tightened while Lenore's eyes widened. "You would not do that!" Lenore hissed. "You cannot lock us away. Jane would not let you!"

It took all of Tor's strength not to lash out at her for that statement. His jaw ticked dangerously. "Be glad that you are a woman, Lenore," he said. "Were you a man, I would plaster your body all over this chamber. As it is, keep your mouth shut. Mention Jane again, in any way, and I will turn you out of these walls and forget I ever knew you."

Lenore gasped, recoiling, but Barbara remained immobile. "You needn't worry about us, Tor," Barbara said evenly. "We understand your terms."

"Obey them or everything you know is at an end."

Barbara nodded shortly, pinching Lenore until the woman nodded unhappily. But she didn't do as he had told her – she didn't keep her mouth shut.

That had always been Lenore's problem.

"But you do not understand," Lenore hissed. "What we do, we do to protect Jane's memory. You are *her* husband, Tor. You only belong to her and we must preserve that."

Tor stared at her. It was a very good thing she wasn't a man because if she had been, she would be dead right now. As it was, he had to take a step back. He was closer to losing his composure than he had ever been in his life.

"Jane is dead," he said simply. "She has been dead for nearly seventeen years. I do not belong to anyone at the moment, but I soon shall. Thank you for reminding me that you cannot continue to live with me. It takes away any lingering guilt I might have felt for sending you away."

Lenore's eyes widened. Even Barbara had a reaction. "Send us away?" she gasped. "But… but we live here!"

Tor wasn't going to argue the point with them. This wasn't the time. In fact, he'd said too much already, but he didn't regret it.

He was finally seeing what everyone else saw in The Vipers.

He pointed to the bed.

"Tend to that man," he said. "You have the freedom to move about the castle within reason. I have your keys and I will not return them to you, so if you need to go anywhere that requires a key, you must get my permission. Do you understand?"

They still weren't over the shock of him speaking of sending them away, but they both nodded. "Aye," Barbara said. "We… we are grateful for your mercy, Tor."

He didn't believe that for one minute. Barbara was the ringleader, the chief manipulator, and she was good at telling people what she wanted them to hear. Stepping away from them, Tor motioned to Fraser and the soldiers to follow.

"Come," he said. "We shall leave the man to Barbara and Lenore, but do not let the man wander. He is to remain to this room."

"Do you want us to stand guard, my lord?" one of the soldiers asked.

Tor shook his head. "Nay," he said. "He appears too sick to move, so that is not necessary for now. Barbara and Lenore will keep him restricted to this chamber."

He said it for all to hear, including Barbara and Lenore. They were bent over the man, preparing to decide what they would need to help him, as Tor shut the door and left them alone with their patient.

When he was gone, Lenore's eyes welled with tears.

"Did you hear that?" she sniffled. "He is going to send us away!"

Barbara was beginning to pull off the man's tunic, a simple tunic that bore no colors. "Help me," she said, and Lenore rushed to lift the man's arms. "And you should not have said what you did, you fool. You confessed everything to him when you told him that we were preserving Jane's memory."

Lenore continued to sniffle. "It is true."

"But you do not want him to know that," she snapped. "That is our mission in life, not his. *We* must preserve our sister's memory."

They managed to yank the man's tunic over his head, tossing it aside. That left a mail coat that needed to come off and they began to struggle with it.

"All because of her," Lenore seethed. "She had no business coming here. This is *her* fault."

She was speaking of Isalyn. Barbara was well aware. As they heaved the man into a sitting position so they could remove the coat, Barbara replied.

"Her father came here because his son was betrothed to Isabella," Barbara grunted as she held the man up for Lenore. "You know that. You know that Tor is attempting to smooth over the fact that he killed the man's son. But the daughter… you saw the way Tor looked at her."

"She looks at him the same way!" Lenore screeched and the man fell back to the mattress as they yanked the mail coat from his arms. "She will make him forget Jane. She *wants* him to forget Jane, I know it!"

Between the two of them, they tossed the mail coat to the floor. Barbara brushed back the hair that had fallen in her face and bent over the unconscious man again.

"Mayhap that is true, but we cannot touch her," she said. "If we do, you heard what he will do to us. I do not want to spend the rest of my life in a vault."

"Then we have to make her leave," Lenore said as if that were the obvious solution. "We have to make her *want* to leave."

"Or pay someone to remove her."

Lenore looked at her sister in shock. "Remove her? How?"

"Abduct her."

Lenore gasped. "Do you think we should?"

Barbara shrugged. "We may not need to," she said. "But time will tell. She is only here for a visit, after all. It is not as if she is a permanent resident, but we must keep a close watch. If it looks as if she and her father are staying too long, then mayhap we can motivate them to leave. Mayhap we can even motivate them to leave… sooner."

"How?"

"I do not know," Barbara said, but the thoughts were churning behind those dark eyes. "But it will come to me. Until then, I intend to keep a close watch on Isalyn de Featherstone."

Lenore agreed. "And what about Isabella? What about her?"

Barbara shrugged. "She is no longer to be trusted," she said. "But we cannot seek any vengeance against her, as much as I would like to. She is a de Wolfe and if something happens to her, the entire clan will come down around us. We would provoke their wrath."

Lenore understood. "I like Bella a great deal, but she should not have spoken out against us."

Barbara lifted her eyebrows. "It is clear she has been watching us. I should have been more aware that she would have seen the signs. But for now… we do nothing. We cannot."

With Tor's threat hanging over their heads, their hands were tied. They were conniving but they weren't stupid.

They didn't want to end up in the vault.

Lenore sighed heavily. "Very well," she said, reluctantly pushing that subject aside. "Now, for this man – what would you have me do?"

Barbara turned her focus away from treacherous women and on to the unconscious man. "Come with me to the kitchens," she said. "We will gather a few things to help him."

Lenore nodded, following her sister from the chamber and shutting the door softly. Only when their footsteps faded did the man on the bed open one eye to make sure that he was alone.

Joah de Brayton was quite alone.

And he'd gotten an earful.

CHAPTER SIXTEEN

GOD'S BONES, HE thought. *Did I truly just hear all of that?*

He was still in shock.

It had taken Joah a few days of hard riding to arrive at Blackpool Castle, and given the fact that neither he nor his horse had barely rested, it gave the perfect illusion of a man who was desperately ill. He was exhausted and sweaty, and warm beneath all of that armor, so he was the very picture of a man who needed help.

Already, he had received a good deal of it.

Pretending to be unconscious had its advantages. People would speak of things in front of him that they wouldn't have had he been awake, so all he had to do was lay there and pretend to be oblivious. He'd begun that particular performance about the time he reached the first of two gatehouses of Blackpool Castle.

At the first gatehouse, all he had to do was faint and the rest was easy. Men came out of the gatehouse to see what the trouble was and after he pretended to be incoherent, he further pretended to pass out completely. Given that it was an expected hospitality practice to tend to the health and well-being of an ill traveler, he was picked up and carried into the gatehouse and set gently on the floor inside of the guard shack.

That was where he learned quite a bit.

Although Joah had known the Blackpool Castle was a de Wolfe property, he hadn't known who was in command. He was not surprised to discover that the son of the Earl of Warenton was the commander, the man called Tor. One of the same men who had been in the Hunting Party that had murdered Steffan, according to Powell.

Joah could not have planned this better.

Already, he was where he needed to be, in the fortress of a murderer. It was a perfect place to start, but what made it more perfect – and also a little puzzling – was the fact that Isalyn de Featherstone and her father were evidently here as well and, according to the two women, Isalyn was betrothed to Tor, or sweet on him, or something that those two women disapproved of.

But there was some connection there.

Pretending to be unconscious had given him more information than he could have hoped for, but he was particularly interested in the fact that the two women had also mentioned Isabella, none other than the woman Steffan had been betrothed to.

She was here, too.

That told Joah that almost everyone with a connection to Steffan and the man's death was here at Blackpool for one reason or another. He was in a nest of them. A son of the Earl of Warenton, Gilbert de Featherstone and his daughter, and Steffan's betrothed, Isabella. So many pieces to a greater puzzle that he planned to fit together for his own particular needs. He wasn't sure how he was going to do it yet, but something those two women said stuck in his mind, even now.

We will pay someone to remove her.

They had been referring to Steffan's sister, Isalyn. Their

entire conversation revolved around their evident dislike of her, which made more sense when they spoke of the woman in relation to Tor de Wolfe. Tor had an eye for her, or she had an eye for him, and the two women were incensed about it. They had spoken of removing her, of even paying someone to abduct her. Fairly strong words coming from two well-bred women, but it gave Joah an idea.

Militarily, he could not hope to hurt the House of the Wolf. He couldn't even take on one of them in a personal challenge because everybody knew de Wolfe knights for the most elite knights in England. Not that he was any slouch, but challenging a de Wolfe knight would be suicide.

Nay, he had to be far more clever than that.

He had come here to seek revenge for something they took from him. They took Steffan from him, the only man he had ever loved. Given that they had taken something from him, it would stand to reason that the best way to seek vengeance against them would be to take something from them.

The dynamic between Tor de Wolfe and Isalyn de Featherstone had his focus.

If those two women really wanted someone to abduct her, then perhaps they did not have to look any further than the man they were about to help. It was true that Lady Isalyn was his beloved's sister, but Steffan had never spoken fondly of her or of his father, so there did not seem to be any love lost between them. In fact, Joah couldn't remember Steffan ever speaking kindly of his sister.

Therefore, Joah had no sense of hesitation when it came to an abduction.

Perhaps this was the best way to avenge Steffan, not only against the House of de Wolfe, but against the family who never really cared for him.

That's what Joah was.

An avenging angel.

And the time for retribution had come.

"YOU HAVE *AGREED*?"

Gilbert had to sit down. He was feeling lightheaded. He'd just been informed that Isalyn had agreed to the betrothal between her and Tor de Wolfe, and Gilbert was having trouble breathing. As he sat heavily, he could hear his daughter snort.

"Father, this is what you wanted, is it not?" she asked, amused. "Why are you taking it so hard?"

They were in the chamber Isalyn was sharing with Isabella. Tor had just returned from the task Isabella had summoned him for and he had then sent Isabella to find Gilbert, but the man had only been lingering in another chamber nearby. He'd never left the building, fearful of his daughter's behavior. In case she decided to attack Tor in a betrothal-induced rage, Gilbert wanted to be there to stop it.

Now, Gilbert had entered the chamber to find Isalyn smiling, Tor smiling, and a pleasant atmosphere all around.

He was stunned.

"I am not taking it hard," he said after a moment. "I am simply surprised."

Isalyn glanced at Tor before replying. "But this *is* what you wanted, isn't it?" she said. "I thought you would be going mad with celebration."

Gilbert cast her a long look. "Daughter, where you are involved, nothing is for certain," he said. Then, he gestured at the corridor outside. "Why do you think I was in the other chamber? I was certain a fight was going to break out and, suddenly, we were going to find ourselves permanent residents of the Blackpool vault."

Isalyn started laughing, looking at Tor, who was also chuckling. "It is not like that at all, my lord, I assure you," he said. "Your daughter and I have come to a fine understanding. I feel confident to say that this betrothal is sealed."

Gilbert stared at him as if still in disbelief. This is exactly what he'd hoped for, what he'd planned for, and now it was happening. His daughter *was* going to marry Tor de Wolfe. As the realization sank in, he broke down into a grin.

"Bloody hell," he muttered. "She *did* agree, didn't she? Now all we need is the wedding and a feast to end all feasts. It shall be the greatest feast the north has ever seen and we shall have it in Carlisle, at my manse of Etterby House. Men will speak of this feast for years to come!"

He was becoming terribly excited for a man who, moments earlier, barely registered emotion.

"As the father of the bride, that is your right, of course," Tor said. "But as a de Wolfe groom, my family is quite large. Unless your manse can hold hundreds, then mayhap we should reconsider and have it at Castle Questing. I know my father would be grateful. When my brother and I married the first time, it was very far away and he was unable to attend. Would you give my father the privilege of hosting the feast?"

Gilbert thought on that a moment before nodding. "Of course," he said. "Etterby's hall can hold about one hundred men, mayhap less, so it might be better to have it at one of your larger fortresses."

"It will still be a feast that men will speak of for years to come."

Gilbert was clearly very excited about the prospect. He stood up, rubbing his hands together with glee.

"When shall we have this marriage?" he asked. "Have either

of you discussed the time and day?"

Tor and Isalyn looked at each other. "Nay, Father," Isalyn said. "We have not gotten that far, to be truthful. I suppose there is no reason to wait except I am sure we would like guests to have time to travel to the feast."

Gilbert waved her off. "You are thinking of your aunt and friends in London," he said. "You can get married now and have the wedding feast at a later time. It will give Warenton and me time to plan the greatest event in the north."

Tor could see there was no stopping Gilbert's excitement. "I am agreeable to that if Isalyn is," he said. "My father will want to invite every ally, you know."

Gilbert threw up his hands. "Let him," he said. "I will invite everyone I can think of. I'll invite the bloody pope. My daughter's wedding is reason enough to celebrate because she is older than most brides and a reckless woman at times, and I never thought she would get married."

When he realized what he'd said in the heat of the moment, he looked at Isalyn in horror, but she started laughing. Tor burst into laughter and, soon, all of them were infected with it.

"Have no fear," Tor said. "We shall have the wedding before the week is out, but I must inform my father so that my immediate family can attend. He would never forgive me if I did not."

"Where will we be married?" Isalyn asked.

Tor looked at her, hardly believing he was discussing this very subject with such joy. After Jane, he never imagined he'd look at a remarriage with anything other than duty and sorrow, but now… now, that wasn't the case. He was as elated as he could possibly be. Looking at Isalyn's lovely face, he was more excited about something than he had been in a very long time.

Perhaps even ever.

"We can summon a priest from Kelso Abbey," he said. "My

grandparents were patrons. We can marry in the great hall and have a family feast afterwards. Is that acceptable?"

Isalyn nodded, looking at him with an expression he'd never seen on her before. It was like… hope.

It was the most beautiful thing he'd ever seen.

"Most acceptable, Tor," she said quietly. "It will give me time to retrieve my good dress. I left it behind at Featherstone."

"I should like to buy you your wedding dress, if I may."

It was a sweet offer, but she looked at him curiously. "Why? I have a perfectly serviceable one back at Featherstone."

Tor was hesitant to say anything more in front of Gilbert because he was about to say something personal, meant only for Isalyn's ears. Truth be told, he was something of a romantic at heart and he'd been very romantic with Jane those years ago – bringing her flowers, a tame bird in a cage, buying her little things, engaging in little gestures that made her happy. Much like his ability to feel emotion again, he thought his romantic soul had died out long ago.

But it was pulsing with life again.

He threw caution to the wind.

"Because I want you to wear something I have given you as a token of my happiness for our marriage," he said. "It will be a dress that you will look at in the years to come and know that the first time you wore it was when we were married. It will mean something to us both. Mayhap I am not explaining it well enough, but that is why I would like to purchase your dress – because it will be new and beautiful, like our marriage. And I would also like to purchase a wedding ring for you."

Isalyn smiled faintly. "I would be happy to wear a dress you gave me for our wedding," she said. "Truly, Tor, I would be honored. It is very thoughtful of you."

"You need not buy her anything," Gilbert said, spoiling the sweet moment. "My stall is in Carlisle. We shall go there and you can pick anything you wish, and it will not cost you a pence. I have several dresses for sale, made by seamstresses to sell to women who like to do the final sewing on them. They are very popular because most of the work is already done. They just need to be finished to the size of the woman who wears them."

Tor looked at him. "Let me be plain," he said. "Whatever I select, I shall pay for. To take it from you without cost defeats the purpose. I must buy it."

Gilbert didn't really understand the need, but he didn't argue with him. "As you wish."

"Do you have rings also?"

"Many."

That made up Tor's mind. "Then it is decided," he said. "We shall go on the morrow."

Gilbert was so happy that he was nearly bursting with it. "Excellent," he said. "Let us celebrate with some of your good wine. We must send word to your father immediately. I am to be related to the House of de Wolfe!"

He was already through the door, rattling off all of the missives he needed to send. Tor grinned at the man, who was quite literally skipping from the building, before turning to Isalyn. She was laughing at her father, hand over her mouth.

"You would think *he* was marrying into the family," she said. "I swear to you that I have never seen him so excited."

Tor snorted. "Wait until you see *my* father," he said. "He may give your father competition for who can be the happiest about this marriage."

"I am looking forward to it."

Tor's gaze lingered on her for a moment before taking a few steps and ending up standing next to her. Reaching out, he took her hand, a touch that sent bolts of excitement through his body. It was quite amazing to him because he never truly thought he would feel like this ever again. Life, once again, was thrilling and for the first time in a very long while, he was looking forward to the future.

He felt as if he were awakening from a very long and very dark slumber.

"As am I," he said, his voice low and hoarse as he lifted her hand and kissed it sweetly. "I am looking forward to all of it. This day has turned out to be quite remarkable. When I awoke this morning, I did not imagine I would have a bride by nightfall."

The kiss to her hand wasn't enough. One moment, he was holding her hand and in the next, he was holding her. It happened so fast. She was in his arms and nothing in the world had ever felt so right or so true. She was soft and supple, her body against his, and he slanted his lips over hers.

He could feel her tremble.

It wasn't a lusty kiss, not at first. He simply wanted to taste her. But she was collapsing against him, her flesh quivering in his embrace, and his kiss turned hungry. It had been close to seventeen years since he'd last kissed a woman, close to seventeen years since his body had known the pleasure of the female form, and that need inside of him came roaring back to life.

Time stood still as he feasted on her lips, feeling her arms wrap around his neck, smelling her sweet scent in his nostrils. The kiss had been as unexpected as the betrothal itself, and he forced to himself to release her before he lost control completely. As he loosened his grip, she very nearly fell to her knees.

Tor grabbed her.

"Are you well?" he asked.

She grinned, mortified and lightheaded. "Of course," she said. "I… I just need to catch my breath."

He smiled at her. "So do I."

She laughed softly. "You are at least on your feet," she said. "I think the last time I was in your arms was when you saved me from that wild horse. It was a different situation."

"Aye, quite."

"I like this one better."

"So do I."

They smiled at each other for a moment and Isalyn reached up, wiping away the saliva from his bottom lip. Her heart was thumping so hard that she could hear it in her ears.

"It has been a momentous day, to be sure," she murmured, her hand on his face. "A long ride this morning led me to Blackpool where I have fallen from a window, covered myself in mud, fought with harpies, and found a husband all in one day."

Tor laughed softly, kissing the hand on his cheek before lowering it. But he didn't let it go. "And the day is not over yet," he said. "Imagine what we will discover by the end of the evening."

"I am waiting with anticipation."

His smile faded. "Your mention of harpies has reminded me that I must tell you why Isabella summoned me earlier," he said. "We had an ill traveler at the gatehouse and I turned him over to Barbara and Lenore to tend. In order to accomplish this, they must be allowed to move about freely, but I have warned them. If they so much as look at you in a manner you do not like, you will tell me. I have threatened them with the vault for the slightest infraction, so they should be on their best behaviors. You will see them moving about Blackpool, so I wanted you to know."

That wasn't something Isalyn wanted to hear, but she understood. "Not to worry," she said. "I can take care of myself, but Isabella… she turned against them and I am certain they did not take kindly to that."

Tor squeezed her hand. "Bella has her father and brother

here," he said. "They wouldn't dare make a move against her with those two about. But you are sweet to worry about her."

"She is a sweet lass," she said. "I like her very much. I have apologized to her for what my brother did… I cannot imagine him jilting a lady as sweet as Isabella."

"Truthfully, she does not seem all that torn up about it," he said. "We all thought she was quite devastated when your brother left her, but she does not seem that way at all."

They were heading from the chamber and Isalyn tucked her hand into the crook of his elbow, as if it were the most natural thing in the world. They had started off as acquaintances, perhaps became fast friends, and now their relationship was progressing naturally, if not quickly. Isalyn had never felt anything more natural or normal than she did when her arm was in his.

As if they had always belonged together.

"Isabella has a good head on her shoulders," Isalyn said. "She is young, but she has a maturity beyond her years. She told me that she was devastated when Steffan left her but that her grandmother told her that he wasn't worth weeping over. Any honorable man worth his weight would not have left her at all."

Tor took her out into the corridor, heading for the open entry door. "That would be my grandmother, Jordan," he said. "We all call her *Matha*, meaning 'mother' in Gaelic. She is our rock. All of these big, powerful sons and grandsons, and she is our foundation. A stronger, wiser woman you will never meet."

"Another de Wolfe family member I am looking forward to meeting."

"I am anxious to introduce you," he said. "But until that time, I believe your father expects us to celebrate with him. I had better tell my Uncle Blayth personally of our betrothal. He would not forgive me if he heard it from someone else."

She looked at him, her eyes glimmering. "You are a considerate soul," she said. "I do believe I like that about you."

He glanced at her, that sweet little face, that glorious blonde hair. He felt like a giddy squire. "I hope there are other things you like about me," he said softly.

She looked away, coyly. "I do, too," she said. "I surely intend to find out."

She could hear him laughing as they made their way out into the sunshine.

CHAPTER SEVENTEEN

THEY WERE IN the room.

Joah had fallen asleep, but he was awoken to the sounds of someone moving around in his chamber. He could hear voices, women speaking softly, and he peeped an eye open to see what was going on.

Two women were moving around in the chamber, both of them with bright red hair and pale skin. One was taller and larger than the other, and she seemed to be the one giving the orders because she would point and whisper and the smaller one would do her bidding.

Joah suspected that these were the two women he had heard when he had first been brought into this chamber. The ones that spoke of Tor de Wolfe and Steffan's sister. He thought perhaps to open his eyes and show them that he was awake but, on second thought, perhaps it was better if he didn't. They had been forthcoming with a great deal of information the last time he feigned unconsciousness, so he was curious to know just how much more he could learn if he continued to play a witless lump.

So, he lay there and pretended to be unconscious as they moved around the room. Someone put another blanket on him and someone else begin washing his face and arms with cool water, which felt very nice. They didn't seem to be as talkative this time around, so Joah decided to show them that he was awake. He wasn't learning anything this way.

He twitched and one of the women gasped. He twitched again and both of them wondered aloud if he was finally awakening. One of them leaned in and spoke softly to him, asking him if he could hear them.

Slowly, he opened his eyes.

"Where… where am I?" he asked weakly.

"You are at Blackpool Castle," the larger woman said. "What is your name?"

Joah closed his eyes, feigning weakness. "My name is Joah," he muttered, seeing no issue in giving them his real name. "How long have I been here?"

"You came earlier today," the woman said. "Do you not remember?"

Joah opened his eyes again. "I think so," he said. "But it all seems like a… dream. A painful dream. Where is my horse?"

The second woman leaned over him from the other side. "In the stables, I would imagine," she said. "Do not worry about him, for he is being tended to. It is you that we must tend now. Where are you from, Joah?"

He grunted as if in pain. "South," he rasped. "I… I am a knight errant in search of my next liege. I thought to come north… de Wolfe has many knights… did I make it to a de Wolfe holding?"

The larger woman nodded. "You did," she said. "I am Lady Barbara and this is my sister, Lady Lenore. Blackpool Castle is the holding of Sir Tor de Wolfe, son of the Earl of Warenton. Do you think you could take some nourishment, Sir Joah?"

Joah nodded, letting both women hold him up as he sipped at a bowl of beef broth. He had a few sips before falling back on the bed, as if sitting up just those short few seconds were all he could bear.

He had to keep up the act.

"Thank you, my ladies," he said, sounding a little more lucid. "You are most gracious."

"Will you take more nourishment?"

He waved them off, weakly. "Later," he said. "I find that conversation might help me to regain my strength just as much as your food. Will you simply speak with me? It has been such a long time since I have spoken to anyone and it is rare when I am in such lovely company."

Barbara smiled faintly, looking over at Lenore, who was smiling quite brightly. Flattery went a long way with Lenore. As Barbara stood up and went to set the bowl of broth down, Lenore took her place next to Joah's bedside.

"How long have you been without a liege?" she asked.

Joah closed his eyes wearily. "Long enough," he said. "My former liege was a cruel man, so I left him to seek my fortune."

Lenore was interested. "Have you been to many exciting places in your travels?"

He looked at her, young and pale and pretty. "A few."

"Did you have exciting adventures?"

"More than a few," he said. "But not without purpose."

"What do you mean?"

"I mean that I have done many things over the years, things that a man of my skill set is capable of," he said. "I do what I can to earn money. You see, I have a sickly mother I send all of my money to, so anything I earn goes to her."

Lenore was greatly sympathetic. "How noble of you," she said sincerely. "You are a very good son to be kind to your mother."

He sighed. "She is my mother, after all," he said. "I have been forced to take some… unsavory tasks that pay very well just so that I can send her the money she needs. I was hoping to find steady work with the House of de Wolfe so I am not forced to take small and terrible tasks any longer."

Lenore looked uncertain. "I do not know if Tor needs any knights, but I will ask," she said. "I will ask him to come and see you."

"Would you?" he said, hope in his voice. "I would be very grateful. But if you hear of anyone needing something, a knight to complete a task of any kind, I would be interested to know what it is. I will do anything for money for my dear mother."

"What *kind* of task?"

It was Barbara asking the question, standing behind Lenore and wiping out a bowl. Joah turned his attention to the lass with the eyes as dark as sin.

"Anything," he said. "If there is a dispute, I have been paid to kill the lord causing it. I have been paid for my sword to fight other men's battles. I have been paid to abduct a bride for men who wanted one. I have been paid for many things."

Barbara stopped wiping the bowl. "You have been paid to abduct women?"

"Many times."

"Where do you take them?"

"Wherever I am told to," he said. "I've dumped women off at nunneries, taken them to men who paid me to abduct them, even taken them to brothels to work off a debt. If you pay me enough, I will take a woman wherever you want me to."

Barbara stared at him for a moment, pausing in wiping the bowl, before slowly resuming. "It must be well-paying work, then," she said.

"It is," he said. "As I said, I have done many things, so if you know of anyone who needs my services, I would be grateful if you could pass along the information."

Barbara didn't reply. She simply turned back to the table

that contained the bowls and cups and medicaments she had brought to tend to the sick man. As Lenore picked up a wet cloth to put on his forehead, Joah lay back and wondered if his words had any impact.

It was difficult to tell.

They had spoken of wanting Steffan's sister abducted or, at the very least, removed from Blackpool. The reasons behind it didn't concern him. All that mattered was that they had unknowingly opened the door for him and he had stepped through, planting an idea in their minds.

Time would tell as to whether or not their talk was just idle chatter.

Or, if they were serious.

BUILT ALONG THE banks of the River Eden, the city of Carlisle was a large, bustling burg. Being that it was so close to the border with Scotland, it had its fair share of Scots. The farmers from the borders would bring their produce and livestock to the Carlisle market every Saturday because a buyer was a buyer as far as they were concerned, and they didn't care if a man was English or Scottish as long as his money was good.

The city had a cosmopolitan flavor to it because it was the largest city this far north, and it also had a large fish market because of its proximity to the Solway Firth. There had been a heavy rain the night before and black clouds were still hanging in the sky to the north but, for the moment, the rain stopped. The inhabitants of the city quickly went about their business before the next round of rain began.

The party from Blackpool Castle had departed at dawn, just

as the rain was letting up. Tor brought a contingent of thirty heavily armed men, not including himself and Fraser, and they were armed to the teeth. Tor did not travel outside of the walls of Blackpool without being heavily armed because the Scots were so volatile in this area. Given that they were going into a town that was known to have a heavy Scottish presence, he wasn't going to take any chances with Isalyn and her father along.

It was a bit of a dichotomy with Gilbert because he was a man who did business in Carlisle on a regular basis, Scots and English alike, and he didn't see the need for such a heavily armed contingent. He had his own knight in Fraser, and he had a personal fifty-man army that was one of the most well supplied armies in all the north to protect his goods, but that was completely different than riding into town escorted by a de Wolfe contingent with enough weapons to start a small war. As he had commented more than once, he felt like the king and his own personal escort.

Isalyn, on the other hand, was even worse. She hated riding with an escort and Tor knew it, so he kept glancing at her, winking at her now and again. Isalyn was certain that he was waiting for her to ride off and escape the escort, but she had no intention of doing so. Even if she *did* hate having a bunch of armed men around her.

But she settled down quickly and, in truth, she really didn't mind. She was flattered that Tor thought enough of her to ensure that she was well taken care of. The previous day had been such a whirlwind and she was still trying to come to grips with a drastic change her life had taken and just a few short hours.

When she had come to Blackpool, it had been with the intention of seeing Tor again and perhaps getting to know him better, but a betrothal had never been on her mind. She could still hardly believe it, but every time Tor turned around to look at her and give her a saucy wink, her excitement in the path that her life had taken was even greater than the moment before.

It all seemed like a dream.

Isalyn had spent the previous evening in the great hall of Blackpool, the center of a celebration with her father leading the toasts. There had been very little conversation between her and Tor because her father seemed intent to monopolize all of the conversation. He was quite drunk early on and, in truth, she didn't blame him. The man had had a week of excessive upheaval, losing a son and now losing a daughter in marriage.

Gilbert's emotions were at the extremes and the alcohol helped him vent those emotions, and even embrace them, because it was a week that had seen both grief and joy. Although Isalyn didn't know her father as well as she probably should have, she knew him well enough to know that he was still reeling from the events of the week and trying to find his footing.

Tor seemed to know that, too. Her betrothed was a man of few words, but he was also a man who seemed quite intuitive. He let Gilbert carry on, cheering the coming wedding and telling stories of Isalyn when she was very young in an attempt to poke fun at her. Considering he and his wife had split when Isalyn had been young, those were the only stories of his daughter that he knew. Isalyn relived stories that she didn't quite remember in some cases, like a little girl who had hoarded a litter of messy kittens in her chamber, or the child who liked to steal pickled onions.

As much as she wanted to stay up all night with Tor and enjoy the celebration, unfortunately, Isalyn grew quite weary early on and was forced to retire when she simply couldn't keep her eyes open any longer. Isabella, who was also at the feast, retired with her and the two of them retreated back to the chamber they now shared. Isalyn was so tired that she fell asleep somewhere in the middle of Isabella's excited chatter about Fraser and how handsome the man was.

Poor Isabella was left talking to herself.

But this morning, she was feeling quite rested, and she had dressed carefully in a sapphire blue gown that reflected the color of her eyes. Her long blonde hair was carefully dressed as it always was, with braids and ribbons, and she knew that she must have done a good job because Tor kept looking at her. By the time they reached the merchant district of Carlisle, he could hardly wait to pull her off her horse.

While a few of the soldiers took the horses to the nearest livery, Gilbert took off down the avenue as he headed for his merchant's stall. As he had explained to Tor, he had an army of servants who manned his stall because he was not there on a daily basis, so his large merchant business had a majordomo and a clerk who essentially ran the day-to-day operations. They were very good at business and had made Gilbert quite rich.

Gilbert's stall was the largest one in the merchant district, directly south of Carlisle Castle. The building was a two-storied structure with every manner of goods that one could wish for, and there was a board over the entry that had the word "Featherstone" burned into it. Once they reached the wattle and daub building, Gilbert welcomed Tor into his stall in the grandest fashion.

As the de Wolfe escort took up positions outside, Tor entered the establishment with Isalyn on his arm. Fraser brought up the rear, as his usual position was to shadow Gilbert everywhere he went as the man's personal protection.

The interior of the stall was very crowded. Tor had been to Carlisle, many times, but he'd never stopped at de Featherstone's stall, so both the size and the content was of some surprise to him. Everything seemed to be in organized sections – items for women, fabric, combs, and things of that nature, and even items for men – but there was so much of it that it was overwhelming. It wasn't so much a single merchant's stall as it was a great bazaar.

But Tor knew what he wanted so it was simply a matter of having Gilbert point him in the right direction. At this hour of the morning, the stall was already full of women shopping. Most of what Gilbert had seemed to be for women and when Tor question him about it, he stated that women were the ones that usually controlled the purse strings in a family, so everything he carried was designed to catch their attention.

And that included the pre-made dresses.

One entire wall was full of such garments. There was a rope strung from one end of the wall to the other with a few posts in the middle to help support the weight of all of the garments that were hanging on the rope. Gilbert had invented a type of hanging frame for these garments that filled them out so women could see them as they were meant to be. It looked like a square made out of wood that hung from a rope.

It was quite inventive and Tor went to the hanging dresses to look for one that he liked. He could have had Isalyn select the dress but as he had told her, he wanted to do it. He wanted to select it and he wanted to pay for it because it was a gift to his wife on their wedding day, and he didn't want any help in selecting it.

He wanted it to be special.

There were quite a few dresses strung up on the rope and there were a few women looking at them. Isalyn was still attached to his arm but he pulled her hand from his elbow and clutched her fingers tightly as he walked from one end of the display to the other.

As he walked, he visually inspected every garment. Some of them were quite spectacular, while others were simple and durable. They were loosely basted, with no hem on the bottom, so they were essentially an unfinished product. He swept the line of dresses twice and was considering a pale blue silk when Gilbert suddenly appeared with his majordomo, both of them carrying garments from the rear of the stall.

"I have been saving this one for someone who could afford it," Gilbert said, holding up the dress. "This is a fine and expensive dress, all the way from Venice. The fabric is called *nacrè*. It is made from two different colors of silk, in this case blue and pink, to give the fabric an iridescent look, like a butterfly's wing."

When Tor heard Isalyn gasp at the sight, he knew he'd found the dress. It was a truly spectacular piece – figure-hugging, with embroidered seed pearls along the neckline and down the sleeves, which were split from mid-arm and trailed well past the hands. The combination of the two colors gave the fabric a lavender color, truly something spectacular to behold.

The majordomo had the matching shift, which he held up for Tor's inspection. It was white, made from silk, and both sleeves were covered with the same seed pearls that were around the neck. When worn with the dress, the shift sleeves would peek out from the split silk sleeves of the gown.

It was a dress made for a queen.

"How much is it?" Tor asked.

Gilbert looked at the dress. "For a garment this rare?" he said. "Very expensive. One hundred and twenty pounds."

"I will take it," Tor said without missing a beat. "She will need slippers to match. Do you have them?"

"Of course," Gilbert said. "I will send her with my majordomo to select everything she needs."

"Good," Tor said. "But first, let me look at your rings."

Gilbert was motioning them to follow and Tor still had Isalyn tightly by the hand because, at this point, she was content to be led around. Tor was the man with a plan and she was happy to let him carry it out. As they followed Gilbert to the rear of the stall, Tor turned to look at her, receiving a sweet smile for his effort. There was something in the air between them, now more powerful than ever before. He smiled in return just as Gilbert reached his destination.

It looked like an enormous wardrobe, but when he opened it, it was full of treasures. In fact, there was an armed guard standing in the shadows nearby, positioned to protect the contents. Gilbert didn't even let Tor look through his stock because he had something in mind right away.

"There is something here I want you to see," he said, looking through the boxes. "Unless it has been sold, but I do not think so. It is rather unique and… here it is!"

He pulled forth a big, teardrop-shaped garnet set in dark yellow gold and handed it to Tor, who studied it carefully. Isalyn was looking over his shoulder, thinking that it was quite lovely but also quite big. She had never envisioned herself wearing a boulder-sized gem on her finger, but she didn't want to spoil Tor's fun. If he wanted her to have it, then she would wear it happily.

But that wasn't the end of it. Gilbert pulled out another ring and held it up to the light.

"I am glad we've not sold this one, either," he said. "The color of the gold is similar to the garnet's setting, but this ring is very, very old. I got it from a man in Brampton whose family has owned their lands for centuries. The story I was told was that the man's great-grandfather, many times over, had found this in the remains of an old Roman house on their property, and the man brought it to me to trade for some goods he needed. It is solid gold and there is an inscription on the inside of the ring."

Tor took it from him, peering closely at it. It was a thin,

dark gold band. There wasn't anything spectacular about it, but he could see the faint outlines of flowers etched into the surface. The more he looked at it, the more he saw a delicate woman's ring. When Gilbert mentioned the inscription, he looked on the inside, barely making out the faded Roman letters.

"*Libet te*," he said softly. "I choose thee."

"Exactly," Gilbert said, beaming. "I thought you might like to give it to my daughter, since you did choose her."

Tor gave him a half-grin, looking at Isalyn to see that she was utterly enchanted by the ring and the inscription. Lifting her hand, he slid it over the third finger on her left hand.

It fit perfectly.

"The Romans believed that a wedding ring should be worn on the third finger of the left hand because there is a vein that goes directly to the heart," Tor said softly. "Whether or not that is true, I do not know, but I remember reading that long ago. This is where it belongs."

Isalyn held up the beautiful ring, watching it gleam in the light. She, too, could see the worn etching, but instead of an old ring with faded flowers, she saw something strong and timeless and romantic.

"I wonder who this belonged to," she said softly. "Whoever it was, her husband must have loved her very much."

Tor was smiling at her expression. That bold, reckless woman he'd first met was a poet and a romantic at heart. He should have known, given the fact that she wrote dramas, but he could see it written with naked abandon all over her face.

"I am certain of it," he said quietly. "Do you like it?"

She nodded eagerly. "I love it."

"And the garnet."

She looked at it, still in Tor's fingers. "I would rather have this simple ring than all the jewels in the world," she said. "This ring has lasted for centuries, and now it is to be upon my hand.

It has endured, as marriage should. As love should. If you are agreeable, I'll have this one."

Tor could see that she meant it. Lifting her hand, he kissed the ring upon it before turning to Gilbert and handing him back the garnet.

"Just this one," he said. "The lady has spoken."

Gilbert shrugged and put it back in the box, but he immediately dug into another box and pulled forth a delicate necklace of small, perfect pearls.

"This is a gift from me to my daughter," he said. "It goes well with the dress."

Tor inspected it, agreeing to accept the gift without even consulting Isalyn. Gilbert, an excellent salesman, also talked Tor into a heavy golden cross with pearls on it and a big, golden chain. He bought that one and didn't even ask about the price, which turned out to be a tidy sum. In all, Tor was going to be out a small fortune, but he didn't care in the least.

They weren't even finished shopping yet.

With the ring still on her finger, Isalyn went about gathering the rest of the things she needed for her wedding dress even as Gilbert tried to talk Tor into purchasing half his stall. Combs, hose, slippers made in The Levant, hair pins… Gilbert walked Tor through all of them, insisting that a lady needed such things, while Tor kept an eye on Isalyn halfway across the stall. Every once in a while, he'd see her roll her eyes at her father's sales pitch.

That only made Tor grin.

A pleasant trip into town that morning turned into a long and expensive day, and Tor couldn't have been happier about it, for one very good reason –

I choose thee.

He had chosen her, indeed.

CHAPTER EIGHTEEN

HER FATHER WANTED to leave today.

That was the entire reason that Isabella was not allowed to go into Carlisle with Tor and Isalyn. Blayth wanted to return home today, or at least start home, and he didn't want to have to wait for Isabella to return from Carlisle.

It was a two-day ride back to Roxburgh Castle and at least another day to Castle Questing, so Blayth wanted to get started. His business here was finished, but he was thrilled at his nephew's betrothal and had spent most of the night sitting up with Tor, celebrating the event and trying to keep the man from reflecting too much on Jane.

Isabella had gone to bed long before her father and Ronan had. Ronan had told Isabella this morning that Tor had become drunk enough to the point where he was starting to lament Jane's passing again, nearly seventeen years after the woman had died.

Although he had not expressed his lament to Gilbert, he had expressed it to Blayth and Ronan. It wasn't that the man had any regrets, nor was he sorry that he was moving on with his life, but it was more a gentle reflection on what could have been. Since Tor's father wasn't there to help his son, Blayth was more than happy to fill that role with his gentle, firm guidance.

This morning, her father and brother were still in bed even as Tor and the rest of the party rode out for Carlisle. Isabella was awake because she had slept all night long, but given that she had seen Barbara and Lenore moving about freely last night, she was not particularly eager to leave her chamber.

She had stayed to her room.

Tor had assured her that Barbara and Lenore were on their best behavior and that they would be of no threat to her, but Isabella was sorry to say that she did not believe him. She had known the pair for far too long and knew what they were capable of, and she knew that they would not forgive her for bearing witness against them. Therefore, she thought it wise to stay out of their way until she left Blackpool.

But that meant a very lonely morning. Fraser had gone into Carlisle with Tor and Isalyn but, in his case, it was because he was Gilbert's knight and he was paid to protect his lord and to go wherever Gilbert did. Isabella understood that, but she wished she had been able to go along simply to be near him.

She was becoming quite enamored with the man.

Fraser was kind and intelligent and wildly handsome, and she had spent a good deal of the feast the previous night speaking to him. He was very proper with her, which was quite a change from her last suitor, who went out of his way to steal kisses or pat her on the bottom. Steffan's behavior had been quite scandalous and she was certain her father did not know the extent of it, but that was for the best. Steffan's actions were hollow and she realized that now. At the time, however, she had felt flattered by his interest.

But Fraser was showing her how an honorable knight really behaved.

He didn't try to steal kisses and he did not try to get her alone. Everything he did was in full view of her father who, somewhere during feast, began to realize that Fraser and Isabella were engaged in a rather long and somewhat flirtatious conversation. At least, Isabella was flirting.

Fraser was simply smiling.

Isabella had a feeling she was going to have to do some explaining to her father once he awoke, but his chamber was next to hers and she could still hear his heavy snoring. Her father was usually a night owl, even at home, so it wasn't unusual for him to be up all night and then sleep until midday.

Ronan was still in his chamber as well, but she could hear nothing coming from his room. Ronan was like their father and had been known to sleep quite a long time if given the opportunity. Isabella could remember the times when her mother would take a bowl of water and throw it on him simply to wake him up. It was something of a running joke with the family, how much Ronan liked his sleep. The older knights were convinced that would end on his first battle march.

There was no sleeping on the battle march.

Therefore, Isabella had no one to talk to and no one to entertain her as she waited for her father and brother to rise. The windows of her chamber faced the inner wall and part of the yew tree, so she didn't even have a good view. By late morning, she was becoming quite restless, restless enough to dare to leave her chamber just so she could walk around and stretch her legs. She had to do something to stave off the bone-numbing boredom. She figured if she saw Barbara and Lenore, she could simply walk the other way.

Quickly.

Boredom was forcing her to take the risk.

Slipping from the chamber, she made her way outside into the cloudy morning. It had rained the night before so the ground was muddy in parts, but she avoided the puddles as she made her way to the great hall. She had a servant bring her some food early that morning, but she was hungry now and she wanted to see if there was food available in the hall.

There was a fairly good chance that she would see Barbara and Lenore there but, somehow, she just wasn't worried about it any longer. The more she thought about it, the more she realized that she wasn't going to let those two women make her a prisoner in her cousin's home.

As she walked, she looked around the bailey and could see Christian over by the inner gatehouse. He hadn't gone to Carlisle that morning, but had remained behind in command. He waved to her and she waved back. She was starting to feel better, more confident and happy. She was about to step into the hall when she heard a voice from behind.

"Good morn to you, Isabella."

Unfortunately, she knew the voice. Startled, she turned to see Barbara standing behind her. What upset her the most was that she never saw or heard the woman coming and, suddenly, she was there.

Isabella's happy mood plummeted.

"Good morn," she said shortly. "I was told you were tending a sick man."

"I am," Barbara said steadily, but her dark eyes were glittering. "He will recover."

"That is good," Isabella said. "I… I was just going to get something to eat. Please excuse me."

She turned around to leave but a word from Barbara stopped her.

"Wait," she said. "Please. I wanted to speak with you."

Isabella stiffened. "Barbara, there is nothing we have to say to one another," she said. "I do not need to hear anything you wish to say to me."

She tried to turn away again but Barbara followed her. "Isabella, we have known each other a very long time," she said. "I thought we were friends. I do not know what Lenore and I ever did that should make you hate us so."

Isabella was becoming impatient. "I do not hate you, but you know that everything I said was true," she said. "You *did* put the oil on the floor of Heather d'Umfraville's chamber and you *did* push Violet le Marr down the stairs. Now that I think on it, there was that lass from Helmsley Castle who awoke one morning with her hair tangled up in the bedframe. Half of her hair had to be cut off and, somehow, I do not think that was an accident because I know you and Lenore were around her that night. You tried to befriend her."

Barbara sighed faintly, averting her gaze when she realized that Isabella had known far more than she had let on. There was no use in denying it.

"You would not understand," she said quietly.

Isabella rolled her eyes. "Understand what?" she said, annoyed. "Understand that you would hurt any woman who would so much as look at Tor? The entire family knows what you and Lenore are capable of. Do you know what they call you? The Vipers. They all say that poor Tor lives with vipers. So if I were you, I would be very careful from now on. One more offense and you will provoke the wrath of Warenton. That is something you would not survive and you know it."

Barbara looked at her in horror. "How can they say such things about us?"

"Because it is true, Barbara," Isabella said. "You and Lenore have dark hearts, although I do not know why. You were raised with people who tried to love you. You had the best education, the best of everything. No one knows why you and your sister turned out the way you have."

Barbara, who was usually so emotionless, began to appear hurt. With that hurt came a weakened composure.

"You do not understand," she said, her voice trembling. "It

did not matter that the House of de Wolfe tried to love us. We were only wards. We were not part of the de Wolfe family. We had lost everything and the only thing we had left was my sister's husband. You have never lost a sister, Isabella. You do not know what it is like to preserve the memory of a loved one."

Isabella looked at her as if she had gone mad. "I thought my father was dead at a young age," she said. "Even though he returned to us, still, I did not try to prevent my mother from remarrying simply to preserve his memory. Life goes on, Barbara. You cannot live in the past and you cannot hurt people to manipulate the future."

"Life should *not* go on," Barbara snapped. "Don't you understand? Tor is all we have to remember our sister. He is *her* husband. He belongs to her!"

Isabella sighed sharply. "He is going to marry Isalyn," she said, watching Barbara's eyes widen. "I am sure he will tell you himself, but I am telling you now. He is marrying her and there is nothing you can do about it. All of your attempts to control him and to keep women away from him haven't worked. He will find happiness in spite of you."

Barbara's hand went to her mouth in shock. "It is not true!"

"It *is* true," Isabella insisted. "He is in Carlisle right now purchasing a few things for their wedding. You had better reconcile yourself to the fact that Tor is marrying again. If you do not, you will only incur his wrath."

Barbara's eyes started to fill with tears. "He does not love her," she muttered. "He only loves Jane. I have heard him say he only loves Jane!"

Isabella could see that the woman was shaken, but she didn't have any sympathy. "What he feels for Isalyn has nothing to do with Jane," she said. "It does not affect his feelings for her. I am sure he will always love Jane, but he has a right to be happy again with a living, breathing wife. Why would you try and take that away from him?"

Barbara blinked, tears splattering. "He said… he said that he did not belong to anyone at the moment, but he soon would," she said, more to herself than to Isabella. "This has happened so fast… Lady Isalyn… it is too fast. He meant *her.* This must not happen!"

With that, she stumbled away, rushing back towards the apartment block.

Isabella watched her go with concern. It was more emotion than she had ever seen from Barbara, speaking as if her heart were broken. As if, somehow, Tor had jilted *her.* To Isabella, it simply didn't seem rational. Barbara didn't seem rational in the least. As she stood there, watching Barbara rush off, Christian suddenly appeared beside her.

"Are you well?" he asked, his eyes on the retreating Barbara.

Isabella turned to the man. He was tensed up, ready to protect her.

But she still felt uneasy.

"I am," she said. "She did not try to harm me in any way. She simply wanted to talk."

"What about?"

Isabella sighed. "I'm not sure," she said. "She thinks I hate her. I told her I do not hate her, but she does not have a good heart. Christian, she said something strange. She said that Tor only loves Jane and when I told her he was marrying Isalyn, she said it must not happen."

Christian sighed heavily. "You told her about the betrothal?"

"She was going to find out sooner or later."

Christian couldn't argue with that. "True, I suppose," he said. "But until Tor and the others return, stay where I can see you. Or go to your chamber and bolt the door. Will you please do that for me?"

Isabella nodded. “I will,” she said. “I want to stay out here in the sunshine for a little while. The walls of my chamber have been closing in around me all morning. I wish I’d gone to Carlisle, too.”

He smiled, patting her on the shoulder. “They’ll be back soon,” he said. “I mean, Fraser will be back soon.”

She looked at him sharply. “Why would you say that?”

He was looking at her, an annoying look like a taunting brother would give a sister. “Mayhap because that’s what you want to hear,” he said. “I saw the two of you talking last night at the feast. You have the man captivated, Bella.”

Isabella turned her nose up at him. “You think you’re so smart, Christian Hage,” she said. “I was supposed to be married only last week and now you have me married to someone else so soon?”

Christian scowled. “Who said anything about marriage?” he said. “But Fraser seems like a good man. You can have a nice, long betrothal before the marriage so people will not talk and say you flitted too soon from one man to another.”

She stuck her tongue out at him. “Go away, you big dolt,” she said. “I’m going to sit over by the keep and wait for Tor and Isalyn to return.”

“And Fraser.”

She took a swing at him but he laughed and easily ducked, darting off and leaving his cousin frustrated.

But she wasn’t really frustrated. Isabella grinned when Christian couldn’t see her, knowing the man was on to something but refusing to admit it.

Still, she would stay where he could see her.

Wandering over to a stone bench by the keep, her thoughts turned from Fraser back to Barbara. She was anxious to tell Tor about their conversation so the man could be prepared.

This must not happen!

Something told her that there was going to be trouble.

CHAPTER NINETEEN

When Tor and Isalyn returned from Carlisle, Isabella was waiting for them.

It was early afternoon and the clouds overhead were gathering and threatening more rain as the party left their horses in the outer bailey and made the trek to the inner bailey on foot. Isabella had been sitting in the intermittent sunshine on the stone bench next to the keep, with a direct view of the gatehouse, and the moment they passed through, she was up and moving swiftly for them.

Isalyn saw her first.

"I can hardly wait to show Isabella my dress," she said. But then, she sobered a little. "You do not think it will upset her, do you? She was so recently supposed to marry and that was taken away from her. I do not want to make her sad."

Tor could see his cousin heading in their direction, her braids lifting in the wind. "I think she would very much like to see your new things," he said. "She is not a selfish girl. She would not begrudge you your happiness. You *are* happy, aren't you?"

Isalyn gazed up at him, a smile playing on her lips. "Very much, my provincial knight," she teased. "And you?"

"Very much, my reckless old bride."

They laughed at each other as Isabella came near. "Stop looking so deliriously happy," she snapped, though it was in good fun. "You two make me sick and I am certain it is only going to get worse."

Tor snorted. "It will, I am positive," he said. "What are you still doing here? I thought you were going home with your father."

Isabella cocked an eyebrow. "He drank too much last night and is only now breaking his fast," she said. "I do not think we will be leaving before tomorrow. Ronan is even worse. He is still in bed."

Tor grinned. "Where is Uncle Blayth?"

"In his chamber," Isabella said. "How was your visit to town?"

"Productive."

Isabella looked around at the party, lugging heavy chests. "Where is Lord de Featherstone?"

"He chose to remain in Carlisle," he said. "He sent Fraser back with us, however. You should be grateful."

Isabella looked at him, her eyes narrowing when she saw that he was smirking. "I have no idea what you mean," she said dismissively, but she quickly changed the subject and tucked her hand into the crook of his free elbow. "Tor… I saw Barbara this morning. She did not know that you and Lady Isalyn are getting married and she… well, may we go somewhere and speak about it?"

It was an unhappy change of focus and Tor lost some of his good mood. "You were not threatened, were you?"

Isabella shook her head. "Nay," she said. "My father and brother are here. Christian was here also, so I was well protected. But… I must speak to you about it, please."

He was relieved that Barbara had at least behaved herself

while he was away, but he was concerned with the urgency in Isabella's tone.

"Certainly," he said. "Let us take these treasures to your chamber and then we may speak."

"Good," Isabella said, looking to Isalyn. "Did you get some beautiful things?"

Isalyn nodded eagerly as the focus shifted to her. "The dress Tor selected for me is exquisite," she said. Then, she held up her hand to show her the wedding ring. "And he bought this for me, too."

Isabella looked at it closely. "A pretty gold band," she said. "But no stone?"

Isalyn took the ring off. "No stone," she said. "This is an ancient Roman wedding ring and what is inscribed inside of it is more valuable to me than any stone. Can you see it?"

Isabella was trying to get a look at it. "*Libet te*?"

"I choose thee."

Isabella's mouth popped open. "Oh, Isalyn," she gasped. "How beautiful. How sweet!"

Isalyn took the ring and put it back on her finger. "It is both of those things," she said. "I cannot wait to unpack the trunks so you can see the other things Tor has purchased. He was quite generous."

Isabella nodded eagerly as Tor turned to the soldiers following them and whistled, motioning towards the apartment block. They headed in that direction and Isabella caught sight of Fraser, bringing up the rear. She let go of Tor and stood aside as the column passed, waiting for Fraser to catch up to her.

His smile upon her was warm.

"Good day, my lady," he said. "I thought you were going home with your father."

She took up pace beside him, walking towards the apartment block. "He had too much drink last night," she said. "Our trip is delayed until tomorrow."

"Good," Fraser said. "That gives me more time to talk to you. I was rather lamenting the fact that you would soon be back at Castle Questing."

Isabella looked at him coyly. "You can always come and visit."

He grunted. "I would need to speak to your father first before doing that."

"Just to visit?"

He averted his gaze, struggling with a reply, when he suddenly came to a halt and grasped her by the elbow, pulling her to a halt as well. The soldiers carrying the trunks continued on, following Tor and Isalyn, and Fraser waited until they were far enough away before speaking again.

"I only know to be direct, so I shall be direct now," he said. "I have been thinking about this all morning. Though we have only known each other for a single day, I found our conversation last night to be most… pleasant. Before you retired for the evening, it was one of the better conversations I have ever had. I found myself quite distressed when your father said that he would be taking you home today."

Isabella was trying to play it casual. The last time she got excited over a man speaking sweetly to her, she ended up betrothed to a man who left her at the church. Therefore, she wasn't about to get too excited, as much as she wanted to.

"As I said, you may visit," she said. "You do not need my father's permission to visit Castle Questing."

"I need it if I am to visit you."

"For what purpose?"

He just stared at her for a moment before lowering his gaze. "Forgive me," he said. "I thought… surely you are not ready for another man to call upon you so soon after Steffan's death. But last night, I thought… it does not matter what I thought. That was horribly inconsiderate of me and I deeply apologize."

He started to back away from her, but Isabella followed, realizing her attempts not to become overexcited had the opposite effect. She put her hand on his arm, grasping him before he could get away.

"Stop," she commanded softly. "Fraser, I would like very much for you to come to Castle Questing and call on me. I was only trying to coerce you into saying what was on your mind."

He paused, looking at her rather guardedly. "You need not coerce me into saying what is on my mind," he said. "Ask me and I shall tell you."

"Then I am asking. What are your intentions?"

"I would like to court you."

A smile spread across her lips. "I would like that, too."

He blinked as if surprised by her answer. "But… Steffan…"

She shook her head. "It was never meant to be," she said. "He was overwhelming in his pursuit, insincere in his flattering, and probably told me more lies than I care to admit. At the time… well, I had never really had a suitor before and I suppose I fell into the flattery trap. I believed what he told me, but when he did not show up for our marriage, I realized I'd been tricked. It was foolish of me, but it did one thing – any emotion I felt for him was quickly gone until humiliation was the only thing left."

Fraser's gaze lingered on her a moment. "You were not the fool," he said quietly. "*He* was."

"That is sweet of you to say so."

"It is the truth," Fraser said, lowering his gaze again and taking a deep breath. "I must be further honest, my lady. We spoke briefly on my family last night, but I did not tell you all of it. My family is not wealthy. In fact, I serve de Featherstone because he pays well and I must earn my way in life, so if your father is thinking to marry you to a prestigious knight from a great family, I am afraid that is not me. But I am honorable, loyal, and have worked hard to accumulate what money I have earned. Upon the passing of my father, I will inherit Welton Castle and the title of Lord Faldingworth, and I intend to return my family's estate to the powerful bastion it used to be, but for now… now, I must serve de Featherstone."

She was looking at him with an amused twinkle in her eyes. "Are you proud of your position, then?"

"I am."

"Then so am I. Fraser, truly, you need not worry."

"But I fear your father may not approve because I do not have a great name, nor do I serve a great house."

She laughed softly. "I am the eldest, and only, daughter of Blayth de Wolfe, brother to the Earl of Warenton," she said. "Warenton lands are four times the size of any other earldom in the north and my father commands thousands. We are the largest family in the north."

"I am aware."

"Then you must realize that we do not need wealth or lands, for we have enough of our own," she said. "A man of good character is worth more than money or lands, and should you and I marry, you would serve the Earl of Warenton. That is much better than serving de Featherstone."

Fraser didn't say anything for a moment. It was clear that he was mulling over what she had said.

"Then I must be plain before this goes any further," he said. "It is true that, someday, I would like to serve a big house. That has always been my desire. But you… I do not court you because you are a de Wolfe and my path to service would be a simple thing. I would court you simply because you are who you are, and for no other reason. You could be the daughter of a peasant for all I care and I would still want to court you. What you are makes no difference to me – it is *who* you are. Do you understand?"

Isabella nodded. "I do," she said, smiling. "And the same thing can be said for you. I do not care that you do not come from a great family. It is your heart I care about and nothing more."

A smile tugged at the corner of Fraser's mouth. "Then we understand one another."

"We do."

"Then I would speak to your father before you leave."

Reaching out, she looped her hand into the crook of his elbow. "I happen to know where he is."

Fraser had never been prouder than he was at that moment, heading towards the apartment block with Isabella on his arm. It fortified him for what was to come.

But what was to come was not what he had expected.

The day was about to take a dark turn.

"SHE SAID THAT?"

Isabella nodded solemnly. "She did."

Tor simply shook his head in disgust and turned away.

Isabella and Fraser entered the apartment block to find Blayth standing in the chamber that Isabella had shared with Isalyn, speaking to Tor as Isalyn removed all of the pretty things he'd purchased for her in Carlisle and placed them across the bed. Fraser had hoped to speak to Blayth privately and, in truth, he was a little intimidated by the big, scarred warrior, but his plans were thwarted when Tor asked Isabella to elaborate on her concerns with Barbara.

So, she told him. As Fraser shut the door quietly so the conversation wouldn't be overheard, Tor wasn't surprised by what Isabella said.

But like her, he was concerned.

"I am sorry I told her, Tor," Isabella said, thinking he was miffed at her. "But I knew that she and Lenore would know soon enough, so I saw no harm in telling her, yet when I did, it was as if she went mad. She muttered to herself and ran off. I thought you should know."

Tor sighed heavily and reached out, putting a hand on her soft cheek. "Not to worry, Bella," he said. "I am not angry with you. It is true that Barbara and Lenore would know soon enough, but I do not like what she said to you. She really said that it must not happen?"

Isabella nodded. "I would not lie to you."

"I know you wouldn't," he said quickly. "I simply meant… that was a concerning thing to say. I would have hoped that she would have at least accepted the news stoically, but it seems that she did not."

Isabella shook her head. "Nay, she did not," she said. "Tor… I have seen Barbara and Lenore at their most wicked. They are capable of almost anything and it seems to me that they may try to do something to Isalyn to prevent her from marrying you."

Tor looked at Isalyn, who was smoothing out the white silk shift with the pearl sleeves on the bed, pretending that she wasn't listening. She was going on as if nothing could bother her, but Tor knew she must have been distressed listening to the conversation. She was simply trying to be brave. Scratching his head, he looked at his uncle.

"Help me," he pleaded softly. "I fear I have lost my perspective in this situation. They are Jane's sisters and I do not want to harm them, but I do not want them here at Blackpool any longer. They are a danger and I will not allow them to threaten Isalyn. You have the advantage of being neutral in this circumstance, so tell me what you would do."

Blayth could hear the distress in his nephew's voice, unusual for the usually composed man. Truth be told, he was very glad he was being asked that question because he had some opinions on the matter.

He had for a long time.

"Do you want my honest opinion, Tor?" he asked.

Tor nodded firmly. "Please," he said. "Tell me and I shall do as you say."

"Are you certain?"

"I am."

Blayth rubbed his hands together thoughtfully. He'd been waiting for this very question for years and he was prepared. Tor had been in denial for so long that this was an unexpected moment, but not entirely unexpected considering the way Tor kept looking at Isalyn.

He had a bride to protect.

"Do not take what I am about to say as an insult, but from the start, you failed where Barbara and Lenore were concerned," he said. "They were quite young when you brought them to Castle Questing and you turned them over to Scott's wife and told her to do with them as she pleased. Avrielle molded them, taught them, guided them, but you were their only family and you essentially cast them off. I am not trying to hurt you, but what I am about to tell you is the only solution as I see it."

"What is that?"

"Send them away," he said flatly. "Armathwaite Nunnery is near Carlisle. Barbara and Lenore have been able to do whatever they please since they were brought into our family and you have not held them in check, nor have you disciplined them. They do not know what discipline is. You must send them to the nuns at Armathwaite and let them impose their strict rules upon them. They are Benedictines, Tor. That means their order is one of obedience and strict discipline. Unless you want your new wife looking over her shoulder for the rest of her life, it is the only solution. Let those two vipers atone for their sins, of which they have many."

Tor knew he was right and tried not to feel like a failure because of it. He had created a pair of monsters and now he had to deal with the consequences. He glanced at Isalyn, who was holding up a sheer gossamer scarf so Isabella could see it and he knew there was no other choice. He realized that he was quite eager to get rid of them, especially when Barbara's words to Isabella sounded like a threat.

He couldn't let any lingering guilt for Jane muddle him any longer.

"I thought about finding the pair husbands to solve the problem, but that will take time," he said. "Moreover, I do not want to saddle any man with women like that. It would be a cruel trick to play on my worst enemy, so you are correct. Armathwaite is an excellent suggestion."

"I am glad you think so," Blayth said, but his manner softened. He really wasn't trying to be cruel. "Tor, we know you thought you were doing what Jane wanted by taking care of her sisters, but you were so young at the time. We know you did what you thought was best, but there is an old saying – *nati sut mala*. Do you know what that means?"

"Evil born?"

Blayth nodded. "It means that some people are just born wicked," he said. "Mayhap Barbara and Lenore were just born that way and there was nothing you could have done about it even had you known. Jane was a good and true wife, but sometimes that does not always carry over to the rest of the siblings. It is not something you should blame yourself for, but ignoring it *was* your fault. I am proud of you for finally facing the reality of those two and doing as you must. Do not feel guilty for it."

Tor smiled weakly. "I am trying not to," he said. "But I know that Jane would have been appalled at what they have done. She did not have an evil bone in her body."

Blayth had never met Jane, but he knew Tor was a man of character. He surrounded himself with people of character, the exception being Barbara and Lenore. Out of guilt, they had been his blind spot.

But the blind man could now see.

"I am sure she was a fine woman," Blayth said. "That was never in dispute. As for her sisters, would you like me to send a missive to Armathwaite and relay the situation? We can send Barbara and Lenore to the nunnery as soon as you wish."

Tor thought on that a moment. "Nay," he said. "No missive. I will personally escort Barbara and Lenore to the nunnery and explain the situation myself to the nuns. I shall also leave a sizable donation for their care. This is something I must see to myself. They are my problem, after all."

Blayth understood. "You should do it sooner rather than later."

Tor nodded. "I will. Tomorrow, if I can."

Blayth smiled at him, patting him on the shoulder and calling to his daughter to attend him so the betrothed couple could be alone. Isabella went, but slowly, until Blayth grasped her by the hand and dragged her out of the chamber. Fraser, who had been lingering by the door, followed close behind. When he shut the door quietly behind him, Tor turned to Isalyn.

"I am sure you heard all of that," he said quietly.

Isalyn was in the process of draping the gossamer scarf over her shoulders, admiring the glistening material. "I did," she said. "But it was not my place to interrupt you or give my opinion. May I do that now?"

"Of course."

"Your uncle's suggestion is an excellent one," she said. "Barbara and Lenore will be well tended at the nunnery. They will have a life of purpose and discipline. You said yourself that they did not wish to marry, and they cannot remain here, so the nunnery is a logical solution. I do not mean to sound callous, but let Armathwaite have the harpies."

Tor gave her a half-grin at the name she used for the pair, true as it was. "I suppose I should have done it long ago," he said. "This entire situation has me ashamed."

Isalyn shook her head. "You should not be," she said. "No matter how hard you try, you cannot control the thoughts and actions of others. Barbara and Lenore have made their own choices."

"True," he said. "But I feel as if I should make amends to the young women they injured. Poor Heather d'Umfraville lost three front teeth because of them."

Isalyn winced, putting her hand to her mouth at the ghastly thought. "Poor woman," she said. "But everyone believed it was an accident, correct?"

"They did."

"Then mayhap you should simply let things lie. What good will it do to let her know it was deliberate? It will only hurt her more."

He sighed. "I suppose that is true," he said. "I saw her a year after the accident and her father had taken her to a surgeon in London who had made an appliance for her with the teeth of corpses. She could put it in her mouth and it looked as if she had never lost those front teeth, so thank God the damage was somewhat repairable."

"What a remarkable thing," Isalyn agreed. "Since she has been restored, I would just let her continue to think the incident was an unfortunate accident. But you are very sweet to want to make amends."

Tor smiled at her and, as if suddenly realizing they were alone, reached out and pulled her into his embrace. It was the first time he'd ever done that, freely and without reserve, and Isalyn wrapped her arms around his neck. He was so tall that he had to bend over in order to hold her and she clung to him tightly.

For a moment, they simply held one another, feeling warmth against warmth.

It was a magical moment.

"I want to take care of Lenore and Barbara before we wed," he said huskily, his face in the side of her head. "I hope you do not mind, but I do not want them hanging over our heads or interfering with our marriage in any way. Let me take them to Armathwaite first so that we may only focus on our life together. That is all I want to think about."

Isalyn's fingers were in his hair. "I understand and I agree," she said. "Do you really intend to take them to the nunnery tomorrow?"

"I would do it tonight, but I suppose it is the compassionate thing to give them time to choose which possessions they wish to take," he said. "But truthfully, I have lost my perspective with this. What do you suggest?"

She pulled back to look him in the eyes. "You are worrying too much," she said softly. "It seems to me that you went through years of inactivity where they were concerned and now, you are concerned that you are not reacting swiftly enough. Taking them in the next day or two is fine."

He smiled faintly, leaning forward to kiss her soft mouth. "Thank you," he murmured. "When they are safely away and all is well again, we shall go to Castle Questing so you can meet my father."

She chuckled. "Then you must retrieve my father from Carlisle first. He will not forgive you if you visit Warenton without him."

"Why did he stay in Carlisle, anyway?"

She shrugged. "Something about his majordomo stealing from him," she said. "The last time I visited, years ago, he said the same thing, so I think it is something he accuses the man of on a regular basis."

"But still, the majordomo remains."

She nodded, giggling. "He does."

Tor pulled her close once again, feeling her body molding against his. He could feel her breasts against him, her belly. She was round and pleasing, and he could feel himself becoming aroused. It had been years since he'd last had a woman, and being a man in his prime, had all of the normal needs of a man.

Especially where Isalyn was concerned.

She made him feel like his entire body was awakening from a long and dark slumber.

"Let us not speak of your father or of the harpies any longer," he muttered, burying his face in the side of her head again. "Let us only speak of us."

Isalyn gave in to his overwhelming heat, his power. She closed her eyes, savoring his embrace.

"What do you wish to speak of?" she whispered.

He sighed with great contentment before picking her up and carrying her, her body trailing down his, over to the bed so he could sit down. He sat, putting her on his lap.

"Of you," he murmured, kissing her neck. "Of us. My father has ten children. I should like to have at least that many."

Her eyes flew open and she looked at him in horror. "*Ten* children?"

He fought off a grin. "Too many?"

She could see that he was teasing her, so she played along.

"Nay," she said. "But I think they should all be girls."

Now, his eyes opened wide. "All girls?"

She nodded confidently. "Girls are much easier to manage than boys."

He grunted. "I have not done very well with girls in my care in the past."

Her smile faded. "You will when I am in charge of them," she said. "They will be disciplined and loved and encouraged to be creative. They will be the most cherished and well-mannered lasses in the north."

His smile returned, just a little. "You'll have them writing dramas?"

"Mayhap," she said, a twinkle in her eyes. "Riding wild horses, writing dramas, and forging their way in this world. That was how you met me, after all. It is not such a bad thing."

He leaned forward to kiss the tip of her nose. "It is not," he said. "And after we are married, we will make plans to go to London and look for property to purchase. I will speak with my Uncle Edward. He spends most of his time in London and will know who we may speak with. Mayhap there is an old earl somewhere, selling his London townhome."

"I am looking forward to it."

"Are you really?"

Her answer was to lean forward, kissing his lips sweetly. That was the only answer Tor needed. He lost himself, winding his fingers in her carefully styled hair, but she didn't stop him. He pulled her down to him and she let him. She was soft and sweet, and he feasted on her like a man who hadn't tasted a woman in many years.

Truth be told, he'd only had one sexual experience before he met Jane and he hadn't had any since. Oh, there had been urges, but he hadn't given in to them simply because he felt as if touching another woman was betraying Jane. He was confused and sad, and considered celibacy a necessary evil.

But he didn't feel that way any longer.

He was prepared to feast on a woman he would be faithful to until the end of his life.

That delicious figure was calling to him, those full breasts and generous hips. His kisses became more forceful, his tongue sliding into her mouth as she gasped. But he suckled on her tongue, settling her down, and she began to mimic his movements. Her body became boneless and pliable.

In a short amount of time, Tor was on fire.

Laying Isalyn on the bed beside him, his big, warm body partially covering her, his weight bearing down on her, but she didn't resist. Her arms around his neck held him fast. When he tried to pull away a little so his weight would not be so heavy on her, she wouldn't let him move. She suckled on his tongue as he has suckled on hers.

The fire began to burn out of control.

Tor didn't keep her waiting. As his lips feasted on hers, a big hand closed gently over a full breast, feeling the silken texture against his palm. The action startled Isalyn but she didn't pull away from him, not even when he pulled the top of her gown and shift down, down to the point where he nearly exposed the nipple. Still, she didn't resist and he pulled the dress down a little further.

The nipple sprung free.

His mouth clamped over it.

Isalyn gasped in both surprise and ecstasy as he began to suckle. Every tug sent bolts of excitement shooting through her body and between her legs, a flame ignited that she'd never before experienced. She had no idea what it was, but something was pulsing to life. The more he fondled her, the more Isalyn seemed to respond.

The gown was coming off.

Isalyn didn't even know how it came off, only that it had. The ties were unfastened and she lifted her arms so he could pull it over her head, and suddenly it was on the floor. She was nude, with only her hose on her legs, tied with matching ribbons, and the mere sight drove Tor mad with desire. His mouth left her breasts, his lips feasting over her belly and her hips. His mouth, his hands, were everywhere.

Isalyn lay there and let him.

Tor was being consumed by a wildfire now. He returned to her plump breasts, nursing against them hungrily as his fingers sought out the dark curls between her legs. She was already wet and swollen, her body preparing for his entry, and he pushed a finger into her tight, wet passage, slowly moving in and out of her, mimicking the thrusting that would soon be taking place. Isalyn groaned and opened her legs to him, instinctively, and Tor could wait no longer.

As fast as lightning, he ripped off what clothing he had on – a mail coat, padded tunic, belt, breeches – they all ended up on the floor and he threw himself down on top of her again, listening to her grunt as his weight came down. Carefully, he positioned his heavy phallus at her threshold, pushing into her slick and waiting body. He was so big that Isalyn groaned at his sensual intrusion, wriggling her hips as she tried to make it more comfortable, to ease the sting of possession. But her body was so prepared for this moment that a sting was all it was as he thrust into her, breaking her maiden's barrier, claiming this woman for his own as he'd never claimed another. She was his, body and soul, and nothing on this earth could ever separate them.

She belonged to him, forever.

Carefully, Tor began to thrust, his arms going around her as he gathered her up tightly against him, her chest to his, the feel of her soft breasts against his flesh feeding his lust. Beneath him, Isalyn groaned and gasped at the new sensations, her legs opening wider for him as her nails dug crescent-shaped wounds into his broad back. Her body was responding to his as if she were made for him and him alone.

She wanted more.

Tor had never experienced anything so sweet in his entire life. His body pounded into hers and she accepted all of him, her pelvis instinctively moving against his. It was pure magic, his manhood burying itself into her wet folds as her body tried to coax forth his seed. Her hands, soft and warm, moved from his back to his buttocks timidly. At first, her touch was light, like butterfly wings, becoming acquainted with the feel of his rock-hard backside. After a moment, her touch became bolder and she squeezed his cheeks in a gloriously delicious move.

Tor surrendered without a fight.

His hot seed exploded into her body and Isalyn felt him shudder as he released. He kept moving within her, however, his hand moving to the junction between her legs, stroking her until she, too, experienced her first release. It was as if her entire body exploded, gasping as waves of pleasure rolled over her.

As the ripples died down, Tor remained buried in her, kissing her gently, showing her without words how much he was coming to adore her. An unexpected woman at the most unexpected time in his life had quickly become part of him.

He'd never been overwhelmed like this before.

"I'm sorry," she whispered in his ear.

He stopped kissing her and looked at her. "For what?"

Isalyn looked rather dazed, but there was no mistaking the warmth in her eyes. "For not putting up more of a fight," she murmured. "We are not even married yet and I let you… I pray you do not think too poorly of me."

He looked at her strangely. "I pray you do not think too poorly of *me*," he said. "We should not have taken such liberty and I know that, but the moment I touched you, common sense and reason seemed to vanish. What I have come to feel for you,

Isalyn… I am overwhelmed with you. All of you."

She smiled, her hands going to his face, stroking his brow gently. "Then mayhap we had better marry as soon as possible so that we do not feel guilty should we become overwhelmed with each other again."

He snorted. "So your father does not turn Fraser loose on me if he realizes I cannot keep my hands from you."

"I think you can defeat Fraser."

"I can, but if I hurt him, Isabella would never forgive me."

Isalyn chuckled, throwing her arms around his neck again and pulling him close. Tor wrapped her up in his big arms, savoring her flesh against his, closing his eyes as he inhaled her delicious female musk.

"Isalyn?"

"Aye?"

"What would you say if I told you that I adore you?"

"I would say that I adore you, too."

"I may even love you."

"I may even love you, too."

That was all Tor wanted to hear. He'd been waiting his whole life for this moment and he didn't even know it.

He would have liked to have taken more time with her, but there would be all the time in the world after they married. They were in a rather risky position at the moment, so with a final kiss, Tor pushed himself off her and pulled her into a sitting position. He went around gathering clothes that had been thrown off in the heat of passion and they quickly dressed. He'd barely finished pulling his boots on when Isabella was knocking at the door, demanding to come in.

With a final wink to Isalyn, Tor opened the door for Isabella and ducked out as she ran in.

And Isabella was none the wiser as to what had just occurred.

Magic.

CHAPTER TWENTY

"DID YOU MEAN what you said?"

Lying on the uncomfortable mattress in the borrowed chamber, Joah looked at Barbara curiously.

"I do not know," he said. "What did I say?"

Barbara was upset. Her face was pale and there were tears in her eyes, and she stood over Joah twisting her fingers nervously. A few feet behind her, Lenore watched her sister with concern.

"You said that you could be hired for a… task," Barbara said.

Joah nodded. "I can, my lady," he said. "Do you know of someone who needs my skills?"

Barbara nodded shortly. "I do," she said. "*Me.*"

Joah's eyebrows lifted. "You?" he repeated. "What can I possibly do for you, my lady?"

Barbara was trying very hard to control her emotions, but she wasn't doing a good job. She was so cold most of that time that when she did feel something, it shot out of her like sparks out of a snapping log.

Pop… pop…

"I want you to remove someone from Blackpool."

Behind her, Lenore gasped, but Joah was fixed on Barbara.

"As you wish," he said steadily. "Who am I removing?"

Barbara's jaw ticked. "A lady," she said. "I will pay you well but ask no questions. I want you to take her somewhere and sell her to men who will take her far away. Sailors, mayhap, or a merchant caravan. I do not care who. But I want her taken away so that she will never return."

Joah could see she meant it and he had a suspicion as to who it was. He couldn't have planned this better if he had tried and as he lay there, he tried not to look too pleased about it.

Finally… the seeds he had planted were taking root.

"I will need a name of the lady, at least," he said evenly. "But I will not ask for your reasons, as they are your own. Who am I to remove?"

Barbara took a deep breath, mulling over her answer, before replying. "A woman named Isalyn de Featherstone," she said. "She must be removed from here, quietly and efficiently. Can you do this?"

"I can."

"Now?"

Since he really wasn't sick or injured, he gave up the ruse altogether. He propped himself up on his elbows. "I suppose so," he said. "Do you have a plan in mind?"

Barbara nodded stiffly. "I will pay you twenty pounds," she said. "It is almost all of the money I have, but it will be worth it to be rid of her. My sister will take a horse around the inner wall and back to the postern gate. You will be waiting there and I will lure Isalyn to the kitchen yard where you will take her through the postern gates and escape."

Joah frowned. "Will there not be soldiers about to see this?"

Barbara shook her head. "They mostly congregate near the main gatehouses and most especially at the outer gatehouse," she said. "They will probably not think much of Lenore going out for a ride around the inner wall and their attention will be on her while you slip out through the postern gates."

He still looked doubtful. "Gates," he repeated, emphasizing the plural. "There are *two* postern gates?"

Barbara nodded. "There are, but they are not heavily guarded," she said. "They are manned by the servants and the inner gate is usually kept unlocked, but I know where the keys are kept. I can open both gates. The servants will not question me, as I usually oversee the kitchens as part of my duties. They will not think twice about what I am doing."

It seemed foolproof enough and Joah reluctantly nodded. "Very well," he said. "How do I get to the gate without being seen?"

"You are very close to the kitchen yard now," Barbara said. "You can stay to the shadows from the wall and make your way to the gate. It will not be that difficult."

"As you say," he said. "But I want my own horse."

Barbara shook her head. "It will look strange if Lenore takes your horse out for a ride, so she must take another." She was starting to look desperate. "Please… will you do this?"

Of course he would. This was the best of all worlds for Joah, having fallen right into his lap. He'd primed the women based on the conversations he had overheard from them and now his plan was coming to fruition. He'd take Steffan's sister far away and then he could probably make more money ransoming her back to de Wolfe. Or, he'd sell her to the highest bidder, as Barbara had suggested.

Either way, his vengeance would prove lucrative.

He would make sure of it.

"I told you that I will," he said after a moment. "When do you wish for this to take place?"

"Today," Barbara said. "Now, if you are able. I saw Isalyn come through the gatehouse with Tor and men bearing trunks, so she is here, somewhere. Probably in the chamber downstairs that she shares with Isabella."

"She will not go with you, Barbara," Lenore said, her voice trembling. "If you try to lure her away, she will not trust you."

That was very true and Barbara knew that, but she was desperate. "But someone must lure her to the postern gate," she said to her sister. "Will you do it? She is not as mistrustful of you."

Lenore nodded unsteadily. "Aye," she said. "But what should I say?"

"Tell her that you wish to show her something," she said, sounding annoyed. "Tell her that you are very sorry for everything we have done and we wish to show her something… nay… *give* her something. Tell her you wish to give her something and it is in the kitchen yard near the postern gate. If she demands to know what it is, tell her that it is a surprise. Beg her forgiveness if you must, but get her out to that postern gate."

By the time she was finished, her voice was lifting and she was becoming animated. Lenore nodded, cowering in the face of her sister's irritation.

"I will," she said. "Shall I go now?"

Barbara looked at Joah, propped up on his elbows. "Can you do this now?"

Joah sat up completely, swinging his legs over the side of the bed. "As soon as you pay me, I can."

Barbara ran for the door. Her money was in the chamber she shared with Lenore in the keep, one of those massive chambers that was luxurious but too vast to hold a goodly amount of heat in the wintertime. Even so, she and Lenore had shared one since their arrival to Blackpool and it was where they kept all of their precious possessions.

"I will return," she said as she put her hand on the latch. "Lenore, help him with whatever he needs so that he is well prepared. I will locate Isalyn so that you know where to seek her. We must do this swiftly and silently, before Tor discovers what has happened. And, Sir Joah… you must flee faster than you have ever fled in your life. If Tor catches you, he will kill you."

Joah didn't seem too concerned. "I need my possessions," he said. "I need my sword. Where are they?"

"They were brought here," Lenore said, pointing quickly to a corner where Joah's possessions had been dumped when he was brought to the chamber. "Everything is here."

Joah hadn't noticed them because he'd been in a supine position, but now his gaze drifted over the pile, visually inspecting it.

"Excellent," he said, returning his attention to Barbara. "Go and get my money. And do not worry… I will make sure Lady Isalyn does not return. You have my word."

That was all Barbara wanted to hear and she fled the chamber.

The plans were in motion.

ISALYN KEPT LOOKING at the ring on her finger, smiling and daydreaming even as Isabella was chatting up a storm about the beautiful dress that Tor had purchased for their wedding. Already, she was pulling out her sewing kit, a grand one that she traveled with, preparing to help Isalyn hem up the bottom and reinforce the stitching on both the shift and the dress. Isalyn didn't have a sewing kit and, worse, she was forced to admit that she wasn't a very good seamstress.

But Isabella was an excellent seamstress and she was armed

with her trusty needle. She was preparing to go to work when a knock in the door interrupted them. Isabella was closer to the door so she went to open it, revealing a pale-looking Lenore on the other side.

Immediately, there was tension in the air.

Isabella and Isalyn knew that Barbara and Lenore were moving freely at Blackpool and they further knew that the sick traveler the women were tending was in the chamber that Isalyn had escaped from on the first floor, but with the heavy density of the stone walls and the way the stairs were built into the walls themselves, they hadn't heard any of the comings and goings from upstairs. The chamber shared by Isalyn and Isabella was tucked away from the entry door to the apartment building, so they had been quite happy forgetting about the harpies, as Isalyn called them.

Perhaps viper was a kinder name.

But perhaps not.

"What do you want, Lenore?" Isalyn asked impatiently.

Lenore didn't try to come into the chamber. She stood in the doorway, her gaze moving from Isalyn to Isabella and back again.

"I… I came to speak to you, my lady," she said, her voice trembling. "May we speak in private?"

Isalyn shook her head. "Nay," she said. "If you have something to say, you may say it in front of Isabella. We have no secrets."

Lenore's features tightened with uncertainty but realizing she had no choice, she nodded and swallowed hard.

"I wanted to say," she said, stopped, and then started again. "I wanted to tell you how sorry my sister and I are for what we have done. We have no excuse other than to say… well, I suppose you know that my sister and I are orphans. Our parents died of the same fever many years ago and we came to live with our only sibling, Jane, and her husband. When Jane died, Tor was all we had left. He is all we have. Sometimes, when you try to hold tightly to something, it can make one a little… mad."

Isalyn was listening with a good deal of doubt, but Lenore seemed sincere enough. She looked at Isabella, who looked back at her with the same doubtful expression.

"There are many people who have lost loved ones and they do not go mad," Isabella said. "What you did wasn't just madness, Lenore. It was wickedness."

Lenore looked at Isabella in distress. "I know," she said. "We know that now. Bella, you do not know what it was like when we were young. My mother and father did not have any servants to take care of them when they were ill, so it was left to Barbara and me. Can you imagine what it was like to watch your parents die as you tried to help them, not knowing what to do? We were just children. We were alone with dying parents and no way to help them. That did something to us. It made us panic with the thought of losing someone. I think… I think that is why we try to hold on to Tor so tightly, any way we can."

She sounded quite pathetic and her tale, in truth, was a sad one. Neither Isabella nor Isalyn were immune to it. Being women of feeling and compassion, it was natural that they should feel some pity.

"But you are not losing Tor," Isalyn said, less hostile than before. "If you would just stop to think that when Tor marries, you would be gaining another family member who wants to love you, then your fears would be for naught. But you treat every woman who wants to get close to Tor like an enemy."

Lenore's eyes welled. "That is not true."

"It is."

"Mayhap… mayhap they are our enemy," she sniffled. "Look at what is happening – Tor is marrying you and sending us away because of you."

"He is sending you away because of the way you are behaving," Isalyn said sternly. "You have left him no choice and I will not be living my life in fear, wondering what you are going to try to do to me next. Your behavior has dictated his actions."

Lenore sniffled again, wiping her nose with the back of her hand. "I-I know you are right," she said. "I suppose I have always known. Barbara and I had a long discussion about it and we are both very sorry for what we have done and we would like to make amends to you."

Isalyn wasn't so sure she wanted any part of this but, on the other hand, she didn't want to be cruel. It was possible that Lenore meant what she said, that the threat of being sent away had scared them into good behavior.

Still, she was understandably doubtful.

"I am not sure that is possible or even advisable," she said. "But for the sake of argument, what amends do you mean?"

Lenore pointed towards the inner bailey. "Would you come with me?" she said. "I have something to show you."

"What is it?"

"Please, my lady. It is a surprise. It is our gift to you, but I could not bring it inside."

"Where is your sister?"

"She is holding the gift."

A warning bell went off in Isalyn's mind. She looked at Isabella, who was equally unsure, but being women of kindness, and forgiveness, that propensity weighed heavily on their decision. They would be hard women, indeed, not to allow a chance for forgiveness. It was against her better judgment, but Isalyn could feel herself relenting.

"Where is she?" she asked.

Lenore started to move away, towards the apartment door that led out into the inner bailey. "I will show you," she said.

"Please? Will you come with me?"

"*Where* is your sister?"

"Outside of the postern gate," Lenore said. "What we have for you was really too big to be brought inside. I promise I will not touch you or lay hands upon you in any way if that is what you are concerned with. We simply want to give you something as a token of our sincerity. Will you not come?"

Isalyn and Isabella looked at each other before Isalyn finally shrugged. "Very well," she said reluctantly. "But Isabella is coming, too."

Lenore nodded her head. "Please," she said. "She is welcome to see it, too. Truly, my lady, we are very sorry. We hope to prove it to you."

She was rushing out into the inner bailey with Isalyn and Isabella reluctantly following. The dark clouds from the north were starting to move southward, so another storm was on its way. But for the most part, it was still a sunny day. Lenore was up ahead, leading the way, as Isalyn and Isabella walked arm in arm.

"What do you think she has for me?" Isalyn whispered.

Isabella shook her head. "I do not know," she said honestly. "It could be a hive full of bees."

"Or rabid dog."

"A gang of angry Scotsmen?"

"A pack of hungry wolves?"

They started laughing, though the subject was quite serious. They were both wary and trying to pretend that they weren't. Isalyn finally sobered.

"This probably is not the smartest thing we could be doing," she said. "But I suppose everyone deserves another chance. Although this goes against my better judgment, I would not be happy with myself if I simply denied them and turned away. Already, I feel like the wicked new wife, sending the younger sisters of the first wife away even though I know they brought it upon themselves. What do you think about their need for forgiveness?"

Isabella sighed heavily. "I think they are capable of anything," she said. "Whatever happens, I would advise not going outside of the gate until we know just what this 'gift' is."

Isalyn looked up to the wall walk of Blackpool. The inner wall was slightly taller than the outer wall and it had a walk that went all the way around, including the kitchen yards and the postern gate. In fact, she could see Christian on the wall over near the great hall and she pointed.

"Look," she said. "There is Christian. We are being watched, so I feel a little better."

Isabella could see Christian, too. He was armed with a crossbow, as most of the sentries were on the wall walk to be able to act on an attack at a moment's notice. That was the usual weapon from the walls.

"I suppose," she said. "But let us get this over with and return to your dress."

The women were in the kitchen yard by this time. Over to their left was the infamous pigsty that butted up against the apartment block. The last time Isalyn was here, she had been covered with mud and rushing to find Barbara and Lenore, so she hadn't really given the kitchen yard much of an inspection.

It was a very large yard, one that covered about one third of the entire inner bailey. Off to the right was the actual kitchen, a large outbuilding that had kilns built into the walls and a massive fire pit several feet away from it. Even as Isalyn and Isabella walked through the yard on Lenore's tail, they could see that there was a butchered hog on a spit, roasting over an open flame in preparation for the evening feast that was still several hours away.

All of the servants seemed to be collected over on that side of the yard, working for the coming meal, and the section that Isalyn and Isabella were passing through was vacant. There were a few small outbuildings, the buttery and another shed, and once they neared the postern gate, the view to the kitchens was blocked.

The postern gate was ahead. It was a heavy iron door, incredibly dense and reinforced because at the rear of the fortress was where the outer wall and the inner wall were the closest proximity. The outer wall was mostly the ancient wall built by the Romans more than a century ago and, in this section, it followed the natural slope of the landscape so that it was much lower than the inner wall. There was a moat between the inner and outer wall here, with a path and a small bridge that led to a second postern gate, built into a small gatehouse that was heavily reinforced.

Because the land beyond was a marsh mostly, and the tree line was about a half-mile away, anyone crossing it would be a sitting duck for the crossbows on the wall, so this area wasn't considered much of a threat and was therefore not heavily watched. Lenore was far enough ahead that she reached the gate built into the tall inner wall first, shoving it open, and Isalyn and Isabella slowed their pace as they neared the open gate.

That was their undoing.

Suddenly, there was as dull thud and Isabella fell to the ground. As Isalyn bent over to see what the matter was, someone grabbed her by the arm. It was a strong, biting grip and Isalyn found herself looking into the face of a man she didn't recognize.

He was older, with graying hair and a sloppy beard, and his gaze focused intently on her.

"You look like him," he muttered, his breath foul. "I see Steffan in you, Lady Isalyn."

He was holding something in his hand and it took Isalyn a

second to realize that it was a sword, but he was holding it hilt upward, like a hammer. As Isabella groaned, it occurred to Isalyn what had happened.

Panic surged.

"You *hit* her," she hissed, trying to yank her arm free. "Why did you hit her? Who are you?"

The man was trying to sheathe his sword and hold on to Isalyn at the same time. "Shut your mouth, Woman!" he hissed. "You're coming with me."

Isalyn went from stunned to panic to full-blown hysteria. She began to twist and fight, trying to yank her arm from him as he held her fast.

"I'm not going anywhere!" she yelled. "Let me go!"

The fight was on.

The man, whoever he was, was strong. Unable to sheathe his sword, he tried to hit Isalyn in the head with it as he'd hit Isabella, but Isalyn dodged and kicked and scratched. She started to scream and he was forced to drop the sword, pushing her roughly against the wall, hard enough to knock the wind out of her.

He clamped a dirty hand over her mouth.

"Be quiet or I will kill you where you stand," he growled. "You're coming with me."

In her terror, Isalyn brought up a knee and rammed it into the man's privates. He faltered and loosened his grip enough so that she was able to break free, but he was on her in an instant, grabbing her by her long hair and falling on top of her when she tripped and fell forward.

Using his body to pin her down, his hands went around her neck, squeezing as she struggled to breathe and scream. Unfortunately for Isalyn, she couldn't get her hands up from the way he was pinning her and the world was starting to go black. She tried her hardest to scream, to fight, but he was heavy and strong, and he had her trapped. The world began to fade and her struggles lessened.

Soon enough, everything went black.

CHAPTER TWENTY-ONE

HE THOUGHT IT looked rather odd.

Barbara had taken a horse from the stables to the inner gatehouse, telling the soldiers that she wished to ride around the inner wall and collect some wildflowers. Since that wasn't unusual behavior from Barbara, the soldiers let her through, but Fraser was watching from the yard when she'd ridden through and he thought that something about her looked strange.

Then, it occurred to him.

She had two big, heavy saddlebags on the back of the horse. Those types of bags belonged to knights, as he had a pair of his own. They were custom made, durable pieces of equipment, tailored to each owner. They weren't something that young women out to gather flowers would normally carry, nor would any bags she carried have a three-point shield burned into the leather.

... shield?

Suspicious, he followed.

Fraser was looking for Tor or Christian or any other knight as he ran to the stable yard, but he didn't see anyone. He thought they were probably in the great hall at this time of day, but he didn't want to take the time to find them. He did, however, grab a stable servant and sent him with a message for Tor – that Barbara had left through the inner gatehouse and Fraser was following her.

Satisfied, he grabbed the nearest horse, threw on a bridle, and leapt onto the back of the skittish beast. Digging his heels in, he took off across the outer bailey, heading for the inner gatehouse.

The men on the wall were pointing to the east, the direction that Barbara had gone, and Fraser followed. There was a path around the castle inner walls with the moat down below, so he followed that trail as quickly as he could, rounding the southeast corner and then finally the northeast corner, coming around the bend only to see something quite confusing over near the postern gate.

He could see the horse that Barbara had ridden out on, but she was off the horse now and simply standing there holding it. Lenore was there, too, but she looked worried. She was wringing her hands. As Fraser drew near, a man suddenly appeared carrying a limp woman in his arms, and Fraser recognized him as the sick man who had come to Blackpool for help. The same man that Barbara and Lenore were supposed to be tending.

Only he wasn't sick any longer.

It took Fraser less than a second to see that the woman in his arms was Isalyn.

He spurred his horse into a gallop.

Suddenly, he was plowing through Barbara and the horse she was holding, and he could hear screams as Barbara went rolling down the embankment towards the moat. The horse, too, slid down the embankment and Fraser heard a big splash as the animal fell into the water. Lenore screamed and ran back inside the postern gate as the man with unconscious Isalyn in his arms lost his balance and dumped Isalyn down the slope. Fraser leapt from this horse and onto the man, and the fight was on.

Since Fraser wasn't armed, all he could do was throw punches at the man he had believed to be deathly ill. They all had. But clearly, the man was well enough and certainly hearty enough to fight back. Big fists were flying as Fraser got the upper hand, pummeling the man as he tripped over his own feet and fell to the ground. But the minute Fraser threw himself onto the man to finally subdue him, the man produced a dagger and Fraser leapt right on it.

It sank into his body, by his hip.

Momentarily stunned by the pain, it was enough of a pause for his opponent to throw a fist into Fraser's face. As Fraser snapped back, the man charged him, slamming him against the inner wall. Furious and in pain, Fraser ripped the dagger out of his body and turned it on the man, stabbing him in the shoulder by his neck. The man screamed as Fraser drove the dagger deep. It was disabling, but not crippling.

The battle went on.

Isabella awoke to the sounds of a scream, but not just any scream. There was a man screaming, somewhere, and she lifted her head, having no idea why she was laying in the mud. The last she remembered, she was walking with Isalyn towards the postern gate and then… nothing.

Lifting her head, she could see the postern gate in front of her, open, with Lenore standing there, weeping hysterically.

Something terrible was going on.

Head pounding, and feeling nauseous, Isabella staggered to her feet. She could hear sounds of a fight and Isalyn wasn't anywhere to be found, so she went into panic mode. The buttery was immediately to her right and there were a couple of old wooden butter churns, one used to make the butter. They were big and heavy, but one of the paddles was partially chipped, which was why it wasn't currently used. Grabbing the heavy butter paddle, Isabella wielded it like a club and staggered to the postern gate.

The first thing she saw was Lenore, weeping and gasping, and Isabella didn't hesitate. She swung the paddle at Lenore's head and hit her squarely on the side of her skull, sending the woman down the embankment towards the moat. Down below, Isabella could see a horse swimming in the moat, trying to pull itself up on the other side, and Barbara up to her waist in the murky water, trying to claw her way out.

But the noise was coming from the fight to her left and Isabella turned to see Fraser in a vicious fight with a man she didn't recognize. They were both covered in blood and Isabella screamed at the sight, but her shock didn't prevent her from acting. Convinced that Fraser's life was in danger, she lifted the paddle high and charged the men fighting, bringing that heavy paddle to bear on the man locked in mortal combat with Fraser. She whacked him on the back of the skull, twice, and he released his grip on Fraser. But as he started to fall, a nasty-looking bolt plunged right into his back.

Down he went, face-first into the mud, never to rise again.

Still in panic mode, Isabella looked to see where the arrow had come from and she could see Christian on the wall above, crossbow in-hand. Realizing there were soldiers now rushing to help and protect them, Isabella threw the paddle aside and ran to Fraser, who was just rising to his knees. She fell down beside him, her hands reaching out to steady him.

"Fraser!" she gasped. "What happened?"

Fraser was beaten and bleeding, but he was alive. Breathing heavily, he had one hand over the dagger wound near his hip, but the other one came up to cup Isabella's panicked face.

"Easy, Bella," he said softly, breathlessly. "I am not as bad as I look, I promise."

Her eyes filled with tears. "What happened? Who is he?"

"That is the sick man we brought in for Barbara and Lenore to heal," Fraser said between heavy breaths. "I saw Barbara ride out on a horse with what I am guessing are that man's saddle-bags and I discovered him taking Isalyn outside of the postern gate, so I… *Isalyn!* Where is she?"

Isabella shrieked as she and Fraser started looking around in a panic for Isalyn. Men were starting to spill out from the postern gate, including Blayth, Ronan, and finally Tor, who had been summoned from the great hall by a terrified servant. Tor saw a bloodied Fraser, a dead man with an arrow in his back, a wet horse on the other side of the moat, and Barbara and Lenore down by the moat's edge.

"Tor!" Isabella screamed. "We must find Isalyn! She must have fallen down the slope!"

Tor was on the move. He had no idea what had happened. But at the mention of Isalyn, he was moving, sliding down the slope, searching for Isalyn somewhere in the grass and muck. He finally caught sight of her lifting her head out of the tall grass down by the moat's edge. She had a hand to her head, and her dirty hair was all over her face. Tor rushed towards her as fast as his legs would carry him. He ended up slipping because of the angle of the slope, falling heavily on his left side, but he scrambled and clawed his way over to Isalyn.

His arms finally went around her, holding her tightly as if to never let her go.

"Isalyn," he said, his voice trembling. "What in the hell is going on? What happened to you?"

Isalyn was groggy, a hand on her aching head. "Lenore," she muttered, trying to remember what had gone on. "She said that she and Barbara wanted my forgiveness. They wanted to make amends. She said they had a gift for me and they brought me out to the postern gate, but a man grabbed me. I don't know who he was and… God's Bones, where is Isabella? He hit Isabella!"

"She is well," Tor said, feeling lightheaded with both relief and fear. Fear of what could have been. "She is with Fraser. You said that Lenore and Barbara brought you out here?"

Isalyn collapsed against him. "They tried," she said, closing her eyes because her head was killing her. "That man was waiting for me and he tried to kill me. Tor, they brought me right to him."

Tor still didn't really know what was going on, but he had heard enough. He turned to see his uncle halfway down the slope and he called to the man.

"Uncle Blayth!" he shouted. "Barbara and Lenore – get them to the vault!"

Blayth was on the move and, along with Ronan, managed to grab Barbara and Lenore. Tor could hear them screaming but he didn't care. They could have drowned in the moat at that very moment and he wouldn't have cared. Any semblance of concern he'd ever had for them was gone forever.

Forgive me, Jane.

They had committed the last crime they were ever going to.

CHAPTER TWENTY-TWO

Armathwaite Nunnery
One week later

THE MOON WAS full overhead, the stars beyond like a sea of diamonds against the black expanse of sky. As Tor walked away from the walls of the ancient nunnery, he could still hear the sobs of Barbara and Lenore as the nuns took them away, pleading with him not to leave them. Begging him to reconsider. Telling him how Jane would not have wanted it this way.

But he was immune to it.

For the first time in almost seventeen years, he was numb to it.

Barbara and Lenore were dead to him now.

Blayth, Fraser, Ronan, and Christian were waiting for him in a group. They were mounted, with Ronan holding the reins of Enbarr and the two other horses that had brought Barbara and Lenore to their final destination. Tor took his beloved steed from Ronan and deftly climbed into the saddle.

As the party began to move north, he didn't look back.

"How do you feel, Tor?" Blayth asked quietly. "I know that this was difficult, but it was the right thing to do."

The moon was so bright that it appeared as if the entire land were lit by a million white torches, everything so bright that it was like daytime.

For Tor, it was, indeed, as if a new day had dawned.

The first day of the rest of his life.

"I feel fine," he said. "I feel as if a great burden has been lifted. I'm only sorry it took me so long to come to my senses."

Blayth glanced at Ronan and Christian, the men who had known Tor better than most. "It was quite a burden," he agreed. "And quite complicated. Who knew that the sick man who had come to Blackpool was a rogue de Royans knight? We would have never known had I not recognized the body. I had seen the man come with Kelton de Royans to the gathering of the northern warlords last year. I feel badly that I did not see him when he first came to Blackpool. Mayhap we could have avoided this whole situation."

Tor held up a hand to ease him. "It was not your fault, Uncle Blayth," he said. "We took him in, as it was the right thing to do, having no idea that he was only pretending to be ill to gain access to Blackpool and to the House of de Wolfe. Barbara and Lenore played right into his hands."

"Kelton de Royans said that it was rumored that Joah de Brayton and Steffan de Featherstone were lovers," Blayth said quietly. "I care not who a man loves, but I do care about his character and de Brayton seemed to be lacking, according to Kelton. To seek revenge for a foul scheme gone wrong only comes from a man with poor standards and even worse judgment."

Tor glanced at his uncle. "Sometimes, it can happen in the best of families," he said. "Look at Steffan. Gilbert is a good man and Isalyn, of course, is beyond reproach, but Steffan had a distinct lack of character. Kelton pressed one of his other knights, a friend of Steffan's, who said that Steffan only sought the betrothal with Isabella to gain access to the de Wolfe war machine. He had promised Joah a great position once he married her. Thank God he didn't."

They all turned to look at Fraser, riding along silently, listening to everything that was being said. When he saw all of the attention on him, including Blayth's, he smiled weakly.

"Thank God, indeed," he repeated, a smile on his lips. "I would not have the great honor of becoming her husband next week."

As Blayth cocked a stern eyebrow at the man, the others started laughing. "We are fortunate to have you in the family, Fraser, and do not let Papa make you think otherwise," Ronan said. "He may look like a terrible barbarian, but he already loves you. I can tell."

"Shut up," Blayth grumbled to his son. "You are not to make him feel so welcome until he has been married to Bella for a while. If you make him feel comfortable, he will not fear me."

"I will always fear you, my lord," Fraser said smoothly.

Now, Blayth was trying not to smile as the others laughed. "Smart man," he muttered.

The party continued on, the mood lighter than it had been in some time, ever since Barbara and Lenore nearly carried out their final, terrible plan to remove Isalyn forever. After the scare, Tor had summoned his father and married Isalyn in the man's presence three days later, and she had worn the gorgeous wedding dress that he had purchased for her. Upon her finger, never to be removed, was the ancient posy ring they so cherished.

I choose thee.

"Did you tell Gilbert what Kelton de Royans told you, Uncle Blayth?" Tor asked, anxious to return to Blackpool and to his new wife, who was in the care of his father and her father at the moment. "He knows that Joah came from Netherghyll, but I was not sure how much more you told him."

Blayth shook his head. "There is no reason to tell him anything more," he said. "Would it do any good to tell him that his son's lover was seeking revenge for his death? That he was mad with rage and that his son was trying to dupe the House of de Wolfe by marrying Isabella? Nay, I did not tell him. Steffan may have been a terrible son, but he was Gilbert's only son. He knows that the man was a coward and a scoundrel. I do not want to pile on and tell him even more than that."

It was a compassionate decision on Blayth's part. Tor faced forward, watching the road ahead, calculating that they would make it home just before dawn. Just in time for him to climb into bed with Isalyn and make love to her while the sun rose.

His wife.

He never thought he could be so happy again. But he hadn't reached this point without help.

He'd had a lot of it.

"I want to thank you all for everything you have done," he said after a moment. "Uncle Blayth, my thanks to you for your wisdom and advice. Ronan, you are my younger cousin, but you are more like a brother to me. Christian, you are my cousin and my second in command, but you are the best friend a man could have. And Fraser… you have quickly integrated yourself into the House of de Wolfe. I have a feeling you and I will be spending many years together, closely, because it has become apparent that Isalyn and Isabella cannot be separated. Isabella very nearly sacrificed her life for Isalyn and I will never forget her bravery. And you… you nearly died trying to protect Isalyn. I will never forget that, either. Not ever."

Fraser smiled faintly. "My position with Gilbert was a long and lucrative one," he said. "But now… now I feel that I finally belong somewhere, and to someone. Thank you for accepting my fealty at Blackpool. I will not fail you."

"I know you won't," Tor said. "But we see a good deal of

action from the Scots. If you wanted a post that will see action, you got one." He paused, looking up at the brilliant sky again. "You know, the last time I was riding in a group with my de Wolfe brethren, it was to hunt down Steffan de Featherstone. We were there to right an injustice and tonight… I feel like we've done the same thing, only differently. We righted another kind of injustice."

"True, lad," Blayth said. "We did, indeed. Did you give Armathwaite the donation you brought?"

Tor nodded. "It is more money than they'll see in ten years of donations," he said. "And it is something I do not ever wish to speak of again. I only wish to speak of the future, which includes a wedding next week for Fraser and Isabella. I will get blindingly drunk on Uncle Blayth's fine wine, dance with the bride, and also with my wife, and enjoy myself immensely."

Ronan grinned at Fraser, who simply lifted his eyebrows at his future brother-in-law whom he was coming to like a great deal. Riding next to Ronan, Blayth cocked his head thoughtfully.

"Did I ever tell you about Alys and Gerard de Wolfe's wedding so many years ago?" he said. "Oddly enough, it is one of the few things I remember from the past, although I have no idea why. They were married at The Lyceum, the de Royans castle south of Wolfe's Lair, and everything was proceeding wonderfully until I was attacked."

They all turned to look at him. "Attacked by whom?" Tor asked.

"My own mother," Blayth said, his eyes twinkling at the hazy memory. "All because of a song I sang for the guests."

Tor started to laugh. "I do not believe it," he said. "Matha attacked you for singing?"

Blayth nodded. "She was not at your wedding, so I did not sing the special song for her, but she will be at Isabella's," he said. "I will teach you the song so we can all sing it to her."

"A song that makes her attack?" Tor said, dubiously. "I do not think I want to learn that song."

"Learn it!" Blayth bellowed, watching his nephew laugh. He began to sing it in his beautiful baritone.

"There once was a lady fair,
With silver bells in her hair.
I knew her to have,
A luscious kiss… it drove me mad!
But she denied me… and I was so terribly sad.
Lily, my girl,
Your flower, I will unfurl
With my cock and a bit of good luck!
Your kiss divine,
I'll make you mine,
And keep you a-bed for a fuck!"

Tor and Fraser refused to learn it, but Ronan and Christian did. When Fraser married Isabella in the great hall of Castle Questing a week later, they happily sang it with Blayth's urging.

True to form, elderly Jordan de Wolfe was fairly spry for her age and took after them with a switch. When her grandsons moved too fast, she went after Blayth because she knew who had taught them the song. Blayth ran, too, spending the rest of the evening dodging his angry mother.

And he loved every moment of it.

EPILOGUE

Trimontium Amphitheater
Kelso, Scotland

THEY WERE LITERALLY on the edge of their seats.

The entire audience at the Trimontium Amphitheater was on the edge of their seats, having just watched two hours of a drama that had them riveted. It was called *The Harpies of Blackpool*, and the stars of the show were two evil women who destroyed everything they touched and would have succeeded in destroying the city of Edinburgh had the hero, an English knight, not stopped them by virtue of his magic sword.

It was the climax of the drama, performed to an audience full of men where over half were Scots from the borders. Only men were allowed to attend dramas, and act in them, so it was a female-free environment. The Scots were furious that the harpies tried to destroy Edinburgh and not too thrilled when an English knight came to their rescue, but in the very last moment when the harpies were drowning in the Firth of Forth, the knight ripped off his tunic to reveal that he had been a Scotsman all along.

The crowd went wild.

All but the English, of course, although they had greatly

enjoyed the drama of the wicked harpies. Sitting on the grass of the ancient amphitheater, the men from the House of de Wolfe refrained from booing when the English knight revealed himself to be Scottish because the play changed nightly. Two nights ago, it had been a Scotsman who had ripped off his *leine* to reveal that he was an English knight.

On the borders, one must cater to both crowds.

Tonight, however, the drama favored the Scots, who cheered and yelled and even threw coins onto the stage below, which was just a vast dirt area. The amphitheater had been built by the Romans a thousand years before and although a good portion of it still stood, it wasn't nearly what it had been when dramas had once entertained Roman troops.

But for tonight, it served its purpose.

The Harpies of Blackpool Castle was another rousing success.

There was no one more proud of the drama than Tor, who sat with his brother, Will, his cousins, and his uncles, Scott, Troy, and Blayth. They had all come to Kelso to see Isalyn de Wolfe's drama, although only the family knew that she was the one who had written it. For all anyone else knew, London playwright Wellesley Fairhurst had penned the piece.

It had been four years in the making.

The birth of two children during that time had slowed Isalyn's determination to continue her beloved hobby, but it didn't stop it completely. Between the births of Tristan de Wolfe and Merrett de Wolfe, Isalyn had written the drama that had the villains as bad as they could possibly be and the hero akin to Jesus Christ. It had been dramatic and sappy at times, and Tor had been greatly amused by it, but the crowd loved it and that was all that mattered.

And his wife was in her glory.

Because Isalyn couldn't travel to London with the babies,

she had convinced some of her friends to come north and perform it for the masses in the wilds. They had happily come, and now two harpies were dying terrible deaths as the audience screamed for more.

But there wouldn't be any more until tomorrow night.

With the drama ended and the crowds thinning out, Tor left his family still seated on the grass to hunt down his wife, who was backstage where the actors were. She was dressed in clothes a usually well-bred noblewoman wouldn't wear, like breeches and tunics and cloaks, and her glorious hair was pinned back under the hood of the cloak because she didn't want to appear like a woman to the casual observer. Women weren't allowed at these dramas, so she was trying to stay hidden.

But it didn't work very well. The birth of two children had left her even more gloriously round and supple, and Tor snuck up behind his wife as she was speaking to one of the actors made up to look like a harpy. He grabbed her from behind, pulling that lush body against him.

"Another remarkable night, Lady de Wolfe," he murmured in her ear. "You have two hundred clansmen out there cheering happily because Edinburgh is saved."

Isalyn turned in his arms, her face alight with joy. "They *did* like it, didn't they?" she said. "I think some of those men have been here every single night."

Tor snorted. "Of course they have," he said. "Some of them are Scotts, from Matha's clan. They know this is a de Wolfe production, so they have come to support their English branch of the family."

"And that is why I let them have a Scots hero part of the time."

Tor leaned forward to kiss her but, suddenly, they were surrounded by other de Wolfes, all of them congratulating

Isalyn on a job well done. Scott was the first one to hug her tightly. He adored his daughter-in-law, who had been the perfect match for his strong, silent, and brilliant son.

"Another success, Isalyn," Scott said. "Tonight was positively magnificent. I thought we were going to have a battle, however, when you brought out the knight to save Edinburgh. There were a few men from Clan Kerr out there and they took particular exception to that."

Isalyn started laughing. "I know," she said. "I was watching from the shadows. They started throwing things. Did you see them?"

Scott laughed. "I did," he said. "They were throwing pieces of jerky. Did you not see the knight pluck one that had hit him on the chest and eat it?"

They all started laughing. It had been an eventful night, a moment for the House of de Wolfe to bond over something other than a battle. Times such as this, with laughter and joy and pleasure, were rare. Troy de Wolfe, Scott's twin, who had also married into Clan Kerr, pushed his way to the front so he could kiss Isalyn on the cheek.

"You are lucky that is all they threw," he said. "If the Kerrs become enraged, they'll start throwing knives."

"There is always tomorrow night," Isalyn said, a twinkle in her eyes. "I'll put my knight in real armor so he can protect himself should the dirks start to fly."

She was joking. Sort of. The Scots and the English in the same amphitheater had been dicey from the start, but Isalyn had been determined to use a theater that the Romans had once used and unite the border through entertainment. It somehow gave validation to her dramas, performed in the same space that had once been a backdrop for Greek and Roman tragedies.

All she knew was that she was happier than she had ever been.

Thanks to a certain provincial knight.

But the hour was growing late and they needed to head back to Castle Questing, which was about ten miles to the southeast. It would take them little more than an hour to get there, traveling beneath the light of the half-moon during a summer's night that had been mild and calm.

The de Wolfe men helped Isalyn shut down the amphitheater for the night, collecting costumes and props that were being stored in a livery across the road, one that bordered the River Tweed. Fraser was hauling things particularly quickly because he wanted to get back to Castle Questing where his wife was waiting for him.

At nine months pregnant, Isabella was round and rosy, hungry and grumpy, and ready for the child to be born. She had demanded to come to Castle Questing when Isalyn's drama opened and they had been at Castle Questing for two weeks. But they were also there for another reason – Isabella had been born at Castle Questing and she wanted her baby to be born there as well, so everyone, including Blayth, was playing a waiting game for his first grandchild to be born.

"Come on, now!" Fraser was clapping his hands to get men moving. "Hurry up. We must head back to Castle Questing."

That made Will drag his feet. Big, dark, and handsome, Will was the image of his grandfather, William de Wolfe, but he had a touch of the de Norville sense of humor thanks to his mother, the eldest daughter of Paris de Norville. He had a pillar made of plaster in his hands as he crossed the avenue to the livery, pausing next to Fraser.

"Do you think you're the only man who has a wife he wants to return to?" he asked, incredulous. "She has probably already had the child."

Fraser frowned. "She promised not to have it while I was away."

Scott and Troy heard him and started laughing. Even Will grinned. "She may not have a choice," he said. "Women have babies when they have them. It is not something they can plan."

Fraser cocked an eyebrow. "Then we had better hurry."

They did. A little more than an hour later, the party from Kelso entered the massive bailey of Castle Questing, turning their horses over to the stable servants as they headed into the equally enormous keep.

Isalyn was half-asleep as she walked in, staggering to the point where Tor picked her up, cradling her so she wouldn't fall. There was a steady hum of chatter going on as men went about removing helms and gear. Tor was about to take Isalyn up to their chamber to check on their two young sons when he was blocked by his grandmother descending the stairs.

Jordan Scott de Wolfe was wrapped up in the tattered shawl she always wore, the one her husband swore she would be buried with. She was in her eighth decade but she moved, and looked, like a much younger woman. The shining star of the entire de Wolfe family, she looked at Isalyn with concern when she saw that Tor was carrying her.

"Ish?" she said, using her family nickname. "What's the matter with ye, lass? Are ye ill?"

Isalyn smiled weakly, pushing herself out of Tor's arms. "Nay," she said. "I'm simply weary. Tor was being kind by carrying me. How are my lads?"

Jordan smiled. "Finally in bed," she said. "They remind me of Scott and Troy at that age. I couldna get them tae sleep no matter how hard I tried. I had tae sing for yer lads for an hour tae put them tae sleep and ye know I dunna sing very well."

Isalyn leaned in and kissed the old woman on the cheek. "Thank you, Matha," she said. "You know they love to hear you sing the fairy song."

Jordan grunted. "My throat is raw," she said, watching

Isalyn giggle as she moved past her, heading up the stairs to check on her sons. But Jordan stopped her. "Wait, Ish. Where's Fraser?"

He was towards the rear of the group, removing his gloves, but when he heard his name, his head shot up.

"I am here, Lady de Wolfe," he said.

Jordan beckoned him forward before pointing up the stairs. "Go tae my granddaughter," she said. "She has a little surprise for ye."

Fraser went pale. "She… she does?"

Jordan's old eyes twinkled. "Get," she said. "Dunna keep her waiting."

Fraser bolted. They could hear him running up the stairs, including Isalyn, who looked at Tor's grandmother with wide eyes.

"Did she have her babe?" she asked anxiously.

Jordan nodded. Then, she started to laugh. "I was trying tae get yer two tadpoles tae sleep when I heard Bella calling for me," she said. "I practically had tae tie Tristan down. I promised him that he'd be able tae ride his pony tomorrow if he went tae sleep and that was the only way I could leave him. Remember that, Tor. Tristan rides his pony tomorrow."

As Tor nodded, Isalyn put her hands on Jordan's arm. "But Bella? Is she well? Is the babe well?"

Jordan patted her hands. "Very well," she said. "By the time I went intae the chamber, she was already pushing the first baby out. Her mother and I barely had time tae help her. The lass did it almost all by herself."

Isalyn's eyebrows lifted. "*First* baby?"

Jordan nodded. "She had two," she said, listening to the men mutter their approval. "Two little lads who scream like banshees."

Isalyn squealed with delight. Kissing Jordan on the cheek

again, she rushed up the stairs, listening to her husband call after her and telling her to wait a moment. But Isalyn didn't want to wait; she wanted to see Isabella's babies. For as close as they had become, Isalyn truly felt as if Isabella were her sister.

For all they had been through together, they were in spirit if not by blood.

It was a joyful night at Castle Questing as two new souls were brought into the world. Isalyn stood in the doorway of Isabella and Fraser's chamber, becoming misty-eyed as ever-stoic Fraser had tears streaming down his face at the sight of two healthy boys.

As Tor came to stand behind his wife, he put his arm around her as he admired Fraser and Isabella's boys from afar. Isalyn gazed up at her handsome husband, feeling the love from him more than she ever had. Love was in the air tonight, for them all, with the births of William and Kieran le Kerque, named after both of Isabella's grandfathers.

Four years ago when Isalyn had taken a chance on a horse that had run away with her, she could have never imagined how her life would be changed by the man who had saved her from certain injury or death. A brave knight bearing a de Wolfe tunic who had risked his life for her, in what would be the first of many times. Strong, courageous, and noble, sometimes she wondered if she was worthy of him.

Isalyn had gone from a lonely woman living with her aunt in London to a massive family that spanned most of Northumberland. She had a husband she loved more with each successive breath, two beautiful sons, a father she had finally become closer to, and a life that most women dreamed of. Provincial or not, the wilds of Northumberland had become her home and she loved it there.

She loved her life.

For the lass with a taste for big cities and the widowed

knight who had lost his way in life, they found a strong love that was worth fighting for, because there is no love stronger than that of a de Wolfe and his mate.

Isalyn and Tor had finally found their little bit of heaven.

CS THE END &

Children of Tor and Isalyn

Tristan

Merrett

Jasper

Jane

Emma

Madeline

Gilbert "Gil"

Thomas Scott

Kathryn Le Veque Novels

Medieval Romance:

De Wolfe Pack Series:
Warwolfe
The Wolfe
Nighthawk
ShadowWolfe
DarkWolfe
A Joyous de Wolfe Christmas
BlackWolfe
Serpent
A Wolfe Among Dragons
Scorpion
StormWolfe
Dark Destroyer
The Lion of the North
Walls of Babylon
The Best Is Yet To Be

De Wolfe Pack Generations:
WolfeHeart
WolfeStrike
WolfeSword

The de Russe Legacy:
The Falls of Erith
Lord of War: Black Angel
The Iron Knight
Beast
The Dark One: Dark Knight
The White Lord of Wellesbourne
Dark Moon
Dark Steel
A de Russe Christmas Miracle
Dark Warrior

The de Lohr Dynasty:
While Angels Slept
Rise of the Defender
Steelheart
Shadowmoor
Silversword
Spectre of the Sword
Unending Love
Archangel
A Blessed de Lohr Christmas

Lords of East Anglia:
While Angels Slept
Godspeed

Great Lords of le Bec:
Great Protector

House of de Royans:
Lord of Winter
To the Lady Born
The Centurion

Lords of Eire:
Echoes of Ancient Dreams
Blacksword
The Darkland

Ancient Kings of Anglecynn:
The Whispering Night
Netherworld

Battle Lords of de Velt:
The Dark Lord
Devil's Dominion
Bay of Fear

The Dark Lord's First Christmas

Reign of the House of de Winter:
Lespada
Swords and Shields

De Reyne Domination:
Guardian of Darkness
With Dreams
The Fallen One

House of d'Vant:
Tender is the Knight (House of d'Vant)
The Red Fury (House of d'Vant)

The Dragonblade Series:
Fragments of Grace
Dragonblade
Island of Glass
The Savage Curtain
The Fallen One

Great Marcher Lords of de Lara
Dragonblade

House of St. Hever
Fragments of Grace
Island of Glass
Queen of Lost Stars

Lords of Pembury:
The Savage Curtain

Lords of Thunder: The de Shera Brotherhood Trilogy
The Thunder Lord
The Thunder Warrior
The Thunder Knight

The Great Knights of de Moray:
Shield of Kronos
The Gorgon

The House of De Nerra:
The Promise
The Falls of Erith
Vestiges of Valor
Realm of Angels

Highland Warriors of Munro:
The Red Lion
Deep Into Darkness

The House of de Garr:
Lord of Light
Realm of Angels

Saxon Lords of Hage:
The Crusader
Kingdom Come

High Warriors of Rohan:
High Warrior

The House of Ashbourne:
Upon a Midnight Dream

The House of D'Aurilliac:
Valiant Chaos

The House of De Dere:
Of Love and Legend

St. John and de Gare Clans:
The Warrior Poet

The House of de Bretagne:
The Questing

The House of Summerlin:
The Legend

The Kingdom of Hendocia:
Kingdom by the Sea

The Executioner Knights:
By the Unholy Hand
The Mountain Dark

Starless
The Promise (also Noble Knights of de Nerra)
A Time of End
Winter of Solace
Lord of the Shadows
Lord of the Sky

Contemporary Romance:

Kathlyn Trent/Marcus Burton Series:
Valley of the Shadow
The Eden Factor
Canyon of the Sphinx

The American Heroes Anthology Series:
The Lucius Robe
Fires of Autumn
Evenshade
Sea of Dreams
Purgatory

Other non-connected Contemporary Romance:
Lady of Heaven
Darkling, I Listen
In the Dreaming Hour
River's End
The Fountain

Sons of Poseidon:
The Immortal Sea

Pirates of Britannia Series (with Eliza Knight):
Savage of the Sea by Eliza Knight
Leader of Titans by Kathryn Le Veque
The Sea Devil by Eliza Knight
Sea Wolfe by Kathryn Le Veque

Note: All Kathryn's novels are designed to be read as stand-alones, although many have cross-over characters or cross-over family groups. Novels that are grouped together have related characters or family groups. You will notice that some series have the same books; that is because they are cross-overs. A hero in one book may be the secondary character in another.

There is NO reading order except by chronology, but even in that case, you can still read the books as stand-alones. No novel is connected to another by a cliff hanger, and every book has an HEA.

Series are clearly marked. All series contain the same characters or family groups except the American Heroes Series, which is an anthology with unrelated characters.

For more information, find it in **A Reader's Guide to the Medieval World of Le Veque**.

About Kathryn Le Veque

Medieval Just Got Real.

KATHRYN LE VEQUE is a USA TODAY Bestselling author, an Amazon All-Star author, and a #1 bestselling, award-winning, multi-published author in Medieval Historical Romance and Historical Fiction. She has been featured in the NEW YORK TIMES and on USA TODAY's HEA blog. In March 2015, Kathryn was the featured cover story for the March issue of InD'Tale Magazine, the premier Indie author magazine. She was also a quadruple nominee (a record!) for the prestigious RONE awards for 2015.

Kathryn's Medieval Romance novels have been called 'detailed', 'highly romantic', and 'character-rich'. She crafts great adventures of love, battles, passion, and romance in the High Middle Ages. More than that, she writes for both women AND men – an unusual crossover for a romance author – and Kathryn has many male readers who enjoy her stories because of the male perspective, the action, and the adventure.

On October 29, 2015, Amazon launched Kathryn's Kindle Worlds Fan Fiction site WORLD OF DE WOLFE PACK. Please visit Kindle Worlds for Kathryn Le Veque's World of de Wolfe Pack and find many action-packed adventures written by some of the top authors in their genre using Kathryn's characters from the de Wolfe Pack series. As Kindle World's FIRST Historical Romance fan fiction world, Kathryn Le Veque's World of de Wolfe Pack will contain all of the great storytelling you have come to expect.

Kathryn loves to hear from her readers. Please find Kathryn on Facebook at Kathryn Le Veque, Author, or join her on Twitter @kathrynleveque, and don't forget to visit her website and sign up for her blog at www.kathrynleveque.com.

Please follow Kathryn on Bookbub for the latest releases and sales: bookbub.com/authors/kathryn-le-veque.